'What happens when we are forced to leave what we love? Our life's work, our marriage, our homeland? *The Teacher's Secret* is a delicately woven tapestry of interlinking stories that reveal the ordinary struggles of decent people in the small town of Brindle. Built of richly conceived characters—teachers, mothers, wives—it draws you in to the web of relationships in and around a little public school, its dramas, crises and victories, as people navigate their own and bear witness to each other's struggles. It is a story of rupture and repair, about the betrayals of the past, and what happens when the systems and institutions we trust to guide our lives fail the humans within them. This is a big-hearted book about a small community and how small acts of kindness and courage, and the willingness to face the truth, restore the human spirit to a sense of new belonging.' JOANNE FEDLER

Also by Suzanne Leal
Border Street

Praise for *Border Street*

'Utterly engrossing and moving...An exquisitely poised and intelligent unveiling of secrets; a book honouring the hidden, the intimate and the painfully unresolved.' GAIL JONES

'A book that looms closer with every page . . . By the end, you start seeing the characters on the street, and you hear their voices in your sleep.' MARKUS ZUSAK

The Teacher's Secret

SUZANNE LEAL

ALLEN&UNWIN

SYDNEY • MELBOURNE • AUCKLAND • LONDON

The extracts from Roald Dahl's *Charlie and the Chocolate Factory* on pages 225, 226 and 227 are reproduced with the kind permission of the Roald Dahl Literary Estate LLP and the Penguin Group.

First published in 2016

Allen & Unwin
83 Alexander Street
Crows Nest NSW 2065
Australia
Phone: (61 2) 8425 0100
Email: info@allenandunwin.com
Web: www.allenandunwin.com

Cataloguing-in-Publication details are available
from the National Library of Australia
www.trove.nla.gov.au

ISBN 978 1 76029 055 9

Set in 12/18 pt Minion Pro by Post Pre-press Group, Australia
Printed and bound in Australia by Griffin Press

10 9 8 7 6 5 4 3 2 1

for my parents, Barry and Roslyn Leal
and
for my husband, David Barrow

Terra I

Term 1

Terry

His eyes spring open and, in the minutes before the alarm rings, he thinks about the day ahead. He looks forward to the first day of term the way the kids look forward to the first day of holidays—with a jump of excitement.

Beside him, Michelle is still sleeping. He smiles as he looks across at her. In sleep, there's something that takes away all the years so that she seems little more than a girl. He's a lucky man, that's for sure. He only needs to look at her to remember that.

When the alarm rings, she stirs. Drawing a deep breath, she moves her head and, with the brush of her hand, pushes a lock of hair from her face. She rubs her eyes before, very slowly, she opens them.

'Good morning, sweetheart,' he says softly.

It takes her a moment to focus. 'Hello,' she says, her voice thick with sleep. 'What's the time?'

'Ten past seven, love.'

'Already?' She yawns. 'Can't be.'

While she stretches, he gets himself dressed. Today he chooses his orange shirt, because it's cheerful, teams it with a pair of long trousers and his Rockports and he's done.

In the kitchen, he works his way through a bowl of cornflakes, drinks a couple of mouthfuls of tea and heads for the bathroom. As always, it's a surprise to see himself in the mirror: a figure on the way to becoming an old man. There's even silver in his moustache these days.

All in all, though, it's been a good life; a fortunate life, even. He's not saying it's been plain sailing, that's not what he means. And certainly, there are things he'd have changed if he'd had the choice.

Like being a dad.

Because he'd have liked that. It's one of the things he'd have most liked.

The kids at school, they're pretty upfront with the questions. 'Sir,' they'll say—especially the new ones; the ones that don't know him so well—'how many kids have you got, sir?'

Mostly, he'll just shake his head and play it straight. 'No kids,' he'll say. Other times, he'll make a zero out of his thumb and index finger and hold it up. 'Zero,' he'll say. 'I have zero kids and one dog.' That normally works a treat. It always does when you add a dog into the mix. Because in the end, nine out of ten kids are more interested in dogs than babies.

Sometimes, though, he'll squat down and crook a finger to draw the kid close. 'You know how many kids I've got?' he'll whisper. 'Hundreds.'

Michelle isn't so good on the questions. Of course she tries; she says all the things he's heard other people say—other people like him and Michelle, people without kids. *Kids?* she'll say. *It's a full-time job just looking after Terry.* That's his cue to look a bit guilty and hopeless, like he's owning up to it: that she's right, he's the reason why. Truth is, they tried and they tried: the natural way, the medical way. Nothing worked. For a while, they spoke about adopting, but in the end nothing came of it. Strange to admit it now, but he can't quite remember what happened: whether it all got too complicated with the forms and the procedures and the waiting and what have you, or whether, in the end, they just got tired of it and called it a day. It's all a long time ago.

And now's not the time to be thinking about it anyway; now's the time to get going. But first he pops back into the bedroom, a fresh cup of tea in his hand. It's part of the morning ritual: he gets up and gets himself ready, then makes Michelle a cuppa to have in bed. And although her eyes are closed again when he comes in, her lips curve in a smile as soon as he puts the cup down on her bedside table, a soft chink of ceramic on the wooden coaster. 'You all ready?' she asks, her voice throaty.

'All ready,' he says. 'Funny, though, to think of the year without Diane.'

Eyes open now, Michelle gives a stretch. 'They'll have a ball, the two of them,' she says, stifling a yawn. 'A year travelling the world. What's not to like about that? I'd do it in a flash.' She sits up and reaches for the tea. 'I still think you should have put your hand up for the job.'

It's not the first time they've had this discussion. 'It's not my thing, love,' he tells her again. 'You know that. When have I ever fancied myself as head honcho?'

'They'd have given it to you, you know that, don't you? I mean, you are the assistant principal. Diane said you would have been a shoo-in.'

He dismisses this with a grunt. 'Elsie's reading now,' he says. 'Got to make sure she doesn't forget how.'

～

He finds himself whistling as he drives. As usual, there's no traffic. It's one of the things he likes about living in Jinda. Because it's at the tip of the peninsula, it's a bit like living at the end of a railway line: everyone else gets off first so you end up with the carriage to yourself. It's a tranquil place to be. And it's by the water, which he loves. From their balcony, they look straight across the bay to the shipyards and the loading docks. At night, it's a picture, with everything lit up and bouncing and sparkling off the water.

There's only one road out of Jinda. It starts small but eventually fans out into the three lanes that head straight for the city, which is why there are so many commuters living in Jinda. Terry's just glad he's not one of them: all that traffic and hoo-ha in the morning and the crowds of people spilling out onto the footpath once you're there. It's not for him. Even Raleigh—only a fifteen-minute drive from Jinda—is getting too busy for him these days. That's where Michelle works, three days a week, as the receptionist in the medical practice.

Terry works in Brindle, which is just before Raleigh, and if he takes the direct route—straight along the main road, then right at the lights—he can be at the school in less than ten minutes. He prefers the scenic route, though, so he turns off earlier, just before the jail, and heads down towards the water. When they first arrived, it used to give him the heebie-jeebies, having a jail so close by— and a big one too, so big it was almost a little suburb in itself—but Michelle never minded. At least it kept the house prices down, she'd say. Otherwise what chance would they have had of buying a place so close to the water? And as for the odd escapee: what sort of idiot would hang around in Brindle or Jinda rather than hop-skipping it as far away as they could?

Further down from the jail, closer to the water, are clusters of public housing. The flats themselves are rundown and there are always the louts and the drunks—that's a given—but there are worse places to live. Elsie and Len, for example, they've done all right, and out of habit he slows down to look for them. Whenever he sees Elsie walking to school, he'll stop to give her a lift. It gives her a buzz to drive into school with him and he likes to make her happy.

After the flats, the road dips down and swings around past the golf course. Bright green at its best, the summer has brutalised most of the course this year, leaving the edges of it pale and dry. But perched on a cliff, almost falling into the ocean as it does, it's still his favourite place to be, drought-stricken or not. From here, he can see past the rock pool and across to the skinny little inlet they call Brindle Bay. It's not fancy so it's never attracted a crowd, and only on the wildest days does it bring the surfers down from Raleigh. Which leaves it pretty much free for the Brindle Public kids.

The school itself is a block up from the beach, on the corner between the football oval and Brindle Memorial Park, which, years back, used to be a dump. Hard to imagine that now, he thinks, as he swings into the staff car park and turns into what is, unofficially, his space.

He grabs his battered old briefcase from the seat beside him and gets out of the car, slamming the door hard to make sure it shuts properly. He's halfway to the staffroom before, remembering, he turns back. There, on the back seat of the car, is a batch of Michelle's cupcakes: a tradition for the first day back.

The walk up to the staffroom is slower this time, what with trying to balance the cakes and hang on to his briefcase at the same time. Luckily, the playground is quiet. Not for long, though: tomorrow, when the kids start back, the noise will be deafening. He misses them over the summer break, and he's always dead keen to see them all again, to hear what they've been up to. Which is not to say he doesn't appreciate having the first day without them, so he can get ready for the onslaught. Pupil-free day, that's what they used to call it. Until someone in head office decided there was a problem with that—disrespectful to the kids or some such rot—so now it's become a 'staff development day' instead.

Voices float down from the staffroom. As he reaches the doorway, he pauses for effect, holding the plate of cupcakes in front of him.

When Tania sees him, she starts to clap. 'It's Michelle's cakes,' she calls out.

Terry feigns outrage. 'Sometimes I think that's all I am: a courier for Michelle's cakes.'

Tania hoots. 'Not true, Terry, not true. We love you as much as we love Michelle's cakes.'

Terry puts the cakes down at the far end of the large table that nearly fills the room.

'Can we have one now, sir?' Tania asks him, her voice a high-pitched whine although, as ever, her eyes are sparkling. She's had some sun over the break—the last of the idiot sunbakers—and her skin is glowing. She reminds him of a hazelnut, everything about her a shade of brown: dark brown hair, light brown eyes, soft brown skin. 'It's the Koori in me,' she says. 'That and the wog.' The Koori from her mum, the wog from her dad, who calls himself Italian even though he was born in Brindle.

8

'You still shouldn't bake yourself.' That's what he tells her, year in, year out. And he knows that makes him sound like her father but he can't stop himself. 'None of it's going to save you from a melanoma.'

Tania, though, seems to thinks her heritage gives her some sort of immunity. 'You burn, I absorb.'

Well, that's rubbish, he thinks to himself, but he lets it go for today. Instead, he shakes his head at her. 'Ms Rossi,' he says, 'you know the rules at Brindle Public. Michelle's cakes are not to be eaten before ten-thirty.'

Tania slumps back in her seat. 'But I'm hungry now, sir. Have some pity—I'm on Year 5 this year.'

He's not budging. 'Ten-thirty, Ms Rossi. Then you can have two.'

Beside her, Belinda is laughing. Terry gives her a wink. 'Welcome back, Ms Coote.'

He has a soft spot for little Belinda. He knows he shouldn't think of her like that, as little Belinda; she's a colleague and colleagues need to be treated with respect and all that palaver. But he can't help it. She's little Belinda to him and that's all there is to it. And she's a sweetie. She really is. Just what you'd want in a kindy teacher. She's probably not much more than twenty-five—she's only been out for three years—but it's hard to guess her age just by looking at her. Because she's so little and round. Like a dumpling.

'Good holiday?'

She beams back at him. 'Terrific,' she says.

He knows she's single and he's always waiting to hear if there's someone on the horizon. Not that he'd ask her, not straight out like that, but Tania gives him an update every now and then. It always astonishes him how women talk. About everything. Nothing too personal, nothing too intimate to share with the sisterhood. And he's surrounded by them. Everywhere he bloody looks, there they are, the sisterhood again. Not that he minds being the only man on staff. *Just me and the girls*, that's what he says.

There's a small kitchen area in the staffroom and before he sits down, he makes himself a cup of coffee. 'Anyone else?' He turns to do a head count, but there aren't any takers. Nor is there any sugar. He makes a mental note to pick some up during the break. Without it, the Nescafé's bloody awful, but at least it's hot.

He sits down between Belinda and Tania, with Helen and Elaine opposite him. 'So here we are again.'

Helen gives him a dry smile. 'Least I get to escape next year.'

She's been threatening to retire for years now. 'Really?'

'One more year,' she says, 'that's all I've got in me. Then I'll cash in the super and take off travelling.'

Himself, he's never had the travelling bug. In all the years, he's never wanted to leave Jinda—or Brindle, for that matter. 'How long's it been for you then?'

Helen taps the table with the back of her rings. 'If I make it through this year, I'll be up to twenty-five.'

'Twenty-five.' He makes a whistling sound through his teeth. 'That's some sort of anniversary, isn't it?' He elbows Tania. 'Help me out, will you, love? Twenty-five years—what sort of anniversary is that?'

'Silver, Terry. It's silver. I can't believe you don't know that.'

Terry nods at Helen. 'See, love? Silver. We'll have to get you a silver tray or a watch or something to mark the moment.'

But Helen just shakes her head at him. She's let her hair turn grey and now she reminds him of a sparrow. It's the haircut as much as the colour: flicked back and layered so that it looks like she's growing wings at the side of her head. Her clothes are sparrow-like, too, all browns and beiges, without a splash of something to brighten them up.

Beside her, Elaine Toomey is almost the polar opposite. A real fashion plate. Today she's in white trousers and a loose silvery top. As always, her hair is long and blonde, even though, after Helen and Terry himself, she'd be third in line for the prize of longest-serving teacher at Brindle Public.

She's brought her coffee with her, takeaway from downtown Henley—eight kilometres north of Brindle but a world away—because she's still not convinced that anyone in Brindle can make a decent brew.

He watches her cradle the cup in her hands as she takes a sip. 'How is it?' he asks her.

The resumption of their morning ritual makes her smile. 'Perfect,' she says in a soft cultured tone that's out of place in this little enclave where, for the thirteenth year running, she'll be taking the Year 1/2 class.

His eye on the empty doorway, he leans across to her. 'So,' he says, his voice a stage whisper, 'have you seen her yet?'

Elaine purses her lips and, her eyes also on the doorway, pretends to shush him.

He turns to the rest of them. 'Anyone seen the new boss yet?'

'Acting boss.' That's all Helen says. The others look blank. They know her name—Laurie Mathews—and they know she's come not as a school transfer, but straight from head office, from some management position. Policy or something.

Checking his watch, Terry raises an eyebrow. 'Well, by my reckoning, she's late.'

That makes Belinda titter but Tania just rolls her eyes. And as though it's all been scripted, that's when they hear footsteps coming down the hallway. Quick, heeled footsteps. Regular, not rushed, not tripping up in haste. Click, click, click, click, click, click, stop. And then, there she is, in the doorway.

God, she's young. That's his first thought. So young that, for a split second, he wonders whether she's a student teacher. But her face is set with a look of authority that immediately puts him straight.

She's wearing a suit, which is odd, given that the last person to wear a suit to Brindle Public was the pollie who popped in a couple of years ago to talk to the kids about Anzac Day. Or Remembrance Day. He can't remember which.

Like the pollie, she's fully kitted out. Only she's in a skirt, not trousers. She's got the suit jacket buttoned right up although it's still the middle of summer. Christ, she's even wearing stockings. If he could get away with it, he'd lean over to Tania and whisper to her, *Think she's missed her stop, don't you?*

The woman's eyes flick around the table. There's space for her to sit close to the door but instead she walks right around the room until she's at the head of the table, just where the cupcakes are. For a minute, Terry thinks that's why she's chosen that spot—so she'll be closest to the cupcakes. Instead, without a word, she reaches over, picks them up and takes them over to the kitchen bench.

Oi, he wants to call out, *oi*. He can't believe she's done that, just up and moved his cupcakes without even a *mind if I pop these over on the bench?*

She sits down at the table, opens her laptop and turns it on. Only then does she address the group.

'Good morning,' she says, 'I'm Laurie Mathews. I'm looking forward to being your principal for this year.'

'Acting,' Terry mumbles under his breath. *Acting principal.*

Across the way, Elaine's smile is nervous. 'I'm Elaine,' she says, 'Elaine Toomey. On behalf of our little school, I'd like to welcome you here.'

Laurie nods. 'Thank you, Elaine,' she says. 'It's good to be here.' Her voice is louder and lower than he would have expected, and he wonders if that's a learnt thing or natural. He pictures her, then, as a ten-year-old, with a booming voice that's loud enough to knock you flying. The thought of it tickles him and he glances at Helen, to see whether she's with him, to see whether she's thinking what he's thinking. But she's already off somewhere else, her eyes glassy.

And well might she dream the hour away, because that's how long Laurie Mathews takes to go through all the bloody departmental facts and figures. Relevant stuff, he'll give her that—enrolments and funding and budgets and the like—but he's never really been interested in the numbers and now, quite frankly, he just wants her to finish up so he can head off to his classroom and start getting ready for the little rats. Year 6, it's not an easy gig, even if it's only a small class this year.

Thinking about them makes him lose track, so when Laurie Mathews hands him a sheet, he's got no idea what it's all about. Holding it out in front of him, he rears his head back, trying to read it. But it's no good. Without his glasses, he can't make head nor tail of it. It's just a piece of paper with a whole lot of rectangles all over it. And he can pretend all he likes that he's still in his thirties, but it's the eyes that make a liar of him. To think he used to have 20/20 vision. Hawkeye Pritchard. Could have been a pilot if he'd wanted. Not anymore, though.

But even with his specs on, none of it makes any sense.

Laurie keeps quiet until everyone has a sheet. Funny how the room stays silent while they wait for her. Normally, it's non-stop chatter. Especially after the holidays when there's so much to talk about. But not today.

He sneaks a look at Tania, who's frowning at the sheet. She leans forward to say something but Laurie gets in first.

'As you can see,' she says, 'this is a diagram of the school, to show classroom allocations for the year.'

Terry lifts his head up. He's had the same classroom for years. When he takes a closer look at the diagram, he strains to find his name. When he does, he snorts in disbelief. She's put him in one of the bloody demountables, right up at the top end of the school. It's the last place he'd have chosen.

'There's a bit of a problem with your diagram,' he says, holding the sheet up in front of him.

Laurie tilts her face towards his, another tight smile on her lips. 'I'm sorry . . .' her eyes flick down to her computer screen '. . . Terry. What's the problem you've found?'

The tone of her voice—cool but with an edge to it—gets him even more agitated. 'The room in this diagram,' he says, 'is not my room.'

She nods her head slowly, as if to agree with him, as if to concede that there's been a mistake. 'Given that yours is the smallest class, Terry,' she says, 'I thought it was better to give you the smaller demountable and Belinda one of the larger fixed classrooms.'

At this, Belinda flushes bright red and shoots Terry a grimace.

He's started to colour too. It's like he's been sideswiped. Keep it calm, he counsels himself, keep it calm. It's not Belinda's fault. She didn't ask for it.

Although they've never actually been articulated, there are a few unofficial rules at Brindle Public. One is about the classrooms. If you're one of the new teachers, you get whatever classroom is left over. The longer you've been at Brindle, the longer you've had to work your way up the ladder to classroom heaven. There's no dressing it up: Terry has been at the top of the ladder now for the best part of a decade. And for each of those years, he's had the pick of the rooms—one of the old wooden ones that runs along the side of the school, with a balcony at the front. Nice and light and, with the windows up, enough of a breeze to keep the temperature manageable, even in February. Clean white walls that he paints himself at the end of each year. His canvases, that's how he thinks of them. Ready to be covered with next year's paintings and collages and projects and mobiles. It's his room. And everyone knows it. Whatever this new one says, everyone knows it's his room.

'I'll take the demountable,' Belinda says, her voice wavering.

But Laurie is resolute. 'Thanks, Belinda,' she says, 'but I think the new allocation will work better in terms of class management and interaction.'

Class management and interaction? What the hell is she talking about?

He opens his mouth to say something, but Tania gets in first. 'Thanks for taking the time to draw up the diagram, Laurie,' she says. 'The thing is, some of us have been at the school for a long time and we've got used to a particular classroom: we know how to set them up so they work best for the kids. There's never been any conflict over it. It's always seemed to work well.'

She looks around the table for support. Belinda looks like she's on the verge of tears and Elaine has her mouth pursed. Only Helen seems unperturbed. Terry checks the diagram again. By coincidence, Helen is still in her old room. So she's all right. But Tania's up in Siberia with him, at the far end of the school, right up near the hall.

Once Tania has finished, Laurie clasps her hands together. 'Thank you, Tania. I'm sure the system has worked well enough in the past, but I think you'll find that we'll be in a better position to meet our strategic direction and student outcomes with the proposed configuration.'

He'll explode if he hears another word of bloody management-speak rubbish. His neck has tightened up—he can feel it—and his hands are clenched into hard little balls.

The anger must be radiating out of him because now Tania has got a hand clamped over his. 'Good to have you next to me,' she whispers. Her tone is light, but the pressure of her hand is heavy. Anyone else and he'd just shake it away and keep on going, but Tania can always slow him down.

With her free hand, she shows him her sheet. 'Look,' she says, still in a whisper, 'side by side, so we'll be able to team teach.'

He grunts. On the upside, it couldn't be further away from the principal's office. *Acting* principal. But he still can't believe it. That she has the gall to just barge in and turn the place on its head. Well, there's one thing he can guarantee her: he won't be taking that sort of thing lying down.

Meanwhile, Tania's managed to negotiate a fifteen-minute tea break. And she's taken charge of the cupcakes, too, returning them to the table and, with a flourish, ripping off the cling wrap to reveal the little masterpieces. Except that she's pulled the cling wrap off so quickly she's taken half the frosting with it.

'Terry's wife made them,' she tells Laurie. 'Help yourself.'

Well, Terry's not too sure Laurie deserves one. Quite frankly, he'd prefer her to keep her mitts off them.

As it happens, Laurie's already shaking her head. 'I keep away from cakes,' she says with a laugh.

What, Terry wants to snap at her, *not even a bloody cupcake?* Instead, he reaches over to choose the one he wants: the one that's still well covered in dark chocolate frosting and sprinkled with hundreds and thousands. 'More for the rest of us, then.' He says it as an aside, but the words come out so clipped and angry that Tania stares at him in astonishment.

Okay, he gestures to her, his mouth full of cake. He's been looking forward to the cakes all morning, but now he's too annoyed to enjoy them. And where's Diane when they need her? Off drinking cocktails in bloody Hawaii.

❦

When at last the meeting is finished, Tania gives him a poke. 'Come on, grumpy, let's do a recce of the classrooms.'

'Who the hell does she think she is?' he says, spitting the words out as they walk up towards the hall. 'No discussion, nothing. A done deal. Soon as she bloody walked in. Before she even walked in. All sorted before she'd even laid eyes on us.'

Tania squeezes his elbow. 'She's just got a bit carried away trying to show who's boss, that's all.'

'If I knew we were going to get her, I'd have applied for the bloody job myself.'

'But you didn't. And you know why you didn't: because you can't stand administration. Face it, Terry, you're a classroom man.'

The demountables—his, now, and Tania's—face away from the rest of the school and look out onto a small patch of grass that used to be a soccer field. A private little space, tucked away from the rest of the school. The senior space, that's how he'll sell it to the kids. Yep. The senior space. At least it's got a bit of a ring to it.

There's a vestibule area at the entrance to the classroom, tiny but with enough space for the kids to hang up their bags. It's the classroom itself that distresses him. Everything's wrong about it. It's small, it's hot and the walls have been painted in a yellow so bright it's going to have the kids bouncing around. They need a calm colour. Something that's not going to hype them up. He checks his watch. Eleven o'clock. There's still time. If he's quick, that is.

Tania's got bright yellow in her room, too, and she hates it even more than he does. So they jump in the car and make their way to Jim's hardware store. The store is close enough that they could walk, but time's in short supply. Once inside, they decide on a white that's called something else and head straight back to school.

By the afternoon, the rooms have been transformed. Tania has moved her tables into cluster groups but he's not convinced. He prefers a horseshoe. Makes the kids concentrate better and leaves a big space in the middle of the classroom for his rug.

Now is as good a time as any to retrieve it from his old room. It's a heavy bastard and he has to hoick it up over his shoulder. Even then, it almost kills him and he needs a break before he's even got up to the hall. The sun's still vicious, although it's already after three, and he can feel the sweat dripping down the back of his neck. He sits down to catch his breath but stands up again when he catches sight of Elaine coming round the corner. Quickly, he heaves the rug back onto his shoulder and, one hand pulling on the railing, climbs up the stairs.

'Already giving it a homey touch, are you, Terry?'

He gives her a wink and tries not to wince with the weight of the damned thing. 'You know what they say, Elaine, hard to make a silk purse out of a sow's ear.' He loves that saying. Because it's so idiotic. Last year, it took him a whole afternoon to explain it to the class. Poor Elsie was still puzzling over it the next day.

Once he's manoeuvred the rug into the classroom, he rolls it onto the floor then steps back to check how it looks. Leaning back on his desk, he surveys the room. Better, he thinks, with a touch of pride. Much better.

༄

Just up the street from the school is a small strip of shops. Nothing fancy—a chemist, a corner shop, a bakery and a cafe—but it's enough to get what you need. That afternoon, once he's made a bit of headway in the classroom, he pops up to the cafe and orders a coffee. There's a new lass serving, he notices. There's also a new display on the counter: a series of handmade cards, each with a different photograph. When he looks a bit closer, he sees that the photos are of Brindle: the boat ramp, the pool, the beach, the headland. Fancy that, he thinks to himself. Brindle cards. Who would have thought it? Only a couple of years ago and the only thing people knew about Brindle was the jail. He chooses a table at the far end of the cafe, and when the coffee comes he's happy to find that they've made it the way he likes it, strong and hot.

He sees Len and Elsie as soon as they walk in but neither of them sees him. He's about to call Elsie's name when something stops him. Instead, he leans back in his chair to watch them, funny pair that they are.

Together they amble down the passageway, both of them looking like they got their clothes from a bin somewhere. Len's T-shirt is marked and his trousers must once have belonged to a much bigger man. On his feet, he wears a pair of dirty white Volleys without socks. Light brown hair falls around his face in jagged edges, as though it's simply been lopped off to keep it out of his eyes. His face is large and square, his mouth narrow and his eyes small and dark.

Elsie looks so much like him even a stranger would pick them as father and daughter. She has the same large, square face, the same light brown hair, the same dark eyes, only hers are more blank than watchful. Her hair is also badly cut: too long to look neat, too short to tie back. She is dressed in a light green T-shirt and ill-fitting royal blue shorts with the Brindle Public logo embroidered on one leg. She wears nothing under the T-shirt, and the outline of early breasts is all too clear. She needs to be fitted for a bra, Terry thinks. But this isn't something that's going to occur to Len.

'We want a milkshake!' Len shouts at the woman behind the counter.

When she shrinks back, Len steps forward. 'We want a milk-shake,' he repeats.

The woman keeps her distance. 'What flavour?' she asks.

Len swivels back to Elsie. 'Elsie,' he bellows, 'what flavour?'

Elsie crooks her finger and sticks it into her mouth. 'Caramel,' she says.

'What?' Len yells. 'What'd you say, Elsie?'

Elsie pulls her finger out. 'I said *caramel*!' she yells back.

Everyone in the shop is watching them and the woman's face has turned red with embarrassment. 'One caramel milkshake, then?'

Len starts to shake his head. 'Not one,' he yells, 'two! We want two caramel milkshakes.'

'Takeaway?' Her voice is hopeful.

Len shakes his head. 'Nup. We're going to drink them here, at one of your tables here.' He turns back to his daughter. 'Isn't that right, Elsie? We're going to have our milkshakes here, aren't we?'

'Our caramel milkshakes, Dad.'

Len gives her a big smile. 'You've got it right there, Elsie.'

Although this is not the usual practice, the woman makes Len pay upfront. This doesn't worry him—he just gets out his wallet and hands over a note. But he's vigilant about his change, counting it out slowly and loudly to make sure she's got it right.

There's a row of booths along one wall of the cafe. Len and Elsie choose one and sit opposite each other, a steel-topped table between them. The seats are covered in vinyl, which, when they first sit down, is slippery enough for them to slide on until they bump into the wall. It's so much fun they do it twice, then Elsie does it again.

When the milkshakes come, neither of them hold back. They both just put their heads over the metal cups and suck up as fast as they can, right to the bottom. Terry swallows a smile.

Once they've finished their milkshakes, they don't hang around: they're up and at it. Only on their way out does Elsie spy Terry.

'Mr P!' she shouts. 'Mr P!'

Terry puts up a hand and gives her a little wave. 'Hi, Elsie.'

The two of them shuffle between tables to get to him. 'I'm in Year 6 now,' Elsie tells him.

Terry smiles. 'Are you just?'

'I think so, Mr P. But what do you reckon? Do you reckon I'm already in Year 6 even though school hasn't started yet? Or am I still in Year 5 until tomorrow?'

Terry pretends to give it some serious thought. 'I'd say you're already in Year 6, Elsie. That's what I'd be saying.'

Elsie is puffed up with pleasure. 'That's what I was thinking too, Mr P. That's exactly what I was thinking.'

As he makes his way back to the classroom, it's Elsie who fills his head. She's come a long way, that's for sure, but he still can't help but worry about how she'll go in high school. Kids can be cruel, and Elsie's an easy target. But it's still a year away and a lot can happen in a year. Like reading. Like getting Elsie's reading right up to speed. And not just Elsie, the lot of them.

It's late by the time he's got the classroom sorted. Michelle just shakes her head when he finally makes it home. She's not annoyed, though. She's used to it. And she's made him that chicken casserole he loves, the one they just call 'Michelle's casserole'. She's had the day at home and the place looks a treat.

'Diane's replacement, what's she like?' she asks him.

He's not in the mood to think about it.

'She wore a suit,' he tells her. That's about as much as he can manage.

Michelle laughs. 'A suit? At Brindle Public? Good luck with that.'

Nina

Nina wakes early. When she opens her eyes, she sees that a slice of summer sunshine has pushed through a slit in the curtains, beaming light across the bed. Gently, she wriggles around to face Steve then props her head up with her hand to watch him. She often watches him sleeping. She likes to wonder at him, this handsome man, who, somehow, is also her husband.

Her hair falls in her face. With her free hand, she tucks it behind her ear. Because there is so much of it, half of it falls back again. This time, she twists the errant strands into a coil then pushes it away. She has curly hair, long blonde-brown curly hair that turns to frizz when she brushes it. So she rarely brushes it at all.

His hair—Steve's hair—is curly too, but darker; in the sun it has a copper sheen. Beautiful hair, she thinks.

When he stirs, she moves closer to him, close enough for her foot to rub against his. Smiling, she kisses him on the lips then rubs her nose against his cheekbone. He wakes slowly. A stretching sort of waking that makes her smile widen. When, finally, his eyes open, they lock on her face, so close to his, and he draws back. She pretends this is not what has happened.

'Hi,' she says softly, her smile more hesitant now.

With a grunt, he turns onto his side, away from her. He's been working late, she reminds herself; he's tired, he needs to sleep. He should sleep.

And she should get up. If she's to get to school on time, she should get up now.

So that's what she does.

She slips a light dressing-gown over her nightie and quietly leaves the bedroom. Next door is Emily's room. Emily doesn't like to fall asleep in the dark and so, as always, her door has been left ajar. Now, Nina opens it wider, just wide enough to look inside. Her daughter—their daughter—is still sleeping, her face tilting up on the pillow, her tiny rosebud mouth closed. Nina's heart widens as she watches her: this little girl, no longer a baby, who sleeps not in a cot but in her own bed now. Except that she hasn't completely got the hang of it yet, and there are nights when, woken by a thud, Nina will rush in to find her on the floor, still asleep, her little brow unfurrowed by her fall.

It is half past six and Emily will certainly wake soon. But not, Nina hopes, before she has had a coffee.

The kitchen itself is small but the alcove beside it is large enough for a table. This is where Nina loves to sit, mostly because it has a view out onto the yard. Not that it's a beautiful yard: just patchy grass with a concrete path that leads up to the washing line. But Nina tries to see how it might be, with a new deck coming off the kitchen and the yard filled with trees. That would be lovely, she thinks. Steve isn't so keen. A money thing, mostly, but he's never really been one for home renovations. He thinks they should be happy to have got into the market at all, with prices rising so quickly. And she *is* happy about that, even if Claremont wouldn't have been her first choice. But Claremont is Steve's stamping ground and he likes it here, so who is she to complain?

She does miss the sea, though. Not that it's so very far away; they could drive to the beach in forty minutes. But they don't.

Before they'd bought in Claremont, they'd lived within reach of the water. Up north—right up north, ten hours north—and so close to the ocean she could almost taste the salt water when she woke in the morning. She'd loved living there. And she'd loved working there. Of course she was only ever a casual teacher—permanent placements almost never come up on the north coast—but she'd been lucky: one term had turned into two, then into a year, then two, then three.

Midway through the second year, she met Steve. It was at a party at the local surf club; not one Nina had been invited to—one of the other teachers had dragged her along, *to get you out a bit*. Nina had never been a party girl; in a crowd, she was shy and awkward.

She heard him before she saw him. He had the type of voice that could carry a party. The type of voice Nina didn't have. When he came into view, she found herself watching him. He stood out. At the time, she would have guessed he was well over six foot. In fact, he is only just five eleven. Still taller than her, though, if only just.

When he caught her eye, she blushed, and when he made his way over to her—of all the people there, it was her he chose—she'd felt her palms become sweaty. And although she became tongue-tied, he seemed not to notice; he just stayed and talked. About what, she can't remember anymore, just that there had been a steady stream of words, steady and comforting, almost without a break, so that she didn't need to say much in reply. She loved that: loved that her quietness was not a problem. When, at the end of the night, he asked her out, she looked around the room, filled as it was with bronzed and buxom locals, and was amazed he should opt for her. And when, less than a year later, he proposed to her, she answered quickly: so quickly there was no chance for him to reconsider.

Later, after they were married, he decided it was time for a change. Instead of serving drinks at the club, he'd try to get into management. For this, he needed to study, and for him to study, they needed to move. So they moved to Claremont.

And now, from the hallway of their house in Claremont, she hears the patter of little feet headed her way. Emily is up. There she is, poking her head through the doorway. Standing up, Nina holds her arms out. 'Good morning, blossom,' she says.

Emily stays by the door. 'I'm not a blossom, Mummy, you know that, don't you?' Her voice is severe.

Nina tries not to laugh. 'What are you then?'

'I'm an Emily Foreman,' she says.

Nina murmurs in agreement. 'Yes,' she says, 'that's exactly what you are: you're an Emily Foreman.'

One foot balanced on the other, the little girl looks pleased. Quickly, Nina checks the clock on the wall. It's almost seven: time to get a move on.

Today they are out of the house just after eight, which isn't bad. Quietly, carefully, Nina closes the front door so as not to wake Steve. Emily, too, knows to be quiet in the mornings. *Because Daddy is sleeping,* she tells Nina on the way to the car, her voice a whisper-hiss.

Nina fumbles in her bag for the car keys. 'Because Daddy worked late last night, didn't he?'

Emily nods, her eyes wide. Daddy's work is important. Already she knows this.

It's Tuesday; Tuesdays and Wednesdays aren't childcare days; they're Poppy days. Today when they arrive at Poppy's house, the front door is closed. Nina gives only a cursory knock before she turns the handle and walks in.

'Hi, Colin!' she calls out to her father-in-law.

'That must be my two favourite girls!' he calls back.

Nina smiles to see him.

'What about Auntie Jen?' Emily pipes up. 'Is she your favourite girl too?'

Colin tugs at his ear, which has tufts of grey hair growing out of it. This fascinates Emily. It fascinates Nina, too, who often catches herself staring. 'You're right,' he says now. 'Auntie Jen is my favourite girl too. You're all my favourite girls.'

From Colin's place, it's only a short drive to Stenton Public School. This is Nina's third year there as the learning and support teacher. It's a good job—especially because it's part-time—and although she misses the bustle of the classroom, she loves the one-on-one teaching. She even wonders if she'd be able to cope with a whole classful of kids again. Not to mention how she'd ever manage a return to full-time work.

As she nears the school, she scours the street for a park. There isn't any staff parking at the school so it's simply a matter of finding a spot wherever she can. Today she's lucky and gets one right outside the gate. She takes it as a sign that the day will be a good one.

In her boot is a plastic crate full of books and a carton of milk.

Leaning over, she swings her handbag over her shoulder, lifts out the crate and carries it over to her classroom. Well, classroom is something of an overstatement. In reality, it's an old storage area. There aren't enough classrooms to go around, and because Nina isn't on class and works part-time, she got what was left over.

She doesn't mind. In fact, she's grown to love it. And even though it's small and narrow, a wall of windows keeps the room bright and sunny.

From two of the windows, she has hung tear-shaped crystals that throw strips of rainbow across the room and onto the walls. She is especially pleased with the walls: pleased she painted them light blue and white, like a piece of sky drifting in through the windows.

The only table in the room is covered in a tablecloth to hide the fact that it's actually just two old school desks pushed together. In the corner of the room is an old filing cabinet covered with a silver-blue scarf. On top of it is an electric jug, a tin of chocolate powder and a packet of marshmallows. She adds the carton of milk. If Nina has a drawcard, this is it: when they are working with her, the kids can have a hot chocolate with a marshmallow.

She turns the kettle on, but before it's boiled there's a knock on the door. 'Come in,' she calls out, but no one does. So she walks over and opens the door herself.

In front of her is a student she doesn't recognise; the new girl, she presumes. 'Paige?' she asks.

The girl nods. She doesn't return Nina's smile but she does look her in the eye. This, in itself, is unusual. On a first meeting, the new kids tend to just shuffle their feet and look at the floor. It's embarrassing to be hauled out of class to see Mrs Foreman. It's as good as holding up a sign saying *I'm stupid*. That's why no one ever comes to her with their head held high. Except this one. She's a stocky kid: broad shoulders, chunky little legs and a barrel-shaped tummy. Freckles, too; not just across her nose but a whole face full of them, from her forehead right down past her chin. Her hair, light brown and long, could do with a cut.

'I'm Mrs Foreman,' she says. 'Nina Foreman.'

This makes the girl flick her head up in surprise. It's an introduction Nina gives deliberately. To create an intimacy, to give out a bit of a secret. To make up for the embarrassment of being sent out of the classroom and over to her in the first place.

'Come in,' she says. 'Have a seat.'

The kettle starts to whistle as it boils, and already Paige is looking past Nina and across to the tea corner.

Nina makes her a hot chocolate. 'White marshmallow or pink one?'

The girl's lips twist up. 'Pink.'

Nina hands her an exercise book, which is already covered in red-and-green-striped contact. Nina covers all her students' books, to make it seem a bit less like schoolwork and a bit more like fun.

'Do me a title page,' she tells the girl. 'Just your name and your class.' Nina has three pencil cases: a green one filled with coloured pencils, a red one with textas, and a blue one with lead pencils and biros. She places them all on the table and leaves the girl to it. She always starts with something easy, something she knows they'll be able to manage, so they don't panic.

Paige looks doubtful but opens her book to the first page then runs a finger down the edge to make it stay flat. She chooses the red pencil case and tips it up so that the textas roll out of it and onto the table. For her name, she uses purple. *Paige Peters* she writes in careful bubble writing. To make a border, she draws green zigzags along the edge of the page then repeats the pattern in red and then blue. When she has finished the last zigzag, she looks up at Nina.

Nina nods. 'Good,' she says. 'And now I want you to tell me a story about yourself. Just a short one. Two or three sentences, that's all.' It's a test to gauge the girl's writing level, only she doesn't want to say that. But the girl isn't fooled, and her face falls.

Nina hands her a lead pencil. 'It's just for me,' she says, 'so I can get to know you.'

The girl bites her lip but takes the pencil and starts to write. She is left-handed, like Emily. For this reason alone, Nina feels a sudden affection for her.

She writes slowly, her first attempt at each word crossed out then rewritten. Most of the words, even on a second attempt, are misspelt.

'So,' she says, 'you'll be eleven this year?' This is what the girl has written—that she'll be eleven on 11 August; that she has a cat at her mum's place; that her dad lives in an apartment where they aren't allowed pets.

Next, Nina hands her a book. It's a simple text, widely enough spaced to make it seem like a chapter book. The girl's reading is stilted and laborious and she baulks at many of the words. She's well behind where she needs to be. Which means that she and Nina will be spending a lot of time together this year.

Terry

A new day, 29 January. First day back for the kids. And, he remembers with a start, Clare's birthday.

Clare.

Oh God.

And although it's been years—decades—she's still crystal clear to him. Even now, he can picture her as if she were right there in front of him: her lithe little body, her light pink lips, the watery blue of her eyes.

Lovely eyes.

Lovely Clare.

It makes him tremble to conjure her up like that. Even now.

Best not to, then.

Best to push her right away again.

So he does. He gets into his car, gives himself a shake and pushes Clare Sorenson back into the far recesses of his mind.

The new term, that's what he needs to focus on now.

And sure enough, he feels it the moment he steps into the playground: the crackle in the air that signals the true start to the school year. An energetic feeling, that's what it is. That's what's special about it. Because there's nothing better than watching the kids tumble in through the gate and, like magnets, click back into their little posses.

Except for Elsie, who doesn't attach herself to anyone much. Today, she's hovering around the play equipment, half watching the other kids, half daydreaming, one finger in her mouth.

He hears Trina before he sees her. 'Elsie!' she screams. 'Elsie!' He follows the sound of the voice and spies her down by the front gate. It's been a while—years—since she last came to school. And she's not looking great. Everything about her is unwashed and her dress, cotton and stretchy at the bodice, has a wet stain down the front. Her feet are bare, her face is grimy and her hair is dry and unkempt.

When she catches sight of Elsie, she starts screaming louder. 'Come here, you little bitch,' she cries out as she makes her way over to the play equipment. 'Get over here, you stupid bitch.'

Terry hurries over. Before he can reach them, Trina is already on top of her daughter, her hands lashing out to slap the girl. Elsie wraps her arms around her head and tries to curl herself into a ball. She is shouting now but her voice is hoarse and muffled.

'Get off her!' Terry shouts, but Trina just keeps going.

'Trina! Trina, leave her!' This time, his voice is so loud it cuts through, halting Trina in her frenzy.

Elsie is no longer shouting; now she's just crying. Mucus pours out of her nostrils and when she tries to wipe it away, she streaks it across her face instead. Her crying is loud. 'Mum,' she cries, her voice rough. 'What was that for?'

Trina, defeated now, has her shoulders hunched forward. 'Because,' she says, her voice a low growl, 'you're a little bitch. You've always been a little bitch.'

Elsie doesn't reply at first. Instead she rubs her fingers hard into her nose. 'Not always, Mum,' she says. 'I'm not always a bitch, Mum.'

Putting his arm around the girl, Terry presses her to him so that she's facing away from her mother. 'Go now, Trina,' he says. 'The bell's about to ring so you should just go now.'

A crowd of kids has started to gather around them. Still holding Elsie, Terry shoos them away with his free hand. 'There's nothing to see,' he says, 'nothing to see.'

To Trina he hisses a final warning, 'I said go, Trina. Now.'

Trina shoots her daughter a vicious glare before she makes her way back to the front gate.

Once she has left, Terry crouches down in front of Elsie and tries to soothe her. When, after some minutes, he stands up, Elsie leans her head into his chest and puts her arms around him. Softly, and with one arm around the girl's waist, Terry strokes the back of her head. They stay like that for a long time—until the girl's shoulders are no longer heaving. Slowly, then, and with a great gentleness, Terry breaks the embrace and, taking Elsie's hand in his, walks her over to the staffroom.

She's still sobbing quietly when they get there. The door is closed and Terry hopes to God that Laurie isn't in there so he won't have to go through the rigmarole of explaining what's happened and what bloody form needs to be filled in. Because it's Elsie, what they really need to do is to keep head office right out of it. Give the kid a bit of TLC and leave it at that.

He's in luck: only Tania and Belinda are in the staffroom. He gives a tiny shake of the head so they won't ask what happened—not now, not while Elsie's there—and they don't. Instead, Tania rubs Elsie's back while Terry looks for something he can use to clean the girl's face.

He can't find any tissues, but there's a roll of paper towel in a metal dispenser near the sink. He rips off a length of it, wets it under the tap so it won't be too harsh on her skin and starts to clean her face. Any other eleven-year-old would resist, but Elsie lifts her face up to make it easier for him. Slowly, then, her tears subside. Thinking that it might be helping—his wiping her face—he goes back to the sink, takes a fresh piece of paper towel, wets it with warm water and again runs it over her skin. 'Shush, love,' he whispers, 'it's okay now, it's okay.'

A moment later, the bell rings. Although it's not a bell anymore. Now it's a recording that gets played through the loudspeakers. With Diane in charge, it was always going to be the Stones and, in a show of hands in the staffroom, 'Jumpin' Jack Flash' won by a vote. Every morning, Terry has a little smile as he watches the kids hurrying to the sound of those bad boys. This morning, his smile is smaller than usual, but that's not surprising. Bloody Trina.

Just when things had finally been sorted out; just when Family Services had agreed that even if Len wasn't the sharpest knife in the drawer, it didn't mean he couldn't look after his daughter—and this happens. All the work he'd put into it—his work, Diane's work— and now this. He'll kill Trina if it unravels now. If it all gets dragged up again, he'll come after her with an axe. It's been a lesson, though, and this is the lesson he's learnt: sometimes it's better to fly under the radar and keep Family Services well out of the picture. With any luck, Trina'll take off again and never come back.

Enough of that. He turns to give Elsie a wink. 'Come on,' he says, holding out his hand. 'Let's go.'

Outside, there's mayhem in the playground.

'Last year's classes,' Terry calls out. 'Lining up in last year's classes.'

Running the length of Terry's old classroom is a balcony that looks over the morning assembly area. It's a good place to address the school, provided the PA system works. Terry calls it the Diane Thomas soapbox. But today, Laurie's up there instead, in a suit again. Grey this time, instead of black. Still must be stinking hot, he thinks. His shirt is short-sleeved and already he's sweating.

Bringing the microphone up to her mouth, Laurie starts to speak. But no one can hear a word she's saying. Stifling a smile, Terry climbs the stairs to give her a hand. Sure enough, she hasn't switched the thing on. Granted, the button's on the bottom of the mic instead of at the side, but still. He turns it on for her, gives it a tap to check it's working, then hands it back. She says thanks but shoots him a half-hostile look, like it was his fault all along. And that's enough to make him want to yank out the cable on his way back down the stairs.

'Good morning, Brindle Public,' says Laurie, and this time, because she puts her mouth so close to the microphone, it emits a sharp whistling sound. 'My name is Ms Mathews and I will be the acting principal while Ms Thomas is on leave this year.'

The announcement gets the kids whispering to each other, although Terry's got no idea why. Diane must have warned them thirty times that she'd be away for the year. Still, it seems the penny's only just dropped.

And then it's over to the main game: all students are to go with their old teachers, who'll talk to them about their new classes.

So far, so good, until Terry starts to lead his class up the stairs and over to the demountables.

'Mr P,' Kurt calls out, his voice already deeper than it was last year. His hair, thick and dark, sits neatly over his ears after what, to go by past experience, might well be his only haircut for the year. 'Mr P,' he repeats, 'where we going? We're going the wrong way.'

'Yeah, Mr P,' Ethan chips in. 'This is the wrong way.'

Terry turns around. 'Let's just say there's been a couple of changes since last year. Can't tell you just yet—I'll explain once we're there.' At least that makes it sound exciting. And sure enough, they fall silent as they follow Terry up the stairs, past the hall and over to the demountables.

'Here we are, ladies and gentlemen,' he announces as they enter the vestibule. 'Find a hook—don't fight about it, remember it's only a hook—hang your bag on it then go and sit on the rug.'

Once they're all inside, Terry drags his chair across so he's sitting in front of them all. 'As you can see,' he says, 'I've been given a new room.'

Kurt puts up a hand. 'But it's not your room, it's Ms Coote's room.'

Terry gives his hair a scratch. He can't have nits already, surely; not on the first day back. 'Good point, Kurt,' he replies, 'and nice observation. It has indeed been Ms Coote's room for some years now. But this year we've swapped.'

'Your old room's much better than this room, Mr P.' Ethan is sitting beside Kurt. He doesn't raise his hand, he just calls out.

'Hand up, please, Mr Thompson, otherwise it'll all descend into chaos before the day is done.'

Ethan shoots up a hand and keeps on talking. 'The other room, it's heaps better. For one thing, it's got a balcony.' He's a freckly kid, is Ethan, and he talks with his face scrunched up so tight he seems to have his eyes closed. Brindle is league territory and Ethan and Kurt are the school's star players. Kurt because he's built like a brick and Ethan because he's fast.

'That's correct, Ethan, it does have a balcony.'

'So why did you swap then, Mr P?' It's Jade this time. For a kid who mostly zones out in class, every now and then she's spot on with her questions.

He stops to think about it. *Ms Mathews made me* isn't going to be the most helpful answer, even if it's the honest one.

'Well, because Ms Coote's class will be a big one this year. And Ms Mathews thought it would be better if Ms Coote had some more space.'

'So Ms Mathews made you swap?' Cody sits just behind Kurt and Ethan, his little head peeping out from between them. He's thin and wiry and small, his hair bleached close to white from a summer spent, no doubt, on his surfboard.

Terry shakes his head. This is one of those times when lying's the only way to go. 'No. It was more an agreement.'

Cody leans forward, a hand on each of his mates' shoulders. 'I wouldn't've agreed, Mr P,' he says, his voice earnest. 'I would've just said, *This is my room and I'm going to keep my room.* That's what I would've said.'

'Me too,' Ethan calls out. 'I would've just stayed.'

Time to move on, Terry thinks. 'So, ladies and gentlemen,' he says, 'today I'm going to be telling you about your new classes.'

A nervous ripple passes through the group. He could draw it out a bit, call them out name by name to keep the suspense going, but what for? Best just serve it straight up.

'So,' he says, 'here's the news: I'll be your teacher again this year.'

He watches as they digest the information. Kurt is the first to react, punching the air with his fist as he lets out a whistling, '*Yes-s-sss.*'

The rest of them are quieter. Cody nods his head like one of those dolls on a spring and Ethan just looks pleased. Behind him, Jade leans back on her hands and gives Terry one of her lazy grins. Even though she's not yet twelve, she's as sassy as an eighteen-year-old. Out of school uniform, you'd think she was fourteen, fifteen even. Already she's a head-turner. Her hair, naturally a very light brown, has lightened with the summer, and there's a new smattering of freckles across her nose.

Beside her, Bridie doesn't do or say anything. She just stays as she is: cross-legged on the rug, her hands in her lap. Only when Terry gives her a wink does she venture a tiny smile, her eyes big and watery behind her thick glasses.

Elsie is sitting right in front of Terry and, like a big puppy, she jumps up and runs to him, falling over him with her arms outstretched. A few of the kids snigger, but they're all used to Elsie.

'So then,' Terry says, once he's sent Elsie back to the rug, 'welcome back to Brindle Public, 6P.'

That's all he says, but it's enough to send a buzz across the classroom.

'And now, 6P—' he repeats the word deliberately, to keep the excitement up, to highlight the elevation it represents, this rise to the top of the ranks of Brindle Public School '—we're going to start the new year with some holiday news. Each of you will stand up and tell us, in a couple of sentences, something good about the holidays.' With exaggerated movements, he takes a stopwatch out of his trouser pocket. 'You know the drill: one minute on the stopwatch and I'll give you a warning when you've got ten seconds left.' It's a technique he's been using for a couple of years now—ever since Anthony Longman wouldn't shut up.

Today, Jade is first cab off the rank. Unfazed by the stopwatch, she spends the first ten seconds fiddling with her hem, which, in Terry's view, should come down a couple of centimetres. More than that. What she really needs is a new school uniform. One that isn't so tight across her chest. Puberty has come to her in a rush and, as she lets go of her hem to face the class properly, it's clear she's pleased about it. He's never seen her stand up so straight: so straight that her newly grown breasts press hard against the blue-and-white ging-ham of her tunic. He opens his mouth to say something, but what's he going to say? Stop standing so tall; stop being so provocative?

'We stayed at a caravan park down the coast,' she tells the class, 'and one night my sister didn't come back until one in the morning so now she's grounded for two weeks and she can't even go to her best friend's birthday party. And we hung around with a whole lot of high school kids and we pretended I was in Year 8 and they all believed us.'

She stops and Terry counts down the remaining seconds: fifty-six, fifty-seven, fifty-eight, fifty-nine, sixty. 'Thank you, Jade.'

Bridie has a new uniform but really, he thinks, she and Jade should just swap. Poor little Bridie's tunic is two sizes too big for her and hangs off her tiny frame. What was Vonnie thinking? Not a fly-ing chance in hell Bridie's going to grow into it this year.

She pushes her glasses up before she starts, her eyes on the stop-watch as nerves and the time limit make her gabble. 'My dad made me a pencil case and it's got my name on it.' She holds up a glazed wooden box that has the word BRIDIE burnt into the top, the writ-ing sloping and shaky. She slides the top panel open to reveal a rubber, a sharpener and two pencils so new they haven't yet been sharpened to a point. Terry makes an encouraging sound so she'll keep going and she does, her words tumbling together. 'And my dad and me, we went on a holiday and we went to this fun park and we went on every ride.' She looks down as she speaks, and only when the time is up does she give Terry a cautious look. He taps his fingers against his leg, swallows, then gives the girl a nod. Still wary, she colours as she makes her way back to the rug.

Kurt swaggers his way to the front of the classroom. He's turned brown-red with too much sun, the skin across his nose peeled back to a baby-doll pink. Standing with one leg bent, he gives his hair a scratch before he starts. 'We went overseas with me dad and we stayed in these hut things that have got poles on them so they aren't on the ground, they're, like, on poles. And we went to the jungle and that and then, my brother and me, we caught the plane back by ourselves and there was this snack bar at the end of the plane and you can go there whenever you want, and whenever you want a hot chocolate, you just press this button and they bring it to you.'

Terry holds up a finger to give him the fifteen-second warning. This makes Kurt stop still for a second before he gets the rest of his story out in a rush. 'And they've got this Xbox thing on the plane, and we played it the whole time. And you could even play it while you eat your meal because the screen's stuck to the back of the chair in front of you.' He looks over to Terry to check how he's done, giving himself the victory sign as Terry mouths fifty-eight then fifty-nine before he draws an imaginary line across his neck.

'So why did you and Jordan catch the plane home without your dad?' Terry asks the question lightly.

''Cause me dad, he's moved there now. 'Cause his fiancée, that's where she lives. So we get to go there on the holidays.' Kurt scratches his head again. 'Not the next holidays—'cause it's really expensive to go there—but probably after that.'

When Terry nods, Kurt gives him a smile that's half proud and half like he wants to say something else before he squashes himself back down between Cody and Ethan, and Cody gives a yell because Kurt's sitting on his ankle and Cody reckons it's twisted.

Terry surveys his brood with a satisfied smile. It's good to be back, he thinks. It's really good to be back.

Sid

Sid doesn't need an alarm clock. Like a bird, he wakes as soon as it's daylight. He doesn't get up straightaway, though; he just lies in bed for a bit and lets the day catch up with him.

It's promising to be a hot one, already he can feel it in the air. He doesn't mind the heat. He's not a fan of humid, sticky days, but a bit of heat, that's another thing. Now he throws the sheet off, pulls himself up and swivels around until his feet are on the ground.

Under his toes, the carpet is thin. And no wonder; it's done its time. He was a kid when they laid it and now he's sixty-seven.

Although he takes his pyjamas off, he leaves his singlet on. From the wardrobe, he chooses a short-sleeved shirt. He's never been a man for a T-shirt. In a T-shirt he feels half dressed. He needs a collar to feel right.

His swimmers are hanging up in the bathroom. He pulls them on, then backtracks into the bedroom for yesterday's walk shorts. All he needs is a towel, his sandals, a pair of underpants to put in his pocket, and he's set.

He never locks the door. He doesn't see the point in it. There's nothing much worth stealing inside and, from what he sees on the telly, locks don't seem to deter anyone much anyway. If they want to get in, they'll get in all right.

Ahead of him, the laneway is quiet. Four doors down, there's a passionfruit vine that, as best as Sid can tell, is the only thing keeping the back fence up. A hammer and a couple of nails would do the trick, but the owners are new and he's not sure they'd appreciate him just getting in and fixing it up. Still, his hands itch to do it each time he passes by.

He turns left at the end of the street and walks down until he hits the bay. It doesn't matter how often he sees it, every time it makes him go quiet, just looking at it. It's so beautiful.

The pool—Brindle Rock Pool, according to the new council sign—is just past the boat ramp. Every morning, Sid is down at the pool by 7.45 am. A lot of the regulars are earlier than that. Six am, even, some of them. Not him. He can't see the point of it. Especially as he doesn't need to be at the school until just before nine.

On Tuesdays and Thursdays, Ray motors down to meet him at the pool. Ever since he got the ride-on buggy, he's had a new lease of life. It's an electric thing, the buggy, something of a cross between a motorbike and a golf cart. Ray plugs it in at night, and by the morning he's ready to go. And it's a sight, all right, to see Ray heading past the golf club then careering down the footpath until he reaches the pool itself.

They've always got on well, he and Ray, even when they were kids. When they were little, they'd get mistaken for twins. Which was fair enough, from Sid's perspective at least, given that there's only eighteen months between them. But Ray hated being mistaken for his little brother's twin. Not that it would happen now. Now people would give Ray an extra ten years over him. Sometimes, you've got to be careful what you wish for.

Sid doesn't wish for much. He's more inclined to let life deal out its cards and get on with it. There are worse places to find yourself than Brindle. And here he is, still living in the house he was born in. Unlike Ray, who took off as soon as he could. But someone had to stay—especially after their father dropped dead. So Sid stayed to keep their mother company, and then, as time went on, there was never a good enough reason to move out. If he'd had a family, things would have been different—he wouldn't have expected them all to bunk in with his mother—but, somehow the family thing never happened. That's the truth of it. It just never happened.

And since his mother's been gone, it's just him at the house now.

Today, the first touch of water on him is cold. Climbing backwards down the metal ladder, he lowers himself into the water until he is covered to his neck. Most of the young ones wear goggles and a cap—even the men—but he's never done either. He just closes his eyes for the first couple of seconds then keeps them open for the rest of the time. A bit of salt water never hurt anyone.

He mostly swims overarm, two strokes to a breath. As a nipper, he'd keep his face right out of the water, but they don't do it like that anymore. Now, they keep the face in. Left side or right side—it used to be you got a choice—but he's noticed that it's gone and changed again among the young ones. Now it's one side three breaths, the other side three breaths and on you go. He'd got used to breathing on the left, but the whole swapping sides thing is a bridge too far.

The first lap is a bit nippy, but by the second lap, it's perfect. Today, the pool's an aquarium and as he makes his way back up the length of the pool, he's following a blackfish. He's a big one, bigger than others Sid has seen, and he thinks of him as the chief. Chief blackfish, trailing a school of smaller fish, tiny blue and yellow ones that disappear in a clap of colour when Sid gets too close.

After his third lap, he stops to have a break. Leaning his elbows up on the concrete edge of the pool, his eyes follow the waterline across the narrow bay that stretches out in front of him and across to Sandy Rock. For the locals, it's the best fishing spot around. Sid used to do some fishing there himself, though he hasn't done it in a while. Tom, who lives five doors down, he still gets around there. And every week or so, there'll be a knock on Sid's door, and it'll be Tom with a couple of fish in a bag for him. Sometimes he'll stay while Sid cooks them up and they'll have dinner together. Other times, Tom will just hand him the fish and be off. Either way, it's okay by Sid; he likes Tom's company, but he likes his own company, too.

For his fourth lap, he floats on his back and looks up at the sky. It's a clear sky. Clear and sunny. A good way to start the school year. Yes, he repeats to himself. A good way to start the school year.

He floats his way back to the shallow end, his head full of nothing much, so much so that he misjudges the length of the pool and bumps his head against the end. It doesn't hurt so much as knock him out of his reverie. With a bit of a start, he straightens up.

From over near the pool shower, he hears Ray calling out to him. 'Bump yer head, did you, mate?'

When Sid looks up, Ray is speeding down the pathway on his buggy, walking stick poking out of the back. As always, he's in a pair of board shorts, his calves red and tight from the infection that's already put paid to movement in his feet. Not that it's stopped him smoking. *Might make me cut down a bit*, he says, *but buggered if it's going to make me stop*. He's a rollies man and he rolls them up tightly so they're as thin as a straw; so thin the filter bulges. That's another concession to the leg problem: the cigarette filter. Something to keep the doctors off his back.

'The pool take you by surprise, did it, mate?' he yells. He's always been louder than Sid.

Sid puts his hands up on the top edge of the pool and laughs. 'Lost in me thoughts,' he calls back.

Ray parks the buggy in the usual spot: just beside one of the bench seats that's been concreted into the sandstone that surrounds the pool.

Getting off the buggy should be a simple enough manoeuvre, but for Ray it's a bit of a business and he needs more than a minute to manage it. Now, a minute's not a lot of a time unless you're watching your big brother do something that should take a couple of seconds, his face screwed up in concentration and in something that isn't quite pain but looks pretty close to it. That's when, as always, Sid wants to shout out to him to check he's okay, to check if he needs any help. But, as always, he stays quiet and carries on like nothing's wrong. That's what he's learnt to do.

Once he's off, Ray pulls his walking stick from the back of the buggy and leans on it. He can handle some weight on his feet, but not a lot. *Because of the flamin' gangrene.* That's how Ray tells it. Sid's pretty sure it's not actually gangrene, but it's still not much chop. Still means that his feet won't work the way they should. Except in the water. They flip along okay in the water. That's why he likes coming to the pool, no matter what the water temperature is.

'You coming in, mate?' It's an offhand question, but Sid times it carefully, waiting until he can see that Ray has got his balance and will be able to get over to the pool without too much drama.

Ray's got the script going too. 'Hold your bloody horses.'

Standing still in the water is making him cold, but Sid stays put as he waits for his brother to get over to the pool's edge. It upsets him to watch it—the winch-drag of Ray's steps—and sometimes he looks away, pretending to check out the headland instead.

When he's at the edge of the pool, Ray holds on to the ladder to lower himself down to a sitting position. At the same time, he throws his walking stick aside, so that it clatters on the ground behind him.

Once he's finally in, it's like he's been reborn. He's a breaststroke man, not an overarm man, and he never puts his face in the water; he just keeps his head up the whole time, even if there's a school of sparkling fish swimming right under him.

Sometimes, they stop at the end of the pool—the far end, not the ladder end—and look across the bay, across Sandy Rock and up onto the headland. It's a low rise of bush scrub covering loose sandy soil that, at its point, turns to hard sandstone shale. When they were nippers, he and Ray would scour the place for bullet shells left by the shooters after a day on the rifle range. It's still there now, the rifle range—smack bang in the middle of the headland—and the shooters still come of a weekend, but it's been a while since he and Ray were up there. No chance for Ray now, but Sid could still do it; have a wander, even take the path all the way over to Raleigh Beach. If he had a mind to, that is.

And as if he can hear what his brother is thinking, Ray uses his chin to point up to the headland. 'You been up there lately?'

Sid gives his chuckle—a quiet, fruity sort of chuckle—and shakes his head. 'Can't remember the last time.'

After a bit, they battle their way back down the length of the pool. Once they get there, Ray flips on his back—face up to the sky, hands out, feet up—while Sid gets out to take a shower. It's just a wooden post holding up a copper pipe with a shower head at the end of it, but for Sid it's the best shower in the world: every morning, there it is, all laid out in front of him: a magnificent vista of sandstone, ocean and bush.

Once he's rinsed himself, he turns the shower off and reaches for his towel. He has the dressing technique down pat. With the towel wrapped around him, he walks across to the bench where he's laid out his clothes. Then, checking the towel's still wrapped tight around his waist, he slides his swimmers down until they fall to the ground. He takes his underpants out from the front pocket of his shorts and manoeuvres them up his legs, all the while making sure that the towel's still around him okay, that it's not going to come loose and leave him starkers. Then he does the same with his shorts. Only then does he let the towel drop.

His shirt he leaves to last. He keeps a comb in his shirt pocket and he runs it through his hair so that his side part is straight and the rest of his hair is slicked down. He's still got it—his hair, that is—but it's started to thin out, there's no denying that. Surprisingly, though, it's stayed black, although a bit of grey has started to creep up around the sides. Better than Ray, though. He's grey through and through.

Now Ray's pulling himself up the ladder. With a twist, he plops himself onto the edge of the pool and, gripping one side of the ladder, pulls hard until he is standing up. His hand still on the ladder, he bends over to grab his walking stick then lumbers back to the bench and the buggy. When he gets there, he takes his towel, gives himself a cursory wipe down, then reaches over for his T-shirt. When he's got it back on again, he dips his hand into the front basket of the buggy to fish out his cigarette.

Now it's getting late, and it's time for Sid to go. It's only a ten-minute walk to the school and he goes straight there. There's no reason to go home first; the school is close enough that he can nip home for lunch so there's nothing he needs to take with him.

Officially, he's the general assistant—the GA—but for everyone there, he's just Sid. Diane calls him an institution. He supposes that's because he's been there longer than anyone else. Longer than Diane and Helen, and Terry, too, for that matter. And that's only counting his working time; that's not counting all the years he went to school there. Ray says that in all his life, Sid's never moved outside a five-hundred-yard radius: house, school, shops, pool. That's an exaggeration, of course; for years he worked on building sites, laying bricks all around the place, until it started playing havoc with his back. Luckily, he came across the job at the school.

He's always there well before the bell goes. He uses the time to walk around the place and check what needs doing. Most of the kids say hello, just a passing hello as they're running around doing their thing, whether it's chasing each other or kicking a soccer ball or playing handball with a tennis ball—that's been the big thing for the past couple of years: handball. He likes watching it all.

Now he can see young Melinda Saunders coming in through the gate, her boys in front of her, heading for the play equipment. Young Melinda, already a mother of two. And doesn't it just seem like yesterday that she was in school uniform herself? Dark-haired, blue-eyed little thing that she was, pigtails flying as she'd run for the equipment, the same way her boys do now. Of course, the equipment's changed, hasn't it? When one of the Lumsden boys broke his arm flipping down from the climbing frame, well, that was the last straw. First the frame itself came down, then the slippery dip that was so steep it was more like a roller-coaster, and finally the roundabout. That was the one that puzzled him. How was the roundabout a danger to the kids? The momentum, that's what someone told him: with a couple of kids pushing, it could go so fast that a kid or two might fly off if they weren't holding on hard enough.

Sure the kids needed to be a bit careful, but by gosh they had fun. There's not the same sense of excitement on the new stuff, even if Melinda's boys still manage to whip up a storm on it. When Ethan first tried his balancing stunt on the new monkey bars, he couldn't have been more than nine. Elaine was on playground duty, he remembers that much. Sid watched her face go white when she saw Ethan, standing right up there with his hands in the air. Then her voice got so husky she couldn't even order him down. In the end, Sid had to go over there himself.

'Good job,' he called out to the boy. 'How about showing me how you get down again?'

When he got no answer to that, he tried a different tack. 'Can't you do it, mate? Can't you get down, is that the problem?'

That wasn't the problem; even then he had Ethan's measure and he knew that, more than anything, the boy needed to prove himself. Just as he'd hoped, Ethan had started to climb down, bending slowly until he was close enough to grab on to the bar before, with a flourish, he dropped down and jumped off.

You had to admire the kid's agility. He got that from his dad, Adam. Adam Thompson. One of the local builders. A nice-enough fellow, too. Friendly. One of the parents who always takes the time to say hi when he comes to pick up the boys. And when they come to school together, Adam and Melinda, for assemblies or concerts or what have you, he's got a nice way with her, holding her hand or linking arms. Things are good between them, that's pretty clear. It makes Sid happy to see it, even if it is strange to think of young Melinda Saunders as a wife and mother. Not that she's even Melinda Saunders anymore, of course. She's Mel Thompson now.

For a moment he watches her, before he heads over to the little stand-alone building everyone just calls 'Sid's place'. It's not big— most of the building is given over to storage, which leaves him only the front room—but it's enough for his needs. A workbench spans the width of the room, the wood thick and weathered and gouged. Sid keeps his tools directly above the bench, each tool on its own hook. On the wall opposite the bench he hangs his brooms, and in the corner there's a table pushed up against the wall with a chair on either side. On the table is a tin Sid fills with the chocolate-chip biscuits they sell at the bakery.

His little place is tucked in between the school office and the car park. To get there, he has to pass by the back of Diane's office. There are two windows—one behind the desk, another to the side of it— and whenever Sid walks by, he tilts his head to check whether she's there. If she is, he always gives her a little wave.

That's what he does now: he tilts his head up to check if she's there. When, instead of Diane's shock of dark hair, he sees a head of blonde hair, his head jolts back in surprise. It takes him a moment to remember. It's still only early, so he can't even blame it on a busy day. *Silly old codger*, he tells himself.

He wonders where Diane is now, what corner of the world. She gave him the rundown before she left but there were that many places, she lost him halfway. She'll be having fun, wherever she is, that's one thing he can say for sure.

This new one, she's a different kettle of fish. Too young to be in charge, but too serious to be so young. A funny combination.

He watches her through the window, frowning at the computer screen. Already she's made big changes to Diane's office. All the kids' paintings that were stuck to the wall have gone. The lot of them. All that's left is clean, white walls.

He's still peering in when Laurie Mathews flicks her head up from her computer—it reminds him of a rabbit, she does it so quickly. Just as quickly, her eyes meet his and she jumps—fair jumps out of her seat—like she's spied an axe-murderer. To try to settle her, he smiles, raises a hand and mouths *hi*. When he does that, there's an immediate change in her expression. Now she's not looking frightened anymore; now she's looking annoyed, so annoyed his hand freezes in a half-wave and his smile fades.

She'll take a bit of getting used to, this one.

Terry

The end of the day and Terry's in his own world as he makes his way down to the car park, briefcase swinging against his side. It's Kurt he's thinking about mostly, and why the hell Sean got it into his head to move himself overseas when he's got two young boys. If now's not the time they need their father, well, when is? One thing he knows for sure is this: a holiday twice a year isn't going to cut it once the novelty wears off. He wishes he'd known about it before-hand. Then he'd have kicked some sense into Sean's head. Or at least given it a shot. Too late now, though, by the sounds of it. Strange how much can happen over the holidays.

He's so busy mulling it over he doesn't hear her at first and starts when he finds her right there beside him.

'Can I have a word?' she asks.

He's got to be at the club at four and it's already quarter to, but it's clear that 'no' isn't the answer Laurie's looking for, so he gives her a nod and waits for her to speak.

'I thought we could have a talk in my office,' is what she says.

His body sags. 'I'm afraid I've got an appointment at four,' he says. The word appointment is a good one. Makes it sound like it's something pressing, something urgent.

She starts to walk towards the admin building. 'It won't take long.'

He falls into step with her. This would be the moment to start up with a bit of small talk, he knows, but he can't be bothered.

When they reach her office, she closes the door behind them. She takes a seat behind the desk and offers him one in front of it.

'I wanted to talk to you about the incident this morning,' she says.

He looks at her blankly.

'The incident with Elsie Burnett.'

He can't believe it'd already slipped his mind. 'Yes,' he says, 'of course.' She'll be wanting to thank him for stepping in. Not that he expects thanks. He always keeps an eye out for Elsie.

'You're aware of the departmental regulations in relation to physical contact between teachers and students?'

He stares at her, not sure what she's getting at. 'Sorry?'

She leans back. He seems to have upset her but he's got no idea why. Her voice is more clipped this time. 'Departmental regulations prohibit physical contact between teachers and students. You've been teaching for a long time, Terry, surely you must know that.'

He's still not sure where this is going.

'Your conduct with Elsie this morning—it was inappropriate.'

'What do you mean?'

'Your physical contact with her was inappropriate.'

Now it's his turn to get upset. 'What are you trying to say, Laurie? That I shouldn't have comforted the child? Is that what you're saying?'

'I'm not saying you shouldn't have comforted her. You just shouldn't have touched her the way you did. It's in breach of the department's code of conduct.'

That does it. 'What the hell are you talking about?' He can hear his voice rising. 'I gave the kid a cuddle. Her mad, drug-addled mother had just lashed into her in front of the whole school—and on the first day of term, no less. Unsurprisingly, the girl was distraught. Wouldn't you be? She didn't need me to stand back and tell her it would be all right—because, let's face it, Laurie, it's not going to be all right, is it? She didn't need me to give her some bloody mean-ingless platitude. She just needed a cuddle, for Christ's sake. And if you're waiting for an apology for that, then you'll be waiting a while.'

❧

He grits his teeth as he makes his way to the car park, so angry he can't think. On autopilot, he starts the car and drives to the golf club.

He could drive right up to the clubhouse but, as usual, he parks down the bottom where he can look through the scrub and across to the rock pool. God's own country, and it's still a secret.

He turns off the engine but makes no effort to get out of the car. His heart is beating double speed. He can feel it popping its way through his shirt. He'll be on his way to a heart attack if it doesn't slow down soon. And he'll be blowed if he's going to have a heart attack on her account.

Your conduct was inappropriate.

God, just thinking about it makes him want to punch something.

Lady, he should have said, *I was a teacher when you were still at school, and I think I can judge what's appropriate and what's not.*

How dare you question my conduct? How dare you? That's exactly what he should have said.

He's still cursing as he wheels his golf bag up to the clubhouse. But he can't let it spoil his game. On that score he's adamant: he's not going to let it put him off his game.

Sid is already waiting for him, holding his one golf club, his pockets bulging with golf balls.

'Sorry for keeping you, mate,' Terry says.

'I saw you go into the office. Figured you might be held up.'

Terry kicks at the ground. 'Well, she wanted a word, didn't she?'

Sid nods but doesn't ask for the details. It's one of the things Terry most likes about him, that he doesn't push. 'Righto,' he says.

Terry could tell him all of it; there's nothing he can't trust Sid with. Over all the years at Brindle Public, that's something he's learnt: that Sid's a good man. So he opens his mouth to say something. Something like, *You know what she wanted?* But just thinking about it is making him feel sick, like there's a rock in his stomach, so instead he stays quiet.

And silence is okay by Sid, too, so it's in silence that they make their way up to the first hole.

It's a dog of a course in a jewel of a position. That's how Terry describes it. The clubhouse needs a paint and an update, and at the moment there's more sandy soil under foot than there is grass. But the greens are still all right. Even when the rest of the country's in drought, still the greens get looked after. Tank water or something like that. Whatever they do to get around the water restrictions.

Terry steals a glance at Sid. He still doesn't get it. They must have been playing golf together for, what, twelve years? Could be even longer. And in all the years, Sid's stuck to the one golf club. Early on,

Terry didn't comment on it; he figured it must be a financial issue, something like that. So before Sid's birthday one year, he passed the hat around the staff and got enough to buy three decent irons and a good putter. Then he topped up the takings himself so they could throw in a golf bag. A bloody good present. That's what he'd thought: a bloody good present. And, to be fair, Sid used the lot for a bit. But within a matter of months, he was back to his old one-iron game. Except that he used one of the new irons instead of his old one. The bag, the putter and the other irons—by Terry's calculations they haven't seen the light of day in eight years. It ticked him off at first, that they'd gone to such a lot of trouble only to have it all gathering dust in Sid's garage, but not anymore. If Sid wants to play with one iron, good luck to him. More chance of yours truly winning the game that way.

Although now, with the sun still beating down and the air heavy and humid, he thinks that Sid might be on to something. Because today's one of those days Terry would rather not be pulling his bag up the hill through dead grass and dry sand.

Baggage-free, Sid is at the first tee while Terry's still struggling to get up there.

'Come on, mate,' Sid calls. 'Thought you were supposed to be the youngster here?'

The jibe injects Terry with an unexpected spurt of energy that propels him up the hill to the summit. As usual, it's well worth the effort. Looking straight ahead, with the clubhouse on their left, there's nothing but ocean in front of them. An endless stretch of deep blue water—filled, no doubt, with half a million golf balls.

Today, Sid tees off first. Placing the ball down in front of him, he squints in the direction of the hole and, without even a warm-up, hits the ball hard before straightening up to see how it's going.

Terry watches as the ball lands twenty feet short of the hole. Not bad, he thinks. He decides he'll use a three wood for this one. It'll give him the length he needs. Lining himself up beside the tee, he has a few practice shots. When he thinks he's got it right, he moves over to the ball, pulls back and, carefully, carefully, hits the ball up and over towards the green. When it lands in front of Sid's ball, a smile spreads across his face.

'It was about Elsie,' he says as they walk over to the hole. 'She wanted to talk to me about Elsie.'

'Because of Trina?'

Terry gives a short laugh. 'You'd think that'd be it, wouldn't you? But no, not because of Trina—because of me. She says I shouldn't have touched her.'

Sid stops short. 'You didn't lay a hand on her. I saw the whole thing. You didn't touch her. You just told her to leave.'

This time Terry really laughs. 'Not Trina. Elsie. She said I shouldn't have touched *Elsie*.'

'What do you mean?'

'She says I shouldn't have given her a cuddle. It was inappropriate conduct.' Just saying the words brings an awful taste to his mouth. 'She made me sound like a paedophile.'

'What'd she want you to do?'

He shrugs. 'She didn't say. Just told me that my behaviour was inappropriate. In breach of the code of conduct or some rubbish. You know what I should have said to that? I should have asked her what the code of conduct says to do when a kid's falling apart on the first day of school because her mother's just got stuck into her. No, no, better than that—I should have just left it to the bloody code of conduct to sort the whole thing out.'

Sid tips his head to the side. 'She was pretty upset, wasn't she? Elsie, I mean. And she gets a hard time of it anyway, even without Trina turning up again. I'd say you did the right thing, Terry.'

They are up on the green now, and as Sid talks, Terry pushes the toe of his shoe hard into the grass, so hard he makes a hole in it. 'I've got to tell you, Sid, I didn't see that one coming. You know, I'd have thought she'd be thanking me for a job well done, that sort of thing. Could have knocked me for six when she started having a go at me. I sure as hell wasn't expecting that. Merit certificate maybe, but not a bloody ticking-off.'

This makes Sid laugh. 'Tell you what, I can't get you a merit certificate but I can buy you a beer when we finish. That cheer you up?'

Terry gives him half a smile. 'Long as I get a chance to whip you first.'

As they head over the rise towards the next hole, they see a couple of kids coming their way. One's carrying a bucket and, every now and then, the other one bends down to pick something up from the ground. A golf ball, that's what it's got to be. The club pays kids to collect them. Not a bad little earner for the sharp-eyed. He can't see their faces—they're too far away for that—but their gait gives them away: Kurt with his shoulder-first stride, his tough little body moving like a tank, and skinny little Cody with his running walk, jumping around like a rabbit on the headland. Terry stops to watch them. He's still watching when Sid, ahead of him now, turns back to give him a shout to hurry on. At the sound of Sid's voice, the boys look up. And as soon as they catch sight of Terry, they start running over to him.

'Mr P, Mr P!' Cody shouts, his voice shrill. 'We already got fifteen balls. Already!'

Terry smiles. 'Good work,' he says, but Cody's still got more to tell.

'We reckon we'll get thirty, minimum. Dad says they're every-where, golf balls that just get left here.'

Terry hadn't noticed Scott, but there he is, behind the kids, his walk long and slow, his eyes on the ground. He stops when he catches up to the kids but says nothing to Terry. Nor does he meet his eye. It's odd, but Terry's used to him.

'Scott,' he says, 'doing a bit of golf-ball salvaging?'

Scott focuses his bloodshot eyes somewhere between Terry's nose and his mouth. 'Boys wanted to have a go at it. I'd said I'd give them a hand then take them for a late surf.' He pushes a hand through his hair, which is long and blond and curled stiff with salt.

'Great day for a surf,' says Terry although, really, he's got no idea. All he knows is that it's not raining, which has to be a good start.

Scott keeps playing with his hair but doesn't answer. There's an earthy, sweet smell about him. It's the way he always smells. A few years ago, Terry mentioned it to Tania, just in passing. He can still see the astonishment on her face.

'Don't tell me,' she'd said. 'Don't tell me you don't know that smell.'

When he'd looked blank, she'd burst out laughing. 'Dope, Terry, that's the smell. That's what dope smells like. And that's what Scott smells like, because he's always stoned.'

Now he smiles at his naivety, and Cody looks up at him, curious. Terry gives him a wink. 'Here's a lesson, Cody boy: you're never too old to learn something new.'

But Cody's got no idea what he's talking about and Terry's not about to clarify it. Besides, it's already late and they'll need to make a move if they're to get a surf in, so they keep walking, the three of them, Kurt in the lead, Cody scrambling after him and Scott loping behind, as though there's a cushion of air between him and the ground.

As he watches them go, it occurs to him that maybe Scott's too stoned to be driving the kids around. And if he is, what's he, Terry, to do about it? While he's deciding whether to chase after them or just let them go, Kurt circles back so he can join Scott, who slings an arm over the boy's shoulders. They keep on walking then, Scott and Kurt side by side, Cody a bit in front, and soon they're too far to catch anyway.

Sid gives Terry a shout to get a move on and Terry hollers back, 'Hold your horses, I'm on my way!'

Nina

Marina Cincotta is Nina's best friend, and having her at Stenton Public is one of the school's drawcards—especially on Wednesday mornings, when they both have an hour free. They catch up in the staffroom; Nina makes the coffee while Marina stretches out along a row of vinyl armchairs. Today, she's wearing a rainbow-coloured kaftan. Her hair, wild and dark and long, is out, and curls down past her shoulders.

'So, how's cranky Steve?' This is what Marina always calls him—because he always sounds cranky on the phone.

The criticism would rankle if it came from anyone else, but because it's Marina, Nina just laughs. 'Fine,' she says, handing her friend a mug of coffee. 'He's fine.'

Marina sits up to drink it. 'The big new job going okay?'

'I think so. The money's good at least.'

'Got to like a man who brings home the bacon.' She winces as she swallows. 'Did you put any sugar at all in this?'

'Three,' Nina says. 'I shovelled in three teaspoons of the stuff.'

Peering into the cup, Marina looks unconvinced. 'The thing is,' she says, 'I need a bit of a sugar kick to recharge me. I'm still recovering from the weekend.'

Nina gives her the once-over. 'A good one?'

Marina stretches her arms in front of her. 'Let me tell you, Nina Ballerina, the drought has broken!'

Nina laughs. 'Meaning?'

'Meaning, party on Saturday night and there he is: tall, blond, great abs, *great* shoulders—I thought I was hallucinating. But no. Turns out he's hosting the party for a mate of his who works with Cheryl—that's how I got the invite—so there I was, in his house.'

'And?'

'And what?'

'What happened?'

Marina takes a deep breath. 'Well,' she says, 'there's this spa in his backyard—no pool, just a spa—and a whole lot of people start stripping down to their undies and jumping in. Mr Shoulders gives me this look and says, *So, you coming in?* Apart from hello, that's the first thing he's said to me. Then, right in front of me, he whips off his T-shirt and his jeans and there he is, in his boxer shorts.'

'And?'

'And I'm only wearing a G-string under my dress, aren't I?' She says this loudly—too loudly—then lowers her voice to a whisper. 'And I'm not going to be stripping down to my G-string at some party. So I say to him, *I'll come in if you get me a pair of boxer shorts like yours.* He gives me a smile like that's the weirdest thing he's ever heard, but then he disappears upstairs somewhere and, sure enough, when he comes back, he's got another pair of boxers in his hand.'

Nina claps a hand over her mouth. 'Tell me you didn't.'

But Marina's eyes are dancing. 'So, I go into the bathroom, strip down to my bra and undies, put his boxer shorts over my undies and off we go. Next thing, I'm sitting in his spa drinking champagne. After a bit he turns to me and says, straight up, *You got a boyfriend, you got a husband?* I'm not sure how to answer so I just say, *No boyfriend; I used to have a husband.* He clinks my glass and says, *Cheers—I used to have a wife.* And when I ask him how long it's been, he says, *The van just left.* Which is witty, right? So I drink a bit more champagne and stay the night.'

Nina laughs in disbelief. 'With him?'

Marina smiles. 'Yep.'

'The whole night?'

'Yep. Breakfast and everything. I figured it was time to go when he told me his ex was about to come over to—get this—pick up the rest of her stuff.'

But Nina doesn't get it. 'What do you mean?'

'Just what I said: to pick up the rest of her stuff. Because it turns out he wasn't being funny: the van really had just left, just before the party.'

Nina wraps both hands around her coffee mug. 'So he'd been separated for less than a day?'

'Ten hours.'

'No way.'

'Yep. Ten hours.'

'And?'

'He gives me his card—a merchant banker, can you believe it?— puts me in a cab, gives me a kiss and says, *I'll call you.*'

'And?'

Marina shakes her head. 'Not so far.'

'It's only Wednesday.'

'I know. Apparently the rule is if they haven't rung by Thursday, they won't be ringing.'

'And then?'

She gives a bit of a shrug. 'You move on, baby, you move on.'

'Just like that?'

'Where's the choice?'

Nina's eyes widen. 'I couldn't do it. I just couldn't. All that waiting for the call, wondering what's going to happen. It'd kill me.'

Marina gives her a lopsided smile. 'Lucky you've got cranky Steve then, hey?'

Terry

Wednesday morning is assembly time at Brindle Public and, as usual, the national anthem—both verses of it—kick off the proceedings. But even though the words are right in front of them—up on a board to the left of the stage—still only a quarter of the school gets them right, and by the end of the second verse just about everyone's given up the ghost. It's the highlight of Terry's week to see just how wrong they can all get it.

When that's done, Laurie walks up to the lectern and waits for the post-anthem noise to die down. Terry can't remember the last time the lectern was used. In fact, he can't even remember having seen it for, what, ten years or more? He wonders where she could have found it. In the music room? The storeroom? God knows. Anyway, there it is, smack bang in the centre of the stage, and there she is, right behind it.

'Good morning, students,' she says.

'Good morning, Miss Mathews.' And although they answer in singsong unison, most of them falter over her name.

'Last week,' she tells them, 'I noticed that a lot of students were not wearing full school uniform. And as I look around me now, I can see that many of you are still not wearing full school uniform.'

When she says this, Kurt elbows Cody in the side and gives him a low victory sign. Theirs is a loose interpretation of the uniform requirement. Instead of black leather lace-up school shoes with white socks, Kurt is wearing his old favourites: a pair of battered white Volleys that have begun to split at the sides. As usual, he wears them straight, without socks. Sometimes Cody turns up in thongs, but today he's wearing a pair of his brother's Nikes. Whenever he has them on, he struts around like he's the king of cool, although privately Terry thinks he looks ridiculous flapping around in shoes four sizes too big for him. But Nikes are Nikes, whatever the size.

'You should all be proud to be students of Brindle Public School. And you should show pride in your school by wearing your full school uniform. So from now on, I expect you all to come to school dressed appropriately—and that includes the proper footwear.'

Terry swallows a smile as his eyes sweep the room. Of the hundred and sixty kids sitting there—give or take a few—he reckons maybe thirty are wearing black leather school shoes. Good luck, lady, he thinks to himself.

Himself, he's all for having a uniform—it keeps things easy and it stops the playground from becoming a fashion parade—but as for doing army checks to make sure it's all to regulation, well, he'd say that's going too far.

And the uniform chat is all she's got for the kids on this occasion, so then it's over to Terry to MC the rest of the show. Unclipping the microphone from the side of the lectern, he walks right up to the front of the stage.

'Good morning, Brindle Public,' he says, using his stage voice.

As the kids start to reply, he takes another step forward, then pretends to take another, one that will send him tumbling off the stage and into the sea of faces in front of him. His foot in mid-air, he puts a hand behind one of his ears. 'Can't hear you, Brindle Public.'

The kids are laughing now but they don't say anything until he counts them down. 'One, two, three: good morning, Brindle Public.'

This time the kids scream it out. 'Good morning, Mr Pritchard!'

He steps back. 'That's better, Brindle Public. Sounds like you might be ready for a bit of music then?'

It's a Brindle Public tradition, the assembly singalong, and something Diane and he used to do together. This year, for the first time, he's flying solo. Pointing the control button at the back of the stage, he waits for the projection screen to unroll until, finally, it completely covers the left-hand side of the stage. With the press of another button, lyrics cover the screen; one more button and crackly music fills the hall. The kids start to nudge each other. He's chosen a goody: Diane's favourite and probably the school favourite, too.

Over-excited, some of the kids come in too soon, shut up, then try again. Feigning disappointment, Terry shakes his head and, with another press of the button, cuts the music.

Let's give it another shot, Brindle Public,' he cajoles them. '"Blame It on the Boogie". From the top.'

When the music starts again, Terry sing-speaks into the mic to keep them all together. Mostly it's a mess, but God, it makes him laugh. Shame about the other stuff, but there's still a lot to like about Mr Michael Jackson.

As the chorus approaches, there's a build-up of momentum, then an eruption of singing and arm-waving and sitting-down dancing.

For the kindergarten kids, and for anyone else who's forgotten, Terry mimes out the actions: a half-circle for sunshine, hands stretched out for moonlight, twinkling fingers for good times and a bit of arm- and hand-twisting for the boogie.

By the end, it's bordering on a fiasco, and for Terry, there's always magic in that. So he lets them go for a bit until he calls them back to order.

'Steady on,' he tells them. 'Steady on.' Then he waits for the place to quieten down before he hands the mic to Laurie so she can sign off and send the kids back to their classes.

Laurie carries the microphone back to the lectern and tries to push it back into the holder. Once she's got it, she yells into it, her voice so unexpectedly loud it makes even Terry jump. 'Students,' she says, 'your behaviour is unacceptable. You are not in a school disco, you are in your school assembly and I expect you to show some respect for your teachers and for your school. From now on, during assembly, I will expect only to see and hear quiet singing without any actions. At your disco you can dance, but at your assembly I expect more appropriate behaviour.'

The student body stare up in astonishment. Beside her, Terry struggles to keep his expression neutral. He can't trust himself to look at her, and staring down at all the little faces in front of him will only make him more irate. Instead, he chooses a point at the far end of the hall and keeps his eyes fixed on it.

Laurie keeps talking but he doesn't hear any of it. Only when the kindergarten kids stand up and file out of the hall does he register that the assembly's over and he should get off the stage to retrieve his class.

He mulls over it as he walks the kids back to the demountable.

A year of it, he thinks. How the hell is he going to manage a year of this woman?

Back in the classroom, Kurt sticks up a hand. 'Mr P,' he asks, 'how come we aren't allowed to do the actions at assembly anymore?'

Terry considers how to answer that one. *Because Laurie Mathews is an uptight upstart with no sense of humour.* His lips twitch with the urge to blurt it out.

'Ms Mathews thinks it makes you too rowdy. She thinks assemblies should be quiet, genteel affairs.'

Kurt keeps his hand up. 'What do you reckon, sir?'

Terry pulls at his ear. Bugger it. 'Actually, Kurt, I really like songs with actions,' he says.

A murmur ripples through the class as Cody shoots up his hand. 'So, Mr P, does that mean we can still do actions at assembly because you're in charge of singing and that, or does that mean we can only do them when Miss Mathews is away?'

Terry cocks his head to one side. 'I'd say that's a watching brief at this stage. That's what I'd be saying.' And there's no follow-up on that, even though he's pretty sure none of them knows what he's talking about. He makes a mental note to explain it next lesson: *a watching brief—something to look out for when you've got no bloody idea what's going on.*

Nina

As she turns into Colin's street that afternoon, Nina sees Jen's car parked outside the house. Good. She loves Steve's sister as much as she does his dad.

The two of them—Colin and Jen—are sitting at the kitchen table. When Colin sees her, he stands up to give her a kiss. 'Sit yourself down while I make you a cuppa,' he says.

Nina gives him a hug before she turns to Jen. 'Hi, stranger.'

Jen's face crinkles up. 'Hi, yourself.'

In the backyard, Emily is playing with Jen's little girl, Yvette. With only fifteen weeks between them, the cousins could pass for twins.

As Nina slips into a seat beside Jen, Colin says, 'So give us the update.'

Nina laughs. 'The update?' she says. 'Not much—I think that's the update.'

On the kitchen table is a pile of cork coasters. Colin puts one in front of Nina then places a cup of coffee on top of it.

'There you go, love.' As always, the coffee is instant and, as always, he has added sugar to it, even though Nina only takes milk. Still, there is a comfort in sugary coffee when Colin is the one to make it for her.

'How's the boy?' This is what he always calls Steve.

Nina nods as she false sips on her coffee so it won't scald her tongue. 'Good,' she says, 'he's good. The new job's going well as far as I can tell.'

Colin makes a clicking sound with his tongue. 'Well, he's got you to thank for it, hasn't he, love? Getting him through all the study and the rest of it. More than I managed when he was at school, I can tell you that much.'

Nina smiles. 'It was worth it, wasn't it? He likes the job and the pay's almost double.'

'Like I said, love, and it's all thanks to you. The best thing that's ever happened to him, that's what you are.'

Pleased, ridiculously pleased even, Nina repeats the words to herself. *The best thing. The best thing that's ever happened to him.*

Out in the backyard, the girls are getting louder. Jen starts to rise but Nina puts a hand on her shoulder. 'I'll go,' she says.

The dispute is over a Barbie doll: that much is clear. The girls have one each but now the argument is about whether they should swap. Emily's face is determined, her fat little fingers clenched around her doll, so focused on the argument she doesn't notice her mother until Nina is right beside her.

'Mummy!' she cries when she sees her. 'Mummy, you're back!' The doll forgotten now, she lets it slip to the ground as she flings her arms around Nina's legs.

Nina lifts her daughter up into her arms. 'Hello, my darling.'

Emily wraps her arms tight around Nina's neck and nuzzles into her ear. 'Hello, my mummy.'

While Emily is distracted, Yvette bobs down to grab the doll.

Trying not to smile, Nina holds Emily even closer so she won't see what's happened. 'Let's go home,' she whispers.

Emily keeps her head burrowed into Nina's shoulder. 'To see Daddy?' she asks.

'Soon,' Nina tells her, 'soon.'

⁓

In the car, Emily squirms as Nina tries to fasten the seatbelt. 'It's too tight, Mummy,' she says, 'too tight.'

Nina checks but it's not too tight. Giving it a bit of a fiddle, she pretends to adjust it. 'Better?' she asks.

Emily nods. 'Better.'

When they get home, there's a message on the answering machine. It's Meg, wanting to see when they're free for dinner. They're good friends, Meg and Paul, and it would be nice to catch up.

Nina is in the shower when Steve gets home. Turning the water off, she wraps a towel around herself and hurries out to greet him. Emily is already in his arms, clinging tight to him. 'Daddy's home,' she says.

Nina reaches over to kiss him. 'We need to be out by seven,' she reminds him.

A slight frown crosses his face. 'It'll be all right,' he says, 'we've got heaps of time.'

That's not true, but she doesn't want to push it. Instead, she heads off to get herself ready. Her dress is new and she's pleased with it. It's a simple style, black, almost to the knee with capped sleeves and a scoop neck. There are black fishnet stockings to go with it—the fine ones, not the tarty ones—and her jewellery, as always, is silver: a chunky beaten necklace with matching earrings and bracelet.

She has ironed Steve's shirt and left it hanging on the wardrobe door beside the tie she's chosen: the blue one with a shot of green through it.

But later, when he's showered and dressed, she sees this isn't the tie he's wearing. Instead he's wearing the Simpsons tie someone gave him: rows and rows of yellow-skinned Barts running across a red background. As she opens her mouth to say something, the doorbell rings.

It's the babysitter, Josie, but to Nina's surprise, she's not alone. With her is a boy Nina has never seen before—more than a boy; a man, really.

'Hi there,' she says to Nina, flicking her hair in the man's direction. 'This is Nathan.'

Nathan smiles and offers Nina his hand. It is then she sees he has piercings running right up his ear. Startled by this, she fumbles the handshake. When she hears Steve's footsteps coming up behind her, she turns to him for help.

'Steve,' she says, her tone pointed, 'this is Nathan. He's come to babysit with Josie.'

She wants him to go into bat for her, to say to Nathan—man-to-man style—that perhaps it would be better for Josie to babysit without him, seeing as he's a stranger to them, and no one wants a stranger minding their child. But Steve just puts out his hand and gives the boy—the man, the stranger—a loud clap on the arm. 'How you doing, Nathan?'

Nathan homes in on Steve's ridiculous tie. 'Like your tie.'

Steve holds it out in front of him and gives a chuckle. 'Not bad, is it?'

Josie leans in to have a look. 'Cool,' she says, 'got to love a Bart tie.'

When Emily hears Josie's voice, she sprints into the room. Josie gives her a big smile. 'Hello, chicken,' she says.

Emily's eyes sparkle. 'I'm three,' she tells her.

Josie affects surprise. 'Are you sure you're three? I thought you were two.'

Emily shakes her head. 'No, I'm three. And then I'm four.'

Josie bends down to her. 'We'll have fun tonight, won't we?'

Steve slaps Nathan on the back. 'Not too much fun, though, mate. Not too much.' Nina can't believe it. But Steve laughs as Nathan colours.

Nina isn't sure if she wants to go out at all now. 'Ring me if you need anything,' she tells Josie. 'Anything at all.'

The girl nods. 'It'll be sweet,' she says. 'Don't worry.'

Nina's smile is small. 'Okay.'

In the car, she is still troubled. 'I don't like Josie turning up with some boyfriend we don't even know.'

Steve pushes air through his lips. 'He seems all right. And it's not like it's just him—Josie's there, too.'

Nina shakes her head. 'I don't like it, though. I don't think she should just turn up with some stranger.'

'Doesn't look like he's a stranger to her, does it?' He reaches out to run a hand over her leg. 'Just relax, it'll be fine.'

✺

The top floor of the club has been cordoned off for them and two long tables have been set up to one side of the room. On each of the tables, there are place cards.

On the other side of the room, near the bar, drinks are being served. There must be forty or fifty people gathered there. Nina recognises none of them. Suddenly shy, she grips Steve's hand.

A florid man in an open-necked shirt walks over to them. 'Mate,' he says to Steve, 'welcome to your welcome party.' He must like how that sounds because he chuckles and says it again.

Steve chuckles with him and Nina tries to join in, but her laughter sounds forced. She waits for an introduction but none comes. Instead, the two men start talking club politics. Gazing past them, Nina looks over to the other guests. There are more women than men and, from what she can see, hers is the longest dress in the room. The other women wear short, shiny dresses and orange-brown spray tans.

Steve's friend taps her on the arm. 'How about I get you and Steve a drink?'

As they follow him though the crowd and over to the bar, everyone they pass greets Steve with a shout or a tap on the arm. Nina is pleased to see this; pleased to be the wife of the guest of honour.

Steve, too, is in his element. She can tell by his walk—jaunty and confident—and by the way he wraps his arm around her when they get to the bar.

Steve's friend orders for them. The drinks are free so it's simply a gesture, but a nice one. There's too much cordial in her lemon, lime and bitters and she winces at the sweetness of it. Steve has a beer and after his first sip, she leans in to tell him he's got froth on his moustache. He scowls as he wipes it off and she wonders if she's spoken too loudly.

Before she can ask him, before she can shoot him anything more than a puzzled look, a woman sidles up to them and slips an arm around Steve's friend, who leans back to rub cheeks with her. She looks much younger than he is and her hair, a startling blonde, is piled on the top of her head in starched curls. Her dress is short and stretchy and lolly-pink. Her shoes, high and strappy, match her dress and her bare legs are darker than her face. Beside her, Nina feels like a Greek widow.

Still clutching Steve's friend, the woman smiles at Nina. 'I'm Trudy.' Someone has turned the music up, and she has to yell to be heard. 'Sav's wife.'

Nina smiles back but her mind is elsewhere, trying to work out if she can't just rush home and change into something else. As she mulls it over, Trudy says, 'You must be really proud of Steve. I mean, with the new job and everything.'

Nina nods. She is proud, that's true, proud and happy for him.

Trudy is still talking—something about the dinner—but Nina's no longer listening; she's looking across at Trudy's husband and wondering why he's called Sav, and whether it's short for Salvatore. Not that he looks Italian, with his pink-red skin. But it's got her curious so she leans over to Trudy to ask her. 'So Sav—where does his name come from?'

Trudy gives her a bemused look. 'It's short for Gavin.'

When they sit down for dinner, it turns out the four of them have been seated together. There is wine on each of the tables and Gav stands up to serve it: red for Steve, white for Trudy. He holds the bottle of white over Nina's glass and when she shakes her head, swaps bottles and starts to pour red wine into her glass instead. When she keeps shaking her head, he gives her a knowing look. 'You preggers, are you?'

Somehow she manages a smile. 'No, I'm not.'

Gav looks over at Steve. 'Don't tell me your missus is a bloody teetotaller, mate!' he bellows.

Steve grimaces. ''Fraid she's not much of a drinker, mate.' He nudges her with his elbow. 'One-pot screamer, aren't you, love?'

Nina's mouth tightens into an even smaller smile.

Trudy slaps Gav on the arm. 'Leave her alone and just let her enjoy herself.'

Gav's voice rises in protest. 'That's what I was doing: offering her a bit of social lubricant. Where's the harm in that, babe?'

Trudy looks at Nina and lifts her shoulders, half in apology, half in surrender. It's a kind gesture and Nina smiles to let her know it doesn't matter. Even though it does matter. And it matters because she's completely out of place here. Her hair, her dress, her shoes, her voice, even her drinking: it's all wrong. She checks her watch: 9.15 pm. With any luck, they'll be home by midnight.

It's closer to 1.30 am when Nina finally pulls up in the driveway. Steve has fallen asleep in the passenger seat and she leaves him there while she runs inside.

Josie is watching a movie but Nathan has crashed out beside her and it takes Josie some shaking to wake him. Finally he sits up and, his eyes glazed, mumbles goodnight as Josie leads him out the door. Following them out, Nina slips some money into Josie's hand. Without even looking at it, let alone counting it, Josie pushes the notes into the pocket of her jeans before she directs Nathan towards her car.

When Nina returns to her own car, Steve hasn't moved. At first she shakes him softly, then harder and harder until finally he wakes up. 'We're back,' he says to her, his words blurring. 'We're back home. Home, home, home.' This makes her smile and when he sees that, he smiles too.

Carefully, then, she guides him into the house and across to the bedroom.

As soon as they're in bed, Steve's hands begin to wander over her body. She's not up for sex but she wants him to hold her and tell her she's beautiful even though she wore the wrong dress and said the wrong things. His hands are clumsy, his breath is sharp and his speech is slurred, but he does say she's beautiful and he does hold her. And she's happy to be told and happy to be held.

Joan

The ring of the alarm bell is shrill, so shrill it wakes her with a start. Reaching an arm out across to the table beside her bed, Joan taps the clock to stop it. It is a cool morning, oddly cool for Brindle in February. Her nightie, cotton and lemon-coloured, is too light for such a morning and, with a stifled yawn, she reaches for the dressing-gown at the end of the bed. It is her summer dressing-gown, sky blue chenille and short-sleeved.

The house is still but outside there are bird noises. Some of them come from Billy-boy, but most are from the Indian mynas who come too close to his cage and try to peck at him. Budgerigars have weak hearts, she's been told, but Billy-boy's a tough one. Not even the mynas faze him.

In the kitchen, the table is already set for her breakfast. Unnecessary, she knows, to set the table for herself each night, ready for next morning, but it's a habit she can't break. More than that, even, she finds it comforting to come into the kitchen every morning and see everything waiting for her: the small plate with its matching cup and saucer, the butter knife, the stainless-steel teaspoon, the eggcup; the saucepan already on the stove, half filled with water, so that she need only light the gas and reach into the fridge for an egg. Today, she chooses one that is brown and speckled, testing it in the eggcup first to check it fits, before she puts it in the water. Some eggs are just a touch too big for this, her favourite eggcup.

Hers is a two-cup teapot, and she fills it right up, even though she'll drink only one cup of tea over breakfast. The rest she'll take into the backyard and throw over the parsley plant. It is a habit she has taken over from her mother. Certainly, the parsley seems to thrive on it.

The egg, when she takes it out, is just as she likes it: the white cooked but the yolk still runny. She butters her toast liberally and cuts it into fingers, which she is tempted to dip into the yolk. Instead, she nibbles at her toast, finger by finger, and sips her tea slowly.

Quiet. Too quiet.

She could turn the radio on or bring Billy-boy inside, but she doesn't. Instead, she treats the silence as a test, to see if she can do it; to see if she can manage to live in such a still house. Mostly she can. It is only sometimes she can't.

When she has finished her breakfast, she opens the sliding doors and steps out onto the porch. As usual, Billy-boy is in front of his mirror. When he sees her, he starts to chirp. There are ways of making budgerigars talk; one of them is to remove any mirrors from the cage. But Billy-boy loves the mirror—it makes him think he has company, and she doesn't want to deprive him of that.

After she has cleaned his cage, topped up his water and given him more birdseed, she takes herself off to the shower. Today, instead of using soap, she opens the body wash Judy sent her for

Christmas. When she pumps it into her hand, the smell of rosemary and jasmine fills the room and she regrets not having used it earlier.

She's still thinking about Judy when she steps out of the shower. It's been years since she's seen her. Years. Of course, there are phone calls every now and then, and presents at Christmas, but it's not the same as it used to be, back when they were both still working: heads down over their garments, adding beads and sequins and lace to silk and taffeta and chiffon. It didn't seem to matter how fiddly the task, still Judy could manage to work and talk, while Joan would just work and listen. In that way, they'd made a great team.

They were good years, the years she and Judy worked together. So good it hadn't occurred to her they might stop. Of course, the redundancy package had been generous and the send-off gracious, but, oh dear, how Joan wished they could have stayed on. Not for the money—she would have happily done without the money—but for the work. How she had loved it! Without it, she'd felt quite lost.

It was different for Judy. She had her husband, Frank. And once she got her redundancy, the two of them packed up and moved to the country. They'd invited her down to see them several times, but she'd never quite made it. Her mother, she'd explained; she couldn't leave her mother. But that wasn't the reason. It was more the thought of making her way there alone and not knowing what to say to Frank when she arrived.

Joan didn't have a husband and when, on the odd occasion, people asked her why not, all she could say was that she really didn't know. Which was more or less the truth of it.

Of course, there were some things she did know. She knew she was precious: the miracle child of two people who had found each other late; a child blanketed in a love so protective that, for a long time, it deterred those who might call on her. Later, when such a caller might even have been encouraged, there were none to be found. Especially not in dressmaking. And Joan, a quiet person, was not the type to go looking.

Instead, she had stayed at home with her mother and her father. When her father died, she was grateful to have her confident and gregarious mother still with her. With her mother around, life was vibrant and musical.

Without her, it is quiet and still. Too still.

Once she has dressed, Joan strips the bedclothes and, bundling them up, takes them outside to the laundry, where the rest of the week's washing waits for her. All of it, including the sheets, would fit into a single load, and yet still she separates the items by colour—black, white and mixed—and gives them each a cycle.

She hangs the clothes outside. The clothesline, which has been there since Joan was a child, is a simple affair: a timber post cemented into the ground at either end, with six pieces of coiled wire stretching the length of it. Putting the washing out is a chore Joan likes. She likes to match all the clothes up on the line: shirts pegged under the arms, slacks by the waistband, sheets lined up side by side so that three pegs will do both sheets.

Now a ladybird settles on one of the sheets. Against the white cotton, the tiny bug is vibrant orange. Tentatively, but hopefully, her breath held in, Joan stretches a hand out to the bug, letting the tip of her finger get so close it almost touches the little creature. Slowly, the ladybird moves towards the mountain that is Joan's fingertip, then crawls up and onto it. A smile as she brings her finger, and with it the ladybird, up towards her face. 'Hello there,' she whispers. 'Hello there, little one.'

The ladybird stays, poised. But only for a moment, before it flies away.

On one side of the house is a small park with bench seats and a playground. Most days, Joan spends part of the afternoon sitting on one of the benches, pretending to read her book, when in truth she uses the time to watch the children playing. She would have liked a child. She would have liked to have been a mother. Very much so. Instead, she has spent her life as a daughter. And now that she has no mother and no father, she is no longer a daughter either. It is a thought that hits her hard, for if she is neither daughter nor mother, who exactly is she?

On the other side of the house is Mr Edwards' place; although Mr Edwards himself lives in a nursing home now and the house has been empty for over a year. Only one trip it had taken and everything was gone: his kitchen table and chairs; his sofa; his armchairs; his chest of drawers; his bevelled mirror. If she hadn't been so horrified, she'd have marvelled at how a life could disappear in an afternoon.

A couple of times, they'd gone to visit him, she and her mother. It wasn't far, not really, although it had been tricky changing buses. But Mr Edwards had been pleased to see them and that had made it all worthwhile.

He had come to her mother's funeral. And Joan was touched that he had; touched, too, that his daughter, a busy woman with an important job, had taken the time to bring him.

It was a small funeral. Not because her mother hadn't been loved, but because she had managed to outlive most of her family and almost all of her friends. It still makes Joan sad to think about it.

84

A walk will cheer her up. A walk to the bakery will cheer her up.

She is already halfway down the street when she is startled by a little voice inside her. *Did you turn the stove off?*

Yes, she thinks. Yes, she did. And yet the question makes her uncertain, so uncertain she thinks she should go back, just to check.

She wavers, and as she thinks she will head back, another voice rises inside her. A different voice. This time, it is her mother's voice, gently admonishing. *Joanie, my love*, she says, *the stove is off. You know it; I know it. The stove is off and the back door is locked.*

But, the first voice creeps back, *where is your hat?*

Startled, Joan claps a hand to her head. Her hat is not there. And it's not in her dilly-bag either. 'My hat,' she says out loud.

Forget your hat, Joan Mather, her mother tells her. *It's early so it doesn't matter.*

She is still flustered when she gets to the bakery. The choice in front of her only adds to her confusion so, as usual, she orders a custard slice. The woman who serves her has worked at the bakery for many years now. She knows Joan's name and Joan knows hers: Julia. Since Joan has started to come to the bakery alone, Julia has taken to asking after her mother. Not every time, but often. At first, simply because she couldn't form the words she needed, Joan would say her mother was well. Now, when she could, perhaps, manage to tell her, it is too late; it is like asking the name of a person, who, for years, has been a passing acquaintance. So she finds herself shocked into silence as she waits to see whether this is a day Julia will ask after her mother or one when she will not.

Today Julia just smiles and says, 'With passionfruit icing?'

That's when Joan sees that there is a new type of custard slice on display: one that is simply dusted with icing sugar. Which makes it look more European, or Continental. That's the one she'd like to have for morning tea today: a custard slice dusted with icing sugar.

But it is too late because already Julia has put the other one—the one with passionfruit icing—into a paper bag. Swallowing her disappointment, Joan pulls out her purse and pays for it, silently cursing herself for not speaking up.

Turning around to leave, she collides with the customer behind her. When she looks up, she sees in front of her a man who might be her age. Although she doesn't know him, he isn't exactly a stranger to her. Over the years, she has seen him at the shops, so many times now he has started to nod when he sees her. Although she never nods back, sometimes she does tilt her head in his direction. Because she has been so clumsy, today she can barely look at him.

'I'm sorry,' he says, 'I must have walked into you.' This is not true. It is clear that Joan is the one who has walked into him. But she is too embarrassed to explain. She is too embarrassed to say anything at all. She can only venture a glance at him. There is something pleasant about him. He is a tall man, but not a giant. He has nice eyes, nice blue eyes, and his hair is straight and carefully parted.

He gives her a smile before he turns his attention to Julia. 'Hello there,' he says to her, 'have you got a packet of those beaut chocolate-chip biscuits?'

His question makes Joan feel absurdly happy. She likes chocolate-chip biscuits, too. Only she makes her own.

Rebecca

On waking, Emmanuel's parcel is the first thing she sees, there where she left it, on her bedside table. Sebastian had been at school when it arrived, and although her urge to unwrap it had been strong, still she had waited until he was home. For him, there were two model kits—a fighter jet and a wooden sailing ship; for Rebecca, a smaller package, carefully wrapped. Gently she had tugged at the paper, only to find another wrapping, not paper this time but a length of light cotton folded around something fragile: a glass jar filled with seashells. The card that came with it had a handmade look about it, embossed cardboard with a photograph pasted onto the front. It was a beautiful photograph, of a rock pool, the water blue-green and sparkling, and underneath the handwritten words *Brindle Rock Pool.* Turning it over, she found *Made by Mel* written on the back of the card in the same hand.

Who's Mel? This was the question that immediately sprang into her head. Who was she, this maker of cards from the other side of the world? Her stomach contracted. Were they friends, Mel and her husband? Was she beautiful, this card-making Mel? Catching her breath, she had opened the card cautiously to find it filled with words in her absent husband's hand. Cascading relief somersaulted through her body, a rush of warmth at the sight of those lines and curves, so clear, so familiar they might almost be the shape of him beside her.

My love, he had written, *I hope you like this small gift of shells I have collected for you, and the wrap I have chosen for you. Here, they call it a sarong and it is worn only to the beach—which, can you believe it, is at the end of the street. If I have chosen well, perhaps, when you arrive, you too will wear it on the little beach they have here in Brindle—although I am told August can be chilly! As always, you fill my thoughts. Emmanuel xx*

Brindle Beach is long and narrow, like a small bay. This is what he has told her. On the far side, over by the headland, people fish. The near side has the rock pool. Mel's rock pool. The university, where Emmanuel is based, is not in Brindle itself, but rather a bus trip away. There, in Brindle, he does not have a driver, nor does he have a car. It is not necessary, he has told her, for the transport is good. There is transport, too, here in Fallondale—but not to have a driver, that would never have occurred to her. Clearly, it doesn't seem to bother Emmanuel; his main concern has always been for his work, which, in the field of mining engineering, is important work. He has been much lauded for his fellowship at the university there.

Across the seas where he is now, he is often asked where he is from. In answer to the question, he says he is from Africa, no more than that. This, he has told her, seems to satisfy most people. Only the more curious ask for more. To these people, he speaks of the beauty of the country, and especially their part of it. Of the country's politics he says little—partly because he silently despairs of the regime; partly because they themselves have never had any problems.

It is hard to believe that in a day, February will be over and March will have begun. By then Emmanuel will have been gone two months. Long weeks they have been, for this is the first time they have been apart for so long, and she is still becoming accustomed to the emptiness beside her in bed. Rolling over now, she picks up the phone to check the time. It is already seven o'clock and there are noises coming from the kitchen. Laetitia will be preparing breakfast.

She should get up, she thinks. And get Sebastian up, as well. She isn't due at the studio until eleven—the shoot is a short one today—so she will have time for a walk once Sebastian has left for school. She has taken to walking with her neighbour, Grace, who is new to the area and who, to Rebecca's surprise, is becoming a friend.

Out of bed now, Rebecca looks for something to wear. A sense of order is one of Laety's great strengths, and in the robing room each T-shirt is neatly folded, each pair of socks paired and placed in rows, each dress, each skirt arranged by colour. The shorts she chooses are knee-length. Anything shorter will court attention, which is not what she wants. There is a full-length mirror in the robing room and she ventures a quick look at herself, just enough to confirm that she is still beautiful. This is not a boastful thought. It is simply a fact. She has always been beautiful; indeed, it is for this that she is known. She is Rebecca Vera, actress, model, media personality. And mother to a child who will be late to school if she doesn't rouse him soon.

The door to his room is open and although she has come to wake him, still she steps softly. The curtains are drawn, keeping it night-time dark. Now, when Rebecca opens them, light hurtles in. It will be a hot day, already Rebecca can feel it. From Sebastian's room, there is a view out onto the gardens, which are not only extensive, but also well maintained. Mosy has done a good job, she thinks, and she congratulates herself on having chosen such a diligent and capable gardener. Finding good staff is not always easy.

Slowly, Sebastian is stirring. Although his limbs keep lengthening, still his is the face of a little boy, eyes gently closed, long dark eyelashes curving upwards. Softly, softly, she strokes the side of his face.

'Time to wake up,' she whispers. 'It's well time to be up.'

Eyes still closed, he starts to stretch: legs pushing down under the sheet, stiff arms reaching out to the side.

'Up, up,' she says, 'and perhaps Laety will make you pancakes.'

Hearing this, his eyes open a fraction.

'But you'll need to get up right away,' she says.

Still silent, he blinks and blinks until finally his eyes manage to stay open.

'Get yourself dressed,' she tells him, 'and I'll see if Laety can make a start on the pancakes.'

'Thank you, Mama,' he says, his voice husky with sleep.

In the kitchen, Laety is laying the table. She looks up when Rebecca comes in. 'Good morning, ma'am,' she says.

There is orange juice ready for her and as Rebecca slips into her seat, she takes a quick sip. 'Lovely, Laety,' she says. 'Thank you.'

Laety smiles. She is making the coffee now and Rebecca leans back to savour the smell of it. 'I told Sebastian you'd make pancakes if he's quick.'

Laety gives a snort. 'That boy, he'd do just about anything for pancakes now, wouldn't he?'

'You make great pancakes,' Rebecca tells her.

'I'll make a double batch then, shall I?' It is an offer she makes half in jest, half in earnest. There was a time when Rebecca would eat anything on offer; a time when whatever she ate, still her body stayed pencil-thin. Now she has to be more careful, almost vigilant. So pancakes are out.

Watching Laety as she busies herself at the stove, Rebecca sees that there are grey streaks in her hair. This is something she has not noticed before and it comes as a shock. That Laety should age is something that has never occurred to her. The thought of it unsettles her.

'Are you well, Laety?' she asks.

Her back to Rebecca, Laety is cracking eggs into a bowl. The shell in one hand, she half turns to look at Rebecca. She seems amused by the question. 'Quite well, thank you,' she says. 'And you?'

It is not the response Rebecca is looking for. But neither has she asked the right question. *If you are becoming old, will I also become old?* That is what she wants to know. Even though it is a nonsense question, even though it is the sort of question a child might ask, not a woman who has just turned thirty-six.

'Thank you, Laety,' she says instead, 'I am very well.'

There is a noise behind them. Rebecca doesn't have to turn around to know that Sebastian is at the kitchen door. It is enough to see Laety's face widen with delight. 'Well, young man,' she says, hands on her hips, head cocked to the side, 'your mother tells me you were hoping for pancakes.'

Sebastian takes a seat at the end of the table. 'Yes,' he says, 'I am.' For him, there is also orange juice and, instead of coffee, warm milk.

The pancakes, when they come, are a sight to behold. There are three of them stacked on the plate, topped with banana. Laety brings him the honeypot so he can drizzle honey over the lot. It is a messy business and Laety tucks a tea towel into his collar so that his school uniform won't be soiled. Laety is the only person he allows to do this; or perhaps she is the only person he dares not refuse.

Sebastian has an early start on Tuesdays and he needs to be in the car by quarter to eight, which leaves him less than fifteen minutes to finish getting ready. Laety is the one to hurry him through his last mouthfuls before she whips off the tea towel and sends him to the bathroom to brush his teeth.

Sebastian is in the junior school and during the summer term, the boys wear long navy shorts and knee-length socks. Their shirts are white; their ties blue-and-white striped. Even in summer, the school blazer is to be worn on the way to school and again on the way home. Sebastian complains about this but Rebecca likes to see him wearing it.

The cars are garaged at the side of the property and a wide driveway sweeps around to the front of the house. Benson, their driver, has driven the Mercedes to the door and is standing beside it. Wearing his black suit, he is as smart as Sebastian. Once Sebastian has climbed into the back seat, Benson closes the door after him then walks around the car to get into the driver's seat. When Sebastian was younger, Rebecca would go, too, but now that he is older, she simply waves him off.

❦

As soon as he has gone, Rebecca walks down the road to Grace's house. The electric gate that blocks the house from the street is high and sturdy, with spikes on top to deter agile intruders. To the side of the gate is a bell. Rebecca rings the bell once and waits. For Rebecca, this is a new thing; more often, and particularly in her line of work, she has been the one to keep others waiting. But Grace is a prompt woman and within seconds she is at the gate. She looks tired.

'A restless night,' she tells Rebecca, 'that's all.' But her voice is flat and she seems subdued. Not that she is ever what Rebecca would call vivacious. This, in itself, is something Rebecca likes about her: that she is not a woman prone to gushing. Rather, she is a quiet woman, self-contained even, and she has told Rebecca very little about herself. Only that they had been living abroad, she and her husband, and have recently returned home. And not once has she approached Rebecca with that type of reverence so usually accorded the well-known and instantly recognised. Grace is a trained teacher, although she is now a secretary at the university where her husband, Johnson, also works.

Family money, then, Rebecca had surmised, to warrant such a house in Fallondale.

On occasion, Grace asks her in after their walk. Rebecca likes it when this happens. Today, on the way home, she is more forward than usual. Today, she invites herself in. But when Grace hesitates, she immediately regrets her boldness.

'Actually,' she says quickly, before Grace can respond, 'I probably should get ready instead—it always takes me twice as long as I think.'

This isn't true but Grace's face relaxes when she says it. 'Next time,' she offers.

'Yes,' Rebecca replies, trying not to look disappointed, 'next time.'

Mel

His hands wake her as they brush across her breast, before a finger starts to draw circles around her nipple. She's tired; it's still dark outside, for Christ's sake.

He rolls over, then, so that his mouth is up against her ear. 'Morning, babe,' he whispers, his breath warm.

'Feels like four am,' she says, her voice croaky.

But that doesn't stop him. Instead, his hands move down to her stomach. 'How about I make your day?'

'At four in the morning?' she snorts, but her irritation is feigned. Having his hands on her always feels good. They aren't soft hands, and she likes that: likes that they are rough hands; rough hands that know how to use a hammer and a drill and pour a slab. Hands that haven't been sitting idle in an office.

Again his voice is in her ear. 'Actually, it's just about six,' he tells her as his hand moves down to where her pubic hair used to be. It's a new thing, the Brazilian, and she's still not sure whether she really loves it or really hates it. The first time she got one, it was a surprise for their anniversary. But God, it had killed. Think about it: every clump of pubic hair—the whole lot of it—covered in hot wax and ripped out. And everything on show to Jodie—who, granted, she knows well; she's Brindle's only beauty therapist, after all—but still.

'Why do you want a Brazilian?' Jodie had asked her, wax strip in hand.

Mel shrugged. 'You know, something different.'

'Are you having an affair?'

Mel started to laugh. 'And when am I going to find time for an affair?'

Jodie shook her head. 'You'd be surprised. Where there's a will. Nine out of ten times when a client starts asking for a Brazilian, that's why.'

'Because they're having an affair?'

'Yep.'

'And they tell you?'

'Sometimes, not always. But the Brazilian, that's the giveaway.'

'Anyone I'd know?'

Jodie always has the goss, but generally she's pretty discreet. 'Maybe.'

'Locals?'

Jodie had licked her lips. 'Maybe.'

Interesting. Who? she'd wondered. Not her. In all the years she'd been with Adam, she'd never had an affair. Him either. As far as she knew. No, she did know: there'd never been anyone else for either of them. Christ, she wouldn't know how to start. She'd been a teenager when they got together and now look at them: Mr and Mrs with a mortgage, two kids and a pool in the backyard. Who'd have thought it?

Of course, there are times she would have liked something a bit more exotic thrown into the mix: not so much getting out of the country; she'd have settled for getting out of Brindle for a bit. But she hadn't even managed that, had she? And now look at her: Brindle Public student turned Brindle Public parent. Hardly living on the edge. Hardly an adventurous life.

But when she thinks about another life, a life lived elsewhere, a life of excitement, a life that is more daring, this is what happens: the bay pulls her back, the headland pulls her back, Brindle itself pulls her back until she is forced to give in to it, until she is forced to admit to herself that whatever the pull of the world outside, Brindle is home. And Adam is home, too. For whatever her daydreams, whatever her imaginings of a life lived differently, the truth of it is that Adam is always there, always right there beside her.

Although now he's right there on top of her.

'You like that?' he asks her.

'I like it,' she whispers, although to be honest, she's a bit itchy where her pubic hair is starting to grow back. That's one thing she hadn't thought through, the itchy stubble regrowth thing. Maybe laser it next time? Or maybe just forget the Brazilian altogether?

It's a quickie this morning. But a good one, still. It's always good with Adam—not that she's got much to compare it with. Just what her friends tell her: that a lot of the time they put out because they think they should, even if they don't feel like it. Mel can pretty much be talked into it whenever. Which isn't bad considering it's been—what? Twelve years. Which is already about eleven years longer than everyone gave them at the time.

He was so old, they said, and she was so young. Funny how

quickly that disappeared, how much five years was then and how little it is now.

They met at a nightclub, a dive of a place, but the only one prepared to accept her dodgy ID. Adam and his mate were at the bar, watching as Mel and her friend Bianca sipped on their vodka and lemonade. One drink would get them started, another would keep them going and a third would send them wild.

Back then, he wasn't a dancer. Back then he just stood there watching with a beer in his hand. That's still all he drinks. She likes spirits, especially a gin and tonic with her cigarette once the kids are in bed. Adam doesn't smoke anymore and he's been at her to quit, too. Sooner or later, she probably will. Just not right now.

That first night he played it cool: just watching, drinking, watching. He was still watching when she left the dance floor to get some water from the bar, sweat pouring down her face, hair plastered to her cheeks. He was close enough to her, then, to be heard over the music. 'Bit of a workout up there, hey?'

Mel tilted her head towards him. 'You should try it.'

Without taking his eyes from her, he leant back against the bar and shook his head. 'Not wearing my dancing shoes.'

It was such an odd, old-fashioned thing to say, she just burst out laughing. 'Well, I'm wearing mine—you can borrow them.'

Slowly, his eyes had slipped down her body, past her neck and down to her breasts, then down again until she felt a buzzing in her groin. A brief flicker up, and for a second he met her eyes again before, with another sweep, his eyes were on her shoes: high-heeled and strappy.

'Don't think it's the look I'm after,' he said in a slow sort of drawl.

She'd just about thrown herself on him then and there.

He had a car and a job. Not just a job; he had a trade. He was a builder. He even had his papers. Mel was impressed. So when he offered her and Bianca a lift home, she said yes. His car was a hatchback, a speedy sort of hatchback. In the dark, she couldn't tell the colour, but when he dropped them back at Bianca's place—her parents were away—she saw that it was electric blue.

He was not a teenager. He was twenty. When he told her that, she decided to give herself a bit of a boost. She was seventeen, she told him. In Year 11.

For a surprise one day, he picked her up from school, which, as it happened, was also his old school. There he was, at the end of the day, waiting at the gate for her. He held her hand as they walked back to his car. And that made her so, so proud, that she should be holding hands with her new boyfriend who had both a car and a job.

Inside the car, he pulled her close and kissed her so hard she imagined she might disappear down his throat.

When, finally, they broke apart, his forehead wrinkled.

'Your uniform,' he said, 'why are you wearing that uniform?'

She pretended to be confused. 'What do you mean?'

'That's the junior uniform.'

She'd felt herself turning a deep red.

'You're not in Year 11, are you?'

Eyes down, she shook her head.

'Year 10?' His voice sounded hopeful.

She shook her head.

'Shit, Mel,' he said. 'What, then?'

'Year 7.' She said it as a joke.

'Year 7!' he exploded. 'You can't be bloody serious.'

'Year 9,' she said quickly. 'I'm in Year 9.'

'Year 9? That must make you the only seventeen-year-old in the year, then.'

'I'm fifteen,' she said quietly.

'Fifteen? For Christ's sake, Mel, fifteen?'

She didn't think he'd be back. But he did come back. And he kept coming back. After six months, he bought her a friendship ring. Not silver, like the other girls had, but gold with a tiny, tiny red stone in it.

In the afternoons, after school, he'd drive her up to the headland where there were private places to be. Private places that were big enough for the two of them. Comfortable enough, too, so long as they took the picnic blanket with them. Not that they ever once used it for a picnic.

One time, the condom broke. Just once, but once was enough. Because she wasn't on the pill, was she? How could she be? How could she have asked the doctor for it? He would have been on to her mother in a flash.

It wasn't Adam's fault it had broken. And it wasn't her fault she was so bloody fertile. Now she laughs about it. But she wasn't laughing then. Not when she twigged that something was up. Even that took a while.

No way was she going to buy the test herself; she made Adam do it. They couldn't go back to her house or even his house, so they took it with them up to the headland. When he handed her the specimen jar, she'd just stared at him.

'Pee in it,' he told her. 'You've just got to pee in it.'

But she wouldn't. Not until he'd turned his back, walked away and promised not to look. It was an awkward thing to do, there on the headland, squatting over that stupid jar, her pants around her ankles. The instructions said to dip the stick in and wait three minutes. But within seconds, there were two strong lines.

Perhaps she'd got it wrong, she thought. Perhaps just one line meant yes and two lines meant no. But Adam was holding the instructions and when she held up the stick, she saw his face drop.

Fuck, he was saying, *oh fuck*.

Telling her parents was always going to be tricky; they didn't even know she had a boyfriend. So they didn't tell them. They told Adam's mum instead. And Fran, God love her, she hadn't screamed or shouted or cried. She'd simply turned on the kettle, put her hand over Mel's hand, and said, 'Oh dear, love, that's a bit of a surprise now, isn't it?'

And when Mel, shaking hard, said she couldn't tell her parents, she couldn't possibly—Fran had nodded for a bit then said, 'Well, love, why don't I take you to the doctor so we can find out what's what?'

What's what was a fifteen-week pregnancy, and a belly that, now she knew about it, seemed to be swelling by the second. She wasn't going to have an abortion. She wouldn't even consider it. Adam didn't try to talk her around.

Which meant that Mel's parents would have to be told, and soon. Adam came with her. Fran, too. Because it might be easier that way, she said, for the mothers to talk together.

But the conversation was brief and afterwards there was only silence. From everybody. Thick, thick silence that gave Mel the urge to whistle through her teeth. Instead, she tapped her foot under the table.

'Stop,' her father said finally. 'Stop tapping.'

So she did, she stopped tapping. But once Adam and Fran were gone, leaving her there in a silent, angry house, again she started to tap and tap. This time, her father didn't tell her to stop. This time, he just looked across the table at her and said, 'You disgust me.'

She saw the year out—there were only a few weeks left—but when school started back the next year, she stayed away. She moved out of home, too, and in with Adam and Fran. And after Ethan was born, they became a household of four. And if it was a bit tight at times, it didn't matter so much.

When Mel turned sixteen, they got engaged. Adam bought the rings together—the engagement ring and the wedding ring. Fran didn't think it would be lying to wear them both before they got married. It would be a shame not to, that's what she said, seeing as they'd been designed to be worn that way.

They were married just after her eighteenth birthday. The wedding was small—neither of them wanted to make a fuss. She didn't wear white and her father didn't give her away. Afraid of a refusal, she hadn't asked and he hadn't offered.

After Josh was born, by chance, a house came up for sale at the end of the street. It was old and it was rundown but, though the bank took a bit of convincing, almost affordable. And that's where they've stayed, right there in Brindle. Now, people are even calling it the new hotspot. That always makes Mel laugh. Brindle, by the jail, a hotspot. Who'd have thought it?

Adam is off her now, lying on his back beside her, still catching his breath. 'Thanks for that, Mrs Thompson.'

She smiles as she walks her finger from his belly button down to his groin. 'My pleasure, Mr Thompson.'

There are noises outside. 'Quick,' Adam whispers, 'they're coming.' With a giggle, Mel covers them both with the quilt. Arms wrapped around each other, they wait for the onslaught.

Josh is first in. Theirs is a low bed and even though he is small for a seven-year-old, he can still make it on top of them in one leap. This morning he lands on Adam's groin. 'Go easy, mate,' Adam groans. 'Don't kill your chances of having a sister.'

'What sister?' says Mel. 'I thought we were done.'

Adam makes a popping noise with his mouth. 'Maybe we'll change our minds.'

Now Ethan is launching himself onto them, too. He misses Adam but lands on Mel's legs. 'What are you trying to do, you little monster, break my knees?' She turns to Adam in mock despair. 'How could we possibly bring another child into this madhouse?'

As soon as she says this, the three of them—Adam included—start to grunt and make stupid faces. Pushing them all away from her, she pretends to get up. 'In five seconds,' she says, 'I'll be getting up and—I'm warning you—I'm naked.'

It's the only thing guaranteed to get the kids moving. Now she laughs as she watches them scrambling out of the room, eyes squeezed tight to make sure they won't catch even a glimpse of her.

Adam leans over to kiss her. 'If it's any consolation, babe, I love seeing you naked.'

Nina

It's the middle of March. At the club, that means Aloha time and everywhere Nina looks there are leis linked together to make giant paper chains. Large Chinese parasols hang from the ceiling and giant pieces of papier-mâché fruit are piled on either side of the bar.

Nina enters the room alone, dressed up in a tacky Hawaiian shirt she picked up in an op shop. She recognises no one.

Steve is already here, somewhere. *Steve*, she calls in her head, hoping this will be enough for him to look up and call her over to him.

But there's no sign of him. She could phone him, but the music is so loud he'd be unlikely to hear the ring. Besides, he could be with a client—this is a business function, after all—so he might not even answer.

As it happens, she finds him at the far side of the bar. He, too, is wearing a Hawaiian shirt, but unlike hers, his is the real deal: the cotton is thick and, instead of palm trees, pineapples form a border along it. He wears it with light cotton jeans and a pair of slip-on sandals he must have scored from his father. He looks great, she thinks, like a movie star from the fifties.

Once she has spied him, she picks up her pace. When she reaches him, she stretches out a hand to tap him on the arm. He is in conversation with the barman but when he feels the pressure on his arm, he turns around, his party smile wide. When he sees it is her, his smile seems to drop a little.

In front of them, the barman is pouring a light pink concoction into a cocktail glass. 'Better make it two of those,' says Steve, and she feels happy when he gives her arm a rub.

The drink comes in a martini glass with a short black plastic straw and a paper umbrella pushed into a glacé cherry. Aloha Sunrise, that's what it's called.

Beside her, Steve has dispensed with the straw and is drinking his cocktail straight from the glass. When he has finished, he picks up his umbrella between two fingers and bites into the cherry. She flinches: there is something about a glacé cherry that reminds her of an eyeball. As he starts to chew it, she has to look away.

Once she's finished her drink, she fishes out her umbrella and carefully separates it from the cherry. For Emily, she thinks, as she folds the little umbrella closed and tucks it away into her handbag.

When she looks up again, Steve is reaching into her glass for the cherry. His fingers are too thick for the glass and it takes him a couple of goes before he has it. Quickly, he throws the cherry back into his mouth. She forces out a smile although the action repels her.

With a tilt of his chin, Steve motions to the dance floor and reaches for her hand. She shakes her head but he tugs her towards him anyway. Once they are on the floor, he starts to swing her in and out, in and out. Hot with embarrassment, she tries to resist. She doesn't dance well, especially not rock-and-roll. He does, though, and on their next turn, he gives her a smile as he pulls her back to him. 'Nice moves, Mrs Foreman,' he whispers into her ear. That's enough for her to snuggle into him, but still she's glad when the band stops for a break.

The place is crowded now. Moving through the room are women in grass skirts and bikini tops. They are each carrying small round baskets and one of them is heading for Nina and Steve. From a distance, she is young and beautiful: her hair dark and wavy, her stomach flat and her legs long.

But as she comes closer, Nina sees that the woman is older than she'd first thought and that her face is sun-weathered and lined. When she reaches Nina, she says something Nina doesn't catch.

'Sorry?' Nina mouths. In response, the woman moves in closer, so close Nina can smell the stale tobacco on her breath. 'Choose some tombola tickets,' she says, her voice dry and deep and throaty.

But when Nina starts to search through her handbag for her wallet, the woman shakes her head. 'They're free, you don't have to buy them—just choose them. You can take six.'

And so, sticking her hand into the basket, Nina pulls out six tiny rolls of paper that, when unfurled, each have a letter and a number.

Sliding an arm around Nina, Steve gives the woman a smile. 'Do I get some too?' he asks.

The woman starts to answer before she stops, blinks and stares hard at him. 'You're Steve Foreman, aren't you?'

He nods slowly and, putting his head to one side, purses his lips. 'God help me if it isn't you, Sue Rankin.' At that moment, the music stops and Steve's voice rings out across the room.

The woman keeps staring at him. 'Well, well,' she says. 'Steve Foreman, can you believe it?'

Steve just smiles as his arm slowly slips away from Nina's waist.

Nina has no idea what has them both so transfixed. It is the woman, rather than Steve, who remembers she is still there.

'Sorry, love,' she says. 'Steve and I were at high school together. We haven't seen each other, since . . . when?' She looks to Steve for help.

He has an expression on his face Nina can't quite describe: it's a mixture of fascination and bewilderment. 'Since 1986,' he says. 'December 1986.'

'Not since 1986,' Nina repeats lamely. 'That's a while.'

The music starts up again and it's a song that makes Steve and Sue cry out in recognition. Sue pats Nina's hand as she passes her the tombola basket. 'Gotta dance to this one. Just gotta do it.' She leaves, then, and Steve follows her.

When, after too long, neither of them returns, Nina pushes her way through the party until she's next to the dance floor.

In front of her Steve is playing air guitar, right beside Sue, who's leaning into an invisible microphone, mime-shouting something Nina can't make out, her hair over her face as she shakes her head up and down.

Once the song is over, Nina raises her hand, to show them where she is. When Sue comes to retrieve the tombola basket, she is apologetic.

'Really sorry,' she says. 'Get me on the dance floor and it's just about impossible to get me off again.' She dips a hand into the basket and, pulling out a fistful of tickets, gives them to Nina. 'Here,' she says, 'that's for hanging on to them for me.'

Nina smiles but she doesn't want any more tickets. She just wants to go home.

Sue gives her hand a pat. 'Better get back on the job again. Tell Stevie Wonder I enjoyed catching up.'

It takes Nina a moment to realise she means her Steve. 'Sure,' she says with a weak smile. 'I'll tell him.'

But when she sees him, this isn't what she tells him. 'We shouldn't be too late,' she warns him, 'with the babysitter and everything.'

His eyes are small and glassy. 'The party's just starting, babe, just starting.' And when he puts his arm around her, he leans into her too hard, so hard she thinks she might topple.

Pushing him back, she shakes her head. 'It's already late,' she whispers.

He lets out an annoyed laugh. 'No, babe, the party's just starting.'

So she waits, and when the music stops for good, she could weep with relief.

Except the party's not over yet. Instead, Sue carries a microphone onto the dance floor.

'Well,' she says, 'it's the time you've all been waiting for. It's *tombola* time!' As the room fills with applause, she does a couple of Hawaiian dance moves. Steve raises his hands above his head to keep the crowd clapping. 'Go, Suzi Q!' he shouts. 'Go, Suzi Q!'

She smiles in his direction as she holds the microphone up to her mouth. 'Tonight we have a fabulous selection of prizes for our tombola winners, so dig out those tickets and cross your fingers.'

In all, Nina has sixteen tickets. To her surprise, a quiver of excitement runs through her. With so many tickets, she thinks, she must be in with a chance, especially when there are ten prizes to be won.

But the first five tickets drawn are blue and Nina's tickets are all red. The next four are red but none of them are Nina's numbers. She's not a winner after all. So when Sue calls out the final number—red 34—and Nina sees that it is hers, she stares at the ticket in disbelief. Steve reacts before Nina does. 'Here!' he shouts, grabbing the ticket from her hand and rushing onto the dance floor. 'Here's number thirty-four.'

Sue confirms the win. 'And the final prize winner is Mr Steve Foreman,' she announces, handing him a bottle of Cointreau wrapped in cellophane. With a shout of victory, Steve lifts it up in the air. 'The Cointreau's on me,' he tells the crowd.

By the time the party's finally over it's close to 3 am. Outside the club, Sue fumbles with her phone. 'I'm trying to call a cab,' she says, 'but I can't remember the bloody number.'

Steve spreads out his arms. 'I'll give you a lift home, Suzi Q. I'll take you home.'

Looking up, Sue struggles to focus. 'You can't drive, Stevie Wonder,' she says. 'You're blind.'

And she laughs so hard she starts to cough. She's still laughing as Nina opens the car door for her then walks back around to get into the driver's seat.

When they get to Sue's house, she has a couple of false starts before she manages to get herself out of the car. Once she is out, she leans into the front passenger seat. 'See you round, Stevie Wonder,' she says, her words slurring. 'And you too, Mrs Stevie.'

Steve throws his head and his arms back and laughs like he's never heard anything funnier. 'For sure, Suzi Q. For sure.'

Sue chuckles as she raises her hand to her head in some sort of salute. Nina looks over at Steve and, sure enough, he's saluting her right back.

Sue takes a step towards the kerb then stumbles. She'll end up on the road, Nina thinks to herself. So she puts the car in park, turns off the engine and gets out. Gritting her teeth, Nina takes the woman by the arm and leads her up to the door. A sensor light floods the front porch.

'Where are your keys?' Nina asks.

Sue peers at her. 'You got them?'

'How about I have a look in your handbag?' Nina suggests.

And so, like an obedient child, Sue lifts up her handbag to show Nina. It's a large bag filled with stuff: pens and chip packets and tissues and tampons and make-up and loose change. When Sue shakes the bag, they both hear a jangling sound. Sue gives a satisfied murmur. 'There they are,' she announces. With a grimace, Nina sinks her hand into the bottom of the bag and fishes around until she finds some keys.

'That's them,' Sue tells her, leaning forward until she loses balance and has to press a hand against the front door to steady herself.

'Which one?' asks Nina, holding the keys up in front of her face.

Sue frowns at them. 'I think,' she says indistinctly, 'I think it's a gold one.'

There are three gold keys on the keyring. The second one fits, and once Nina has opened the door, she passes Sue the keys and leaves her there.

When she gets back to the car, Steve is asleep, his head slung back, mouth open. Nina tries not to look at him as she starts the car and drives them home.

Terry

The blinds are still drawn, so he turns his head to listen. When he doesn't hear anything, he's pleased. Nothing worse than a rained-out swimming carnival. Then again, maybe there is. The cock-up they had two years back, now that was worse than a hailstorm. All the kids—the whole lot of them—lined up to be bussed to the carnival. An hour later, they were still there, with not a bus in sight. Belinda had forgotten to confirm with the bus company. Booked the buses, she'd done that all right; all she'd forgotten was the phone call to say it was going ahead. Poor little Belinda was beside herself. Crying—no, sobbing—over it. Devastated.

Ever since, Terry's been booking the buses—and confirming the bloody buses—as well as organising the rest of the carnival. Not that he minds. Truth be told, he loves it.

Now he pulls on his dressing-gown, heads for the kitchen and switches on the radio. And, praise the heavens, it's the weather forecast he's after: sunny and twenty-five. Perfect.

The buses are there on time and by 9.45, a sea of kids are sitting up in the grandstand, poolside. Terry switches on the megaphone and hopes for the best. It's the same bloody megaphone he's been using for the past fifteen years, and it's a bugger of a thing. He's lost count of the number of kids who've missed their races because they couldn't hear what was being said over the static. If they don't get a new one by next year, he'll bloody well fork out for it himself.

But for now, Tania's trying to quieten them all down. *Hands on heads*, she mimes, *on shoulders, on knees, on ears, on lips* over and over again until the kids are so busy following her they stop talking.

Dropping his arm so the megaphone hangs down by his side, Terry sidles up to her mid-routine. 'Stick a finger up each nostril and see what they do then.'

Her mouth twitches. 'How about you call the first race instead, smart-arse?'

Terry claps his hand to his mouth. 'I think Acting Principal Mathews would agree that this is not the sort of language we like to hear at Brindle Public.'

'You know what?' she whispers back, hands on her head, shoulders, waist. 'I'm not sure Acting Principal Mathews would agree with anything you have to say, Mr P.'

Terry takes a bow. 'Thank you, Ms Rossi. I'll take that as a compliment.'

Hands back on her shoulders, Tania flicks him a smile. 'Eight-year-old boys' freestyle, please.'

Terry raises the megaphone back up to his lips. 'First call for eight-year-old boys' freestyle—that's eight-year-old boys' freestyle. Please report to the marshalling area.'

By 11.30, he's ready for a break, so he hands the megaphone to Tania and does a walk through the grandstand to check on the kids. Up the back, Jade is sucking on a Chupa Chup. Below them, Tania's voice is just audible. 'Eleven-year-old girls' fifty-metre freestyle. Eleven-year-old girls' fifty-metre freestyle.'

Terry steps over a bundle of school bags so he can sit beside Jade. 'Come on, love,' he says, 'this is your big chance.'

Jade has another suck of her Chupa Chup before she takes it out of her mouth to have a good look at it. She's sucked it right down into the shape of a tiny brown football. Now she's looking up at him with half-closed eyes, her eyelashes long and dark and, by the looks of it, set in place with mascara. Today her lips are full, too, full and shiny. Must be the lip gloss, he thinks.

'Big chance for what, Mr P?'

'Big chance to do something for your house.'

She cocks her head on an angle. 'Well, I've been cheering, Mr P.'

Terry stifles a smile. 'I'm not talking about cheering, Jade, I'm talking about competing. In the carnival. To get points for your house.'

'Reckon I'm in with a chance for age champion, Mr P?'

She's that dry she could be twenty-five. 'Participation, Jade, that's what I'm talking about. A point for every race you swim in. Jump in the water and there's your point.'

She gives him a half-smile. 'That true, Mr P? I jump in the water, get straight out and I still get my point?'

'Uh-huh. That'll get you a house point. But if you want to earn yourself two class points, you'll need to do a bit more. For the class points, you need to jump in, get to the end of the pool—I don't care how you do it—and get out.'

Elsie is sitting a couple of rows further down. At the mention of class points, she swivels around to face them. 'Two class points, Mr P, just for going in it?' She's got her lunch box on her lap and she's trying to pull open a packet of chips.

Terry shoots a finger at her. 'That's right, Elsie. Long as you go in the race, you get your two points. Go in five races and you've got enough points for a lucky dip.' With that, Elsie lets the chips fall back into her lunch box. 'And, Elsie,' he says, dropping his voice, 'I don't mind telling you, just yesterday I topped up the lucky dip box with some really great prizes.'

Elsie's eyes are wide and trusting. He could tell her he bought an elephant from the zoo and she'd still believe him.

Jade stretches her legs out in front of her. They are long, golden brown and covered in little blonde hairs. Not a blemish on them. 'Bet they're lame, Mr P. The prizes. Bet they're all those lame Lego packs.'

Terry makes a clicking noise with his tongue. 'Wrong,' he says, 'no lame Lego packs. Just a whole lot of terrific surprises.'

This has Elsie almost clapping in delight. 'How many, Mr P? How many prizes are in there?'

Terry lowers his voice to a whisper. 'A carload, Elsie. A carload.'

He's got them both for a moment then; even Jade has straightened up. 'A carload, Mr P?'

'Maybe that's overstating it, Jade, but you get my drift, don't you?'

Jade shakes her head but now she's laughing, so he knows he's got her.

He watches her pull down her denim shorts and take off her little T-shirt. Stripped of them, she's left wearing nothing but a string bikini, the fabric shiny and golden, like the wrapper of a Crunchie bar. She's so clearly not a child anymore: high, round breasts pull at the tiny triangles of her top, leaving a dividing line along the middle of her chest. Her waist, too, has narrowed and her hips are curved now, the skin pressing against the tiny ribbon that joins her little pants together. It's happened so quickly, he thinks yet again, quickly enough for her swimming costume to have suddenly become too small. Even if the shade is beautiful on her lovely brown body.

As she walks over to the marshalling area, goggles over her wrist like a loose bracelet, he keeps his eye on her, marvelling at the confidence of her walk: head high, shoulders back, chest out. Her hips, it seems, have not only given her a new shape, but a new walk too. It's an understated sashay: to the right, to the left, to the right, to the left. Too little to be provocative, too much to go unnoticed.

Elsie has also stripped down to her swimmers. Hers, too, are last year's: a blue pair of racers sun-bleached from navy to mid-blue, the elastic stretched so that the bottom of them droops down and her breasts poke out of them like little cones. Strange to think of Elsie's body forging ahead as her mind struggles to keep up. She searches in her bag until she comes out with a swimming cap. It's a thin plastic one and she has trouble getting it on. He lets her wrestle with it for a couple of minutes before he calls down to her. 'Do you want me to help you?'

Nodding like an eager toddler, she steps heavily across the three rows that separate them until she is standing in front of Terry, the edge of her cap pulled across her forehead, the rest of it flopping down to one side.

Terry pulls the cap off and, using both hands, stretches it out so it will fit over her head. Wisps of hair stick up at the side of her face and, gently, he slips them back with his finger.

'How's that, Elsie?'

The girl smiles as Terry steps back to take a look at her. The cap makes her head look like a big round ball and, together with her belly, the effect is of a Babushka doll. She'll be at the mercy of them all, he thinks. They'll all be laughing at her as hard as they can. Hopefully, she'll be oblivious to it. Hopefully, she'll be so focused on the bloody carload of lucky dip prizes she won't notice.

'Off you go now, Elsie,' he says, his voice tender, 'show me what you've got.'

Still smiling, Elsie turns back to Terry and, pressing the side of her face into his stomach, wraps her arms around him. He rubs her back with his hand and, although he knows he should gently disentangle her, lets her stay there, right up against him. 'Thanks, Mr P,' she says, her voice muffled.

'Looking good, Elsie,' he says softly before he gives her a tap. 'You'd better get up there now.'

Her tread is heavy and awkward as she steps down the concrete stairs that divide the seat rows. When she reaches the last step, she gives a clumsy jump. Still smiling she turns back to Terry to check that he hasn't missed it: that he's watched her jumping down. He gives her a wave to show that he's seen it all. She returns the wave and, with a happy lumbering skip, runs to catch up to Jade.

Across a couple of rows, Bridie is sitting quietly by herself. 'That goes for you, too, Bridie,' Terry tells her. 'You can follow them over to the marshalling area.' At the mention of her name, Bridie's head bobs up. 'Huh?'

'Eleven-year-old girls, Bridie—that's you.'

She shakes her head. 'I'm not swimming, Mr P.'

'Why not, Bridie? You got scarlet fever or something?'

Again she shakes her head. 'Because of my glasses. Nan said I'm not to take them off. Because I'll lose them and she'll have to pay two hundred and fifty dollars for another pair. And that's too much. And I can't swim in them.'

Privately, Terry thinks a new pair of glasses is exactly what Bridie needs. The ones she's got are already too small for her and the frames are too heavy for her little face: mottled blue plastic when she could have a thin metal frame instead. If he thought he could get away with it, he'd get her a new pair himself. But he knows Vonnie: it wouldn't matter if she were down to her last dollar, she still wouldn't be accepting anything from anyone. It'd make a world of difference to Bridie, though.

'Tell you what, Bridie, how about this? Just before you start your race, you give me your glasses. I'll keep them for you until you've finished the race. What do you think?'

When she still looks unconvinced, Terry pats the back pocket of his board shorts. 'I'll put them straight in here—they'll be safe as houses.'

He can see she's still uncertain so he gives it another try. 'Come on, just your age race,' he says, and he's pleased when she stands up and follows him over to the marshalling area.

Helen is dividing the eleven-year-old girls into house groups. Jade has made it to the front of the line and is basking in the sun. When she sees Terry, she gives him a toss of her head and a lazy smile. Any older, and she'd be making him turn bright red with that sort of look.

Behind her, Elsie is sitting up cross-legged like she's the keenest kid in the kindy class. He can just about see her white skin burning up in the sun.

As Bridie slips into line, she hands her glasses to Terry and takes off her shorts. She keeps a T-shirt over her swimming costume.

'It'll weigh you down,' he warns her, but she still won't take it off.

They are all in the same heat: Bridie on the inside lane, Jade in lane four and Elsie beside her in lane five. Only Hayley Timms from Year 5 is standing on the blocks; the rest of them are by the edge of the pool, arms reaching up to meet above their heads, except for Jade, who's got a hand on her hip.

When it comes, the explosion of the starting gun makes him jump a mile.

As expected, Hayley takes the lead from the get-go. The girl's a machine. National titles, here we come. Jade, Elsie and Bridie, on the other hand, well, you'd be hard pressed to say any of them were even aiming for the other end of the pool. Jade might be in with a chance if she'd tied her hair back instead of leaving it out, mermaid-style, so that it's a mess of floating blonde covering her eyes. Despite that, she's making progress until her bikini top comes undone and she has to stop mid-pool to try to keep it around her. Terry laughs. There's a reason why one-piece racer backs are recommended for the girls.

Not that they're helping Elsie, who's ploughing down the lane with all the agility of a submerged truck. Even after her pit stop, Jade's still in front of her.

But this year, Bridie is the favourite for last place. And just as he predicted, the T-shirt isn't doing her any favours. He watches as it balloons up in front of her until somehow it works its way over her head, her arms flailing around until, right in front of him, she starts to sink.

At first, he doesn't register what's happening. Once he does, it takes him less than a second to peel off his own T-shirt and jump into the water. His aim is good and he lands just in front of her.

Her head is underwater now and, putting his arms around her waist, he pulls her up to him so that her face is against his shoulder and her body flat against his. Mid-pool, the water is not as deep as he had thought: over Bridie's head, but just level with his nipples. The little girl coughs into his neck but she doesn't bring up any water; instead she just pants. Her ribs are bony against his chest, her heart is beating fast, too fast, and her breathing is quick and shallow. Pulling her little body tight against him, he murmurs softly to her and she nestles her face into the crook of his neck. When he feels her shivering, he lifts her up onto the side of the pool and, still in the water himself, calls out for a towel.

Immediately, Laurie is beside them, but it's Tania who brings the towel and wraps it around the girl. Laurie turns to Tania. 'Can I leave you to look after her?'

Tania looks surprised, but when she starts to answer, Terry cuts in over her. 'It's fine, Laurie, I'll take care of her.'

Laurie shakes her head. On her face is an expression he can't quite interpret. Something between disapproval and disgust. 'I think it would be better for a female teacher to deal with this.'

'I'm her classroom teacher,' he says, 'so it would make sense for me to deal with it.'

'And I'm the principal,' Laurie replies, her voice curt, 'and I've asked Tania to take over.'

There's a lot he could say back to that. He could begin with the obvious—that she's only the acting principal not the actual principal—and move on from there. He could keep his voice low or he could raise it for emphasis. And he could say this: *I've been here a lot longer than you have, lady, and I'm telling you that I'm her goddamn teacher and I'll decide how to look after her and I won't be taking any advice from someone who probably doesn't even know the kid's name.*

But little Bridie's still shivering and someone's going to have to get her dressed and tell her to warm herself in the sunshine. Having an argument with Laurie Mathews isn't going to speed things up.

So he flicks Tania a disgruntled smile and shrugs his shoulders. 'She's all yours.'

He waits in the pool until they have all gone. Only then does he pull himself up and out. He hears the crack as he sits down on the edge of the pool. For a moment, it doesn't register. Then he remembers. 'Goddamn it,' he says to himself, 'the glasses.'

Cursing himself, he fishes them out of his pocket. To his surprise, the lenses are fine, but one of the arms has completely snapped off. 'Bloody hell,' he whispers. Bridie'll be beside herself when she sees them. Absolutely beside herself.

It's cold out of the water, colder than he would have thought. He'll need a towel to dry himself off. And he's looking in his bag for it when he feels a stinging slap on his back. He turns around in surprise. Behind him, Kurt and his two deputies, Cody and Ethan, are laughing like madmen.

He fixes his attention on Kurt. 'Was that you?' It was a hard bloody slap and he can still feel it.

'It wasn't that bad, Mr P,' says Kurt. 'Just wanted to get your attention, that's all.'

'Well, you've got it now.'

'So, Mr P,' he says, 'did you save Bridie from drowning?'

Terry shakes his head. 'I don't think she would have drowned.'

'But she might've, Mr P. I mean, if she just kept on sinking and she couldn't kick her way up again or something. Then she would've drowned for sure.' Behind him, Cody and Ethan are nodding furiously. 'Because of her T-shirt,' he says.

Terry shades his forehead with a hand to block out the sun. 'Why do you say that?'

'Because it was too big. It was like a dress or something, it was that big on her. It could have gone right over her head and suffocated her. Asphyxiation. That's what it would have been.'

Terry raises an eyebrow. He'd forgotten about Kurt's particular expertise: he's an expert on techniques causing death. Asphyxiation, strangulation, suffocation, dehydration. You name it, he's be able to tell you about it. Just don't ask him to spell it.

'What's asphyxiation?' Cody pipes up.

Kurt makes a choking sound. 'Like when you can't breathe anymore, and if it keeps on happening, you choke and die.'

Cody nods with the air of someone who knows all about it. 'Like what happened yesterday, when I was at your house?'

Terry glances at Kurt, who, quick as a flash, starts shaking his head. 'It wasn't me, sir.'

Cody is with him on that. 'It wasn't even Kurt, Mr P. It was his brother Jordan. He put his arm on my throat, like really hard, and I couldn't even breathe at all.'

Kurt's eyes are wide. 'That's true, Mr P, I swear to God. My brother, he was pressing down so hard Cody started making this noise like he was going to die so I rammed into Jordan so he'd get off him.'

'What do you mean, you rammed him?'

'You know, sir, rammed him. Like rammed right at him.' To show him, Kurt bends over so that his head is level with his backside, and then, his eyes on the floor, arms pinned to his side—so that they, too, are horizontal—he runs hard up the length of the pool. He looks like a bull, all nuggetty shoulders and strong little thighs. When he runs back again, his face is flushed and his eyes are sparkling. 'That's what I did, Mr P. I deadset rammed him.'

Cody's nodding harder now, so hard Terry thinks his head might spring off. 'True as, Mr P,' he says. 'True as, he rammed him just like that.'

'So what did Jordan do?'

Cody opens his mouth to answer but, before he does, flicks his eyes across to Kurt, who gives him the go-ahead with the inclination of his head. 'Well, Mr P, when Kurt rammed into him, suddenly Jordan started, like, yelling and that. And then he turned around and lifted his arm up so it wasn't pressing on my throat anymore and that's when I run.'

Kurt is standing up straight, listening hard, head to the side in case he needs to correct anything. 'I run too, Mr P. I run so friggin' fast I thought I was going to have a heartache.'

''Cause of Jordan,' Cody chips in. ''Cause we thought he'd be after us.'

Terry obliges with the question they're both itching to be asked. 'So, did he get you?'

'Nup, sir, he couldn't catch us, we were that quick,' Kurt says.

Cody's back to his furious nodding. 'And besides, he doesn't know where our headquarters are and that's where we hid out.'

'Your headquarters?' Terry tries to keep his face straight.

'Yeah, Mr P, you should see it. It's sick, we discovered it ourselves, when we were exploring and then we found it, sir, it's near the—' He pulls up short because, sure enough, Kurt is boring a finger into his back.

Terry doesn't pursue the location of the headquarters. Instead, he reaches over to give Ethan a light punch on the shoulder. 'You up soon?'

As if on cue, Laurie's voice trickles out through the megaphone. 'First call for eleven-year-old boys' freestyle. To the marshalling area, please. Eleven-year-old boys' freestyle.'

Ethan's off before she's finished the announcement, feet flapping on the concrete as he rushes to the top end of the pool. Kurt and Cody don't move. Terry points to the marshalling area. 'That's you, boys. Fifty metres. Freestyle. Now.'

Kurt shakes his head and affects an expression of disappointment. 'Can't, sir.'

Terry smiles in anticipation. 'That's bad news, Kurt. Why not?'

'It's me leg, sir. Think I've pulled a muscle or something.'

Terry raises an eyebrow. 'What, just now?'

'Nuh, day before yesterday, sir.' But he turns red when he realises his mistake.

'Seems to be okay now, though, mate. Your ramming run was perfect.'

Kurt gives him a wry smile. It's one of the things Terry likes about him. He'll dish out the tall tales but he's happy to admit it when he's been caught out.

'Both of you. Now.' He's not even going to bother with the lucky dip bribe. Not now he's got Kurt anyway. Because if he's got Kurt, he'll have Cody too.

And sure enough, they both turn and follow Ethan up the concrete to the marshalling area.

Within minutes, the three of them are lined up behind the starting blocks, together with another four from Year 5. Of the seven,

Ethan is the only one wearing a cap. He's stretched out since last year, Terry thinks, stretched right out. And even though his shoulders have started to fill out, he's still a bony little thing. But it's his feet that are the giveaway to the man he'll grow into: long and wide. He'll be six foot by the time he's fifteen. That's Terry's call.

'On your marks.' Laurie's voice, high and thin, doesn't project well. Ethan and Johnny Spiros step up to the starting blocks. The rest of them stand to the side, toes just over the edge of the pool.

Crouched on the blocks, Ethan could be at the Olympics: goggles on, cap slick over his head, arms slightly in front of him, his whole body still and taut, ready to spring.

Then Laurie clears her throat. 'Sorry,' she says.

Ethan keeps in position, swivelling his head only slightly to the left to try to work out what's happened.

'Let's start again,' says Laurie.

Puzzled now, Ethan looks around at the rest of the competitors before he straightens up and waits for the next instruction. But suddenly, and before he is ready, Laurie calls for them, in rapid succession, to get on their marks and get set before she abruptly fires the gun.

In the confusion, Ethan dives badly and for the first ten metres, he's trailing Cody, which is a first. Beside him, Cody's like a little wind-up toy, arms fighting through the water, legs kicking madly. On the other side, Kurt is taking his time; his stroke's good but his breathing's atrocious. But at least he'll make it to the end. By the twenty-metre mark, Ethan has taken the lead, and with ten metres to go, the rest of the field are way back, even Johnny Spiros, who might well have thought himself in with a chance.

For Terry, it's a joy just to watch Ethan go—everything is in sync:

arms, legs, head to the right, head to the left, and again and again. As soon as he finishes, he tilts his head up for his time, but it's not club racing and there's no clock in front of him, so instead he does a half-turn to lean his back up against the tiled wall of the pool while he waits for Cody and Kurt to come in. They're just about neck and neck, but as usual, Kurt manages to get the edge on Cody. Which is just as well, because as long as Kurt's ahead of Cody, everything's all right.

Terry strolls down to the end of the pool to congratulate the lot of them. But especially Ethan.

Crouching down by the edge of the pool, Terry extends an arm to help Ethan out. 'Only fifty metres, sir,' he says. 'I can probably get myself out.'

Terry shrugs. 'My motto, Ethan, is that you should always take a leg up when it's offered because it might not happen again.'

That makes Ethan smile. 'Got a bad start,' he says, relenting, as Terry pulls him out of the water.

'Made up for it, though, didn't you, boy? That's the main thing. That you made up for it.'

Cody is resting his arms on the edge of the pool. 'How about me, Mr P?' he pipes up. 'You going to give me a leg up too?'

With a smile, Terry pulls him up and out of the pool. He's a feather compared to Ethan and his slight body is trembling with the cold. 'Not much of you, is there, mate?'

Teeth chattering, Cody doesn't answer, he just opens up his palm to show Terry a green plastic disc. 'I got fourth, but.'

Kurt is already out of the pool, water dripping onto shoulders that have halfback written all over them. He even walks like a league player: shoulders first, swinging left and right, his neck already thickening into place. A bulldog, that's what he is, a hazel-eyed bulldog.

~

He finds Bridie sitting back in the grandstand. The first time he scans the rows, he misses her. The second time around he spots her bang in the middle of the stand, blinking myopically because she can barely see a thing, poor little love. Funny, though, how different she looks without her glasses; free of the milk-bottle lenses, she's got pretty eyes. And her face is heart-shaped, which is something else he hadn't noticed before. He'd never given it a shape, just skinny. Not that heart-shaped does you a whole lot of good if you can't see a thing in front of you.

'Bridie,' he calls out as he waves his hand towards her. She looks in the direction of his voice but her face stays blank. 'Bridie,' he calls again, then a third time, until she's got him.

He climbs up the stairs to her. 'Well, that's a race I won't be forgetting in a hurry.'

He says it as a joke, but when she drops her head in embarrassment, he kicks himself for saying anything at all.

Keeping her head down, she mumbles something to him.

He puts a hand on her knee. 'What was that, love?' he says gently.

'Can I have my glasses?' The question makes his stomach turn even though he's got his answer ready.

'Okay,' he says. 'I've got some good news and I've got some bad news.'

She raises her head.

'So, the bad news is that I accidentally broke your glasses.' When her face falls, he hurries on. 'The good news is that straight after school, you and me, we're going to go and get you another pair.'

If the good news has registered at all, it's not obvious. Her face is white and drawn. 'Nan's going to kill me,' she whispers.

In his rush to reassure her, his words become clumsy. 'I mean it, Bridie. Today. We'll go today. Straight after school. Before you go home. We'll get it all sorted.'

She's not appeased. 'But what am I going to say to Nan?' Her eyes have filled now and he's scared stiff she's going to cry.

'Nothing, Bridie. You won't have to say anything. I'll do everything.' Placing a hand on each of her arms, he swivels her around so they are face to face. 'I promise, Bridie.'

It's mayhem trying to get them onto the buses and back to school in time for pick-up. Especially when eighty percent of them are hyped up on jelly pythons from the pool kiosk.

Once they're all aboard, Helen and Tania take charge of the school roll so he can finally sit down. He's already thrown his bag on the front window seat to bags it and now he can properly claim it. A bit of quiet, that's what he needs: eyes out the window, watching the world go by. At least until there's some fracas behind him.

But when he returns to his seat, his bag has been moved to the aisle seat and Laurie has planted herself by the window. He feels his body sag in disappointment and has to suppress the urge to reach over and yank her out of the seat. Instead, he lifts his bag off the aisle seat and, cradling it in his lap, reluctantly sits down beside her.

'Pretty successful swimming carnival, all in all,' she says. It's a pronouncement rather than a question and he sees no need to reply. He just looks at his hands and hopes that's all she has to say. 'Lucky the rain held off,' she continues. He nods, but he can't understand why she's making an effort all of a sudden. In any case, he's ticked off about the seat so she's going to be pushing it to get any chitchat out of him today.

Still she keeps on yakking. He waits for her to bring up the fiasco with Bridie but that, at least, seems to have gone clean out of her mind. She's more interested in banning the kids from going to the pool kiosk next year. Not because of the junk food, mind you, but to stop the kids from wandering into the out-of-bounds area beside the men's change rooms. 'You've always got to be on the lookout,' she says.

He's not with her. 'On the lookout for what?'

She lowers her voice so he can scarcely hear her. 'Paedophiles.'

The corners of his mouth twitch. 'What, at the swimming carnival? The place was empty apart from all of us.'

'You can't be too careful.'

'I didn't see a soul, Laurie, not one person. Apart from the lifeguards and the canteen ladies.'

'Systems, Terry,' she says, and her voice is severe. 'We need to be systematic about the kids' safety.'

By God, he thinks, she's a humourless bloody specimen. But he nods and murmurs, 'Systems, yep,' then hopes to hell she'll shut up for the rest of the trip.

The moment the bus pulls up outside the school, all the kids are itching to get out. Quick as a flash, Terry is on his feet as he eyeballs his way down each of the rows. 'Brindle Public students,' he says, his voice rising up from his diaphragm, 'remember their manners at all times. And when Brindle Public students are on a bus they wait quietly in their seats until they are told otherwise.'

There is reshuffling as the kids sit back and Terry waits for the noise to subside before he continues, his voice still booming. 'That's more like it, Brindle Public. Yes, that's much more like it.'

Row by row, he guides the children out of the bus. When Bridie passes him, he taps her on the shoulder to remind her to wait for him by the school gate.

And sure enough, when he gets off, she's waiting there, face pinched. Putting his arm around her, he gives her a squeeze and bends down to whisper in her ear. 'Let's go get you some new glasses.'

Bridie wants to sit in the front seat. She's over ten, and legally that's okay, but it's still safer in the back, doesn't matter how old you are, so that's where Terry puts her. The only drawback is that it's hard to have a conversation when one of you is driving and the other one's sitting in the back seat, so it's a quiet trip. But that's all right. Quiet can be good.

He scores a park close to the optometrist, which is lucky, because it's getting congested in Raleigh these days. Eyes On You, that's what Angelo's shop is called. Terry hates it. What's wrong with something simple and to the point, like Angelo's Optometrist?

As soon as they're inside, Angelo comes over to greet them. His is a vigorous handshake. 'Long time,' he says, squeezing Terry's fingers together. He has a big Italian face and his hair, always jet black and curly, is starting to get some grey in it. 'So what can I do for you? Anything you ask, I'll do it for you, my friend.'

Terry looks solemn. 'The thing is, Angelo, we've got a bit of an emergency on our hands.' From his bag, he pulls out his beach towel and unrolls it to reveal Bridie's broken spectacles.

He hands the broken pieces to Angelo. 'Any chance of fixing them?'

Angelo pushed the severed arm up against the rest of the frame. 'It's not looking good,' he says. 'I could try sticking it but the hinge won't work so the arm won't bend. And I couldn't guarantee it wouldn't snap off again. '

Bridie blinks hard but Terry is happy with the news. 'Perfect,' he says, 'because what we've really come for is a new pair of glasses. We only need to keep the old ones going until the new ones are ready.' He turns to Bridie. 'Purple still your favourite colour?'

When she nods, he selects all the purple frames on display and lays them out in front of her. Tentatively, she picks out a metal pair with pink and lavender sides. When she puts them on, he gives a low whistle. 'Well, aren't they something?'

Her mouth curves up into a smile. 'I like them,' she whispers.

Terry squats down so he's at eye level with her. 'So why don't we get them, then?'

He parks outside the house and before he's even put the hand brake on, Bridie is out, half running, half walking to the door, one hand pressed against the side of her old glasses. The house, he notices, has been recently painted and this reassures him. It's a mushroom sort of colour, but she's left the windowsills white. A nice combination.

He follows Bridie up the pathway then stays behind as she rings the doorbell to be let in. Straightaway the door opens, and there's Vonnie.

Before he can protest, she's bustled him into the house and has him sitting down on the sofa. Soon there's a cup of tea and a plate of cream biscuits in front of him and she won't let up until he's had three.

Bridie sits on the floor between them, her face lifted to catch their conversation as she nibbles at the edge of her biscuit.

There's school to talk about, and Vonnie's health, and how the summer has been. Only then does he ask after Trent.

Vonnie's face falls. 'He's okay,' she says, trying to keep her smile. She starts to say more but stops. Instead she takes hold of the chain around her neck and twists it round and round her finger. 'Remember when he was just a little tyke?'

Terry nods. It's how he always remembers Trent: sitting on the mat at the front of the classroom, hair cut in a number one like a little thug. He'd been warned about him. How he was out of control. How he wouldn't listen. How he was aggressive. And yet there he'd been, sitting down in front of him, good as gold.

Afterwards, people said they weren't surprised.

Bollocks. That was Terry's answer to the bloody psycho-experts. Bollocks. Everyone can be a genius after the event.

Terry glances at Bridie. 'You know that, don't you? That I taught your dad when he was in Year 6?'

'My dad's class, it was the first class you ever taught at Brindle.' There is a quiet edge of pride in her voice.

'My word it was, Bridie, and there he was sitting in front of me, and you know, your Nan here, she'd given him such a short haircut I wasn't sure if he had any hair at all.'

He's told her this before, he's sure of it, but she laughs and laughs like it's the first time she's heard it. Even Vonnie manages a whisper of a smile. 'It's his birthday next week,' she says quietly. 'He'll be thirty-one. Can you believe it?'

He can't really. But that's always the way with his old students. He's always astonished that they grow up instead of just staying put.

'Thirty-one,' he says. 'Wish him a good one for me.' He keeps his voice low and casual and Vonnie nods, her fingers tight around her teacup. She's old, he realises suddenly.

'Vonnie,' he says now, 'there's something I've got to tell you. About Bridie's glasses.'

When he explains, Vonnie's face doesn't register any emotion. 'What do they cost?' she asks. 'The new ones.'

Terry shrugs the question away. 'Angelo's a mate of mine. He gave me a good deal. It's all fixed up. They've just got to be picked up. I can take her up after school tomorrow if you like—check they fit properly.'

'You can't go paying for them, Terry.'

'It was my fault the glasses got broken, so it's up to me to sort out a new pair.'

'They're purple ones, Nan,' Bridie pipes up. 'Really nice purple ones.'

'They look really nice on her, Vonnie.'

Vonnie gives him a rueful smile. 'Thanks,' she says, 'the old ones had just about had it anyway.'

Terry turns to Bridie. 'So what's say you wait for me after school so we can pick them up? Give your nan a bit of a surprise when you come home with them, hey?'

Bridie wraps her arms around her knees and smiles up at him. 'Okay, Mr P,' she says.

As soon as he hears the clicking of heels behind him, he knows it's her.

'Terry,' she calls out, 'Terry.' He pretends he hasn't heard her and keeps walking. 'Terry,' she repeats, her voice becoming sharper.

Slowly, he turns around, feigning surprise that she should be there, right beside him. 'Laurie,' he says. 'I didn't hear you.'

Her face is red from having chased him halfway across the playground. 'I need to have a word with you.'

With quiet deliberation he pulls up the cuff of his shirt to check his watch. It's 8.45 am. Another fifteen minutes until the bell rings. 'Okay,' he says.

'A private word,' she says, 'in my office.'

Christ, he thinks, must we? He loathes the tête-à-têtes in her office. 'Can it wait until lunchtime, Laurie?'

She shakes her head. 'I'd like to see you now, please, Terry.'

As he follows her down to the admin building, a tune gets stuck in his head. It's the Oompa-Loompa song from *Willy Wonka and the Chocolate Factory* and it won't go away. It's still ringing in his head when she starts on him.

'Look, Terry,' she says, 'I'm not going to beat around the bush. I saw one of the students getting into your car yesterday.'

They are both sitting down in her office, only suddenly she's a whole lot bigger than he is. Which is odd, given that he's taller.

Laurie breathes in hard through her nose. The intake of air is so strong her nostrils flare. 'Terry, I said that I saw a student getting into your car yesterday.'

Terry cocks an eyebrow. 'And?'

She drops her chin down a notch. 'What do you mean, *and*? Did you or did you not transport a student in your car yesterday outside of school hours?'

Terry looks bemused. 'Yes, Laurie,' he says, mimicking her clipped speech, 'I did transport a student in my car yesterday. Bridie Taylor, to be exact.'

'You realise that this is in contravention of the regulations?'

He looks just past her to the window behind her desk. From where he is, he can see out to the playground and over to the gum tree in the middle of the front yard. It's an enormous thing now, yet he remembers when it was first planted. A couple of blue wrens are hopping around on one of its branches. They used to be everywhere, until the bloody Indian mynas ran them out of town. Good to see the little critters finally making a comeback.

'Terry?' Laurie's voice is sharp and impatient.

He forces himself to look at her. 'Sorry?'

'It is in strict contravention of the regulations to be alone with a student outside of school hours.'

Not this regulatory crap again. 'What are you talking about, woman?' He knows his voice is raised now, but he doesn't care. 'I took the child to get her glasses fixed.'

Not a flicker from her. 'Did you have her parents' authorisation to do that?'

He leans back against the chair and folds his arms on his chest. 'Bit tricky that, in the circumstances. I presume you've had a look at her details.'

Laurie colours as she leans into her laptop.

That's it, he thinks suddenly. It's the chair. She's got herself a new chair: one of those spacey new office chairs that look like they're made of miniature chicken wire. She must have cranked it as high as it can go. That's why she's suddenly towering over him.

He watches her frown deepen as she rolls the computer mouse

up and down the pad. 'Her grandmother,' she says finally, 'she's the one with custody, is that right?'

His arms still crossed in front of him, Terry nods slowly.

'And her parents? There's nothing on file about them.'

'Her mother died when she was a baby.'

'And her father?'

Terry lifts his shoulders. 'Dunno.'

Laurie's hand hovers over the mouse as she stares at the screen. 'And the grandmother, did she authorise you to take Bridie to the optometrist?'

Terry scratches the side of his mouth. 'She's fine about it. It's just up the road.'

'That's not what I asked, Terry. What I asked was whether she gave you written authority to transport her ward to the optometrist?'

He lets out a loud sigh. 'No, Laurie, Bridie's grandmother did not give me written authority to transport Bridie to the optometrist. I did it because the kid was distraught and she didn't want to go home to her grandmother with broken glasses. And I had to get her a new pair because she can't see a bloody thing without them.'

'Terry, you need permission. It's a child protection issue.'

Not this rubbish. He hasn't got the time or the patience for this bloody departmental gobbledygook. 'What do you mean it's a child protection issue? What do you think I was going to do with her? I took her to the optometrist to get her some new glasses. What's to protect her from, for God's sake? Has everyone gone mad? There's nothing complicated about this, Laurie. The child needed some glasses. I arranged it. I took her back home to her grandmother. Then I went home. End of bloody story.' He stands up. 'And now, Laurie, very sorry to break up the party, but I've got a class to teach.'

∽

He's mid-sentence when the home bell rings. Kurt stands up, ready to grab his bag and run, but Terry keeps talking, all the while eye-balling him back into his chair. Only when the boy is sitting down again does Terry break off. 'We'll finish this off tomorrow, 6P. Off you go.' And he smiles as they stampede out to the foyer to get their bags and take off.

There's a stack of marking to do so he settles himself at his desk to get started on it. He's making headway when he looks up to find Bridie sitting at her desk. She is sitting there quietly, hands clasped, just watching him.

'What are you still doing here?' he asks before he remembers. He can't believe he'd forgotten.

'Sweetheart,' he says to her softly, 'have you been waiting for me all this time?'

He gathers his papers, bundles them into his briefcase then claps his hands together. 'Right,' he says, 'what's say we go and pick up those new glasses right now, then?'

Laurie

It's the part of the day Laurie likes best: when the bell has gone, the playground has emptied, the telephone has stopped ringing and everyone else has gone home. That's when she can get stuck into the paperwork and finally make some progress.

Not that she'd say it openly, but it's strange being back in a school after two years in head office. There's something messy about a school. Everyone always wants something—the children, the staff, the parents. Lately there's been a constant stream of them outside her office, ready to be called in, ready for Laurie to deal with the next thing and the next thing and the next thing. None of it ordered, everything just thrown at her. Just like the office she'd inherited: a shambles. God knows how Diane Thomas managed the filing. Laurie's tried to find some pattern but she's yet to discover it. Reorder, that's what she has to do. Reorder, refile, rearrange. This is Laurie's forte. It's what she was known for at head office: her attention to detail, her sense of order. The systems guru, that's what they called her, and that's what she likes to call herself. Privately, of course.

She often wishes she could be back there. That's a funny thing, considering she hadn't even wanted the job at first. In the end, it was the newness of the work that had convinced her: a new unit— the Child Protection Unit—formed to apply new laws, new policies, new procedures. It would be, they told her, a new way forward in child protection. She would be its pioneer. She liked the idea of that.

And she'd been rigorous with the work. When a complaint came to her, she was meticulous with the evidence, the documentation, the recommendations. She had them all in her sights: those who pounced without warning, those who bullied quietly and those who began with favours and worked their way in from there.

They were all bad eggs, the lot of them. They all needed to be caught early and dealt with quickly.

Who could argue with that? Who could possibly argue with that?

Brad Hillier from Legal could.

Brad was the swaggering sort of man Laurie couldn't abide: the rugged, kayaking type who'd always been part of the in crowd. It was there in everything he did: the way he wore his hair—too long for a lawyer, curling as it did over his collar; the way he leant back in his office chair as though lounging on the beach; the way he held his head to the side as she spoke, appraising her, it seemed, appraising everything about her.

All of it made her contemptuous of him. So why, then, did he also make her nervous, when she was the deputy director of the Child Protection Unit and he was just a legal officer?

She'd have liked to have had a word to the director but could never work out quite how to phrase the complaint. His manner was arrogant, that was clear, yet he was never actually rude to her. His was an unspoken arrogance, one that was difficult to describe. But annoying, so very annoying.

As annoying as having to submit her briefs for his legal opinion. Because more often than not, he would send them straight back to her. More evidence, he'd demand. More evidence, more proof, more information.

What are you talking about? she'd want to scream at him.

Sometimes there is no more evidence. Sometimes you just know. Sometimes you can just smell it. And then what are you supposed to do? Sit on your hands and wait for more evidence, more proof, more information? Or actually do something?

And if she's anything, Laurie is a doer.

'Laurie,' Brad would say to her with a click of his tongue that made her itch to slap him, 'we can't suspend a teacher just because someone didn't like the look of him.'

How could she explain it to him, this cocksure man who had no idea? How could she describe the calls she'd taken day after day— calls from teachers like Brenda Cohen.

Laurie knew to be gentle with people like her. 'Brenda,' she'd said, 'what sort of concerns do you have?'

'He touches the children; he's always touching the children.'

'When you say touching, do you mean fondling?'

For a moment the other woman had been silent. 'I suppose so. On their heads, he's always patting them on the head, putting an arm around them, stroking their backs, that sort of thing.'

'Is there anything more?'

There *was* more.

'He gives things to the children: lollies, toys, things like that. After school, when the bell's gone, he'll encourage the boys to stay in the park. Sometimes there's just a few of them, sometimes there's a crowd. The thing is, he's like a Pied Piper, that's what he's like. And I don't understand why a grown man—and a single man at that— needs to spend all his day in the classroom with the children, then all afternoon in the park with them. I don't like it. I just don't like it.'

'Does he single out any of the children?'

Brenda had hesitated. 'Yes, I'd have to say he does. A little kid, Riley, one of the Year 3 kids.'

'Not one of his own students, then?'

'No. He's on Year 5 this year. But he spends a lot of time with Riley. Gives him things, too.'

Laurie took a deep breath. 'What sort of things, Brenda?'

'Food, mostly: biscuits, fruit, a sandwich sometimes. And clothes, too. Last term, Riley was showing everyone the shoes he bought him. Who knows what else he's given him? I just know I don't like it.'

Laurie didn't like it either. She liaised with the police but they had nothing on him. So often that was the problem: there was enough to know it was a concern but not enough to take it anywhere.

'He's grooming the child,' Laurie told Brad. 'Clear as day that's what he's doing.'

Brad didn't agree.

Sometime later, close to a year later, an unnamed teacher was arrested at an unnamed school up north. Brenda Cohen worked up north, too. And as soon as she read the report, Laurie knew it was him. She didn't need a name, she didn't need anything, she was sure of it. She didn't care what Brad Hillier said. She'd been right. They just hadn't listened. Her colleagues—Ellen, Joanne, Tamara—they all agreed with her: Brad Hillier was completely out of touch.

Laurie had always been hardworking and vigilant, but after that she redoubled her efforts.

Not that hard work had ever been a problem for her. After all, she had been the youngest assistant principal ever appointed to Red Hill Public School. And that doesn't happen without a lot of work. It had been a great achievement and it had taken all her willpower not to flaunt it. For there was a certain poise, a certain gravitas required of an assistant principal.

Not that Terry Pritchard displays any of that, she thinks. A spike of irritation shoots through her body. No poise, no gravitas. In fact, he seems to bring absolutely no respect to the position at all.

And how dare he take a student in his car? How dare he?!

It's people like Terry Pritchard who enrage her, because it's people like him who make the system collapse. What sort of message does it send when the assistant principal acts in blatant disregard of the rules? What sort of message does it send to the other teachers, the parents, the students? She doesn't care how long he's been at the school; Terry Pritchard is a man who needs to learn to toe the line.

'Yes,' she says, aloud this time, 'Terry Pritchard needs to learn to toe the line.'

Resolved now, she leans back and lets her gaze turn to the window. Quickly, so quickly she almost topples in the chair, she sits back up again. It is as though her very thoughts have somehow conjured him up, for there he is, right there in front of her, meandering towards the car park, his awful old briefcase slapping against the side of his leg. Even the way he walks annoys her.

He has no children of his own, that's what she's been told. She wonders why not and why it is that a man like him—a man without children—should choose to be a teacher.

The thought niggles as she watches him. Only then does she notice that he is not alone. There is a child trailing after him. When she leans forward to get a better view, what she sees astounds her. It is the same child, the same little one with the glasses. Brigid. Bree. No, Bridie. Bridie Taylor.

Her head forward, she watches as they make their way to his car.

Stop, she wants to cry out. *Stop*. But her window is closed and difficult to open and they won't hear her through the glass. She could bang on the glass, but this is an idea that comes too late; it comes only after the engine has started and they have driven away.

For the rest of the afternoon, she is too unsettled to focus on her work: too unsettled, too angry and too indignant to do anything but think about Terry Pritchard and his insidious behaviour.

But what, she asks herself, can she do about it?

She could report him, that's what she could do. In fact, she *should* report him. Because already she has plenty to tell: the car trips, the defiance, his persistent touching of the children. It's all there.

And the more she thinks about it, the more certain she is of it.

So she lifts up the phone and dials Ellen's number.

The call goes through but it isn't Ellen who answers. It's Lucy Carboni. Laurie has never heard of her. But when she asks to speak to Ellen Duncan, Lucy tells her that Ellen is no longer at the unit and that she, Lucy, has taken over her caseload.

This comes as a surprise.

'Can I help?' Lucy asks her.

Laurie takes a deep breath. 'I'd like to file a report.'

She tells Lucy everything.

Once she has finished, Lucy is thoughtful. 'I'm not sure there's enough,' she says. 'Especially as he's got the grandmother's permission to travel with the child.'

Laurie is incredulous. 'But I've already told him not to let the child in his car—he blatantly ignores me.'

On the other end of the line, Lucy's voice is calm. 'I'm just saying that, at this stage, it's not something the unit would be able to look into; it would be better dealt with by the school principal.'

'I *am* the principal,' Laurie blurts out. 'I *am* the principal and he won't listen.'

Lucy's voice doesn't change. 'If anything else comes up, please call back. We'll need something more before we can start investigating the matter.'

Laurie is tempted to raise her voice but she knows it won't help.

When she rings off, she is almost rigid with frustration. First, Terry Pritchard won't listen to her and now some upstart from the unit won't listen either.

So what else can she do but watch and wait for him to trip up again?

Term 2

Nina

She does what she can to try to get to sleep. She changes positions. She turns from her front to her back, then to one side. She does some breathing exercises. She tries to clear her mind. She focuses on lying very still.

Nothing works.

Recently, he's been coming home later and later. There's always something at the club that needs his attention. She understands that, of course she does—he's the manager so he needs to be available—she just wishes she could sleep better. But she keeps worrying that something has happened to him on the way home, that this time it's not work, this time it's something worse that is keeping him from coming home.

When sleep still doesn't come, she gets up, puts on her dressing-gown and makes herself a cup of tea. She turns on the television, flicking through the channels until she finds a movie. It's an old one, one she has seen before, and although she keeps her eyes on the screen, she turns the sound down to listen out for his car.

It's 2.13 am and she is on to her second cup of tea when she hears a car pull up outside. Her heart skips faster. Pressing the warm mug against her cheek, she waits for him to turn into the driveway. Instead, the car drives away. *A cab?* It feels like many minutes, but perhaps it is only one or two, before she hears a rattling of keys at the front door. She stays where she is, in the dark, in front of the television. She is agitated, both with relief and—now she knows he is safe—with resentment.

The door opens and he comes through it quickly, as though surprised the door should have given way at all. The smell of tobacco fills the room, all the more pungent in a house that, for years now, has been smoke-free.

He doesn't notice her at first. When he does, he starts. 'What are you doing up?'

'Where's the car?' she asks.

He shrugs. 'Thought I might be over the limit, so I got a lift home.'

'Right.' She wrinkles her nose. It's the wrong time to ask, but she does anyway. 'You haven't been smoking, have you?'

He rocks on the spot. 'And what if I have been? What are you going to do? Ground me?' His voice, loose with alcohol, is spiteful. 'I'm not your son, Nina.'

The sharpness of his tone shocks her and she has to bite the inside of her cheek to stop the tears from forming. He doesn't mean it, she tells herself. He is drunk and tired and she is upset and tired. There is nothing useful to be said tonight. And yet she keeps going. 'But you were doing so well. You know how addictive it is.'

'For Christ's sake, stop badgering me,' he yells. 'For once in your goddamn life, can you just stop badgering me? I'm sick to death of the nagging. Do you hear me? Sick to bloody death of it.'

The tirade feels like a physical attack. 'I was worried,' she whispers. 'I was worried you'd been in a crash or something. I couldn't sleep because I was worried.'

She waits for him to relent, to open his arms to her. It's all he has to do to make things right again. Instead, he stays as he is, fists clenched, jaw clenched, staring at her through narrowed eyes. 'You worry too much,' he says. 'You worry too bloody much.'

It's not the first time he has told her that. But never before has he said it with such anger. This is something new. This is something she doesn't recognise. It unnerves her.

'You coming to bed?' she asks, her voice hesitant.

He shakes his head. 'I'll sleep on the lounge.'

'Please don't,' she says quietly. She needs to feel him beside her. Only then will the worry leave her, only then will her body relax enough to let her fall, finally, into sleep.

But the alcohol has made him belligerent. He refuses to leave the lounge room. She finds him a sheet and a blanket, knowing that otherwise he'd just sleep on the couch without anything to cover him.

Back in bed, Nina tries to keep it together. If she lets herself cry, it will be an admission that all is not okay. And this is an admission she will not make. Because it isn't true. It isn't true. It is a busy time for him, a difficult time. It will pass and things will get better.

There is something at her ear. Something that tickles. Something that makes her shoulder jerk up to stop it, to stop the tickling. A voice, then, a familiar voice.

The tickling is becoming stronger and the voice louder, so loud it vibrates inside her. 'Up, up,' it says. 'Get up.'

There is something at her eyes now, too, something that is both pressing on her eyeballs and pulling at her eyelids. What is it? She feels herself blink, and blink again.

'Hello, Mummy.' Emily is lying on top of her. 'It's morning, Mummy,' she says.

'What time?' Nina asks, her voice throaty. With the curtains drawn, the room is night-time black, but when the little girl jumps down to pull them open, it is already light outside.

Looking over at the window, Nina wonders at that: how one moment it can be night and the next it is morning.

And late, too, as it turns out, so late she scarcely has time for a shower. She has one anyway. But God, she's tired. She's so tired her eyes close in the shower and her body twitches her upright when she threatens to topple.

No complaining, she tells herself as she's getting dressed. *Head up, eyes open, mouth smiling.*

It's a big ask, especially as they tiptoe past Steve and make their way to the door. When she looks at him, she becomes angry: angry that he should still be asleep while she, the walking dead, is not. She has an urge, then, to slam the door hard; to slam it hard enough to startle him out of sleep so that he, too, will be as tired as she feels. But she doesn't. Instead, she closes it softly, a finger to her lips so that Emily, too, will stay quiet.

She makes it to school on time, but only just. Almost immediately, she finds Paige is at her door, an expectant look on her face. When Nina looks at her blankly, her face falls.

'You said to come when the bell went. You said to come

straightaway.' The girl's accent—so broad, so harsh—grates on her, and instead of rushing to reassure her that yes, she has come at the right time, today Nina lets her silence weigh on the child and watches as her brashness gives way to uncertainty.

It is difficult, after that, to get anything out of her.

'Tell me,' she tries, 'what did you do on the weekend?'

Paige keeps her head down. 'Nothin',' she says.

Nina is too tired for this. 'I'm going to need a bit more than that, Paige. Think back. Did you go anywhere?'

The girl shrugs her shoulders and slumps in her seat.

'Your weekend. At least two sentences. Now.'

Her curtness forces an answer from the girl. 'I went to me dad's place and on Saturday we went to the drag racing.'

Drag racing, Nina thinks. God help me.

'And me dad got plastered so Karen had to drive home even though she didn't want to.'

Nina nods. Keep her talking, keep her talking. 'And how do you know Karen didn't want to drive home?'

Baulking at the question, the girl looks over at Nina, her chin tilted down, her lips pushed together. Nina nods her encouragement.

The girl takes a deep breath. 'I knew Karen didn't want to drive home because she said to me dad, *You're a drunk fucker and I'm fuckin' sick of being the fuckin' driver.*'

Leaning back, Nina rubs a finger along her lips. Fair enough, she thinks, she'd asked for that one. 'So,' she says, 'if we were to summarise what you've told me, we could say something like this: *On Saturday, I went to watch the drag racing with Karen and my dad. Karen drove us home but she wasn't happy about that.* Is that a fair way to describe what happened?'

The girl lifts her head so she can take a better look at Nina.

Nina gives her a moment before she taps a hand on the table. 'If you're happy with that as a summary, I'd like you to write it down for me.'

Again the girl hesitates before she opens her exercise book, turns to a fresh page and starts writing. When she is finished, she passes her work across to Nina.

Nina nods as she reads it. 'That's good,' she murmurs, and when she looks up, she sees that the girl's face is flushed with pride. 'You've done well,' she adds, pleased. 'You've done very well.'

That evening, after she's put Emily to bed, Steve rings to say he won't be home for dinner. She doesn't want an argument so she doesn't protest, even though the dinner is in the oven and she has been waiting for him.

When, later, she is in bed alone, she finally lets herself cry; she lets the tears run down the side of her cheeks, lets her nose run until her face is completely covered in tears and mucus. There are no tissues by the bed and, spent now, she is too exhausted even to get up. Taking a corner of the sheet, she wipes her face and blows her nose. *It's okay*, she says to herself. *It's okay, it's okay.* Because tomorrow she'll think of a way to make things better.

Joan

Once a week, on a Wednesday, Joan goes to Brindle Library. It's a small library, and Joan likes that: likes that there are enough books to choose from but not so many as to overwhelm her; likes that there is only one librarian, whose name is Kim and who always greets her with a warm smile. Although Kim is many years her junior, she calls her Joan and not Miss Mather. Part of her wants to be offended by this, but only a small part.

When her mother was alive, the two of them would go to the library in the morning. Only once did they venture there in the afternoon; Joan's mother was so appalled by the behaviour of the schoolchildren, she vowed never again to set foot in the library after 3 pm.

Joan had not been upset by the noise of the children. She had been amused by the snippets of childish conversation trickling past. And now that she is without her mother, she has taken to visiting the library in the afternoon, when it is awash with children. It has become her habit to arrive just before three, return her books, choose a few more then settle down in one of the lounge chairs at the front of the library. There are floor-to-ceiling windows there and even though the weather is starting to cool, still the sun warms her.

By 3.30, the library is filled with children from the local school, each of them in some variation of blue and white.

A book open in front of her, she settles down to watch them. Today, there are two boys waiting at the counter. Kim isn't there— she must be somewhere down the back of the library—but the boys don't seem fussed; they just slouch against the counter and wait. One of them reminds Joan of a bulldog: his shoulders are wide and square and pushed forward. His head, too, is square, and although his legs are long, his torso is even longer. His friend is half his size: small and skinny with bleached hair that needs a wash and a brush and a cut. His school shirt is misbuttoned so that one side of the shirt hangs lower than the other. The bulldog boy hasn't fastened even one button and his shirt hangs open to show a white under-shirt. In her day, students would have been expelled for less.

The little one is still leaning over the counter when he spies a bell on the desk. 'Hey, Kurt,' he says, 'reckon we should give this a ring?'

Kurt—the bulldog—puts a large hand over the bell. 'Looks like a bike bell, eh?'

'Except you don't give it a flick, you just bang it down.' And to demonstrate, the little one does just that. For a small bell, the noise it emits is surprisingly loud: loud enough to fill the library. This makes them laugh so much they start to snort, bits of spittle spraying into the air. Her mother would be horrified but, to be honest, and although she keeps a serious look on her face, Joan thinks it's funny too. And besides, it has the right effect: Kim comes rushing back to the counter.

When she sees the boys just about doubled over with laughter, her face tightens. 'This is a library, boys,' she tells them, her voice severe. 'It's not for mucking around.'

'They giving you strife, Kim?' Now there's a man behind the boys and he's clamped a hand down on each of their shoulders. Joan can't see his face—he has his back to her—but his voice is somehow familiar.

The little one twists up to face the man. 'Mr P told us to come to the library for our assignments and that. To get some books and that.'

Kurt the bulldog nods hard. 'Yep, Sid, about planets. That's what it's about: it's about planets.'

The man keeps a hand on each of the boys. 'Well, I don't know what the ruckus is about then. But I think you should be apologising for the disturbance.'

Joan's not even pretending to read anymore. Instead she's watching as Kim's mouth starts to twitch, as though she herself is trying hard not to smile.

The boys keep their heads down as they mumble something. The man gives them a bit of shake and tells them to look up. They mumble something else, but this time they keep their heads up. Once they're done, the man swings them so they're facing Joan. Embarrassed to have been caught listening, Joan ducks her head and picks up her book. 'And now you can apologise to this lady here for disturbing her peace and quiet.'

Joan feigns surprise as she looks up. 'Sorry for disturbing your peace and quiet,' the boys chorus, almost in unison.

Once they've finished, they keep their eyes on her. They are waiting for her to say something, to make a reply. But what? she wonders. For the truth is this: it is for precisely that reason she has come here—to have her peace and quiet disturbed. And so, as it happens, they have done her a favour rather than a disservice. But she can't actually say that, can she? She needs to think of something more appropriate, something serious. Something like, *Well, I appreciate your apology, boys.* Yes, something like that. So she takes a little breath and lets the words out. Only then does she focus on the man standing between them. It's him, she thinks, her stomach leaping a little, it's him. It's the man from the bakery. The man with the nice eyes. The man who likes chocolate-chip biscuits.

'Well, hello again,' he says as her pulse quickens; not only has she remembered him, he has also remembered her.

She is surprised to hear herself giggle. 'Hello,' she says.

Loosening his grip on the boys, he gives them each a gentle slap on the back. 'Sorry about these two hooligans,' he says. 'Year 6, too, so they should be setting an example for the younger ones.' But his voice is soft now and as he directs them back to Kim, he cups the backs of their heads in a way that is almost tender.

'They're all right,' he says, once they're out of earshot. 'Just a bit energetic, that's all.' He has such a nice voice, sort of slow and calm, a voice that makes Joan feel relaxed; more than relaxed, a voice that makes her feel happy.

He's not speaking anymore but he's still looking at her. He's waiting for a response now, too. Suddenly nervous, she has to swallow before she can answer him. 'They weren't really bothering me,' she says, her voice so thin and soft she has to repeat herself.

He points to the empty chair next to her. 'Is that free?' he asks.

When he sits down, she feels her spine straighten as she tries to think of something else to say. He beats her to it. 'Good book?' he asks, with a nod to the novel on her lap.

Well, she wouldn't know, would she, seeing as she's only been pretending to read it and hasn't got past the first sentence. 'So-so,' she tells him.

'I don't read novels as a rule. Information books, that's what I look for. To educate myself a bit.'

She doesn't like information books. She only likes novels: romance or crime, one or the other. The one she's reading is a romance novel; on the cover, a couple is locked in a tight embrace. She wishes she'd chosen a different book now—something less frivolous. She is careful not to lift the book so he won't see the cover.

But he's not even looking at her book anymore, he's just chatting, and it is with some wonder that she listens to him. She's never been much good at chatting. Words have never just tumbled out of her; she practises everything in her head before she says anything at all. She wishes it wasn't like that; she wishes she was a chatting person, like he is. More than that, she wishes she knew him better, she wishes that they were friends.

But how can she say that, how can she look him in the eye—a stranger, really—and say to him, *I'd like to be your friend?*

Mel

Well, it's a bloody miracle but somehow she manages to pile them into the car by nine and tip them outside the front of the school by seven minutes past.

The moment they're out of the car, a sense of wellbeing fills her and, sinking back into the seat, she closes her eyes to relish it.

A loud banging startles her upright and when she opens her eyes, she finds Ethan's face pressed hard against the front window, his tongue licking up against the glass. She considers pressing the button to lower the window, and wonders whether it would take his face down with it. Instead she just looks at him until, losing interest, he pulls his tongue back into his mouth, moves his face back and opens the door.

'Forgot my lunch,' he announces.

'I left it on the bench for you.'

He shrugs. 'But I still forgot it, didn't I?'

She could whip home and grab it—it wouldn't take her more than ten minutes—and normally she would, but today she doesn't want to. She just doesn't want to. Instead, she rifles through her wallet until she comes up with six dollars.

'Get a lunch order,' she tells him.

His eyes light up. 'Like, anything I want?'

She raises an eyebrow. 'Knock yourself out.'

He's cheering then, cheering and doing the dance they're all doing: the wiggle-your-bum-while-you're-pretending-to-stir-an-enormous-pot dance. It cracks her up to watch it and takes everything she's got not to laugh out loud. Because it's not a laughing-at dance, it's a cool dance. She checks her watch. 'Twelve past nine,' she tells him, 'which means you've got three minutes to get your order in.'

Mid-stir, he stops dancing and, clutching his money, hightails it back into the school grounds. She's happy when he turns back to wave at her. Not that she shows it. Instead, she just flicks her hand up to hurry him on.

Once he's out of sight, she turns on the engine, does a U-turn across the double yellow lines and drives over to the headland. There's a car park at the start of the headland and this is where she parks. It's in the middle of nowhere, really, which is why it's never full but also why it's never completely empty. Because there's always one other car there. Years ago, it used to be Adam's old ute. Today, it's a campervan, curtains covering the windows so whoever's inside can pretend they're not actually in a car park. A brave move, Mel thinks, to spend the night there and risk the after-dark hoons who burn up and down the road then do donuts in the carpark itself. Better just to rock up in the morning when the idiots are sleeping it off. That's when the council workers turn up with their coffee and their egg-and-bacon rolls to watch the sun come up over the water. Because it really is a cracker of a view: straight out to sea and across the bay to Brindle itself.

Although she often doesn't, today she locks the car and, camera in hand, heads over to the wire fence that runs the width of the headland. Attached to it is a sign warning that *Access is prohibited* and *Trespassers will be prosecuted*. Beside the sign, a large hole has been cut into the fence. Mel thinks of it as community action: there are a lot of people in Brindle who are handy with boltcutters. On the other side of the fence, a dirt track leads through the scrub. It doesn't matter if it's only just rained or if it hasn't rained for days or even weeks, for some reason the track is always muddy.

Further on, the scrub dissolves into an enormous expanse of sandstone, flat sheets of it that stretch into cliffs along the water. They are gentle cliffs, though, gentle cliffs that step slowly into the water instead of plunging straight down to it.

Other cliffs, sheer ones, both frighten and fascinate her, and for the same reason: because the closer she comes, the more they seem to call her over, over and over towards the edge.

With these cliffs, it's not the same. Instead, they seem to protect her as she makes her way to the edge; an edge that isn't such a hard edge after all, an edge that's more like the top of a hill, one she can approach, one she can lie down on, part of her leaning over it as she points the camera down, right down to the water so that both the steps of sandstone and a line of blue will fill the frame. It'll make a good card, she thinks. Particularly now that the sun's soft in the sky and the light's good.

Looking north, the land curves out towards the heads. Still lying on her belly, she aims the camera across the water and over to the coastline. Just as she pushes the button, a shot of white spray pushes through the flatness of the water.

'Look!' she cries out, to no one. 'Oh, look!'

Her first whale for the season, and it's not even June! For June's when they start to arrive, when they make their way up north to mate where the water's warm. Mel loves that: loves that they'll travel so far for a root. Except for the poor females who managed to get knocked up the year before; they've got to haul themselves up the bloody coast again just to give birth. And it's not like it's a daytrip. It must be thousands of kilometres. When Mel was pregnant, especially towards the end, it was all she could do to get herself out of bed let alone swim some sort of ultra-marathon.

The sea is still now. She lowers her camera—it's too far away to get a decent picture anyway—but she keeps her eyes focused on the water. And then, suddenly, another spray of water shoots out into the sky. Not just a spray—there's something more, there's something black in front of her. He's breaching, her whale is breaching, up and up, he's breaching. And it's just for her.

Then he's gone again. Completely gone. But there will be more, so many more, up the coast through winter then down again in spring. It's a thought that makes her happy, that always makes her happy, year in, year out.

To her right, the sun has lit up the hillside of Brindle houses. Quickly, she snaps it and then again. The hillside cards are her most popular—the locals get a kick out of seeing their own houses on a card. She has time for only a couple more shots before she scrambles to her feet. It's past ten already and she'll need to start heading back so she won't be late for work.

Back at the car park, the campervan has moved on. In its place is a prison van—one of the big ones, one that can fit a whole army of inmates in the back of it. Not that any of them would be able to see out of it, not with the tiny slits of windows so high you'd have to be King Kong to be able to sit down and look out at the same time. They've got benches rather than car seats inside, she's been told, so they can fit more inmates in, so they can squash them all in the back, close the door and be done with it. She's not sure if they shackle them, too. You'd think they would, just to be on the safe side. Which begs the question: what's a prison van doing parked here in the middle of nowhere? On the patch of grass that separates the car park from the water, she finds her answer: two prison guards are sitting on a rug, both of them tucking into burgers. If they're hoping to hide their identity, it hasn't worked: their sloppy joes do little to disguise the light blue collared shirts and dark blue trousers that scream prison guard. They don't seem too bothered, though; they just seem happy to be munching on their burgers.

What a photo, she thinks. Seriously, what a fantastic photo: the picnickers, the van and the water—perfect. *Lunch at Brindle*, that's what she'd call it.

Back in the car, she finds a bag on the floor of the front seat. When she looks inside it, all she sees is blue. Then she remembers: the school hats. Of the twelve school hats she found at home in the hat basket, only two of them were labelled *Thompson*.

So it's back to school and up to lost property. Hers is a weekly trip and never in vain. Today there's an added satisfaction: today, she won't just be taking, she'll also be giving back. Today, she'll be saving the necks of ten students in the doghouse for losing their hats. Today, too, her own spoils are good: a jacket, two lunch boxes, a drink bottle and a pair of sports shorts. She's popping them into her bag when she hears a familiar voice behind her.

'I'm thinking of a new name,' he says. 'Lost Property—it's a bit bland, don't you think? I was looking for something with a bit more pizazz: something like the Ethan and Josh Thompson Property Department.'

Mel turns to find Terry Pritchard just behind her. She hesitates before she speaks. 'Oh,' she says finally. 'Hi.' Even now, it's an effort not to call him Mr P. Not that he was ever her class teacher, but still.

Call me Terry, that's what he's told her. And she wants to, she really does, but she just can't manage it. And so, as usual, she calls him nothing at all.

'Or maybe we could go a bit wider,' he offers. 'Maybe we could call it the 6P Property Department.'

She laughs when he says that and he laughs, too. 'So, been out and about, have you?' he asks.

When she looks confused, he points a finger at her breasts. Slightly perturbed, she claps a hand to her chest.

'Oh,' she says, 'the camera.' She'd forgotten it was still hanging around her neck. 'I went up to the headland to take some shots.'

He gives her a wink. 'For the next batch of designer cards?'

She thinks he's being sarcastic so she doesn't answer.

'Saw some beauties for sale up at the cafe,' he says. 'Far as I can tell, they seem to be going like hotcakes.'

She pulls a wry face so he'll clock that she's on to him, that she knows he's just having a go at her.

'Really,' he says, his voice softening, 'they were walking out of the place. I reckon you might be on to something there.'

This time he doesn't sound like he's making fun of her. This time he sounds like he's being serious. As she shoots him a look to check, a little part of her lights up with the thought that he might be right, that it might be more than just her own quiet hope: that perhaps she *is* on to something.

'You know,' he says, 'I've started to worry you'll be too busy to keep helping us out here.'

Mel is the closest thing Brindle Public has to a school photographer. For years now, she's been photographing school events. She sees it as her school service; it's what she does instead of covering books for the library or selling ice-blocks on ice-block day. Sports carnivals, presentation days, performance nights: she's at all of them, snapping away.

Embarrassed now, she shakes her head. 'What about the Year 6 show?' she asks him. 'Do you want me for that?'

It isn't just a question, it's also a reminder. Each year, Year 6 does an end-of-year show. For the school, it's the highlight of the year; for Year 6, it's their major performance and farewell concert in one. But so far, she's heard nothing about it.

Terry pulls on his lip. 'The show? Got to be honest, love, I haven't even turned my mind to it what with everything else happening. I s'pose I should get a wriggle on now, shouldn't I?'

Mel gives him a half-smile. 'Happy to help out,' she says.

It was never part of her grand plan to be a house cleaner but it does have its advantages: it's cash in hand, it's flexible and, surprisingly, it manages to provide her with enough job satisfaction to keep her going. Not always, of course. Sometimes, it just pisses her off. But that's more the people than the work itself.

Over the years, she's managed to establish some ground rules to make sure things work the way she wants them to.

First of all, she's a one-man band. For a while, she paid another woman to help her out, but she ended up spending too much time checking up on her and that gave her the shits.

Second, she doesn't bring her own equipment. Either they supply it or they find someone else to clean the house. Because there's nothing worse than hauling a bloody vacuum cleaner and a bucket full of bleach and floor cleaner and window cleaner and the rest of it out of the car boot into the house and back again. So she doesn't do any of that. She just tells them what she needs, even if it means they've got to buy a new vacuum cleaner, new brooms, whatever. And if they don't like that, well, it's the same deal: maybe they'd be better off with someone else.

Third, she doesn't negotiate on rates: thirty dollars an hour, take it or leave it. Most people take it because they know she's good. She gets in, gets the job done and gets out again. Every now and then, there's someone who'll get a bit picky, who'll greet her at the door to point out a bit of dust she missed the previous week. Mel handles complaints as any professional would: she listens, she nods, she rectifies the problem then gets on with the rest of the job. The next day, she texts to advise that, regretfully, her workload is such that she will no longer be able to assist them. She always wishes them the best of luck before she signs off. Yes, good luck. Because they'll be needing it to find a replacement who's better. As for her, it's all win-win: she gets rid of the arseholes and only keeps the people she likes.

Fourth, she needs to have a key to get in. Anyone who baulks at that, well, they're out too. What do they think, that once she's got a key, she'll let herself in and clean the place out? The fact is—and this is something she'd like to explain to them—when you clean houses, you work out pretty quickly where the valuables are. And in Brindle, even in Raleigh, the houses she gets are nice enough but—no offence—they're not worth fleecing. They're the sort of houses with a few nice prints—no originals—and a bit of jewellery that's generally kept in the undies drawer in the main bedroom. And quite frankly, if it's the jewellery she's after, she doesn't need a key to get it. All she needs is a pocket and a minute to herself. And she'll be buggered if she's going to work with someone tailing her to check she's not about to swipe a ring.

Today, she's doing a house in Raleigh. It's a good job because no one's ever there when she arrives; she just lets herself in and gets on with it. The way she attacks the house, you'd think it was a workout. She's dressed for a workout, too: she always is. Not that she ever goes anywhere near a gym, she just likes to look as though she does. Because gym gear solves everything. Running late dropping the kids to school? No problem, so long as you've managed to swap your PJs for a pair of leggings and some sort of zip-up sports top. That way everything thinks you're only late because you managed to fit in a run before breakfast. Why spoil a good story by admitting you just slept in again? Gym gear's the bomb for cleaning, too: it's easy to move in and if you work up a bit of a sweat, who cares? The special gym gear fabric has got that all factored in. And if the owners happen to be home, well, that's good, too; it looks like you're about to get to the housework in an aerobic frenzy, and that's got to make them happy. By the time you make it back to school, if you're still perspiring from the exertion of it all, it'll just look like you've finished your second marathon for the day. Which is yet another reason for not having the car boot filled with cleaning crap: because you don't want to destroy the image with a reality check.

Today Mel's on fire: by 2.30 pm, she's finished everything she needs to do. If she wanted to, she could leave early, but she doesn't. Call it overkill or call it ethics but if the deal's 11 am to 3 pm, then she'll be there from 11 am to 3 pm. She can always find something extra to do. Today she decides to spend the time sorting out the fridge. At home, her own fridge is a nightmare: plates of scraps covered in cling wrap on the off-chance that they'll get a rerun sometime during the week; jam jars with less than a teaspoon of jam left inside that won't get thrown out until Mel discovers them. The Raleigh people are better than that but Mel can still put some order into the shelves and give them a wipe-down with water and vanilla essence to freshen things up. Which means that by 2.55, she can close the door on a fridge that's sparkling and a house that's spotless.

Nina

Nina is in the staffroom when Marina walks in. Today she's all bohemian chic: long earrings and a loose grey shift with a white scarf draped around it. When she sees Nina, she starts. This makes Nina laugh. 'Did I scare you?'

Marina shakes her head but she's still looking unsettled.

'Everything all right?'

Marina shrugs. 'A bit knackered.'

But Nina's not convinced. 'That all?'

Marina gives her a wan smile. 'Maybe it's the start-of-winter thing. Or maybe I just need a cigarette.'

Nina picks up two cups from the draining tray and gives them a shake. 'I'll come with you.'

At the other end of the staffroom is a door that leads to a small, enclosed courtyard. It's a secluded place, unevenly paved with house bricks, its walls covered with overgrown ivy. This is where Marina goes for a smoke, away from everyone else.

Marina waits while Nina makes them each a cup of tea and then together they go outside to the courtyard.

'How's Steve?' Marina asks her.

Nina tries to sound positive. 'He's good.'

Marina looks surprised. 'Really?'

She gives her friend a rueful look: Marina can always see through her. 'Actually, he's been a bit difficult,' she admits. 'It must be the new job. He's been working long hours—I didn't think he'd be so busy.'

Marina lights up then tilts her head away to exhale. She takes a while to answer. 'I saw him on Friday night,' she says, her voice slow.

Nina looks surprised. 'Who, Steve?'

Marina nods. 'Yeah.'

'What, at the club?'

She shakes her head. 'He wasn't at the club.'

Nina gives a puzzled laugh. 'Yes, he was. He would have been there until about eight.'

Again Marina shakes her head. 'Well, at seven o'clock he was in Baranton.'

'*Baranton?* That's nowhere near the club.'

Marina doesn't answer.

'Well, what was he doing there?'

Still Marina says nothing.

'What did he say to you?'

'Nothing.' There is little left of the cigarette now, which has burnt down to the filter. Marina flicks it away with her fingertips. 'He didn't see me. I was walking past this restaurant, I happened to look in, and there he was.'

Nina is still confused. 'What, having dinner?'

'That's what it looked like.'

'By himself?'

Marina stops to light another cigarette before she turns to Nina. 'You want me to tell you stuff, don't you?' Her voice is serious now. 'I mean, you don't want me to keep anything from you, do you?'

Nina feels a weight drop down into her stomach. She forms the question before she says it out loud. 'What are you saying?'

Instead of answering, Marina starts to tap her foot softly. 'Nina, he was with a woman,' she says finally. 'He was having dinner at a restaurant with some woman.'

Nina tries to process this. 'Maybe it was a work thing?' Her voice sounds hollow, so she clears her throat and tries again. 'Maybe they were having a meeting?'

This time, Marina doesn't turn away to smoke. 'They were all over each other,' she says.

Nina repeats the words to herself. *All over each other.* 'What do you mean, *all over each other*?'

Marina's voice, when she responds, is very slow and very clear, as though she is choosing her words carefully. 'They were holding hands and they were kissing.'

'Oh.' Nina says. 'Oh.' She's not sure what else to say. 'Who is she?'

Marina throws the cigarette down in front of her and squashes it with her shoe. 'I don't know.'

'Okay.' Gripping her mug, Nina tries to raise it to her lips but her hands are shaking so hard she spills tea over herself. 'Oh God,' she says, as the hot water seeps through to her skin. 'God.' She stands up quickly, holding her shirt out in front of her. 'Fuck!' she shouts. 'Fuck!'

But she's only wet, not burnt. Even so, the tea has left a faint brown stain down the front of her white shirt, and this distresses her. 'Look at me,' she says, her voice catching. 'Look at me.'

Marina unfurls her scarf and hands it to her. 'This'll cover it.'

But Nina can only stare at it. 'I don't know how to tie scarves,' she says as she starts to cry.

Marina loops the scarf across Nina's shoulders and over her shirt. 'See,' she says, 'now you can't even see the stain. Not at all.' But her voice is so tender it just makes Nina want to cry harder. And here, now, she can't afford to be crying at all.

'Thanks,' Nina whispers as she fingers the scarf. She tries to swallow. 'Marina,' she says softly, 'are you sure it was him? I mean, are you certain?'

Once again Marina is slow to answer. 'It looked a lot like him.'

It looked a lot like him.

Which doesn't mean it was him, does it? But when Nina tilts her head to check this, her friend's eyes are filled with such pity it makes her flinch.

'I have to go,' she says, her voice choked.

Marina nods. 'Do you want me to walk you down?'

Nina shakes her head vehemently. 'No,' she says.

Once she is back in her room, she closes the door, takes her mobile out of her handbag and dials his number. It would be better to wait until they are at home, better to talk to him face to face, but she can't leave it until then. While she waits for the call to connect, her hands start to shake once more. But his phone doesn't ring at all. It doesn't even go to voicemail. Instead, a tinny recorded voice tells her that the service is currently unavailable and she should try again later.

She doesn't want to try later. She wants to try again now. She wants to sort it all out straightaway. So she calls him at work, on his direct line. The switch receptionist answers. Nina finds it hard to keep her voice light and steady. 'Hi,' she says, 'it's Nina Foreman here. Can I speak to my husband, please?'

The woman's voice is pleasant and nasal. 'Just a minute, please.'

There is a long wait until, finally, the woman returns to the phone. 'I'm sorry,' she says, and she does sound apologetic, 'but Mr Foreman called in sick this morning and won't be at work today.'

Nina swallows. 'That's right,' she says with forced gaiety, 'I'd forgotten he was sick. Sorry about that.'

The woman's voice is too gentle to be comforting. 'No problem, love.'

She waits five, maybe ten minutes before trying his mobile again. This time he answers on the second ring. 'Babe,' he says, 'hi.'

'Hi,' she says, 'how's work going?' She has practised the question in her head but now her voice falters as she reaches the end of it.

He, by contrast, doesn't hesitate. 'Busy. It's been full-on all day. Really full-on.'

'Oh.' Her throat is so dry it hurts to swallow. 'So what time will you be home?'

She listens as he calculates aloud what he has left to do. 'Not late,' he decides.

'Sounds good.' She almost chokes on the words. 'I'll see you then.'

When she hangs up, she is numb, so numb she can't even cry. So numb, her mind empties. All she can do is hum to herself: a wandering, tuneless hum that becomes 'Land of Hope and Glory', a song she has never learnt and doesn't really know. In front of her, sunshine pours in through the windows and, caught by the crystal pendants, splinters into rainbows across the room. How does that work? she wonders.

And as she contemplates this, there is a knock at the door. When she checks her watch, she is surprised to see that it is already two o'clock.

Opening the door, she does her best to smile. Immediately, Paige beams back at her. 'Hi, miss, I done my reading homework,' she says.

And although she feels like weeping, Nina keeps smiling as she ushers the girl into the room and sits her down. 'Did you really?'

'All of it,' she says. 'I did all of it.'

'Well, then,' Nina tells her, trying not to let her voice slip into a whisper, 'you'll have to show me, now, won't you? So I know I can believe you.'

The girl's eyes are wide and serious. 'You can completely believe me, miss, completely.' From her bag, she takes out her reader. 'Test me, miss, test me. I swear I can read the whole thing.'

And opening up her book, she starts to read. *The Hare and the Tortoise*, she says. She reads slowly and without expression. But she reads.

'Wonderful,' Nina tells her when she has finished the page. 'Wonderful.'

Paige smiles to herself as she runs her fingers down the page. One eye squinting, she looks up at Nina. 'Bit of a crap story, though, miss, wasn't it? I mean, about talking animals and that. No offence or anything, but I'm a bit past that stuff, don't you think?'

Despite everything, this makes Nina smile. 'Should I find you something harder to read?'

Paige shakes her head. 'Doesn't have to be harder, just better. With people in it and that. Like I said, I'm a bit over talking animals.'

Nina manages a laugh. She hates talking animals too. 'So, what, an adventure story or something like that?'

Paige shrugs. 'Maybe. Depends on the story, doesn't it? Just something that's not really boring.'

To give her a choice, Nina picks out six or seven books. She's pleased when Paige takes her time to look through them all; pleased, too, when she becomes engrossed in her work, so engrossed she seems surprised when the school bell rings. She'll do well, Nina thinks. With more time, she'll do really well.

When she realises it's time to go home, Paige's face falls. 'Miss,' she says softly, 'how come I didn't get a hot chocolate today?'

Her disappointment is so keen Nina wants to wrap her arms around her. 'Paige, I'm sorry,' she says, 'how could I have forgotten? Especially after all your good work.'

So even though it is late, Nina switches on the kettle and makes them each a hot chocolate. As they drink, they are both quiet, and it is a silence Nina savours, a silence that calms her.

A loud knock makes them both jump. When she opens the door, Nina finds herself at eye level with a woman who looks familiar. She is dressed in a cropped jacket with jeans that are tight down to her ankles.

When she sees Nina, her face colours. 'I was told to come here,' she says, and her voice is low and gravelly. 'The teacher said Paige was here.'

Paige's mother, Nina thinks.

But that's not why she's familiar. It's something else. 'We've met, haven't we?' she ventures.

The woman nods. Reluctantly, it seems. 'At the club.'

Then it comes back to her. Steve's friend, his school friend. His stumbling school friend, so drunk she couldn't even open her front door. In her place, Nina would be embarrassed too. She searches for her name. 'Sue?'

Again the woman nods. 'That's it.'

'You went to school with my husband.'

'Something like that,' she says, her voice rushed. 'Come on, Paige,' she calls to her daughter, 'we've got to get a move on.'

Nina needs to go, too. And although it's the last thing she feels like doing, she offers to walk them down to the gate. It's always good to get to know the parents. It can explain a lot. Even reading problems.

But as they walk through the playground, Sue is quiet. When, eventually, she turns to Nina, her voice is puzzled. 'Steve didn't tell me you worked here.'

Nina is surprised by the remark. Why would he?

At the gate, they part ways: Sue and Paige head up the street while Nina walks down towards her car. She's about to open the door when she hears Marina calling.

When she turns around, her friend is hurrying towards her. 'Nina, that woman,' she says, stopping to catch her breath. 'That's her.'

Nina looks at her blankly. 'What do you mean?'

'She's the one,' Marina says. 'She's the one I saw with Steve.'

On a better day, that would make Nina laugh. 'No, she's not. She's Paige Peters' mum.'

But Marina is adamant. 'She was with him. I swear it was her.'

Again Nina shakes her head. 'It couldn't be.'

But as she drives away, she is less certain. And when she thinks back to the party she starts to worry. She shouldn't think about it. Especially not now. Not while she's driving. And not when she's about to pick up Emily. Instead, she turns the radio up high, as high as it will go, high enough to drown out every thought.

But by the time she arrives at Emily's childcare centre, her whole body is cold. Inside the centre, she keeps her head down so she won't have to talk, so she won't have to smile.

She finds Emily, who is playing in home corner, and whispers softly, 'Let's go.'

It is a relief when, in the car, the little girl lets herself be strapped into her car seat without protesting.

It's okay, Nina counsels herself as she puts the keys into the ignition, it's okay.

But as soon as the engine starts, music shoots through the speakers, so suddenly and so loudly that Emily, terrified, begins to scream.

Her fingers clumsy, Nina struggles to turn the volume down until at last she finds the power button and the music is gone.

Emily is still screaming. Depleted, Nina leans back against the headrest. Now what?

She could get out of the car, she could go to Emily, she could cuddle her. That's what she could do.

Instead, she puts the car into gear. And as she drives off, she clears her throat and starts to sing. She sings 'Old MacDonald Had a Farm', softly first, then louder and louder and louder until she is shouting the words out, shouting them out so loudly that Emily's screams no longer penetrate. 'Old MacDonald had a PIG,' she bellows. 'E-i-e-i-o.'

Finally, it works. Finally, out of sheer astonishment, Emily falls silent. Then she starts laughing and soon she is laughing so hard it sounds like she is choking, her little voice straining as she cries, 'More, Mummy, more, more.'

And so Nina gives her more. More cows and more pigs and more sheep and more chickens and more geese and more caterpillars and more cockroaches and more worms and more ants until they are home and Nina realises that her fingers are wrapped hard around the steering wheel and she is wet under the armpits.

Once inside, it is all Nina can do to open a can of baked beans, tip the beans into Emily's favourite bowl and zap them in the microwave.

When she calls Emily over to the table, she makes an effort to sound excited. 'Guess what I've made you for dinner?' she says. 'Baked beans!'

Emily looks unimpressed. 'I need noodles.'

'But I've made you baked beans,' Nina tells her.

Emily shakes her head. 'I really need noodles today.'

She doesn't have it in her to argue, so without a word, she covers the baked beans with cling wrap and puts them in the fridge. Then she boils water on the stove, drops a packet of two-minute noodles in it, sprinkles over the contents of the flavour sachet and serves them up.

Nina sits with Emily while she eats. As always, noodles are a messy affair: half of them make it into the little girl's mouth, the other half fall down her front. Watching on, Nina marvels at the mundanity of it all. She wonders, too, at how it can be that everything is both just as it always is and absolutely changed.

It is this thought that follows her through the evening as she bathes their daughter, dresses her, reads to her and puts her to bed.

Only then does she hear Steve's car pull up outside. As though separated by perspex, she watches him come through the door, smiling as he walks over to kiss her.

'Dinner's ready,' she tells him.

Only once they have started eating does she ask, her tone casual, 'Where were you today?'

Confused, he gives her a hesitant, puzzled sort of smile. 'What do you mean?'

'Today—where were you?'

This second time, he takes longer to reply, and his answer, when it comes, is cautious. 'At work, babe.' And then a pause. 'Why?'

She stops to compose herself. When she is sure she is able to continue, she says, 'I rang your work and they said you were off sick today. But, you know, I can see that you weren't home at all today.'

She wants to wait for him to process this but she can't stop herself. 'Are you having an affair with that Sue woman?'

He licks his lips and starts to shake his head.

'That's not very convincing.' This is what she hears herself saying to him. Her composure, her calmness, surprises her.

Inside, a different voice is raging. A sobbing, desperate voice pleading with him to make it better, to tell her that nothing is happening, that all is well, that they are good, that things are fine.

She waits for him to deny it, to reassure her that anything she has heard is wrong, has been misinterpreted, is a mistake. She braces herself, too, for righteous anger in his denial, for indignation and fury.

She gets none of that. At first, he says nothing. He simply sits at the table, his arms on his legs, his hands clasped together, his head bowed. It is a stance that frightens her.

'It's not like that,' he says softly.

She feels panic rising up into her throat. 'It's not like what?'

'It's not like that.' He raises his head and, for a brief instant, meets her eye.

She swallows. 'So tell me what it is like.' She keeps her voice calm, sympathetic even. Later, she will see this as a mistake, this prompt to tell her everything. Everything she doesn't want to hear.

'I had this thing for her, you know, years ago. And then, there she was again. I couldn't help it, Nina. I couldn't help it. '

He reaches over and puts his hand on hers. Rather than moving her hand away, which is what she wants to do, she lets it stay there.

Looking beyond him, past the kitchen table and over to the kitchen bench, she spies a cockroach egg case stuck to the underside of the bench. She'll need to get rid of it. That won't be hard. She could simply dislodge it with a fingernail or a knife or even the edge of a piece of paper. Really, she should do it quickly because otherwise she'll forget about it, the egg will hatch and it will be too late. But she can't do anything with his hand clamped over hers.

He starts to sob, making ugly, gulping sounds. 'I don't know what to do,' he says. 'I don't know what to do.'

Terry

He thought he knew Vonnie's place well. But it's one thing knowing where the bathroom is and another thing altogether remembering where she keeps the chopping board.

They won't be discharging her until Monday. That's what the doctors are saying. And that's about all he's managed to get out of Vonnie. As to the procedure itself, he's still in the dark. Women's business. That's all she had to say about it.

It was a no-brainer when she asked him to look after Bridie while she was out of action. He could have just taken the little one over to their place—that was one option—but with her school books and uniform and the rest of it, it made more sense for Michelle and him to just move in instead. It's not like they haven't done it before. The first time—it was years ago now—Bridie couldn't have been more than six, seven at a pinch. It had been a longer stretch that time. Over a week. Another stint in hospital for Vonnie, but for the life of him he can't remember what for. He can only remember how nice the time had been: how they'd taken Bridie to the movies.

That Nemo one, that's what they'd seen, the three of them. *Finding Nemo.* And gosh, it had been lovely sitting up in the picture theatre together. Ice-creams for everyone and popcorn to share; Bridie's eyes had nearly popped at the size of the bucket. Lovely. A lovely day. Even now he smiles to think back on it. They'd both felt a bit sad when the week was up and Vonnie was back again.

So it's nice to be doing it again, even if it's only for a few days.

Except now he can feel himself starting to get frustrated. He's checked the cupboards, but it's not there. It's not on the draining tray, either, and it's not in any of the drawers.

Finally, he gives up. 'Poppet,' he calls out, 'can you tell me where to find the chopping board?'

He doesn't have to call out twice; Bridie is quick to emerge from her bedroom. 'Nan normally puts it on top of the microwave,' she says. The microwave, an early model—maybe the earliest model ever—sits on a corner of the kitchen bench. When he looks more closely, he sees that Bridie is right: that's exactly where the chopping board is, right there on top of the microwave.

'Funny place to stick a chopping board,' he says. 'I mean, say all that radiation somehow made its way up there? Think what would happen to the chopping board. It'd get completely zapped, wouldn't it?'

Terry smiles as she considers this. Gee, she looks pretty with the new glasses, he thinks.

'I've never seen a chopping board get zapped by a microwave, Mr P,' she decides. As always, her voice is as soft as a whisper.

'Well, Bridie, my friend, there has to be a first time for everything now, doesn't there?'

She's not sure if he's being serious so he gives her a wink to help her out. 'You know,' he says, 'I had a hankering for bangers and mash tonight, something easy, being Friday night and all. What do you think?'

Bridie agrees. She likes sausages, too.

'I was thinking,' he says, 'that if we get a move on now, we should have it all ready by the time Mrs P gets home.'

It's an effort to remember to call her that, but Bridie won't call her Michelle, so Mrs P it is. Everyone else calls her Michelle: she's never been one to stand on ceremony, especially at the surgery. He's biased, of course, but he thinks Michelle would have to be the perfect medical receptionist. She clever, she's organised, she's nice to the patients and always seems to know when someone needs a bit of a pep-up or a bit of TLC, even if it's just a smile and a squeeze of the hand. His only gripe is that she always has to go beyond the call of duty. Like now, for example. It's already a quarter past six, long past her knock-off time, but she's still there. Some crisis or other. Yet again. *But, love,* he keeps saying to her, *you're the receptionist. Can't you leave it to the doctors to sort out their after-hours crises?* But it's like talking to a brick wall, isn't it, because whatever the circumstances, you can rest assured that Michelle will always go the extra mile. Which means they'll be eating late tonight. Late, at least, by Bridie and Vonnie's standards; they're usually done and dusted by six-thirty, and both in bed by eight.

Bridie's a good little helper in the kitchen, and she's a whiz with the peeler—even the blunt old thing Vonnie has—so he lets her take care of the potatoes while he strings the beans.

'I thought we could catch up with your dad tomorrow.' He tries to keep his voice casual. 'When we finish up at the hospital, that is.'

Bridie keeps peeling. 'You mean after we visit Nan?'

He nods. 'That's what I was thinking. I mean, we won't need to stay at the hospital long—your nan will be home in a couple of days anyway—so it'd give us the rest of the day then, wouldn't it?'

She nods but doesn't look up. 'All right,' she says.

It's a quiet time, then, between them. It would be good to have a bit of music but there isn't a radio in the kitchen.

'You want me to tell you a bit of a story about your dad?'

That piques her interest—he knew it would—and straightaway she looks up. Her expression, though, is guarded.

He smiles to reassure her. 'It's a good story,' he says, 'a funny one.'

'About my dad?' she asks.

'Yes,' he says, 'it's a funny story about your dad. You want to hear it?'

She's stopped peeling now. 'Yes,' she says, 'I want to hear it.'

'All right,' he says, 'so you know I taught your dad when he was in Year 6, but did you know that I was also his housemaster?'

She shakes her head: she didn't know that.

'He was in Bradman House—just like you are now—and in those days, I was Bradman's housemaster, and your dad, he was one of our best runners.'

This seems to surprise her. 'Nan said he played footy.'

Terry nods. 'That's true, but to be good at footy you've got to be a good runner as well.'

How curious it is, he thinks, the whole gene thing: that Trent's daughter should be the spitting image of him looks-wise, but nothing like him in terms of the physical know-how. And didn't he have it in spades? Quick, agile, strong, Trent was the whole package.

'Anyway, it was the school athletics carnival and your dad, he was a red-hot sprinter—the best in Bradman, probably the best in Year 6.

So when the twelve-year-old boys were called up for the hundred-metre race, well, everyone in Bradman had their hopes set on your dad winning the race. That'd mean five points for Bradman and we needed those points to have any chance of winning the carnival. So your dad, he lines up with the rest of the kids, the starting pistol goes and he's off like a shot. I'm up by the finish line and I watch him come, faster and faster, and he's at the head of the pack. You beauty, I think. And there's only fifteen metres left, less even, when it happens.'

Bridie is all agog now. 'What happened?'

'He suddenly petered out, that's what happened.' He shoots her a look. 'You know what it was like?'

She doesn't.

'It was like one of those battery toys that suddenly runs out of power. That's exactly what it was like. What's going on? I thought to myself. Maybe he had a stitch, maybe that was the problem. But it wasn't that at all.'

'What was it?' she asks. 'What was it, Mr P?'

'I'll tell you what it was: it was typical Trent, larrikin that he was. When I looked harder, I saw that instead of leaning forward, he was standing upright, as straight as a soldier. And instead of pushing his legs out behind him, to give himself more speed, he was lifting his legs high up in front of him, so high I thought he'd be able to touch his chin with his knees. You know what your rascal dad was doing, Bridie?'

She looks completely mystified.

'He was showboating—legs up, head up high with a goofy smile on his face—he was showboating for the school. So instead of winning the race by a couple of metres, he pulled in third. I was ropeable, I was absolutely ropeable. And do you know what he said?'

'What, Mr P? What did my dad say?'

It kills him to hear her little voice; so eager, so thirsty to know more about her dad—her silly, silly dad. If he's not careful, it'll even make him teary. Pulling himself together, he makes a pantomime of his face: eyes large, eyebrows raised, mouth pursed. 'This is what your father said: *Well, Mr P*, he said, *I still got third* and *I cracked the whole school up.* He pointed over to the stands and, sure enough, all the kids—all the kids in the whole school—they were laughing and pointing at your dad. And you know what I thought?'

Bridie shakes her head.

'Cranky as I was—and disappointed as I was for him, and for Bradman as well, I suppose—there was a part of me that admired him, too, for just getting out there and giving a performance for the school. Because, you know, that was the other thing about your dad. He was quite the performer. It wouldn't have surprised me if he'd become an actor. Wouldn't have surprised me if I'd seen his name up in lights.'

Charisma, that's what he had, bucketloads of charisma. And for a moment Terry loses himself thinking about it; thinking about Trent, all grown up and walking the red carpet. It wouldn't have been a stretch, not really. Not then, not looking forward like that.

He can't bear thinking about the rest of it. *Trent*, he says to himself, *Trent, you stupid, stupid boy. What were you thinking? What in God's name were you thinking on that day?* Because if ever there was a day to take back in a life, that was the one.

But enough. Enough of Trent. Enough of all of that. It's already quarter to seven and Bridie will be starting to flag.

'Tell you what, love,' he says, 'since we're running a bit late, why don't you whip in and have your shower right now?'

Once she's gone, Terry reaches into the fridge for a beer and sits down to drink it.

Vonnie keeps the curtains closed but Terry likes to keep them open so he can look out onto the garden. It's pretty at night, lit up by the streetlights. He keeps his eye out for Michelle, too. The bus drops her at the top of the street and she just needs to walk down the hill to get to the house. It's safe enough, that's not a problem, even if it's already dark before six now.

Which reminds him: he'll need to switch on the porch light so she doesn't trip up. There are a couple of steps up to the porch and it's like guesswork without the light on.

No sooner has he settled back on the lounge when there comes a cry from the bathroom. Leaving his beer on the coffee table, Terry hurries over. 'What is it?' he calls through the door. 'What's the matter?'

Bridie's little voice is muffled. 'The hot tap—it's stuck, Mr P, it's completely stuck.'

God, he thinks, she'll bloody scald herself if she can't turn the tap off. So he opens the door and rushes into the bathroom. There's no screen or curtain to cover the shower recess and when she sees him there, she covers her body and turns away.

'I'm not looking, love,' he says, 'I'm not looking. I just want to turn off the tap so you won't burn yourself.'

'I can't turn it on, Mr P, I can't turn it on at all.'

Immediately, he relaxes. 'So the water's too cold, love, not too hot, is that the problem?'

The back of her head moves up and down. He lets his eyes scan the length of her body. And what a beautiful body it is, he thinks to himself. Such a lovely little thing. His finger wrapped around the hot tap now, he gives it a wrench.

'There you go, love, done. Probably needs a new washer. I'll see if I can pick one up over the weekend.'

A couple of minutes later, she's calling out again. Because there are no towels. So he grabs her one and, sticking his hand through the door, leaves it on the edge of the vanity.

Then he returns to the lounge room, retrieves his beer and settles back on the sofa to enjoy it.

Laurie

When she looks up from the screen, she's surprised to find it dark outside. And when she checks her watch, she sees that it's already ten to seven. There's enough work to keep her here all night but suddenly she's feeling hungry. It's Friday night and on Friday nights, she rents a DVD from the video store and gets Indian from the take-away shop next door. And now she's craving curry and pappadams. So she switches off her computer, picks up a folder of papers to go through over the weekend and makes her way to the car.

There are a couple of ways to get home to Ashton, but Laurie always turns right up Hart Street then onto the main road that leads her out of Brindle and towards the city. To get to school in the morning, she simply does the trip in reverse: down the main road that runs all the way to Jinda, left down Hart Street, then along the coast until she hits the school. On a good day, she can be there in twenty minutes.

Bridie Taylor lives in Hart Street. Hers is a pleasant-looking house, though the front garden needs some work; there are weeds in the lawn that need to be dug out and dandelions have sprung up on either side of the front steps. Sometimes, Laurie sees the girl playing there by herself. Perhaps this is what has piqued her interest. Laurie is an only child, too.

Lately, when she has been driving past, Bridie has begun to lift her hand up in a wave. The first time, this had surprised Laurie. In truth, she'd felt caught out. It hadn't occurred to her that the child would notice her, just as she had noticed the child. And so, to begin with, she hadn't waved back, not that first time, and not the second time either. The third time, although she didn't wave, she did give a nod. But now she waves back. Once or twice, she's even been tempted to give her a toot. This is something she has resisted; she is the child's principal, after all, and distance is important in such a relationship. So she never toots, she only waves.

This evening, when she drives along the water, the bay is black and beautiful and, above it, the moon is full and high. If she wasn't so hungry, she might even pull up and look out at it for a while. Instead, she turns into Hart Street. And as she drives along the street, she looks across to Bridie's place, lit up by the towering streetlight in front of it.

Tonight, however, what she sees gives her such a jolt it makes her sit bolt upright, swerve into the kerb and pull on the handbrake.

His car—Terry Pritchard's car—is parked outside the little girl's house. After dark and he's at the child's house on a Friday night. What the hell is he doing there?

Hurrying out of the car, Laurie walks across the road so quickly she is almost running. She raps hard on the door.

Almost immediately, the door flies open and there he is, in the doorway. When he sees her, he jumps. He literally jumps. 'What are you doing here?' he blurts out.

What is *she* doing there? Well, that's hardly the question, is it? Behind him, she can see into a lounge room. Sitting on the coffee table is an open can of beer.

'Where's her grandmother?' she asks him.

Immediately, his faces falls. It's all the answer she needs. Clearly, the grandmother is not here and he is alone with the child.

Sure enough, she's right. The grandmother's in hospital, that's what he says. She's in hospital and Terry is minding the fort.

'Vonnie needed someone to look after Bridie,' he tells her, but he's stuttering and stammering so hard she can hardly make out what he's saying, 'so I put up my hand.'

She can feel the heat rising inside her. 'Surely, that's not your job,' she says. 'Surely that's something for her family to do.'

'Sorry?' he says, frowning hard as though he hasn't understood a word she's said.

She repeats herself very slowly and very clearly. 'I said, her family should be looking after her, not you, Terry.'

He licks his lips before he answers her. It irks her to watch it. *Don't lick your lips at me*, she wants to snap at him. She forces herself to stay quiet.

'You've seen the records, Laurie,' he says. 'The mother's dead, the father's AWOL and the grandmother's a widow—where exactly is the family to look after her?'

He's lost the stammering now. Now he's back to his usual arrogant self. Well, two can play at that. She pulls herself up so she's standing very tall. 'There must be someone,' she says.

He crosses his arms in front of him. 'That's right, Laurie,' he says, 'there *is* someone—there's me.' His tone is so patronising she could slap him.

'So you thought it would be a good idea to move in with one of your students without telling me? Is that what you're saying?' She speaks as calmly as she can.

It gives her some satisfaction to watch his face turn red. 'Well, Laurie, that's not how I'd describe it,' he says, 'and quite frankly, I don't know what you're insinuating. All I know is that I've been helping out a family that needed a bit of support.'

She doesn't flinch. Instead, she keeps it very cool. 'Well, Terry,' she responds, 'I'm astounded that you didn't speak to me about this. As your principal, I have a right to be informed of situations like these.'

She can't believe his reply: 'I wasn't aware of that.'

That's when she explodes. 'What do you mean you weren't aware of that? Surely you're familiar with the departmental guidelines on protective practices?'

He just stares at her.

'And you're aware of the policy on home visits, aren't you?'

Slowly, he shakes his head at her. 'Laurie, you're not listening to me,' he says. 'I'm not visiting her, I'm looking after her.'

As if that is an answer. 'Well, that just makes it even more inappropriate.' She's trying hard not to shout now. She's trying as hard as she can. 'That just makes it completely inappropriate.'

At that moment, a voice rings out from behind her. 'What's inappropriate?'

Laurie swings around to find a woman standing in front of her. Before she can say anything, Terry steps in. 'Michelle, love,' he's saying, 'this is Laurie Mathews. Laurie, my wife Michelle.'

It's as if they've all just met at a cocktail party. Laurie is dumbfounded. The woman—Michelle—gives her a smile. 'Would you like to come in?'

Caught off guard, Laurie just stares at her. 'No,' she says, 'I won't stay. I just needed a word with Terry.'

Michelle keeps smiling. 'If you're sure.'

She is sure. She's absolutely sure. Absolutely sure that she wants to get the hell out of here. If she doesn't, she'll throttle Terry Pritchard. So she turns around and marches back to the car. But her hands are shaking so much she can hardly manage to open the door, and once she's inside, she has to try twice to get the key in the ignition. Keep it together, she tells herself, just keep it together. All she needs to do is turn on the engine and start driving home. Then she can decide what to do next.

The audacity, the sheer audacity of the man: that's what she can't believe. How is she supposed to deal with someone like that? How can she be expected to supervise a man who shows nothing but contempt for her and who openly defies departmental guidelines?

And what in God's name has he been doing with that little girl?

And what was he doing drinking beer there, at night, alone, in her house?

She should have called the police. That's what she should have done. And if his wife hadn't turned up, she would have. She'd have called the police on him, then and there.

Now, as she makes her way home, she wonders whether she shouldn't have done it anyway. Whether she should have just called the police and been done with it. Wife or no wife.

Too late now.

But not too late to put in a call to the unit. And this time, she'll be insisting that Lucy Carboni take her seriously.

Nina

In bed that night, the night of his confession, Steve clings to her like a baby. She lets herself be held, lets herself be moulded to his body shape, lets herself be gentle with him. He sleeps before she does, well before she does.

In the morning, he is the one to wake her. Gently, his hand on her shoulder. But she won't be woken easily and it takes some time before she can manage to keep her eyes open. He brings her a cup of tea and when she sees this, she gives him a small, sleepy smile. He smiles back, but his smile is wary. It is this that jolts her out of her half-sleep, reminding her that despite the tea, things are not okay.

She starts when she sees the time—it is already after eight. It takes her a moment or two to remember that it is not, in fact, a school day; that it is Saturday. And yet Steve is wearing his suit.

'You working?' she asks, her voice still thick with sleep.

'I told you I was,' he says.

She can't remember this but who knows? And anyway, what does it matter?

What's going to happen to us? This is what she wants to ask him. She doesn't. She just nods. 'Okay,' she says as he leaves. 'Okay.'

But it isn't okay. For how can she be sure that he is, in fact, going to work? How can she be sure he won't be with *her* instead? How can she be sure of anything at all?

She can hear the television blaring in the lounge room, which means that Emily must be in front of it. She should get up, check that Emily has had breakfast. The problem is, she can't get up. She actually can't get up. All her energy has simply evaporated. She should be crying, that's what she should be doing. She should be crying because her marriage is unravelling. But for some reason, she can't even do that. She can't cry and she can't get out of bed. And all she wants to do is pull the quilt over her head and pretend none of this is happening. Sleep it all away, that's what she wants to do, just sleep it all away. And so, her head resting on her pillow, she lets her eyelids close.

They don't stay closed. Instead, they spring open with the sound of footsteps coming towards her. For a small person, Emily has a heavy tread.

'Mummy,' she says, 'are you sick in bed?'

Nina turns her head to look at her daughter. 'I'm just tired in bed, that's all.'

'It's morning time, Mummy,' Emily says. 'You've got to get up because it's morning time.'

Morning time is the last thing Nina wants to face. *Just this once,* she wants to beseech her tiny daughter, *just this once don't make me get up.*

But Emily is absolutely right: it is morning time and so Nina must get up.

'I'll help you,' the little girl tells her, her face earnest and confident. 'I'll help you get up.'

Taking Nina's hand in hers, she tries to pull her up, right up out of bed. To help her, Nina lifts herself up but pretends it is Emily who has done it. Delighted, the girl's face breaks into a smile so broad it forces one out of Nina, too.

Now that she is up, the day ahead looms large and long, and she will need to think of a way to fill it.

She could take Emily around to see Colin. Colin is mostly at home on Saturdays and he's always happy to see them. And yet she hesitates. What will she say if her father-in-law asks her how she is? Colin has never been interested in pat answers, in nothing answers, and Nina has always been honest with him. But how can she be honest about this? How can she tell him that his son is having an affair? She can't, she simply can't. So no, they won't be visiting Poppy today.

Marina sleeps in on Saturdays, especially if she's been out the night before, which means that an early visit is out of the question. In any case, Nina isn't sure she could manage the day with Marina. What if she has more to tell her? More that Nina doesn't want to hear? So they will not visit Marina either.

Instead, they spend the morning at the local park. At the park, Emily is in her element. Nina is not. For Nina, the park is a place where time stands still. There is a group of children there; some adults, too, but no one Nina knows or even recognises. So with a smile planted on her face, Nina stands apart as she watches Emily slide down the slippery dip, rock on a plastic dolphin and steer a bright yellow motorboat. When Emily needs help on the monkey bars, she keeps her smile as she holds her daughter up so she can grab at each rung until she has reached the other side; she keeps her smile, too, as she lunges to save Emily from falling through a gap in the climbing gym.

It is time for lunch when they get home and in the afternoon, they snuggle up on the lounge to watch a DVD. She hears nothing from Steve.

That evening, she feeds Emily early and by seven, the girl has been bathed and put to bed. There is still no word from Steve and she can't face calling to find out when he will be home. Instead, she leaves the dinner in the oven while, stiff-backed, she waits for him to come home. At eight thirty-six, when the car pulls into the drive-way, she freezes, uncertain whether to stay put or go to the front door. She is still deciding when he lets himself in. Immediately, the smell of alcohol hits her.

She doesn't mention it. She doesn't say a word. She doesn't greet him with a kiss. She doesn't greet him at all. All she can manage is a tiny, tight smile.

'I've made dinner,' she tells him.

But when she serves it, the meat is tough and dry from being in the oven too long and although he says nothing, she sees him grimace as he chews. This is what enrages her: that he should be grimacing when it is his fault the dinner is ruined.

The water jug is on the table, closer to her than it is to him. When he asks for water, she stands up without a word, reaches for the jug and begins to fill his glass.

You bastard, she thinks. How dare you stay back drinking while I'm looking after Emily and making your bloody dinner? This is what she wants to scream at him. This, and so many other things. Instead, she keeps pouring. And once the glass is full, still she keeps pouring; pouring and pouring until the glass overfills and water runs first onto the table and then onto the floor. She doesn't stop. Even when Steve yells at her to get a grip, still she keeps pouring, until the jug is empty, the table is drenched and the water continues to spread across the floor. Only then does she put the jug back on the table and leave the room.

She can't think what else to do, so she shuts herself in the bedroom. This would be the time to cry but for some reason she can't; she just can't. By contrast, she feels strangely calm.

She will take a shower, that's what she will do. In the shower stall, she turns the hot tap right up, revelling in the heat of the water, in the fact that it is almost hotter than she can bear. She could stay there forever, but she doesn't. She turns off the taps, reaches for a towel to wrap around herself and returns to the bedroom.

She is surprised to find Steve there, his back to her as he slides open the wardrobe door.

'What are you doing?' she asks him.

He doesn't turn around. 'I'm going to stay with Dad,' he says, his voice clipped.

Panic travels the length of her backbone. 'What, now?'

'I think it'd be a good idea.'

A good idea for who? she wonders.

'What do you mean?'

This time he does turn around. 'I mean, I think we should spend some time apart.'

Nina's heart is beating hard now, so hard and loud it seems to push up against her ribcage. 'What do you mean?' she asks. Her voice is shrill now, even she hears it.

'I just think it would be better.' His voice is not shrill. His voice is terse, but measured.

'How much time?' Her voice is so high-pitched she hardly recognises it.

'I don't know,' he tells her. 'I don't know.'

For some reason, she stays to watch him pack. He doesn't take much—little more than a change of clothes—and she fixes on this as proof that this is just a temporary thing, just a small thing that will soon be sorted.

With that in mind, she sees him to the door. Only when she hears the engine start and the car drive away, does she start to cry. What now? What now?

The night is cold and, alone, the bed is too large for her. And so, sometime in the early hours of the morning, she slips into Emily's bedroom and into her bed. To fit in, she has to curl herself right around her daughter's body. Her breath—Emily's breath—is soft and regular, so soft and so regular it is almost hypnotic.

Steve doesn't come back. He stays away. He rings for the first time on Thursday, when he says he'd like to have Emily for the weekend.

It is a request that floors her. It is the type of request divorced people make. And she is not divorced. She is married. She and Steve are married.

She rings Marina in a panic. For a long time, Marina just listens. 'I know,' she says finally, 'I know. But Emily needs to see him, doesn't she?'

'Couldn't he just come over to see her?' Nina's voice is less than a whisper.

'That won't work, Nina, you know it won't. And anyway, Colin will be there, too, and Emily loves being with Colin.'

The mention of her father-in-law makes Nina want to weep. 'But so do I,' she says.

⁓

It nearly breaks her to do it, but on Friday night, she packs her daughter's suitcase, which is new. The pyjamas she packs are new, too, as is the book she slips in to be read before bedtime.

The next morning, Emily wakes early. She is excited, she tells Nina, excited that Daddy will be picking her up and excited that they will be seeing Poppy.

When Steve arrives, she doesn't know what to say to him: here is her husband, on the doorstep of their house, and she has no idea how to behave. In the end, she gives him a stiff nod as she waits for him to come inside. He doesn't move. She is slow to realise that he is waiting for an invitation—for an invitation to come into his own house. 'Come in,' she hears herself saying, 'please.' Strange words to be speaking; strange words for a wife to say to her husband. But there they are. And so he does come in and then, somehow, they are sitting at the dining table and the kettle is boiling and she is asking him whether he would like tea or coffee.

'Coffee,' he answers, lifting his left hand a little. A hand that somehow looks different, that somehow looks foreign. For a moment she can't work out why. It is a shock when she realises what it is: his wedding ring is gone. Hers is still on her finger, but his is gone. Gone where? This is her thought and it is by mistake that the words leave her lips.

He doesn't answer her.

So they sit at the table in silence. He drinks his coffee quickly, so quickly she's sure he'll scald himself. She wonders how he can even swallow—her throat is so dry now it hurts, and her own coffee stays untouched.

From the hallway, Emily's voice is high and musical. 'Is Daddy here?' she calls. 'Is my daddy here?'

Steve finishes his coffee as he stands up. 'I'll get her,' he says, but it sounds like a question; it sounds like he is asking for her permission.

Her lips tight, Nina nods, and as he makes his way to Emily's bedroom, Nina hears him exhale. It is a long exhalation, the type made at the end of an examination, or worse: at the end of an interrogation. It upsets her to hear it. It upsets her, too, to hear Emily's excited scream when she sees him. *Daddy!* The word is long and drawn out and delighted. For a moment, Nina is envious of her; envious of the three-year-old who is still loved by a man who no longer loves her.

Come back, she wills him. *Come back.*

Instead, he sends Emily into the kitchen to say goodbye. To say goodbye. To her own mother! How can that be? How can her little girl be taken away, just like that? *No*, she wants to scream, *no, no, no.* But she mustn't do that. What she must do is this: she must push out a smile from her tightened lips; she must find a sparkle for her eyes—but from where?—and she must say, *Goodbye, my darling, have lots and lots of fun.* And she must not cry.

She doesn't. Not even a tear. And although her smile feels like a grimace, Emily is fooled by it. 'Goodbye, my silly mummy,' she says, rubbing her hands down Nina's cheeks. 'Goodbye, my silly-billy-willy mummy.'

She should see them out—she should see her daughter and her husband out—but when she tries to stand, her legs won't move. Just won't move. *Steve,* she wants to tell him, *can you believe it? I can't stand up, I can't even move my legs.*

But he doesn't come back into the kitchen; he just calls, 'Come on, Em—let's go.'

And Emily says, 'Okay, Daddy,' and just like that, they are gone.

She is unused to having time to spare. She is unused to being alone. In the afternoon, she hires some DVDs and in the evening she watches them. For dinner, she has a third of a bottle of wine and a packet of chocolate biscuits.

When, finally, she takes herself off to bed, she is scared she won't be able to sleep, that she will lie awake all night. But she does sleep and when she sleeps, she dreams.

In her dream, she is wandering; walking around a building she doesn't recognise. Emily is lying in her arms and Nina holds her, as closely as she can, her head resting in the crook of Nina's arm. Her daughter has been dead for some days, it seems, and for all these days, Nina has been carrying her. The building, she realises, is a hospital and Nina finds herself in a room with a bed and a couple of chairs. A woman is sitting in one of the chairs while Nina sits on the bed, still clasping Emily to her. The woman starts to ask questions of Nina: her name, her address, her religion, her education, her height, her weight.

Nina begins to answer the questions but soon stops. 'This is all very well,' she tells the woman, 'but tell me this: how can I leave her?'

The woman's answer is simple: Nina must completely immerse her daughter in water then go. So Nina does. She leaves Emily immersed in water. Some hours later, when she returns, she sees to her great surprise that Emily is moving, as though waking. As she scoops her out of the water and holds her tight, she can see that her little girl is alive. And even though her joy is all-encompassing, somewhere in her head is a voice warning her that the water will have harmed her daughter and must have damaged her brain.

In the morning, she wakes to confusion and alarm, needing to speak to Emily, needing to check that all is well and she is safe. She calls Steve's mobile and waits anxiously for him to answer it. But the call rings out. She tries again, but there is still no answer. So she rings Colin.

'Colin,' she says, trying to sound upbeat. 'It's me, Nina.'

There is, she thinks, a hesitation before he answers her. 'Hello, love,' he says.

Hearing his voice makes her want to cry. Her only comfort is knowing that Emily is with him.

'Colin,' she says, 'I—can I speak to Emily? I just wanted to say hello to Emily.' Her words are staccato and anxious.

A pause. 'She's not here, love.'

'What?' Panic shoots through her. There has been an accident, she thinks. There has been an accident and no one has told her. 'Is she all right?'

This time the silence is longer. 'She's fine, love. She's just with Steve.'

Confusion dampens her relief. 'But aren't they with you?'

'No, love,' Colin tells her gently. 'They're not.'

She struggles to keep her voice strong. 'Oh,' she says, 'where are they then?' Forcing out the question makes her want to retch.

He doesn't answer.

'Will they be back soon?' she asks.

'I'm not sure, love,' he says quietly. 'I'm really not sure.'

No more questions, she tells herself, *no more*. But she can't stop herself. 'Did they stay over at her place?'

He could feign ignorance. He could pretend not to know what she means. But she knows he won't.

'I think so.'

'Okay.' Her voice is a whisper.

'I'm sorry, love,' he says. But that's not what she wants to hear. She doesn't want to hear that he is sorry. She just wants him to make things right again.

'Do you know her? This woman, do you know her?'

Colin sighs. 'Sweetie, I've known Sue Rankin since she was fifteen years old.'

That, in itself, feels like a betrayal. *Well, don't call me sweetie, then*, she wants to scream. *If you know her so well, don't call me sweetie.*

And in that instant, she sees exactly how it will be. The family gatherings, the dinners, the get-togethers. They will all be the same, only Sue Rankin will be there instead of her. Sue Rankin will get out of the car with Steve, Sue Rankin will chat to Colin and there will be nothing awkward about it because, as it happens, he's known her since she was fifteen years old.

In the distance, Colin's voice is gentle, soothing, apologetic. But Nina listens to none of it. What's the point? Because now it is clear to her. He comes with Steve. That is the truth of it. He is Steve's father: he comes with Steve, and he goes with Steve. Whatever the situation, whatever the circumstances, he belongs with Steve.

But she'd thought he was hers, too.

Only when the call is over does Nina think about what he has told her. That her little girl has been there, overnight, and that she, her mother, has discovered this only by accident.

How could he? How could he take her there? How could he do that? The more she dwells on it, the more infuriated she becomes.

She rings Colin again. 'I need her number,' she says. 'If Emily is there with her, I need the phone number.'

There's a pause, and she hears him draw a breath. 'I might have a number here somewhere, love,' he says to her, 'but you're going to have to give me a minute.'

She hasn't got the patience to wait even a second. She listens as he puts the receiver down—she knows the house so well she can practically see him doing it, laying it face down on the kitchen bench while he rifles through the address book. There is a crackle as he picks up the phone again.

'Love, I've got a number here. I can give you that, if you like.'

If you like—she takes exception to that. This isn't something she wants, this isn't something she would *like*; as a mother, this is something she *needs*. She has no choice. Doesn't he understand that?

'Thanks, Colin,' she says quietly. 'That'd be good.'

She writes the number down on a scrap of paper, then as soon as she's hung up she transfers it into her mobile phone. And because she can't bear to write any part of that woman's name, she writes only her initials: SR.

Now she needs to ring her. Now she needs to ring her to find out what the hell she's doing with a man who is not her husband and a child who is not her daughter. Her heart pounds as she waits for the call to connect, for the number to start ringing.

But it doesn't start ringing.

It's been switched off.

She's turned the bloody phone off, that's what she's done.

Nina has never been an impulsive person and yet, minutes later, she finds herself driving to a house she may not be able to find again. She knows the suburb, but the street name eludes her. She considers asking Colin for it, but how would she explain herself? Instead she tries to think back, tries to search her mind for it; for the address Sue Rankin had given to her. Drunk as she'd been, she'd at least managed that much.

An L. The street name starts with an L, Nina decides. And the more she considers it, the more certain she becomes of it. So she stops the car and, opening up to the index of the street directory, runs a finger down all the streets beginning with the letter L. It must act as a trigger because suddenly the street name spills out of her. It doesn't start with L after all. It starts with V. Sue Rankin lives in Valley Street.

When she gets to the street, she drives slowly, looking for a house that is familiar. As it happens, it's not difficult to find. In the whole street, there is only one red-brick house with a painted porch. In the daylight, it is a plain house; a drab house in need of work.

Once she has parked, she stays in the car, waiting to see what she will do next. She surprises herself by getting out of the car and walking up to the house.

As she approaches the porch, that night returns to her, crystal clear in its focus. She recalls a sensor light, and when she looks for it, there it is. There, too, are the filmy curtains pulled across the floor-length window beside the door. And there, right there, is the doorbell. And there, too, in her mind is Sue Rankin—unsteady beside her, leaning on her as she fumbles for her keys, her breath sharp with alcohol, her hair too dark for such a pale, pinched face.

Her anger, freshly fuelled now, outstrips any last hesitation as Nina lifts up her hand to press the doorbell once and again and again and again.

The urgency of the ringing brings the sound of hurried foot-steps and suddenly, there she is: her husband's mistress, in a purple sloppy joe and a pair of pyjama pants. Without make-up, her face is lined and her skin is aged. At another time, this might give Nina some comfort. Today, it just enrages her further.

At first, Sue Rankin looks blank. Then something clicks and her face changes. Her eyes retreat and her lips part a fraction. 'Nina,' she says.

'Is my daughter here?' Her voice, cold and clipped, makes the woman flinch. Nina is happy to see this. 'Well, is she?'

The woman nods.

'And is my husband here, too?'

She doesn't answer.

Nina hears her voice rise. 'What do you think you're doing? What the hell do you think you're doing in this awful house with my husband and my daughter?' A pause, then, but not for long. Not long enough to wait for an answer. 'Do you know what you are, Sue Rankin? Do you know what you are? You're despicable, that's what you are.'

The woman says nothing. She could slam the door closed but she doesn't. She simply takes a step back and turns her head away from Nina.

A voice comes from inside. 'Suzi, what's happening?'

Suzi. Suzi Q. Again the party returns to her. Is that when he started calling her Suzi? On that night, and on all the other nights she'd known nothing about? Is that how the name stuck? Or did it go back further than that? Has she been his Suzi Q since she was fifteen years old? Is that how long it's been?

He is beside her, then—beside Suzi—and they are at the door together, standing so close they might be arm in arm.

'What's going on, Nina?' he asks her.

His question infuriates her. 'You're asking me what's going on? You're asking me? How about I ask you what's going on? How about I ask you what you're doing standing there with your slut beside you? How about I ask you what the hell you're doing here with this bitch?' These are words she never uses, words she didn't know she had in her. 'Well?' she screams, and only as the tears slip into her mouth does she realise she is crying. 'Answer me!'

It is then she notices that the curtains have parted and that someone is watching them. It is Paige, standing in the gap, her eyes wide, her mouth trembling.

Somehow, she finds herself back in her car and somehow, she manages to get herself back home.

Once inside, she calls Marina to tell her what she has done: that she has behaved like a madwoman in front of her student; that she has called her mother a bitch, and worse; that she doesn't know how she'll be able to face the girl that week, and what she'll say to explain it. Apart from the truth: that her mother has destroyed Nina's marriage and for that Nina hates her.

Marina is silent.

'What do I do?' Nina demands. 'Tell me: what should I do?'

'You shouldn't be teaching Paige,' Marina says finally. 'It's too much for you and it's not fair on her, not now. You know that, don't you?'

She doesn't know that. It's the first time she's even thought about it.

'And, Nina,' Marina continues gently, 'you know the best thing you could do?'

She doesn't know that, either.

'The best thing you could do is to get out of Stenton—get a transfer to somewhere that's well away. In your place, Nina, that's what I'd be doing: I'd be getting right out.'

Rebecca

It would be untrue to say that, over the last months, the time has flown. That is not how it has been. It would be more truthful to say that the time has not been dragging the way it did in the early weeks of Emmanuel's absence. She is unsure why. Perhaps it is simply a matter of acclimatisation: he is there and she is here and she has accepted that this is how it is. For even though their reunion is approaching, still it is not so close that she has begun to count down the days—although she has begun to think of it in weeks, now, instead of months. Today, it is 25 June, the school term will end on 6 August, and three days later, she and Sebastian will fly out. In just over six weeks, then, they will all be by the sea, in Brindle. But only for a couple of days; after that they will venture further afield: up and down the coast, and then inland, too. A grand adventure, this is how he has described it to her, and she likes the thought of that: of a grand adventure before the return home. She and Sebastian already they have their tickets, and their entry visas, too, which, to her surprise, had been no easy thing. Even for a stay as short as theirs, there had been forms and additional forms, followed by a queue at the consulate so long she'd felt like screaming by the time she made it to the front. The whole business of it irked her: why make it so difficult?

Emmanuel had laughed at the question. 'The thing is,' he said, his voice echoing over the phone, 'everyone's desperate to come. Everywhere people tell me this. You know what I think it is? I think it's the whales—I think it's because of the whales.'

That made her giggle. 'What in the world are you talking about?'

'The whales,' he said, 'they're everywhere—every day I'll spot two, maybe three of them. All I have to do is walk down to the end of the street, and there they are.'

Well, the thought of that: the thought of a group of walking whales; that was enough to shake the funk and make her laugh. 'You idiot,' she said.

And now, as she and Grace walk together, this is the picture that comes back to her: the image of a line of whales just ambling down the street; and once more, she finds herself laughing. When Grace turns to her, quizzical, she doesn't know what to say, how to explain such a ridiculous thought to a serious woman. 'Just a stupid thing,' she says, and Grace doesn't ask for more.

They walk for some time—for close to an hour—before Rebecca turns into her house and Grace walks on to hers.

On the stairs to the front door, Rebecca trips up on something soft and dark. Only when she picks it up does she remember what it is: Grace's fleecy top, left there when she'd come to pick Rebecca up that morning. She'll return it after she has showered.

∽

There are quite a few cars parked outside Grace's house, an odd sight in their quiet street, but Rebecca thinks nothing of it. The electric gate is wide open but, unconcerned, she just walks through. And when she gets to the front door to find that it, too, is open, still she is unperturbed. She just knocks and calls out to her friend.

There is no answer, not immediately. And when Grace does come to the door, there is something different about her, something strained. Her demeanour makes Rebecca uncomfortable, so uncomfortable she forgets to say why she has come and just stands there, helpless, at the front door.

From behind Grace comes the sound of footsteps: footsteps made by heavy shoes, footsteps made by a man. Grace's husband, Rebecca thinks, even though it is unusual for him to be home on a weekday. But when she looks up, she sees that the man who is approaching her is not Johnson, nor is it the gardener, nor the driver. He is no one Rebecca recognises. All she recognises is his uniform. So she shouldn't be surprised to see a gun slung over his shoulder. Yet it does surprise her.

When he gestures at her to approach, still she doesn't get it. Only when he steps forward to grab her is she seized with a sudden wave of fright.

Even when the worst of it is over, still the fright stays with her. It stays behind her smile when, some days later, she manages to change their flights. It stays, too, as she packs in secret, as she struggles to maintain her composure in front of Laety, in front of Benson and Mosy, in front of Sebastian. It stays with her at night when she can't sleep, when her mind won't stop hissing at her to *get out, get out, get out.*

She has told no one, not even Emmanuel, that this is what she has decided to do.

⁓

The fright is with her now, too, as she makes her way to the airline counter, Sebastian quiet by her side. A change of plan, she has told him. This is how she has explained their hasty departure. He queries nothing.

Although she has always dressed well, tonight her clothes are loose and baggy, her shoes are flat and unremarkable and her short, chic haircut is hidden under a long, straight wig. No one gives her a passing look.

When they get there, the woman at the counter is neither friendly nor surly. Theirs is a late flight, and the woman seems tired. She asks for their tickets and their passports and Rebecca's heart beats more quickly as she passes them over. But the woman only glances at them before she asks for their luggage. 'Just the two pieces?'

Rebecca nods. Her own bag weighs nineteen kilograms and it is only now she realises she could have packed more—up to twenty-five kilograms. She had thought the limit was twenty. So she had packed carefully. Two books only, two pairs of shoes only. Some photographs, taken out of their frames and kept flat in a folder at the bottom of the suitcase. Toiletries. Not much more than that. And after all that effort, she could have had an extra six kilograms. It upsets her not to have known that. And then it perplexes her that, after everything else, she should be angered by this. By a lost six kilograms.

The woman behind the counter tags the handles of their suit-cases, prints out two boarding passes and, together with the passports, hands them over.

Rebecca tries to keep her hand steady as she takes the documents, clutching them tightly as if they might slip through her fingers.

It is customs that makes her most fearful. This, she knows, is where it might all unravel. But her media training stands her in good stead and, tilting her chin up, she walks into the customs area with a show of confidence that belies the fear pushing up inside her.

There are cards to complete before they line up to clear immigration. Carefully she writes out her name as it appears in her passport: Rebecca Chuma. This is not the name she is known by; Rebecca Vera—the name of her birth—that is the one people know. That is the one she uses when she would like something to be done quickly or well. So it is a good thing, then, that her passport is not in her birth name but in her married name. It is even better than her disguise.

They reach the head of the line quickly. The officer who serves them doesn't return her smile. Instead he looks hard at her passport before he turns to consult the computer screen to his left. Because there is a glass barrier between them, she can't see what is displayed on the computer. She tries to read what she can from his expression, which is solemn and focused. Her heart pounds as she watches him and she has to work to keep her face relaxed.

Shifting in his seat, the officer moves his head closer to the screen, as if to scrutinise it more closely.

He knows, he knows, he knows. These are the words that push out against her ribs. What now? she thinks. What will happen now?

What happens is this: the man behind the glass leans back in his chair, swivels back to face her and, with an expression she can't read, returns their passports and waves them through.

Relief makes her speechless and, in silence, she and Sebastian walk out of customs and into an over-lit dome of duty-free goods.

Gate five is at the end of it and, when they get there, the departure lounge is only half filled even though they're due to board in less than thirty minutes.

When, forty minutes later, there has still been no announcement, it occurs to her that she has made a mistake, and that this is not the right departure lounge after all. In front of them is a television screen that lists, it seems, only arrivals and no departures. She starts to panic. Perhaps they aren't even in the right terminal, she thinks. And God, oh God, oh God, what then?

Calm down, she tells herself, calm down. Now that they are so very close, she needs to stay very, very calm. She turns to speak to Sebastian, but her mouth is so dry no words come out. She clears her throat. 'I'm just going to check about the flight,' she tells him.

He nods, but stays seated when she stands. 'I'll stay here,' he says.

'No,' she replies, her voice urgent, 'come with me.' It is not enough that he should be within sight. She needs to have him within reach, too.

There is a flight attendant behind a desk at the far end of the departure lounge and together they walk over to her. Although Rebecca is not accustomed to waiting, this is what she does until the woman looks up from her computer.

'Oh,' she says, surprised. 'You scared me.' Her accent is not local and when she smiles at Rebecca, her face is young and unguarded. 'Can I help you?'

Rebecca struggles to reply. 'I wanted to make sure I'm in the right place,' she says finally.

'Let me take a look at your boarding passes so I can check.'

Rebecca nods, but when she looks through her handbag, the boarding passes aren't there. Alarm sets in and her hand starts to shake as she searches for them.

'Take your time,' the woman tells her. 'This always happens to me—I know I've put something in my bag, but as soon as I need it, I can't find it for love or money.'

The zippered part, she remembers. She put them in the zippered compartment. And as soon as she slides a hand into it, her fingers rest on the first of two curved edges of cardboard.

'Yep,' says the woman when Rebecca hands them to her, 'right place, right flight. Seats 17A and 17B. We'll be boarding in about twenty minutes.'

They are long minutes and when, finally, the first boarding call comes, Rebecca stands up too soon, for theirs are neither first-class nor business-class tickets.

When the second announcement comes—for economy passengers rows fifteen to thirty—she and Sebastian are at the head of the line.

The flight attendant who guards the walkway entrance shows little interest in either of their passports and as he feeds Rebecca's boarding pass through the machine, he looks not at her but above her, his eyes flat. A sharp beeping from the machine suddenly brings him to life.

'Wait over there, please, madam,' he says without meeting her eyes.

A wave of fear washes through her as she grabs Sebastian and pulls him over to her. As they wait, they watch the others—all the others—pass through the scanner, down the walkway and out of sight.

When there is no one left to process, the flight attendant leaves the scanner and comes over to them, their boarding passes in his hand. His earlier lethargy is gone. Now he is frowning. 'Mrs Chuma,' he says, 'there is a problem with your seats.'

She waits for what she knows will follow. *The plane is full. There is no more room on the plane.*

Instead he puts a hand out towards her and says something she doesn't catch, because his words are quick and mumbled, and hard to understand. 'Sorry?'

This time he speaks loudly and more slowly, exaggerating each syllable. 'We have had to change your seats. These are your new boarding passes.'

Suddenly, it dawns on her that everything will be all right. They will catch the plane and it will be all right. But the flight attendant is looking concerned. 'Do . . . you . . . speak . . . English?'

Rebecca hardly registers the question and so it is Sebastian who answers for her. 'Yes,' he says, in his beautiful accent, 'English is the language we speak.'

And so they pass through the scanner and go down the walkway and onto the aeroplane. At the entrance, another flight attendant greets them with a smile that seems genuine. 'You must be our lucky last.'

Rebecca has been allocated a window seat and through the darkness, the lights of the airport terminal are bright. There are entertainment screens on the back of the seats in front of them and earphones are handed out together with hot towels. For Sebastian there is a children's activity pack and, even though he is already eleven and getting too old for pencils and mazes, still he seems pleased to have been given it.

Rebecca, by contrast, is agitated as she waits for the plane to depart. Reassurance comes in the smallest of increments: the sound of the doors closing, the illumination of the seatbelt sign, the beginning of the safety demonstration and then, finally, the overhead request for cabin crew to take their seats as slowly the plane begins to move. Only when the plane tilts forward to lift off the ground and into the sky does Rebecca start to breathe normally.

Looking out into the night, she watches as the lights of the terminal recede. Gone and gone and gone. The relief nearly cripples her. But though her body is limp with fatigue, her mind won't rest. At first, this is because she is still fearful, but gradually, as the hours pass, her fear fades to resentment then flares into anger. *Where were you?* she wants to scream at him. *Where were you?* But she cannot, because he isn't here. He still isn't here.

If she had the energy, she would cry. But she can't. Instead, leaning her head back, she closes her eyes. Finally, then, she sleeps.

When she wakes, breakfast is being served. Later, hours later, when Sebastian wakes, there is lunch. After that, there is dinner, and then, to her surprise, a descent.

There is no one to greet them at the airport.

In the terminal, they find a cash machine that spits out foreign notes so colourful they might be play money.

Outside, the light is artificial. Night again, so quickly. They follow signs and a line of lights to a taxicab rank. As they wheel their bags to the cab they have been allocated, there is a click as the boot springs open. Rebecca waits for the driver to take their bags but he doesn't get out of the car. Eventually, she heaves the bags into the boot herself.

When she and Sebastian get into the back of the cab, a light comes on but the driver doesn't turn around to address them. Instead, he looks at them in the rear-view mirror. 'Where to?' he asks.

'Brindle,' she says. 'We are going to Arthur Street, Brindle.'

In the mirror, the driver looks put out. 'Two hours,' he says. 'Two hours I've been waiting here and what do I get? Brindle. You might as well ask me to take you to the other side of the airport.' He leans forward to switch on the radio and turns it up loudly.

She bristles at his rudeness.

Sebastian is oblivious to it. He simply slides along to the far side of the back seat and, pressing his face up against the window, looks out. From her own side, she copies him. Within minutes they are on a freeway, banners lit up on the side advertising cars and cameras. As they drive on, the freeway becomes more desolate and they pass waterside industrial works and shipping containers stacked up in piles. A left-hand turn and the freeway is done, another left and another one and suddenly there is no traffic at all, only suburban streets and streetlights.

When she gives him the street number, the driver stops in front of a block of flats. 'Thirty-two dollars,' he says, although the meter reads twenty-five.

'Thirty-two?' Rebecca queries.

The driver looks at her in the mirror. 'Airport tax.'

She doesn't add a tip and he doesn't help her with the bags.

Once he has driven off, she takes a look at the building in front of them. Emmanuel had told her it was an apartment, but still she had imagined a house. And in the street-lit darkness, she sees that it is a street of houses and that this building, this apartment block, is out of place here.

And so, rather than relief and solace, she feels disappointment. This is wrong of her, but she is too tired to chastise herself for it. Too tired, even, to make her way to apartment number four, knock on the door and whisper, 'It's us.'

Sebastian draws close to her. 'Ma?' To her surprise, he is shivering.

'Ma,' he says, 'shouldn't we go in?'

She nods. Of course, they should go in.

There is a glass door at the front of the building and, as they approach it, they are flooded in a light so bright it makes her freeze like an animal.

The line of buzzers beside the glass door is labelled, in descending order, from one to six. Beside most of the numbers there is a name, but beside buzzer number 4, which should read Chuma, there is nothing. Rather than pressing the buzzer, she gives the door a little push, just in case. Surprisingly, it opens, and so, pulling their suitcases behind them, she and Sebastian walk through into a foyer area. It has a strange smell, like that of a hospital, a smell so strong Rebecca has to put a hand up to her nose.

There is no lift in the foyer, only a stairwell. The stairs are not carpeted. Instead, the concrete has simply been painted grey to match the railing she clutches as she drags her bag up the stairs.

At the top of the first flight of stairs there are two doors. A gold number 1 is screwed onto the first door, a silver number 2 to the second door. They rest here between the two numbers, while she catches her breath. Door number 4, with its own metal plate, is at the top of the next flight of stairs. Apart from the number itself, there is nothing to distinguish it from doors 1, 2 or 3.

She knocks softly.

Although the footsteps come quickly, still the door doesn't open. Instead, she hears his voice from behind the door. 'Hello?'

She makes to answer him but finds she has no words.

'Hello?' he repeats as the latch clicks and the door is pulled open.

There he is, then, in the doorway, wearing a grey woollen pullover and grey pleated trousers. No shoes. Just socks.

And in that moment, that first moment, he is completely unfamiliar to her. Perhaps she, too, is as unfamiliar to him for he just stares at her.

'Rebecca,' he says finally, his voice both gentle and confused. 'Rebecca.'

She stays where she is, planted to the spot, while Sebastian pushes in front of her and reaches for his father. 'Dad,' he says, his voice high and panicked. 'Dad.' And in the doorway, his face bewildered, Emmanuel Chuma draws his son to him and holds him tight. As the boy begins to shudder and sob, Rebecca watches on, like an observer moved by curiosity to stop and stare. In her head, she makes simple sentences that a young child might be made to read. *Here are my husband and my son. My husband holds my son and my son cries.*

She does not cry. She doesn't think that she can; indeed, it is possible she has no tears left. Fright, she thinks, might well have dried them all up.

By contrast, Sebastian has many tears and while he cries, Emmanuel keeps a tight hold on him. Only when the boy has stilled does he release him and turn his attention to her. He doesn't enfold her in his arms. Instead, he handles her as one might a nervous animal—slowly and tentatively. Taking her by the hand, he leads her into a room that is simply furnished: a sofa that faces a television on top of a sideboard, a low coffee table in between.

He ushers her to the sofa and leaves her there. He returns with a cup of tea, which he gives to her. Heat radiates from it and this comforts her. 'Drink it, my love,' he tells her.

She hears water running. 'Sebastian?' she asks.

Emmanuel sits down beside her. 'I told him to take a shower. He will feel better with a shower.'

She nods.

'And you too,' he says. 'You will benefit from a shower.'

She is comforted by his words, by how he speaks. Thoughtful, helpful words. Gentle words of suggestion. Not *you must have a shower*. Rather, *you will benefit from a shower*. She has always loved his words.

'Yes,' she says. 'Yes.'

There will be questions, she thinks. Soon, he will ask her all the questions she would expect him to have. She hopes it won't be tonight. She hopes it will be some time before they are asked.

She follows him into an alcove that turns out to be the kitchen. It is a ridiculously small space, little more than an afterthought, it seems. A kitchen should have a table, but there is no room for a table here. And yet there is no table in the other room, either.

And so the first question she asks him is this: 'Where is the table, the dining-room table?'

He looks away when he answers her. 'The apartment was not furnished with a table. With the exchange rate, accommodation is very expensive here. In the smaller bedroom, there is a desk. That is where I have been working.'

'And for eating?'

He gestures out towards the television area. 'Mostly I sit on the sofa to eat,' he says.

He is making toast now, and he spreads it with butter and honey before he cuts it in half, diagonally. 'Have this,' he says.

She sits on the sofa to eat it and the honey runs from the toast onto her fingers, leaving them sticky. She has nothing with which to wipe herself and can only lift her fingers up to him to show him what has happened. He nods gravely, although at another time he might have laughed at her: his elegant, articulate wife, helpless with sticky fingers.

He returns to the kitchen for paper towels, then, sitting beside her, carefully wipes each of her fingers clean.

'So,' he says, when he is done, 'you are here.'

She nods.

'I was not expecting you so soon.'

Again she nods. 'I know.'

She doesn't want to talk anymore and he doesn't ask anything more of her. Instead, he stands in front of her and, putting a hand under each of her arms, lifts her up. 'A shower now, then some sleep.'

Taking her hand, he leads her to the bathroom door. 'Here is the shower, my love. I will see to Sebastian.'

It is an old bathroom. A pink ceramic toilet bowl and a matching pink ceramic bath take up the length of one wall. Opposite the bath is a cheap white vanity, edges of laminate pushed open by water-swollen chipboard. There is a shower hidden behind the vanity and when she steps into it, the small, hexagonal tiles are cool under her feet. When she turns the tap on, the water is hot and plentiful. But as she lifts her face up to the water, exhaustion sets in and it takes all her energy to turn off the taps, step out of the shower and reach for the towel Emmanuel has left for her.

There is a bedroom to her left. It is sparsely furnished, with only a double bed, a bedside table on either side of it, and a built-in wardrobe. Inside the wardrobe are Emmanuel's clothes. She takes his dressing-gown off its hanger, puts it on and walks back into the living room.

Emmanuel smiles. 'I like you in my clothes.'

She passes a hand over the front of the gown but says nothing. Sebastian is sitting on the sofa eating a toasted sandwich. He has a remote control by his side but when he points it at the television, Rebecca shakes her head. 'It is late,' she says, 'and you have already missed a night's sleep.'

He cocks his head to the side, questioning this. True, she thinks, he slept in the plane and true, it is not yet night at home. But still.

'Finish your sandwich, then you should try to sleep. To get used to the time difference.' He is reluctant, but he is an obedient child and, when he has eaten, he takes himself off to the smaller of the two bedrooms: the one with the desk, the one where Emmanuel has been working. She should go in to settle him, to see that he is all right.

She, herself, is not all right and without Sebastian there, the space between them is wide. 'Would you like more to eat?' Emmanuel asks her.

She shakes her head. 'No,' she says.

She knows she should offer him something more: a couple of words, the beginning of a conversation. But she doesn't.

Later, in the bedroom, Emmanuel unties the cord of the dressing-gown and slips the gown off her shoulders. It unsettles her to be naked in front of him—even though he is her husband and even though he knows her body well—and when he reaches for her, she feels herself flinch.

❧

In the morning, she wakes early: before Emmanuel and before Sebastian. In the living room, her suitcase still stands beside the front door and she rummages through it until she finds a pair of trousers and a pullover.

Once she is dressed, she slips outside.

The morning is cold and she has to tuck her hands up in her sleeves to keep herself warm. But she needs to walk. This is what she needs to do. It doesn't matter where. So she walks along Arthur Street and when, at the end of it, she finds a road that slopes downwards, she takes it. To her great surprise, she finds that what Emmanuel has told her is not a joke: the ocean is at the end of the street, right there.

A footpath follows the line of the water past a driveway that becomes a boat ramp. On the embankment beside the ramp, there are rows of tin boats. Some are tied up to metal stakes driven into the ground while others are just there, unattended and unprotected. If she knew what to do, and if she dared to do it, she would take one and row it out onto the water.

Instead, she follows the footpath along until she comes to a swimming pool, which is not a pool in its own right, but rather part of the ocean itself. There is only one swimmer in the pool—a large, pale man who swims with long, slow strokes—and Rebecca stops to watch him.

On his sixth lap, he stops for a rest and, leaning his elbows up on the edge of the pool, pushes his hair away from his face. She sees then that he is older than she first thought. Sixty, maybe more. 'Bit fresh today,' he says.

When she nods, he smiles and waves. 'Hooroo then,' he says to her.

She's not sure what to say back. Hesitantly, she returns the wave. 'Hooroo,' she repeats, her voice quiet, self-conscious.

This makes him laugh before he turns away from her to swim to the other end of the pool.

As she watches him go, she lifts her gaze beyond him, beyond the pool, and across to the open water of the narrow bay; so narrow it seems no distance at all to the sandstone plateau on the other side of it. Were it warmer, she might make her way across, stroke by stroke, until, reaching the rock, she would pull herself up on it, turn herself around and quietly look out. That's what she would do, she thinks. And yet the truth of it is that while there are so many things she can do, swimming is not one of them: she would be as capable of crossing the bay as she would be of flapping her way into space. And so, instead, she returns her gaze to the lone swimmer and marvels that, after everything, this is where she should find herself.

Terry

Thirty minutes until lunch and there's a lot of fidgeting going on. Then again, that's how it always is at the end of term, with everyone just itching to get started on the holidays.

Terry's got his back to the class while he writes up the topic for the day but from the corner of his eye, he sees Ethan lunge at Kurt, his fingers wrapped around a sharpened pencil.

'Ethan Thompson,' he bellows, 'keep your pencils to yourself or I'll sharpen my own and stick it in your eye.'

Silence then, and things stay quiet until he calls the kids to the rug. When he grabs a dog-eared paperback from his desk and pulls his chair over, they all start to wriggle in anticipation.

'So,' he says, 'I think we need a bit of a recap. Can anyone tell me what's happened so far?'

Ethan's hand shoots up. He stretches it up hard, and when he can't reach any higher, starts to groan to be chosen. Terry lets him have it. 'Ethan?'

'Well, Mr P, there's these golden tickets hidden inside of some chocolate bars. And Charlie, he really wants to get a golden ticket so his grandpa buys him a chocolate bar, but there's no golden ticket in it and so Charlie's really gutted.'

Terry's eyes circle the room and land on Jade. 'And what's the golden ticket for?' he asks her.

She rolls her eyes. 'For a stupid visit to a stupid chocolate factory.'

Terry looks thoughtful. 'For a stupid visit to a stupid chocolate factory. Thank you, Jade. Anyone else?'

Bridie's voice is thin but insistent. 'If you win a golden ticket, you get to go to Willy Wonka's Chocolate Factory.'

'That's exactly right, Bridie. And as Ethan so ably put it, so far our Charlie has been out of luck, hasn't he?' With that, he starts to read.

Charlie entered the shop and laid the damp fifty pence on the counter.

'One Wonka's Whipple-Scrumptious Fudgemallow Delight,' he said, remembering how much he had loved the one he had on his birthday.

The man behind the counter looked fat and well-fed. He had big lips and fat cheeks and a very fat neck. The fat around his neck bulged out all around the top of his collar like a rubber ring. He turned and reached behind him for the chocolate bar, then he turned back again and handed it to Charlie. Charlie grabbed it and quickly tore off the wrapper and took an enormous bite. Then he took another . . . and another . . . and oh, the joy of being able to cram large pieces of something sweet and solid into one's mouth! The sheer blissful joy of being able to fill one's mouth with rich, solid food!

Terry lifts his eyes off the page to take a look at the kids. They're quiet now, each of them intent on the story. It's always the same, whenever he reads to them, they're all little angels. Because in the end, that's what everyone wants, isn't it, to be read a story?

'You look like you wanted that one, sonny,' the shopkeeper said pleasantly.

Charlie nodded, his mouth bulging with chocolate.

The shopkeeper put Charlie's change on the counter. 'Take it easy,' he said. 'It'll give you a tummy-ache if you swallow it like that without chewing.'

Charlie went on wolfing the chocolate. He couldn't stop. And in less than half a minute, the whole thing had disappeared down his throat. He was quite out of breath, but he felt marvellously, extraordinarily happy. He reached out a hand to take the change. Then he paused. His eyes were just above the level of the counter. They were staring at the silver coins lying there. The coins were all five-penny pieces. There were nine of them altogether. Surely it wouldn't matter if he spent just one more . . .

There's a knock at the door. Terry frowns. Marking the page with his finger, he stops reading. 'Come in!' he calls out, his voice sharp.

It's one of the Thomas kids. The littlest one. Joel. No, Jake. There's that many of them, he has to think about it. 'Yes, Jake?'

But with the whole class staring at him, the poor kid gets so nervous he can't say a thing.

So Terry tries again. 'What can I do for you, Jake?'

Looking straight at Terry, the boy spills out the words. 'Ms Mathews wants to see you in her office straightaway.'

Terry lifts an eyebrow. 'Is that what Ms Mathews said?'

The boy nods.

Terry tries not to sound annoyed. 'Thank you, Jake,' he says, making an effort to choose his words carefully. 'Please tell Ms Mathews that I'm not able to come *straightaway* but that I'll be there once the lunch bell has gone.' And turning back to the class, he opens his mouth to resume reading.

The boy doesn't move. 'Ms Mathews, she said straightaway.'

Terry doesn't look at him. 'Yes, Jake, I heard you.' It's an effort to keep the irritation out of his voice. 'But I won't be able to come down to see Ms Mathews until after the lunch bell has gone.'

It's too much for the boy this time and although he loiters at the door a little longer, eventually he turns around and leaves the room. Only then does Terry return to the story.

'I think,' he said quietly, 'I think . . . I'll have just one more of those chocolate bars. The same kind as before, please.'

'Why not?' the fat shopkeeper said, reaching behind him again and taking another Whipple-Scrumptious Fudgemallow Delight from the shelf. He laid it on the counter.

Charlie picked it up and tore off the wrapper . . . and suddenly . . . from underneath the wrapper . . . there came . . .

And before he's finished the sentence, the lunch bell rings. No one moves. No one jumps up to grab their lunch, no one stands up, no one calls out. They all just stay seated, waiting for him to keep going.

But Terry decides not to give it to them, not even that one sentence that will set their minds at rest. No, instead he'll make them wait. Then, as a surprise, he'll read for longer on Friday.

❧

School rules stipulate that all children sit in their classrooms to eat their lunch quietly. Only after they have finished eating are they allowed outside to play. It's a new initiative, brought in under Laurie's leadership. Occupational health and safety, she reckons.

Terry guffawed when she came up with that one. *Occupational health and safety to make them eat their lunch at their desks? You've got to be flaming joking.*

The reason students were to eat their lunches in the classroom instead of out in the playground, Laurie advised, was so they wouldn't choke.

So they wouldn't choke? Choke on what? A cheese sandwich?

Well, he wouldn't be having it. He wouldn't be following some ridiculous directive to keep the kids inside at their desks when they could be outside in the fresh air. The way he got around it was a masterstroke. Even Tania agreed the outside classroom was an act of genius.

So every day, now, as soon as the lunch bell goes, his kids and Tania's all sit down on the lawn—aka the outside classroom—to eat their lunch. It's also a chance to catch up with Tania and have a bit of a chat.

Except for today. Because today, he has to report to the tin-pot dictator.

Irene, the school administrator, is at the computer when he walks into the office. Like Terry, she's been at the school forever.

'Don't they give you a lunch hour anymore?' he asks her.

Normally that would make her laugh or at least smile. Today, she does neither.

'You okay, love?' he asks her, the *love* out before he can stop himself. It's another thing he's been told not to do: no loves, no darlings, no sweethearts, no dears. In terms of inappropriate behaviour, it seems to be up there with having sex with a colleague. So he's going to have to bite his tongue next time. But for now, he just tips his head towards the principal's office. 'She in?'

Irene nods. 'She's expecting you.'

'Is she just?' Pulling a face, Terry waits for a reaction: a smile or a raised eyebrow or something. But she gives him nothing at all.

'Everything all right?' he asks.

She scratches the side of her nose. 'So-so,' she says, without meeting his eyes.

It's unlike her to be curt, but he doesn't want to pry, so he just gives her a smile. 'Better not keep her waiting then, hey?'

He taps on the door and, without waiting for an answer, turns the handle and pushes it open.

Laurie frowns as she looks up from her desk. 'Oh, Terry,' she says. She doesn't ask him in so he finds himself stuck in the doorway, waiting for an invitation to approach. God, he hates being part of the hierarchy game. With Diane, it had never been an issue: he'd just bowl on in, take a seat and start talking.

This one, she'd like him to dip his head before he enters the sacred space. Young enough to be his daughter and here she is expecting the *yes, ma'am, no ma'am* routine. Well, she won't be getting it from him, that's for sure.

'I'm told you wanted to see me,' he says, the words already angry in his mouth.

Laurie extends an arm. 'Take a seat, Terry.'

Now he's been asked, he'd rather not, quite frankly. He'd rather stay standing, hear what she's got to say, then take off back to the kids. But he wants to make this quick so he does what he's told.

'Thanks for coming, Terry.' Sitting forward in her big chair, she passes him a letter. 'I've received some correspondence from head office,' she says.

He takes the letter but, rather than looking at it, holds it loosely in his hand. 'What is it?'

She doesn't answer him; she just tells him to read it.

He's nonplussed by the request. 'What, now?'

When she nods, he gives a grunt as he feels in his pocket for his reading glasses.

The letter itself is hard to read—the ink is light and the font small. He frowns as he tries to work it out. It's addressed to Laurie.

As you are aware, the Prohibited Persons Act was enacted earlier this year. The Act aims to prevent anyone who is found to be a 'prohibited person' from undertaking or remaining in child-related employment.

For the purposes of this Act, a 'prohibited person' means a person convicted of a serious sex offence.

Following your inquiry and the recent consolidation of interjurisdictional databases, it has come to the Department's attention that Mr Terence John Pritchard is a 'prohibited person' in accordance with the Act.

As a consequence of this, any further child-related employment engaged in by Mr Pritchard would be in breach of section 7 of the Act which carries a maximum penalty of 2 years imprisonment.

The Department has determined to advise you of this situation as a matter of urgency to enable you to make alternative arrangements for Mr Pritchard's current teaching commitments, effective immediately.

Mr Pritchard will be advised in writing of this situation. To enable an early resolution to this matter, the Department has determined to allow Mr Pritchard to take immediate retirement. He would otherwise be required to take leave pending the commencement of termination procedures by the Department.

The second page is a computer printout with a soft watermark in the shape of a shield. Below it is Terry's full name and his date of birth. Underneath are details that make the bile rise in his stomach.

So, he thinks, it's not finished, after all. After all this time, it's come to get him.

He drops the letter into his lap and turns his head to the side, so he doesn't have to look at the words, so he doesn't have to look at her.

The room is quiet but noise from the playground comes in through the window behind her. It must be playtime already. Funny, he didn't hear the second bell ring.

He clears his throat. 'So,' he says, and his voice comes out phlegmy, 'what does that mean? Now. What happens now?'

Her voice is crisp but the words are rushed. 'You'll need to retire or take leave.'

'What do you mean?' His mouth, suddenly dry, makes it hard to swallow. 'I've got to get back to the kids.'

She shakes her head. 'You can't go back to the kids, Terry.'

'Eighteen years. I've been here for eighteen years.' His voice is low and hoarse and when he feels a prickling at the back of his eyes, he realises, with horror, that he's about to cry. *No*, he shouts to himself. Not here. Not in front of her. But it's already too late for that.

The expression on Laurie's face softens. It is pity, he realises with a shock. She is looking at him with an expression of pity. 'I'm sorry, Terry, but you'll have to go straightaway.'

At first he doesn't comprehend what she is saying. Only slowly does it dawn on him. That he is being asked to leave. Immediately.

'I can't,' he says, and there is a note of panic in his voice. 'My bag. My things. I've left them all in the classroom.'

'Don't worry,' Laurie tells him, her voice surprisingly soft. 'Irene's sorting that out now. Your briefcase is being brought down to the office. Anything else will be sent home to you.'

'What's happening?' he cries. 'What in God's name is happening?'

Laurie looks down at the desk. He watches her throat move as she swallows. 'I'll arrange for your class to spend the afternoon with Tania,' she says.

As he leaves, he passes Irene at her work station. When she looks up, he brandishes the letter at her. 'You knew about this, didn't you?'

Her face turns an unhappy shade of red as her eyes flick over to the letter then down to the floor.

'How long have we known each other, Irene? Fifteen years? Sixteen? You could have warned me. You could have let me know what was coming.'

Keeping her eyes down, the woman says nothing. Tears drip down onto her keyboard.

When he sees this, he feels ashamed of himself. 'That was unfair, love,' he says as he puts a hand on her shoulder. 'I'm sorry. I'm sorry.'

She shakes her head but says nothing. And so, without another word, he leaves her, and the office.

Back in the playground, he hears Ethan calling out to him. 'You want to play footy with us, Mr P?'

When Terry pretends not to have heard him, Ethan tries again, bellowing as he runs across to him. 'You playing, Mr P?'

The letter is still in Terry's hand. Folding it up, he sticks it in his shirt pocket. Squeezing his eyes tight, he takes a deep breath. 'Mate, can't think of anything I'd rather do than thrash you all right now. Unfortunately, there's a bit of a problem I've got to sort out at home.'

Ethan's face drops. 'It's not Bouncer, is it?'

Terry rubs the boy's back. Despite all the swimming, he's still such a little thing: he can feel the shoulder blades sticking out from under his shirt. 'No, mate. Nothing wrong with Bouncer.'

Ethan looks relieved. 'That's good, Mr P. Glad Bouncer's okay. And, Mr P, my mum told me to remind you about the show—you know, the Year 6 show. If you want any help with it.'

The back of Terry's eyes start to sting. 'Listen, mate,' he says, trying hard to keep his voice firm, 'can't stop right now.'

The moment he gets into the car, Terry feels his body sag. It's all he can do to start the engine and get moving.

How strange to be returning home in the middle of the day. When he turns the key in the lock, there's a galloping inside the house that becomes a scratching and a whining at the door. And as soon as he pushes the door open, Bouncer's wet, sniffing nose buries itself in his hand.

They make their way to the kitchen, man and dog, Bouncer jumping around in circles, beside himself.

It's lunchtime, Terry remembers then. In the fridge he finds left-over bolognese to have on toast. But when the toast is done and the meat reheated, his stomach turns at the thought of it. So he leaves it on the kitchen bench, walks into the lounge room, falls into an armchair and starts to shake. *What now?* This is the question that pulsates through him. This is the question that promises to bring him undone.

❧

Later that afternoon, he hears Michelle's voice float down the hallway. 'Hello, Bouncer boy, hello, Bouncer boy, boy, boy.'

Terry listens as she makes her way down to the kitchen: another murmured word to Bouncer, a humming noise to herself, the jingling of the keys as she throws them on the key dish on the kitchen bench. Only then does she notice him.

'God, Terry,' she cries, 'you scared me. I thought you were staying back to finish the reports.'

He shapes his lips into a smile. 'Changed my mind.'

She looks confused. 'Why, you sick or something?'

He shakes his head. 'No, love, I'm fine. Just changed my mind.'

Michelle raises an eyebrow. 'Well, that's a first for Mr-can't-get-me-out-of-the-school-even-when-it's-holidays.' She spies the chicken on the bench. 'What's this?'

'Made a bit of a marinade. Honey and soy. Thought I'd put them on the barbie.'

Michelle lifts the bowl and, giving it a swish, peers through the cling wrap. 'Good for you, chef man.' She rests a hand on his back. 'Cuppa?'

He nods. 'A cuppa sounds good, love.'

She has to raise her voice to be heard over the kettle. 'How was your day, then, apart from the early mark?'

He shrugs. 'You know, nothing special.'

'Elsie okay?'

He shakes his head. 'Getting there. The reading's coming on, so that's something.'

'Good. That's good. You've done some great work with that girl, you really have.'

He doesn't trust himself to answer her. Instead, he sticks his head in the fridge, eyes blinking hard so they won't give him away, and comes out with a couple of zucchini. 'I'll put these on too,' he mumbles.

Michelle has a cup of tea in each hand. She sips one, grimaces, then hands it to him. 'This must be yours.' He follows her into the lounge room and joins her on the sofa.

'What's with the thinking ahead for dinner?' she asks him. 'You trying to butter me up for something?'

His laugh is forced but she doesn't seem to notice. 'Don't you trust me to do something nice once in a while?'

'Well, you're hardly Mr Metrosexual, are you, love?' Her hand is soft on the back of his neck and he has a sudden urge to curl up in a ball and, like a child, bury his head in her lap.

'Metro-what?' he asks, but his throat is tight and he has to cough before he can get the words out.

'Metrosexual. You know, Mr Can-do-it—in the kitchen, in the laundry, in the bedroom, in the garden. Mr Metrosexual can do a bit of everything.'

Terry pretends to ponder that while he tries to compose himself. 'Think you're right, love. I really don't think you've married a Mr Metrosexual.'

Michelle rests her head on his shoulder. 'Don't think I'm after a Mr Metrosexual. You'll have to do.'

But will I? It is a new thought, and one that makes his stomach turn. Will I still do? Even now?

She knows nothing of it. Nothing at all. Because he's never spoken about it. Because it's never come up. Because he thought he'd never have to think about it again. Because he thought it was over.

The phone rings and, as usual, Michelle leaps up to get it. *Let it go*, he always tells her. *If it's important, they'll leave a message. If it's not, they'll hang up.* But she never listens.

She's a long time on the phone, which isn't so unusual, but when she comes back to him, she is pale and her face is creased with confusion.

'What's happened?' she asks, her voice panic-stricken. 'What's happened?'

Hearing her makes him sit bolt upright.

'What do you mean, love?' He tries to keep his voice steady, but it comes out shrill.

'That was Tania,' she says. 'Laurie Mathews told her you won't be coming back to school.' Her face crumples. 'Terry, what's happened? What's going on?'

Term 3

Joan

Joan is in the kitchen when she hears the commotion. She hurries to her bedroom—the one room that looks onto the street. When she draws back the curtains, she sees a large removalist's truck, the words *Quality Removals* written on the side in pink and black letters. The back of the truck has folded down to form a ramp to the road. Out of it comes a household's worth of furniture: a lounge suite, a dining room suite, a washing machine, a dryer, beds, a refrigerator, a sideboard, a couple of chests of drawers, a bookcase. Who, she asks herself with a flutter of excitement, is moving into Mr Edwards' house?

∞

The next morning, as she is buttering her toast, Joan hears voices in Mr Edwards' garden. She stops, mid-action, the knife in the air, and listens. There is a woman's voice and a child's voice. A girl, she thinks. She can't make out the words, only the melody of their voices. Funny to hear a young voice in Mr Edwards' garden. Before, there had only been the sound of his transistor radio, the volume up loud as he pottered around.

Hearing these new voices makes her feel happy. There is a family next door, she thinks. A family.

As she finishes her breakfast, she tries to imagine who they might be. They will be a family of four, she decides. An older boy and a younger girl. They will have friends over and the house will come alive with the noise of children playing. And Joan will sit on the porch, on the swing seat, and she will listen to them.

But first, she thinks, she should meet them, her new neighbours. She should welcome them. This, she knows, is what neighbours do. Her mother wouldn't have hesitated for a minute. Her mother would have simply gone over, knocked on the door and invited herself in for a cup of tea. Joan doesn't have this in her, but surely she could do something. She could shout across the back fence. *Hello,* she could call out. *I'm Joan, your neighbour.* Or she could watch from her bedroom window and, when she sees them leave the house, she could leave her house too, so they would all meet on the footpath, as if by accident.

Or, she hears her mother whisper, *you could make them a cake, Joanie.*

A tray of biscuits she can manage, but baking cakes has never been her forte and Joan shakes her head at the idea.

Come on, Joanie, her mother insists. *Nothing fancy, just a little something.*

As she washes up the breakfast dishes, she manages to talk herself into it. A sultana cake, she decides, that's what she will make. So she takes out her mother's cookbook and gets started. She measures out the sultanas, whips up the butter and the sugar, adds the eggs and the flour and she's done. Carefully, she pours the mixture into a loaf pan.

To her surprise and delight, when she pulls it out of the oven it looks absolutely beautiful.

Just a little something to welcome you to the street. That's what she'll say.

But when, both nervous and excited, she walks next door to Mr Edwards' house and rings the doorbell—once and then again— there is no answer.

It is some time later when Joan hears a car pull up. A spark of nervousness shoots through her as she rushes to her bedroom to take a look. As she has hoped, the car parks outside Mr Edwards' house. But for a long time, the car doors stay closed until, finally, a woman gets out. She walks slowly to the house. She seems tired. Small wonder, after such a move.

And although Joan is itching to run over with the cake, she knows she can't just land on the woman's doorstep like that. Not when she's just arrived home. She'll need to give her a bit of time.

So she waits an hour before she makes her way over. But at Mr Edwards' front gate, she falters. What if she forgets what to say? What if she just stands at the door with the cake in her hand and can't manage to say a word?

She is so nervous she almost turns back. And yet she doesn't. Instead, she opens the latch on the little gate and, after such a long time, walks through it once more.

She rings the doorbell.

Nothing at first, then footsteps up the hallway. Quick footsteps, much quicker than Mr Edwards, who, for the last few years, had limped slowly to the door. And the image of Mr Edwards is so vivid that when the door does open, she is surprised not to see him there in front of her. Confusion makes her stumble on her words. 'Hello,' she says in a rush, her arms outstretched, 'here's a cake.'

The young woman at the door looks completely bewildered.

I've mucked it up, Joan admonishes herself. I've mucked it all up. 'Sorry,' she says, and her voice catches.

But the woman's eyes are gentle. 'Hello,' she says. 'I'm Nina— Nina Foreman.'

She is a pretty woman, Joan sees, with curly hair that falls over her shoulders. For a woman she is tall, a good foot taller than Joan, and she has a boyish body: thin, with long arms and long legs. Her face is pale and her eyes, a watery blue, have dark shadows under them.

Joan swallows before she tries again. 'I'm Joan. I'm just next door. I thought you might like a sultana cake.'

The woman smiles as she takes the cake. 'I love sultana cake.'

Tentatively, Joan smiles back. 'I've heard your little girl,' she ventures.

'My Emily?' the woman asks.

Emily, Joan thinks. So her name is Emily. It is a name she has always liked.

Over Nina's shoulder, she can see into the house and is curious to know how it looks without Mr Edwards' furniture. She would love to be asked in. Not for long, just for a cup of tea. So she hovers on the doorstep hopefully, waiting for the invitation. But instead of ushering her in, Nina Foreman excuses herself: Emily is away and she needs to use the time to get things sorted. 'Because it's school holidays,' she explains, 'and I'm a teacher so I need to get ready for the new term.'

A teacher, Joan thinks to herself, fancy that—her new next-door neighbour is a teacher. How wonderful! There is so much she would like to ask her: where she teaches, what class she has, what she likes most about it. If she were a chatting sort of person, these are the things she would ask.

But Nina is edging back now—just a little step back into the doorway—so Joan steps back too.

'I'll leave you be, then,' she says quickly as she turns to go.

Nina

She feels guilty not inviting the woman in, but the truth is she's not ready for the questions that will come up over a cup of tea and a piece of cake. Questions like: *So where has she gone, your daughter?* Or, worse still: *Where is your husband?* Better just to keep to herself.

And besides, she is tired.

The next day, she drives over to the new school to pick up a key to the classroom. The principal will be working through the holidays, that's what she's told her. So she's welcome to pop in any time.

She knocks loudly on the door of the admin building. When there is no answer, she knocks again before she tries the handle. When it turns, she pushes the door open, walks in and finds herself in an unlit hallway. 'Hello,' she calls out tentatively, 'hello?'

As she keeps walking, she comes to a door marked *Principal*. When she knocks on the door, a voice calls out, 'Come in.'

Sitting behind a large desk is a very young woman. Nina baulks when she sees her. 'Sorry,' she says, 'I was looking for the school principal.'

The woman looks across at her. 'I am the school principal,' she says coolly. 'How can I help you?'

Nina tries not to look surprised. 'I'm Nina Foreman,' she says, but it comes out too softly, so she has to clear her throat and start again. 'I'm taking over the Year 6 class.'

'Nina—of course—we've spoken.' The woman stands up to greet her, surprising her with a handshake that Nina somehow fumbles. She is dressed, Nina sees, not in jeans, as she is, but in tailored trousers and a button-up shirt.

'I'm Laurie,' she says, 'Laurie Mathews. It's good to meet you.' Reaching into her trouser pocket, she takes out a key. 'I've been carrying this around with me all week,' she says, 'waiting for you to come in.'

It sounds like a rebuke so Nina starts to apologise for not coming earlier. Laurie waves the apology away as she hands her the key. 'Don't worry about it,' she says, 'it's not like I've been anywhere else.'

The classroom is just near the hall, Laurie explains as she walks her up. When they get there, Nina finds a big smiley face stuck to the classroom door. Underneath it are the words *Welcome to 6P*. And although the foyer area leading into the classroom is empty, the classroom itself is not, and Nina is surprised to find it filled with books and paintings and artwork and handwritten projects. Even the teacher's desk, at the front of her classroom, is still covered in papers held down by a mug that says *World's Greatest Teacher*. Instead of retiring, it looks like her predecessor has simply stepped out for a moment.

'Didn't he take anything with him?' she asks, trying to hide her dismay.

Laurie surveys the room. 'Doesn't look like it, does it? But feel free to do what you want in here: rearrange, reconfigure, whatever you like. And anything you don't want, just throw it out.'

This is all the encouragement Nina needs: by the afternoon, the walls are bare, the ceiling is clear and the teacher's desk—her desk— is free of papers and pens and pencils. The mug is gone, too. All that's left are the children's desks, their chairs and a dirty red rug.

The rug can go, too, she thinks. And rolling it up as tightly as she can, she drags it into the foyer, props it up against the wall and pins a note to it. *Please dispose of this rug*, it says.

Without the rug, the classroom seems twice as big and she sets about rearranging the desks into clusters of four, a configuration recommended by the department to encourage teamwork and cooperative learning.

When she has finished, she sits at her desk to consider the room. Its emptiness is soothing and, for the first time, she finds herself looking forward to the new term.

She jumps to hear a voice behind her. When she turns around, she finds Laurie in the doorway. 'Thank God you've got rid of the rug,' she says. 'I was thinking of placing it in quarantine.'

Nina smiles. 'You don't want it, then?'

'I'd be scared I might catch something.'

She gives Nina the briefest of smiles before she clears her throat. 'Do you have a minute?' she asks. 'There're a few things I should tell you.'

What the principal tells her are things to be kept in confidence: things the rest of the staff don't know. Things about Terry Pritchard that Nina, as his replacement, really should be told. To be so trusted makes Nina feel special, but what Laurie tells her leaves her reeling.

When she has finished, Laurie gives her a lopsided smile. 'I should have warned you it wasn't pretty. But I needed to be frank with you, because you're going to have to keep an eye on the kids.

It's what we don't know that's the real concern. There have already been some worrying signs.'

'Among the kids?'

She nods. 'Some inappropriate behaviours; aggression, that sort of thing. I don't want to speculate, but when it comes down to it, a leopard doesn't change its spots, does it? That's what worries me.'

The next Monday, Nina wakes with butterflies in her stomach. She needs to be there early and, carrying Emily in her arms, she hurries to the car. But Emily is too tired for such an early start and once Nina has her strapped in the car seat she immediately falls asleep again.

The childcare centre is a new one—close to Brindle, but not in Brindle—and as luck would have it, Emily is still too sleepy to put up a fight when Nina leaves. Instead, she lets herself be deposited straight into the arms of a carer whose name Nina doesn't catch.

When Nina gets to the classroom—her classroom—she is pleased to see that the rubbish has been taken away; pleased, too, that the rug is gone and the classroom has been cleaned. All that is left is the *Welcome to 6P* sign on the classroom door. Quickly she rips that down, too. The mere thought of him—of Terry Pritchard—sickens her.

The whiteboard in the classroom covers most of the front wall. In careful, rounded letters, Nina writes the date and, under it, her name. As she writes, Marina's voice fills her head: *But why are you still using his name?*

That's right, she thinks. Why is she still using his name?

So she rubs out *Mrs* and replaces it with *Ms.* Then she rubs out *Foreman* and replaces it with *Stewart.*

But when she steps back to check what she has written, it is clear that there is something wrong with it. Something very wrong.

It's not her name, that's what's wrong with it. At least, it isn't her name anymore.

She's no longer Nina Stewart. It's as simple as that. She's Nina Foreman now. Despite everything, that's who she is. And even if he's not sure he wants to be her husband anymore, she's still his wife. And she has a right to his name.

So she rubs the board clean and starts again.

When the bell goes, she stays in the classroom. This is something she and Laurie have decided: that Laurie will bring the class up after rollcall.

They take longer than she has expected; so long she wonders whether there has been a misunderstanding and the class is still stranded at assembly. She is relieved, then, when she hears footsteps—no voices, just footsteps—and happy that hers is a class mindful of the need for silence when walking to the classroom. This, Laurie has told her, is a rule that is enforced throughout the school.

There is a knock on the door. 'Hello?' Laurie calls out as she opens the door and sticks her head in.

Behind her, heads peek through the doorway. Laurie pushes them back again. 'You boys, you can go to the end of the line for that.' Guarding the door, Laurie lets the children through one by one. With the new configuration, there is less room at the front of the classroom and when Laurie tells them to sit down, they have to squash up against each other.

My class, Nina thinks, but all they are is a blur of unfamiliar faces.

'This is Mrs Foreman,' Laurie tells them. 'She'll be your teacher for the rest of the year. Please welcome her to Brindle Public.'

From the floor, there is shuffling and some uncertain clapping.

Laurie tries again. 'Year 6,' she says, 'please say good morning to Mrs Foreman.'

Half-heartedly, they sing out, 'Good morning, Mrs Mormon,' and from somewhere in the group, she hears a loud whisper: 'Where do you reckon she's put all our stuff?'

Laurie zeroes in on a group of boys sitting together. 'Was that you, Kurt Ward?'

A brown-haired boy opens his eyes wide. 'No, miss.'

The freckled kid beside him sniggers.

'Ethan Thompson, is there something you'd like to share with the class?'

The boy—Ethan—shakes his head and looks down, but there's a smile on his face and Nina can see the little blond kid to his right trying not to laugh.

'Any problems, Mrs Foreman,' Laurie says loudly, 'just send them down to me.'

This makes the blond kid lower his head right down while his shoulders keep shaking.

Laurie turns back to the class. 'Well, Year 6, I'll let you get to know your new teacher then.'

Once she is gone, there is a shift in the room, a loosening almost, as a roomful of eyes stare up at Nina.

'Right,' she says, 'I think we'll take the roll.' To her dismay, there is a quiver in her voice. She tries to cough it out. 'Normally when we take the roll, I'd like you just to say *present*. But today, because it's our first day together, I thought we might do something a bit different.'

There's a slight rustling. This has generated some interest.

'As you can see, the classroom has changed a bit. That's because I've divided the class up into teams. Each team will be on the same table.'

When they hear this, Kurt and Ethan start to poke each other.

'So today, when I take the roll,' she continues, 'I'd like you to say *present* then listen for your table number.'

When she calls out 'Cody Archer', the skinny blond boy beside Ethan calls out, 'Present,' in a high voice. When she gives him his table number—table two—he struts across the room, half perform-ing, half self-conscious, his head turning back to look at his mates as he takes a seat.

When Elsie Burnett is also sent to table two, Cody points a finger to the side of his head like he's taking a bullet then slumps down in his seat. Nina is about to reprimand him, but Elsie doesn't seem per-turbed. Instead, with a pleasant, vague sort of smile, she ambles up to the table and sits beside him.

Kurt Ward is directed to table one, which is closest to the front of the classroom. Cody seems disappointed by this, but Kurt him-self makes a victory sign. 'Number one,' he says loudly, 'that's got to be me.'

And when Ethan Thompson gets sent to table one, he's beside himself. 'Yes,' he hisses to the ceiling, eyes closed, fists clenched. 'Yes.'

Jade Maxwell is also on table one, and as she slips into the seat beside Ethan, she gives him a tickle on the back of his neck. Nina sees that she's wearing a necklace with the letter E. They'd be better separated, she thinks.

Beside Bridie Taylor's name is an asterisk. Laurie says she's the one to keep an eye on, so Nina has put her on table one too. When she calls out her name, a tiny scrap of a thing puts up her hand. Nina is dumbfounded. Surely not, she says to herself. Surely not a little thing like her?

ༀ

For their first lesson together, Nina hands out a maths sheet. Nothing too difficult, just something to get them started.

Immediately Kurt's hand shoots up. 'Miss,' he says, 'why did you take down all our paintings and that?'

This makes the rest of the class look up.

She isn't prepared for the question so she just tells them the truth. 'I thought it would be good to start afresh this term.'

Kurt keeps his hand up. 'What do you mean, miss?'

'I thought it would be a good idea to start again this term, to decorate the room together as a new class.'

Kurt shakes his head hard. 'But we didn't ask to be a new class, miss, we just wanted to be the same one. We just wanted to keep on being 6P and that. That's what we wanted, miss.'

Kurt has a pleasant voice, melodic and casual, but Nina feels like he's just slapped her. 'Well, Kurt, I'm sorry, but that's the way it is. You're in 6F now, not 6P. And even though it's a different name, you're all still together, aren't you? You're all still in the same class.'

'But, miss, how come we got you now, instead of Mr P? How come Mr P left?'

She does have an answer to this question, one that she and Laurie nutted out together. 'Well, Kurt, Mr Pritchard has reached an age where he doesn't have to work anymore, so he decided to retire.'

While the others mull this over, Ethan rails against it. 'But he told us all this stuff he was going to do so we'd be good for high school and that. So, I mean, why wouldn't he wait until then? Why didn't he wait and retire next year?'

'I don't know,' Nina says softly. 'I don't know about that.'

Elsie puts her hand up. 'Why don't you ask him, miss? Why don't you ask him and then you can tell us what he said?'

There is murmuring, then a nodding murmuring, and Cody calls out, 'Yeah, miss. You could ask him why he left.'

Nina feels cornered. 'I don't know,' she says, faltering. 'I don't know where he lives.'

Little Bridie holds up a skinny hand and her voice, soft and high, wobbles as she speaks. 'I'll ask my nan,' she says. 'She'll know.'

No! Nina wants to shout. *Not you, not any of you. And especially not you.* But that's not what she says. 'I'll think about it,' she tells them. 'I'll have to think about it.'

❧

After school, she stops by Laurie's office. 'Do you have a moment?' she asks.

Laurie frowns at the computer before she looks up. If there's a look of irritation on her face, it's only a momentary thing. 'Sure,' she says.

'The class want to know what happened to Terry Pritchard. They want to know why he left so suddenly.'

This time the irritation settles on her face. 'I thought we'd dealt with that. He retired, simple as that.'

'But he promised to see them through the year. They want to know why he didn't.'

Laurie shrugs. 'That's too bad. All the students need to know is that Terry Pritchard has retired and you're their new teacher. Nothing more than that.'

The answer doesn't satisfy her. 'But they feel let down because they don't understand what's happened.'

Laurie frowns again. 'What do you want me to say? It's not the last time they'll be let down in their lives. And anyway, getting rid of Terry Pritchard is the best thing that could have happened to them, we both know that. In the long run, they'll be thanking us for it.'

The next day, Laurie is at the classroom door again. This time, she has a boy with her; a boy whose skin is so dark it's practically black. He's new to the school, Laurie tells her. His name is Sebastian, Sebastian Chuma.

He's wearing the school uniform but there's something odd about it. It takes Nina a moment to work out what it is. It's the socks. He's wearing knee-length socks. None of the boys wear knee-length socks.

Sniggers come from table one. Nina fixes on Ethan Thompson and slowly shakes her head at him. It doesn't do any good. Instead, in a whisper that carries over to her, he says, 'You speaka de English?' That sets off the rest of the table again.

'Ethan Thompson,' she announces, 'I'd like you to move over to table two.'

He looks at her in disbelief. 'What do you mean, miss?'

'Just what I said, Ethan: I'd like you to move your things over to table two.' It's the only table with a spare seat. And if Ethan moves there, she'll kill two birds with one stone: she'll separate Ethan and Jade and she'll have the new boy close by if he needs any help.

But Ethan doesn't move. He just screws up his face and stays where he is.

'Ethan,' she says, more sternly this time, 'please move to the seat next to Cody.'

This time, Ethan does move. In fact, he moves so forcefully, his chair scrapes hard along the floor. His face is thunderous as he scoops everything up from his desk. Carrying it all in his hands, he takes it over to table two and dumps it on the spare desk.

Nina tries to keep her voice modulated as she turns to the new boy. 'Sebastian,' she says, 'I'd like you to sit in Ethan's old seat.'

The boy hesitates then slowly makes his way to the seat. When he sits down, he looks so uncomfortable she starts to regret what she's done. Especially when she sees Kurt staring at him strangely. When she looks more closely, she sees that he has turned himself cross-eyed. Sebastian doesn't seem bothered by it; in fact, he's just smiling at Kurt. And that spurs Kurt on, it seems, because when next she glances at him, he's still cross-eyed, but this time he's stretched his mouth wide and stuck out his tongue.

He looks so ridiculous she's tempted to laugh. Instead, she raises her voice. 'Kurt,' she says, 'that's enough.' Then she turns to Jade, who is in the seat beside Sebastian. 'I'd like you to make Sebastian feel welcome,' she says.

Jade seems pleased to have been given the job and immediately moves a little closer to him. She is not as fair as Bridie or even Elsie, but next to Sebastian, her skin seems extraordinarily pale. This is something Jade has to have noticed too, because now she's lining her arm up against his so that they are almost touching. 'Look at that,' she whispers to him, and Nina isn't sure whether to silence her or let her go. The boy doesn't seem upset; he just looks. It's true the contrast is great: he is so very dark, she is so very light and they are both so very beautiful. 'Do you burn, like in summer and that?' she asks him. When he shakes his head, she stretches her arm right out. 'I do,' she says, 'and sometimes I peel and that.' She is leaning over close to him now, her mouth close to his ear, even though her voice still carries across to Nina.

'Thank you, Jade,' she says, 'but perhaps you can leave the talking until after school.'

Jade keeps quiet until the bell rings. Then, instead of making her usual run for the door, she waits for Sebastian. 'How come you're wearing girls' socks?' Nina hears her ask. 'You should push them down,' she advises as they walk out together, 'or everyone's going to think you're a faggot.'

Sid

There's that much commotion going on outside, he can't ignore it any longer so he puts down his hammer and hurries out. But even getting to the door has become a problem now that Terry's rug is propped beside it. There's not enough room for a rug that size, but what was he supposed to do, just toss it on the rubbish heap? Terry's beaut rug? As it was, he'd got the shock of his life to find it outside the classroom, together with the rest of Terry's things, the whole lot of it ready to be thrown out. He couldn't believe it. Just couldn't believe it. But it was the note on the rug that had really got to him. *Please dispose of this rug*, it said. Well, that was easily fixed, wasn't it? He just screwed up the note and put it in the bin.

Then he'd walked into the classroom. That's when he found himself completely lost for words; he could only look around and wonder what the hell had happened. And as he stood there, staring at the scene in front of him, a picture of Elsie Burnett suddenly popped into his head. Not like she is now but when she was still a little tyke. Six or seven, something like that; when Trina and Len were still together. That day—the day that's in his mind now—Elsie was hanging on to Trina's hand as they came through the school gate, her little head down, eyes to the ground. Which wasn't like Elsie, who was always a head-up, looking-around sort of kid. So Sid had looked a bit closer, to check she was okay. Only then did he see what had happened: her head had been shaved, shaved so she was practically bald, so she looked like a mangy old dog.

When he'd looked around at Terry's ruined classroom—everything gone, everything destroyed—that's the only thing he could think of: poor little Elsie's shaved head. And when he couldn't stand gaping at it any longer, he'd had to leave. But he'd taken the rug with him, hadn't he? He'd hauled it right down the stairs and past the hall. In the end he'd even had to drag it along the ground. Almost killed him. But he'd done it.

Outside, the commotion is getting louder. He's not surprised to find Ethan at the centre of it. What does surprise him is seeing him with a kid he doesn't recognise. Black as night, he is, so black Sid can't stop himself from staring.

'Keep away from her,' Ethan is yelling at him. 'You hear me, you stupid arsehole? You just keep away from her.'

It's not the sort of language Sid likes hearing and if Ethan's not careful someone else will hear it and he'll be getting himself another detention. So he hurries over to see if he can't calm the whole thing down.

But things are worse by the time he gets there: they're so bad that Ethan is almost hoarse from screaming. *Fuck*, he's saying, *fucking this* or *fucking that. Fucking something*, at least. Sid can't make it out exactly.

Still yelling, Ethan inches closer to the boy until their noses are almost touching. Sid feels a shot of admiration for the new boy; Ethan's a tough one and it takes some spunk to stand up to him.

'So what are you looking at, huh?' Ethan taunts the boy.

The boy doesn't move. 'Actually,' he says, and he sounds almost British, 'I'm not quite sure what I'm looking at.'

It's then that Ethan launches himself at the boy, arms right around him as he tries to wrestle him to the ground. But the boy won't fall; he just stays planted to the spot.

It's time to step in, Sid thinks, and he grabs Ethan by the collar. 'That's enough now.'

But Ethan is still struggling. In fact, he seems almost out of control. 'You fucking fuck!' he yells. 'You fucking fuck fuck,' as his voice dissolves.

With an almighty effort, Sid lifts him up so that Ethan's just about dangling in front of him. With his free hand, he waves the other boy away. 'Just go,' he tells him, keeping his voice low. 'Just go.'

And to his relief, the boy does. Eyes wide, he turns and walks away.

Only when the boy's well out of sight does Sid let Ethan go. 'What in the world was that all about? What would Mr P say if he saw you carrying on like that?'

Something in the boy's face stiffens. 'Well, Mr P can't say anything, can he, because he's not even here. He's not here so he can't do anything about it. So who cares?'

And then he starts crying. Just like that. Sid can't believe it. And the tears keep on coming, they keep pouring down his face, until his nose is running, too, and he's crying so hard his whole body begins to shake.

Sid puts his hand on the boy's shoulder. 'It's okay, mate,' he says. 'It's okay. Why don't you just tell me what's got you so upset?'

Ethan doesn't answer.

Sid keeps a hand on his shoulder. 'Come on, mate, what's the problem? Why did you get stuck into him?'

His eyes on the ground, Ethan shakes his head.

But Sid keeps pushing. 'Come on, Ethan,' he says, 'tell me what happened.'

And eventually he does. 'Well, how would you feel,' he bursts out, 'if you got moved from your proper table and someone else got your seat just because he's new? And he didn't even say thank you for me moving and now he's going to be friends with all my friends and they probably won't even be my friends anymore. Well, how would you feel about that?'

At first, Sid doesn't say anything. Instead, he just gives Ethan's shoulder a gentle squeeze. 'Well,' he says slowly, 'if something like that happened to me, I think I'd feel confused. Angry, probably, too. I'd say that's how I'd be feeling. That how you're feeling?'

The boy doesn't answer him.

'The thing is, Ethan, maybe you could give him a bit of a chance. I mean, it's not his fault he got your seat, is it? I mean, it wasn't his decision to sit there, was it?'

Reluctantly, Ethan shakes his head.

'So even if you don't really like him that much, you can't really blame him for that, can you?'

Again Ethan shakes his head.

Sid gives his shoulder another squeeze. 'Off you go, then, mate.'

As he watches the boy scamper off, his heart goes out to him. A bad business for the kids, having Terry up and go in the middle of the year like that. And because no one's told him anything about it, he's none the wiser. And Terry's not answering his calls. It's all a bit of a mess really. Tania blames Laurie Mathews—she's made that clear—but she doesn't seem to know much about it either. So they're all in the dark. And if they're all left in the dark, how are they expected to carry on as though nothing's changed? Because it has, hasn't it? Because without Terry, everything's different.

This is what he's thinking about when Laurie Mathews walks up to him. That's a first in itself; she's not usually one to seek him out.

'Sid,' she says, 'just now, there was a lot of shouting.'

He nods. 'Just a bit of an argument between a couple of the kids.'

'More than a bit,' she says. 'I couldn't believe it when I heard it.'

'Ethan can get a bit hot under the collar, that's all. He's calmed down now. He should be all right now.'

She looks unconvinced. 'Well, quite frankly, I was appalled by what I heard. Absolutely appalled.'

The language. She'd be talking about the language.

'And to speak like that to a child of colour, that's what I can't believe.'

Sid's a bit confused by that: swearing's swearing in his book, doesn't matter if it's at a white kid, a brown kid or a black kid. 'He shouldn't be speaking like that,' he agrees. 'I told him as much.'

'Well, I'll be taking it very seriously, I can tell you that much.'

She's getting herself worked up now. Sid doesn't really get it. Give the kid a serve, wash out his mouth, but in the end, it was just a bit of bad language; he's not sure it deserves to be a hanging offence. Then again, he's not the boss, is he?

Mel

The next afternoon, Mel leaves home late and finds herself almost running to get to the principal's office on time. With Diane, there was never any beating around the bush—she'd just come out with it, whatever it was that Ethan had been caught doing that particular time. This one's different.

'It's about Ethan,' she says. 'I'm afraid his behaviour has been unacceptable.' Her tone sounds like she's about to send him off to jail.

Mel waits for more.

'Completely unacceptable,' she says. She's about to say something else when there's a knock at the door. Before she can say anything, the door opens and in walks Adam.

'Sorry I'm late. I was on a job and couldn't get away.' He gives Mel a shamefaced smile. 'Sorry, babe.' There's an empty chair beside her and he plonks himself down on it.

Laurie—Ms Mathews—Mel's not sure what she's supposed to call her—continues talking. 'As I was saying, Ethan's behaviour has been unacceptable today.'

'What—again?' Adam says this with a smile that fades when Mel gives him a warning look. His next question is less flippant. 'How bad?'

'To put it bluntly,' she tells them, 'I was horrified. Horrified to see him picking on a student who's not only new to the school, but new to the country. I was absolutely appalled to hear the racist tirade that came out of your son's mouth.'

Mel arches forward. 'That's a pretty serious accusation. What did he say?'

Ms Mathews shakes her head. 'I don't really want to repeat it.'

But Mel is insistent. 'Well, we need to know what he said. I mean, if it's so bad he could be suspended, we need to know exactly what he said.'

Ms Mathews clears her throat. 'Mr and Mrs Thompson,' she says, 'on Sebastian Chuma's first day at this school, your son called him a fucking black cunt.'

Mel is shocked into silence—Adam too.

'So,' Ms Mathews tells them, 'I'm sure you can understand why I feel it necessary to suspend your son.'

As soon as she's out of the office, Mel turns to Adam. 'I'm going to kill him,' she says. 'I'm going to rip his filthy head off. Then I'm going to ask him what the fuck he was thinking.'

Adam gives her his lazy smile. 'Don't you think it might be a bit tricky to ask him anything, babe, once you've ripped his filthy head off?'

She looks away because she doesn't want him to make her laugh. She wants to stay angry long enough to be able to really give it to Ethan. *Fucking black cunt.* She can't believe it. Can't fucking believe it.

'Give me the keys and I'll wait for you in the ute,' she says. 'I'm too angry to even look at him.'

Adam checks his watch. 'Five minutes until the bell rings,' he says. 'I'll grab them and bring them back to the car.'

Mel nods. 'You'd better warn Ethan he's in for it.'

Adam leans over to kiss her on the lips. 'You look so hot when you're angry, babe.'

She pushes him away from her but not before she gives him the ghost of a smile. 'Make sure you tell him he's in for it, big time.'

Adam nods. 'Sure thing.'

The ute's parked right outside the school office. It's the only good thing about getting hauled into the principal's office half an hour before home time: there's no fight for a parking space. The bad thing is having to deal with all of Adam's shit when she opens the car door and tries to climb up into the front seat: building plans, paint sample sheets, hammers and screwdrivers and the rest of it. She pushes it all onto the floor and kicks it out in front of her so she can stretch her legs out.

Fucking black cunt. Even thinking the words makes her flinch. Where would he have even heard them? Not that it much matters now. Because he's topped it with this one. Little shit. What the hell was he thinking?

There's a small mirror on the back of the sun visor in front of her. Looking in it, she tries to apply a coat of lip gloss without smearing it all over herself. She's still trying to get it right when Josh comes running hard at the ute. He jumps in the back seat but doesn't sit down. Instead he stands up so he can wrap his arms around the back of Mel's head. 'Ethan's in trouble, isn't he?'

In the mirror, Mel gives him the look. 'Oh yeah, Joshy boy,' she says drily. 'Ethan's in big trouble.'

And Adam must have given Ethan the heads-up on that one because he's looking super scared as he makes his way towards the ute. Well, he'll be looking a hell of a lot worse by the time she's done with him.

As soon as they get home, Mel orders him to sit at the kitchen table.

Ethan opens his mouth to say something, then stops.

'Well?' she asks impatiently.

'Can I go to the toilet first, Mum?'

Standing behind him, Adam mouths, *Just say no.*

Mel gives him a hard frown. The last thing she needs is for bloody Adam to turn the whole thing into some comedy routine.

Ignoring him, she fixes her eyes on Ethan. 'Make it quick.'

Josh dumps his bag by the door and escapes up into his bedroom. Adam goes into the kitchen to turn on the kettle and Mel follows him. 'You want to handle this or will I do it?' she asks.

'You're scarier,' he says. 'You do it.'

That just pisses her off. 'Well, that's a bloody copout,' she says. 'A complete bloody copout. Tell you what, I'll do the yelling and you sort out the punishment.'

Adam grins. 'Done.'

He laughs when she scowls back at him.

'It's not funny, you know that, don't you? In fact, it's right up there. I mean, calling some black kid a fucking black cunt, it's pretty bloody outrageous. You hear that in the street and you think, *Who is that racist prick? Hang on, that's our son.* But then again, what would you expect from a loser kid like Ethan? Even his bloody principal thinks that.'

'That's not what she said.'

He's still pissing her off. 'I didn't say she said it, I said she thought it. And what would you know anyway, Mr Sorry-I'm-late-couldn't-get-away?'

Adam keeps his smile. 'I wasn't bullshitting, you know. It was true.'

From the far end of the house, there's the sound of a toilet flushing.

'Get ready,' he whispers. 'Here he comes.'

Back in the kitchen, Ethan gives Mel an uncertain smile.

Mel doesn't smile back.

'Can I, like, have something to eat?' he tries.

Mel crosses her arms in front of her. 'No,' she says evenly, 'you can't. You can just stand there and hear what I've got to say to you.' She keeps her tone pleasant, if a bit cool. It has the right effect. She can see it's putting the fear of God in him. 'So,' she continues, 'your dad and I, we got called up to the principal's office today, didn't we? Turns out you've been having a go at some new kid in the school.'

Ethan doesn't respond.

'Well, is it true? Did you have a go at him?'

When he doesn't answer, she raises her voice. 'Well, did you? Did you have a go at him or not?'

He whispers something she doesn't catch.

'What did you say?'

This time he looks up at her, his face set hard. 'I said, he deserved it.'

Now she really lets fly. 'So he did, did he? On his first day at your school, he deserved to get picked on by you, did he?'

He doesn't answer her.

'And I suppose he deserved to be called a fucking black cunt then, too, did he?'

Ethan looks blank.

'Well?'

Still he looks blank. This just makes her more irate. 'Is there something you aren't understanding, Ethan?'

Hesitantly, his lips part.

'Well,' she snaps, 'what is it?'

'What's a cunt?' he asks.

She just stares at him. 'Sorry?'

'I don't know what a cunt is.' He says the word openly, so openly it suddenly occurs to her that maybe he really doesn't know.

'So why did you call him a cunt if you don't even know what it means?'

He shakes his head. 'I didn't,' he says. 'I didn't call him a cunt.'

'So what did you call him then?'

He looks shamefaced. 'Nothing.'

'Tell me what you said to him.'

'I can't say it to you. You'll get me in trouble if I say the words to you.'

'I'll get you in a whole lot more trouble if you don't.'

He mumbles something she can't understand.

'Loudly and clearly, Ethan, or I'll get your dad to whack it out of you.'

He takes a deep breath and closes his eyes. 'Fucking fuck fuck!' he shouts, his eyes still shut tight. 'I called him a fucking fuck fuck.'

Mel looks at him in astonishment. 'You called him a what?'

Ethan opens his eyes a bit and gives her a wary look. 'I'm sorry, Mum. I just said it. It just sort of all came out.'

But that's not what she wants to know. She lowers her voice so she doesn't sound so cranky. 'Just tell me again, Etho, just tell me what you said. Just exactly what you said.'

'I said, *You're a fucking fuck, you're a fucking fuck fuck*. I'm sorry, Mum, I'm really sorry.'

Mel looks over him to Adam and raises her shoulders in a confused shrug. Adam shrugs back.

'I'm glad you're sorry, Ethan, but your dad is going to have to sort out an appropriate punishment.' She looks back at Adam. 'Aren't you, Adam?'

Adam gives her a fake solemn look. 'That's right, babe.'

❧

It's worth a week's grounding. That's what Adam decides. For picking on a new kid and for using such bad language.

Later, when the kids are asleep and she and Adam are getting ready for bed, Adam comes up from behind and starts to nuzzle her ear. 'You know what you are, babe?'

She leans the side of her face against his. 'What?'

'You're a fuck.'

She laughs. 'No, I'm not.'

'Yes, you are, you're a fuck. Actually, you're not just a fuck, you're a fucking fuck.'

She twists herself around so she's facing him, then wraps her arms around him. 'I am not a fucking fuck.'

'Oh yes you are, babe, you're a fucking fuck fuck. You, my darling, are a real fucking fuck fuck.'

He starts to moves his hand down her backside. 'Oh yeah, baby, that's what you are.'

She smiles into his neck. 'You think?'

'Oh yeah,' he whispers. 'So, you feel like a fuck, then, you fuck-ing fuck, fuck?'

'Fuck yeah,' she whispers back.

Rebecca

The appointment is at ten o'clock. The lawyer Emmanuel has found does not charge for the advice. Rebecca questions how such a lawyer—a lawyer who doesn't charge—could possibly be a good one—but she doesn't argue about it.

When they approach the counter, the receptionist doesn't lift her eyes from her computer. 'Criminal or civil?'

When neither of them answers, the woman raises her head, takes a good look at them, then slows her voice right down. 'Do you have an appointment with a criminal lawyer or a civil lawyer?'

The question irks Rebecca. Surely the woman can see that they are not the sort of people to be in need of a criminal lawyer.

'We have an immigration question,' Emmanuel tells her.

'That's a civil matter, then.' She scrolls down a page on her computer. 'Your name?'

'Chuma,' he says. 'Emmanuel Chuma. And my wife, Rebecca Chuma.'

The woman is looking doubtful. 'So is Tumour your first name or your last name?'

'It is our family name.'

Now she is shaking her head. 'Nothing under T. Have you got the right day?'

'The name is *Chuma*,' says Emmanuel, his voice clipped. 'C-h-u-m-a. And I am certain that our appointment is for this morning.'

The woman is still unwilling to take his word for it. She squints at the computer screen, her mouth tight. 'Emmanuel Chuma,' she says finally. 'That right?'

Emmanuel gives her a small nod.

'Take a seat then and wait for your name to be called out.'

There are plastic bucket seats lined up along the walls of the room and they take a seat beside a girl who seems only a few years older than Sebastian. It is a surprise, then, to see a baby stroller beside her, with a dirty-faced toddler sleeping in it. As Rebecca watches, the girl slides down in her chair and, letting her head fall back, is soon asleep too.

From the front of the room, Emmanuel's name is being called. It is a woman who calls him, and because her voice is thin, she has to speak loudly to be heard. Her hair, Rebecca sees, is unkempt and she wears no make-up. She is dressed casually, in trousers and a shirt under a sleeveless vest, and when Emmanuel lifts his hand to say that, yes, he is Emmanuel Chuma, the woman walks over to them.

At her request, they follow her down a long hallway. This, Rebecca thinks, is where the lawyer's office must be. Instead, they are led into a room that is empty apart from a round table and four chairs. There are no books or bookshelves in it, no files and no lawyer.

'Right,' says the woman, once they are all seated. 'My name's Amanda. How can I help you?'

'We were hoping to see a lawyer,' Rebecca tells her, 'an immigration lawyer.'

The woman nods. 'I'm a lawyer,' she says, 'and a migration agent.'

If this surprises Emmanuel as much as it does Rebecca, he doesn't show it.

'You're on a temporary visa, is that right?'

'I have been researching here,' Emmanuel tells her.

The woman has a notepad in front of her and now she has started to write in it. 'So you're on a student visa, is that right?'

Emmanuel's reply comes so quickly he sounds curt. 'No,' he says, 'not a student visa—a research visa. I am an academic. I am a visiting academic.'

The woman turns to Rebecca. 'And, Rebecca, are you on the same visa as your husband?'

To be addressed like this, by her first name, by a woman she doesn't know—and a white woman, at that—is insulting. 'My son and I were granted visas on the basis of our relationship to my husband,' she says stiffly. 'I can show you our passports.'

The woman tilts her head to the side. 'Sure.'

Reaching into her bag, Rebecca pulls out their three passports.

The woman flicks through the top one. Rebecca cannot see whose it is, whether it is hers, Emmanuel's or Sebastian's. To not know this makes her anxious, immediately and inexplicably anxious.

'Right,' the woman says finally. 'So you're wanting to extend your visa, is that right?'

'Under ordinary circumstances,' Emmanuel tells her, 'that would not be our intention. I have good employment in our country. In addition, I hold an academic post. My wife, equally, has good work there. Unfortunately, since my arrival in Australia, the situation has changed somewhat.' He moves in his chair, shifting his legs. 'In my absence, my wife was detained. Threats were made against her, and against our son.'

Rebecca marvels at her husband's calm delivery of words that make her flinch.

'Are you looking to make a claim for asylum then?'

Emmanuel looks at Rebecca for an answer, but she has nothing for him, nothing to give him. And so, lowering his head a fraction, slowly he lets his eyelids close over his eyes before he opens them again. *I will handle it*, he is telling her. She is grateful for this. No, more than that—she loves him for it.

'Yes,' he says. 'We would like to make a claim for asylum.'

For this, there are forms to complete. Afterwards, there will be an interview with an officer from the immigration department. Amanda the lawyer is happy to help them with the forms but won't be able to accompany them to the interview. Very few applicants bring a lawyer with them, she tells them. And in any case, she adds, most applicants don't have the money for a lawyer. When, then, with a smile, she includes them in the pool of the poverty-stricken, Rebecca has to swallow before she can smile back.

That afternoon, she waits in the schoolyard for the bell to ring and for Sebastian to come to her. Because she knows no one here, she waits by herself. This is why she doesn't turn when a voice calls from behind her, 'Excuse me? Excuse me?'

When, finally, she does turn, there is a woman in front of her. 'The new kid in Year 6,' she says, 'are you his mother?'

Rebecca smiles as she takes in the pale-skinned women around them. 'Yes,' she says, 'I am.'

The woman pulls at her earlobe. 'Listen,' she says, lowering her voice. 'I've got to apologise for my ratbag son. Apparently he had a go at your boy.'

This is the first Rebecca has heard of it. 'I'm sorry?'

'Last week,' the woman tells her, 'we got hauled into the principal's office about it.'

This, too, is news to Rebecca. 'Was it very bad, then, what he did?'

The woman shakes her head. 'What he said, not what he did.'

'And what did he say?'

'Look, the language is bad.' This, it seems, is meant as a warning.

Rebecca smiles. 'I've probably heard it before.'

The woman pauses. 'So you want to hear it then, what he said?'

Bemused, Rebecca nods. 'Yes,' she says, 'I do.'

The words come out in a rush. 'Fucking fuck fuck,' the woman says.

Rebecca thinks she must have misheard her. 'I'm sorry?'

The woman grimaces. 'Yep, a fucking fuck fuck. That's what he called him.'

Rebecca is still confused. 'I'm sorry, what is a fuck-fuck?'

The woman shrugs. 'Fucked if I know.' She gives a bit of a snort. 'Sorry about that. Makes me sound as bad as my no-good son, doesn't it?'

Rebecca tries not to smile.

'Listen to me rabbiting on like a lunatic,' says the woman. 'What I meant to do was give you this.' From her handbag, she pulls out a blank, sealed envelope. 'I don't know your name so I couldn't write it on the envelope. But it's for you. I mean, it's supposed to be for you.'

Intrigued, Rebecca slides a finger under the back flap until it gives. Inside is a card. When Rebecca pulls it out, she can't hold back a small cry of recognition.

It is the rock pool card, the very same one. Slowly she opens it, then reads it.

I wanted to apologise for the bad behaviour of my son, Ethan, towards your son. I'm very sorry it happened.

Best wishes,

Mel Thompson

Mel, Rebecca thinks, *Mel*. And sure enough, when Rebecca turns the card over, there it is, written in the same looping, swirling sort of handwriting: *Made by Mel.*

Rebecca smiles as she looks over at the woman. So this is Mel.

'It's a beautiful card,' she tells her. 'Thank you.'

The woman—Mel—brushes the compliment away. 'Look, my son can be a bit of a ratbag but deep down, he's not a bad kid.' She touches Rebecca's arm with her hand. 'Listen, I know you're new and everything, so why don't you take my number? That way you can call if you need anything.'

When Rebecca nods, suddenly shy, Mel takes out a mobile phone. 'What's your name?'

'Rebecca,' she says softly.

Mel keeps her eyes on the phone screen. 'And your number?'

Her number? She doesn't know it. She doesn't even know her phone number. Taking out her own phone, she scrolls down until she finds it. She hesitates as she reads out the still unfamiliar numbers. Once she is done, the woman rings her. 'There you go,' she says. 'Now you know how to find me.'

Terry

There are a couple of lawyers in Raleigh, but he's not keen on Raleigh people knowing his business. Especially not this, and especially not with Michelle being at the surgery and all. Confidentiality and the rest of it, he knows that's what they'll say to reassure him, but in his experience, confidentiality or no confidentiality, people still talk. And he doesn't want people talking. That's why he's taken the bus into the city to see someone he hopes doesn't know anyone in Brindle or Raleigh—or Jinda, for that matter.

The building itself has an enormous foyer, with a ceiling so high it could house an aeroplane. Why do that? he wonders. Why make a foyer as big as that?

In front of him is a directory listing every business in the building. Among them are a number of law firms. He counts seven, eight, nine: so many of them in just one building.

Clare became a lawyer, that's what he's been told. Little Clare, a lawyer. It had surprised him to hear it. Never in a thousand years would he have pictured her in a law firm. It would have made her mother happy, though, that's for sure. Mrs Sorenson would have been purple with pride about it.

Mrs Sorenson.

God.

He doesn't need to be thinking about Mrs Sorenson.

He needs to be thinking about the task at hand. And to do that, he needs to focus. He needs to find where the hell he's supposed to be in this skyscraper.

Again his eyes scan the directory: level fifteen, that's where he needs to be, for his appointment with Simon Fernandez.

Simon Fernandez, it turns out, is a knowledgeable lawyer with a good understanding of this particular area of the law. There is a lot he can explain to Terry, and he does it well; he is sharp, he is clear and he is pleasant.

But in the end, it's all very simple. There's nothing to be done. There is no one who can reconsider Terry's case; there is no appeal he can lodge. He's a prohibited person and prohibited people can't work with children. Not ever. In short, it's all over, red rover.

He ventures just one question. 'But it was so long ago,' he says. 'Can't they take that into account?'

Simon Fernandez shakes his head. 'Not when it involved a child.'

Terry's face burns. No more, he thinks. He can't stand it any longer. He needs to get out of here—now. But there's still one more thing he needs to know. It's not an easy thing to ask. And the words themselves are hard to form. 'The school,' he says. 'Can I pop into the school—just from time to time—to check how the kids are going?'

The man's eyes flicker. 'I wouldn't advise it,' he says. 'I really wouldn't.'

Terry swallows. 'Just wondering,' he murmurs.

∽

He's back home again by lunchtime.

He has to call Michelle. He'd promised he would.

Bouncer follows him into the lounge room and sits by his feet while Terry tries to work out what the hell he's going to do with himself now. Now that everything's become such a mess.

He misses the kids. God, he misses them. When he can, when it doesn't make him too sad to think about it, he tries to picture them in the classroom, all sitting at their desks, everything the same as it was. Just without him.

The phone is sitting on the coffee table, right there in front of him. He just has to lean forward, pick it up and dial the number. But it's harder than you'd think just to pick up the phone and dial a number. It even makes his hands shake. And yet he does it. He dials the number, she answers and he tells her. 'No good, love,' is all he says. 'No good.' And it kills him to hear the intake of her breath, because what could she possibly say? She's there on reception so she can't move a muscle without the whole world knowing about it. He feels so ashamed, so very ashamed of what he's put her through. The looks, the whispers, the gossip. Because privacy laws or no privacy laws, you can't stop people asking questions about a retirement that's come out of the blue, can you?

∽

When he hears the first knock on the door, he ignores it. A door-to-door salesman, no doubt, and he can't face the inane conversation.

The second knock he ignores, too, then waits for the third one, which, from past experience, he knows will be the last. But this time the bugger doesn't stop. This time he just keeps on rapping at the door until, with an annoyed grunt, Terry gets out of his chair. 'All right, all right!' he yells. 'I'm coming.'

Scowling, he opens the door to find Sid standing there. Too surprised to say anything, Terry just stares at him.

Sid gives him a crooked smile. 'Hello, Terry,' he says. 'Couldn't get you on the blower so I thought I'd better come and see what's what.'

Seeing him there—so matter-of-fact, so unchanged—makes Terry want to cry. Instead he grunts. 'S'pose I'd better let you in then.'

So he leads him down the hallway and into the lounge room. There Terry follows Sid's gaze out over the water and across to the port. 'Last couple of months, there's nothing goes on out there I don't know about. Anything happens, I've seen it.' He tries for a chuckle, to show he's made a joke, but he doesn't get a laugh out of Sid.

'Not the same,' he says, 'at the school. Without you being there.'

Terry chews on the inside of this lip until he can trust himself to speak. 'Every morning, soon as I open my eyes, I'm ready to get up and head off to school. Every bloody morning. Every morning, I forget for a minute or so. You'd think it would click after a bit. No such luck.'

His eyes still on the waterline, he keeps talking, soft talking, like he's talking to himself. 'Days get a bit long, though, just watching what's going on over at the port. Drives Michelle mad, having me moping around the house. She's even started leaving me lists of things to do—a whole lot of fix-it jobs.'

He turns to Sid, arms crossed hard in front of him. 'You know me,' he says. 'Doing them's not the problem. There's still enough of the old chippy in me to turn my hand to whatever needs doing. It's just the starting, Sid.' He coughs, then, to try to cover the faltering of his voice. 'I don't know what's wrong with me. I stare at the bloody list and it doesn't matter what I do, I just can't get going with it. It's like it's in Chinese or something. And I think, Christ, I must be losing my mind.' His eyelids are heavy over his eyes, so heavy his eyes seem closed.

Sid's voice, never rushed, has a flicker of urgency to it. 'You need to get out, Terry,' he says. 'You need to get out of the house. Have a hit with me. That's what you need. Bit of a hit of an afternoon after I knock off.'

Terry shakes his head. He's almost whispering now. 'But I can't even do that. I haven't even got it in me to get on the line and give you a ring. Sounds like a joke, doesn't it? But Christ, Sid, it's all I can do just to haul myself out of bed in the morning. Michelle's at me to get a job. But what can I do, Sid? If I can't teach anymore, what can I do? And who the hell wants a fifty-seven-year-old carpenter who hasn't been on a building site in twenty years?'

He doesn't tell him about the one job he did go for. It wasn't anything great. Just a day or two a week at one of the nursing homes over in Henley, doing all the bits and pieces—any repair work that needed doing, a bit of gardening, a bit of general maintenance. Nothing demanding, just something to get him out of the house. Michelle's words, not his; left to himself, he'd have just stayed put.

So he made the call, then found himself sitting in the manager's office wondering what the hell he was doing there. He sat quietly as John or Dave or Kevin or whatever his name was yabbered on about the rubbish and the garden and the rest of it. The bloke was sounding keen and Terry was answering his questions—when he'd be available, what he'd done before—when, out of the blue, came this one: *Just out of interest, Terry, why did you stop teaching?*

It was a simple enough question, and there was a simple enough answer to it. *I retired.* That's all he needed to say. Nothing more than that.

Instead, he'd yanked his head up in surprise and started to gabble. 'There was a problem,' he heard himself bluster. 'I had a problem at the school. So I left. That's why I left.'

And although the bloke kept on nodding, Terry saw his eyes cool and his head move back. He knew, then, that he wouldn't be getting the job; it didn't matter how good he was, it didn't even matter if there was no one else on offer.

Sid's looking at him, but what's he going to say? That he can't even get himself a job taking out the rubbish?

'I'll keep an ear out,' Sid promises him. 'I'll tell you if something comes up.'

Thanks, he wants to say, but instead of the word that awful taste rises up again. He grimaces as he tries to swallow it back down. Beside him, Sid is quiet.

'At school,' Terry says finally, his voice thick, 'what's news? With the kids, I mean?'

Sid screws his eyes up like he's trying to get a good look at something across the water. 'Ethan Thompson got himself in trouble last week.'

Terry raises an eyebrow. 'What happened?'

Sid shakes his head. 'He was having a go at the new kid.'

'What new kid?'

'Can't remember his name. Something posh. Benedict, Nathaniel, something like that. Foreign kid. Ethan got stuck into him, so the boss hauled young Mel and Adam into the office.'

Terry makes a clicking noise with his tongue. 'Silly little bugger. Thing with Ethan is that he's got to learn how to control his temper; force himself to simmer down. It's always been his problem. Soon as it looks like he's going to blow up, that's when you've got to get in quick, work out what it is that's got him so upset then get him to settle. You know what I used to do with him? I'd make him count. When I'd see he was about to explode, I'd pull him aside and say, *Right, mate, before you do anything, count it down and when you get to ten, work out whether the idea's still a good one.* Oftentimes, that's all you'd need with Ethan. Because he's a good kid, really, just a bit of a hothead. Probably needed running out. Get rid of the excessive energy.'

He looks across at Sid. 'Listen,' he says, 'if you get a chance— don't make it a big thing—just say I told him to keep his nose clean.'

Nina

Friday afternoons are for art, and today Nina has given them the theme *Animals of the Rainforest* for inspiration. On each table she has set out an array of paints, cardboard and craft materials. At the front of the classroom are pictures of rainforest animals. Each child has to choose an animal as a basis for their own painting or collage. It's a good idea, she thinks. More than that, it's part of her plan to slowly transform the room into a fabulous rainforest scene: first, by hanging the animal creations from the ceiling, next, by covering the walls with an assortment of painted trees and vines. She might even get some cheap brown matting to cover the lino. That way, as soon as the kids walk into the room, they'll be stepping into their very own 6F magical rainforest.

But right at the moment, Elsie is demanding most of her time. The project she's chosen is an ambitious one—too ambitious, perhaps, but Nina doesn't tell her this. Instead, she sits beside her and together they trace the outline for a large toucan. It would be easy enough to cut out the toucan and paint it in bright colours, but Elsie is set on making a collage. And so, painstakingly, they rip up yellow, red, blue and green crepe paper, then roll each tiny piece into an even smaller ball. When they have enough of each colour, Nina uses a thick paintbrush to coat the paper toucan with glue and, once she thinks Elsie can manage it alone, leaves her to cover it in paper balls.

At the back of the room, Kurt, Ethan and Cody are huddled together in a group. They have chosen gorillas as their animals and, at Nina's suggestion, are using strips of black crepe paper as fur. Kurt has elected himself the silverback of the group, so, as well as black strips, he needs a line of silver to run down the back of his gorilla. Nina doesn't have silver crepe paper, but she does have a roll of silver ribbon she lets him use. The final result is fantastic, she tells him. It's so fantastic that Cody and Ethan are at her for some silver ribbon, then, too. But because there's only ever one silverback in a group, not three, Kurt vetoes the idea. Cody and Ethan don't push it.

She's already screwed hooks in the ceiling—one for each student—and cut lengths of green ribbon to attach to the artworks so they can be looped onto a hook. That way, instead of leaving them on the desks to dry, each picture can be hung up straight-away. Sid has lent Nina his stepladder and if they stand on the top rung, all of the kids—apart from Bridie, who lets Nina do it for her—can reach high enough to loop their own ribbon onto their own hook.

When Kurt climbs up to hang his silverback, he starts to snort as though trying to swallow back a laugh. And if that's his aim, he's unsuccessful, because soon he's laughing so hard Nina worries he'll lose his footing.

Just dealing with him—day in, day out—is exhausting. 'Enough,' she tells him, 'that's quite enough.' She has no idea what he's finding so funny, but as they take turns to put up their own gorillas, Ethan and Cody also start to guffaw.

Only when the rest of the artworks are up does she notice. It is then she sees that, to each of the three gorillas, a large penis and scrotum have been attached. And because the oversized genitals, all three of them, have carefully been covered in strips of black crepe paper, they're not immediately obvious.

After the surprise of it, her first reaction—if she's honest—is one of admiration: that these boys, so lethargic with the rest of their work, have managed such a creative collaboration. Still, she uses her disappointed voice as she orders the three of them up to stand in front of her desk as she tries to work out what she's going to do: give them a dressing-down there and then, send them straight to Laurie or ask them to take down the gorillas and start again. In the end, she settles on an apology, neatly written and at least five sentences long.

When, later, the bell has gone and the classroom has emptied, Nina lines the stepladder up under each of the gorillas and, scissors in hand, lops off the offending parts.

Immediately, she regrets it. Because, in the end, what exactly was the problem? What exactly had they done wrong? Simply copied, more or less, what they had in front of them: a naked gorilla. And what's the issue with that? Perhaps there is none. Perhaps the problem is hers.

Don't be so stupid. It's Steve's voice that fills her head then. *They're a bunch of idiots who spent the afternoon drawing oversized dicks. I'd be giving them a whack across the ears, not some award for creative bloody effort.*

This makes her smile. For a moment, it almost makes her laugh until, once again, she remembers and, once again, there is a sinking feeling in her stomach.

Sitting down, she takes a deep breath then picks up the first of the three apologies that have been left on her desk.

It is Ethan's and it is short.

dear mrs foreman

    sorry about puting a penis on my gorila. it wasn't the right thing to do. plese don't tell my mum or dad because I already got in troubel to ms mathew and my mum and dad said the shit wil hit the fan if it hapens again. that's what I want to say to you in this leter to say sorry.

    ETHAN

    ps this is 4 senteces not 5, but one of them is quite long.

Cody's is shorter still.

Dear Miss

    This is my apolage for making a penis for my gorilla. I will not do it again. I will take it off if you want. I can do it easy. And it won't take very long.

    Cody

By contrast, Kurt, who usually writes little, has filled the page.

To miss

    You told me to write an apolagy about the penis and balls I made for my gorilla. So this is my apolagy. I'm sorry I made a penis and balls for my gorilla, even if every silverbak gorilla I ever heard of has got a penis and balls anyway. But that's probly just something for real gorillas not ones you make for a stupid rainforest that we didn't even need anyway because we already did really good art stuff with our real teacher Mr P but you just threw that away when you came and we didn't even get to take it home or nothing, even though it took ages to make, most of all my paper mashay planet which was venus. I don't think it's fair that you threw out our stuff when it wasn't your stuff—it was our stuff and Mr P's stuff. Specialy his rug. Because that was a really good rug for sitting on and for having in our clasroom. And it wasn't even your rug and you shouln't throw other poeple's things out.

Kurt Ward

6P (NOT 6F)

The anger that radiates from the page so shocks her she finds herself on the verge of tears. Don't, she mutters, as she lets the page drop from her hands, don't, don't, don't. She's managed worse than this. Kurt is always tricky so she shouldn't take it so personally. She certainly shouldn't be crying about it. But, to her horror, she finds that she is, that she is hunched over her desk, weeping.

A knock on the door startles her upright.

'Come in!' she calls out, trying to stop her voice from catching. As the door handle turns, she picks up the letter and tries to appear busy. When she looks up, she finds Tania Rossi at the door.

'Tania,' she says, surprised. 'Hi.' And as Tania starts to walk over to her, she lowers her eyes so Tania won't see that they're swollen. If the other woman notices, she says nothing. She just hands Nina a school jumper.

'I picked this up in the playground,' she tells her. 'Another Kurt Ward special. I thought I'd leave it with you, ready for him to lose again on Monday.'

Nina gives her a wry smile. 'Thanks.'

Tania looks up at the animal display. 'Nice.'

The compliment warms her. 'You think?'

Tania nods. 'Brightens the room up no end.'

'We only just finished them,' Nina tells her. 'The kids really got into it.' She doesn't mention the penises.

'Good to have a bit of colour back—the room was looking pretty bare there for a while.'

'Thanks,' she says cautiously. She's not sure if Tania's having a go at her or not. 'I'm keen for the kids to connect with the space. You know, feel that it's theirs, as a class.'

Tania purses her lips tight. 'Well, they've always been pretty connected, this group—they're a little bunch. Terry was good at that: getting them all to work together, keeping them motivated.'

Nina fixes a smile on her face. 'Really?'

Tania nods. 'He was a bit of a rock star. To the kids, I mean. Teachers like Terry, they don't come along every day.'

Nina tenses at the slight. 'I thought there were problems,' she ventures.

Tania lifts an eyebrow. 'Problems? What sort of problems?'

Nina can't tell whether she's just playing dumb. 'You know,' she says, trying to keep it vague, 'safety issues, protection.'

Tania stares at her. 'What do you mean?'

Nina hesitates. 'I'm not really sure,' she says. 'I just heard there were some safety issues.'

Tania looks dubious. 'Safety issues?'

When Nina shrugs, Tania shakes her head. 'Don't know about that,' she says drily, 'but there's one thing I can tell you: the only unsafe practice I've seen in here all year is that stepladder stuck in the middle of the room, ready for some kid to fall off and break their arm.'

Nina flushes. 'I needed to get the kids' paintings up before the weekend.' She's sounding defensive but she doesn't care.

'Relax,' Tania tells her. 'I wasn't meaning to have a go at you. I know it must be hard, coming after Terry and all. I mean, they're big shoes to fill, aren't they?'

Nina blinks in astonishment. Clearly, the woman has no idea. *He's not some hero*, she wants to snap. *He's a bloody menace.*

'Especially after what happened,' Tania continues.

Nina says nothing.

'Terry was pushed out,' Tania explains. 'You know that, don't you? That's what happened. Laurie made it impossible for him. Gave him no choice but to get out.'

Nina can't believe what she's hearing. But before she can respond, Tania has started to leave. 'Got to go,' she says, flashing Nina a quick smile. 'Enjoy your weekend.'

Dumbfounded, Nina watches as Tania heads towards the door. When she reaches it, she stops. 'By the way, have you started preparing for the show yet?'

Nina frowns at her, confused. 'What show?'

'The Year 6 show. The Year 6 kids put it on for the rest of the school. Like a farewell concert. It's a big thing.'

Nina feels her heart sink. 'I didn't know.'

Tania smacks her lips together as she turns to leave. 'Better get a move on, then.'

'What sort of show do they do?' Nina calls after her. But Tania has already gone.

Propping her elbows on the table, Nina drops her head into her hands. Another thing. Another thing to think about. She's not sure she's got it in her.

Sid

Sid takes a look at his watch. It's well after four o'clock and with everyone gone for the day, the school is quiet. He's just got to nip up to Terry's room to grab the ladder back from the new teacher, then he'll be off as well. Not too soon, either. It's been a long week already. The truth is, he's not getting any younger, and today he feels his age. Not that he wants to admit it. Because it's not like he's ready to be put out to pasture. He's just a bit tired.

To perk himself up, he breaks into a half-run on the way to the classroom. When he reaches the hall, he starts to pick up the pace. The classroom door, that'll be the finish line, he thinks, but once he reaches the foyer, he decides to push it a bit harder by running through the door and across to Terry's desk. The new teacher has moved it over to the other side of the room, so that'll add a couple of metres and give him a longer home stretch.

Only then does he realise the room isn't empty: the new teacher is still there, sitting at the desk.

He's not sure who jumps higher—him or her.

'Sid,' she says, 'you scared me.'

'Thought you'd have knocked off for the day,' he says, trying not to puff. He notices, then, that she's done something with the classroom. Finally. 'What's this,' he says when he's got his breath back, 'a jungle or something?'

She looks up at the ceiling. 'Rainforest,' she says. 'What do you think?' She sounds nervous, which surprises him. He'd had her picked as one made in Laurie Mathews' mould—tough as nails—what with the way she'd set about demolishing Terry's classroom without so much as an if-you-please. He's been avoiding her ever since.

The jungle or rainforest or whatever it's supposed to be—well, that's something. It's a start.

His ladder is in the middle of the room and he walks over to retrieve it. 'You finished with this?'

She looks embarrassed. 'Sorry,' she says, 'I was going to drop it off on my way to the car.'

She sounds tired and when he takes another look at her, he can see she's exhausted. Maybe she's coming down with something. Always one lurgy or another doing the rounds. They used to joke about it, Terry and him: about how they'd both been at the school so darned long they'd become immune to any of the bugs. But the newbies, they always come down hard in the first couple of years.

'You okay?' he asks.

Immediately, her face crumples. Waving a hand across it, she tries to smile but already there are tears streaming down her face. 'Sorry,' she whispers.

Blimey. What's he supposed to do now?

'The week,' she says, her voice choking up, 'it's been a hard week. I'm finding it a bit difficult. The kids, they seem so, I don't know—so angry. And I know it's hard to have to change teachers mid-year, but I'm trying my best, I really am.' Wiping her eyes, she looks across at him. 'What is it, Sid? What am I doing wrong?'

Sid pulls at his ear. She can't seriously be wanting an answer from him.

But she's staring at him expectantly.

What's she doing wrong? For starters, it's not his place to tell her. He's made a point of never poking his nose into other people's business and he's not going to start now.

'Sid?' she repeats, and this time, it's like she's begging him for an answer.

So what's he supposed to do? Tell her how to do her job? He's not even sure where to begin.

'Look,' he says finally, 'I understand why you might have done it, but clearing the classroom out like you did—everything out—well, it would have come as a shock to the kids. You've got to imagine how it was for them: first Terry's gone, then everything they had in the classroom is gone, too.' He tries to keep his voice steady but it still upsets him to think about it.

She straightens up in her seat, defensive-like. 'I was told they needed a fresh start, after everything that happened. I thought it would make things easier.'

He's got no idea why she would have thought that. 'But you threw out all their work. You didn't even tell them, you just threw it out. Don't I know it,' he adds. 'I had to haul it all down to the bins.'

He's out of line now—he knows he shouldn't be talking to her like that—and he waits for her to slap him down, to tell him to mind his own business. Instead, she just gives him a sad look.

'You're right,' she says. 'I shouldn't have thrown out their work. I should have kept it for them. I was so focused on getting things ready, I just didn't think.'

Hearing it like that, he can see how it might happen.

'The kids and Terry, they went back a long way,' he tells her. 'Years. Terry going like that, it came as a shock to them. To all of us, really.'

She doesn't reply, but it doesn't matter. He's said what he wanted to say, that's the main thing. He's said his piece and he feels better for it. He's not sure she does, though. From the look of her, he'd say she's about to start crying again. That's not what he wants to see.

He looks up at the ceiling. 'The animals look good,' he says. There's a group of gorillas hanging down beside him and he gives one of them a bit of a tug. 'He's the silverback, is he?'

She gives him a tiny smile. 'Kurt Ward's masterpiece.'

This makes Sid laugh out loud. 'Doesn't surprise me, either; he's been the ringleader since kindy. Any trouble and if you follow it long enough, chances are you'll find Kurt's behind it. Either him or one of his mates.'

'I don't think he likes me much,' she says softly. 'I don't think Ethan does either. Or Elsie. In fact, I don't seem to have hit it off with any of them, really. I think they blame me for what happened.'

Sid considers this. 'Maybe they do,' he concedes, 'but they'll get over it.'

'And Ethan's taken a set against Sebastian and I've got no idea how to solve it.'

Sid raises his eyebrows like he doesn't know either. In truth, he knows exactly how she should tackle it; he's just not sure it's up to him to tell her. But what the heck. 'The thing is,' he says, 'Ethan thinks it's Sebastian's fault he got moved from Kurt's table. That's the root of the problem, far as I understand it.'

She stiffens, but he'd expected she might. 'I just wanted to separate Ethan and Jade so they wouldn't muck around all lesson.'

'I don't think that's how Ethan sees it,' he tells her, 'and now he thinks Sebastian is taking all his friends, too. That's why he doesn't like Sebastian.'

'So what do I do about it?'

'You could put him back on his old table.'

She shakes her head. 'There isn't a spare seat.'

'Not if you keep four to a table. But if you put two of the groups together, you'd be right.'

'What, and have one big group and two little ones? That'd be a bit strange, wouldn't it?'

He takes a look around the room, trying to figure out how she could do it. 'You could have two big groups. That way you could run one long table down each side. Or have it in a horseshoe, even.'

She looks doubtful. 'And leave a big gap in the middle of the room?'

'Well, at least you'd have room for a rug, then. The kids always liked it when Terry had his rug. Liked the feel of it—bit of a change from being in their seats all day.'

He waits to be told to pull his head in. Instead she grimaces. 'The thing is,' she says, 'I threw his rug out, too.'

Now he's not sure what to do: whether to say nothing or tell her the truth.

'I've made a bit of a mess of things, haven't I?' she says quietly.

Instead of answering her, Sid clears his throat. 'As it happens,' he tells her, trying to keep it casual, 'I've been holding on to the rug.

Thought it might come in handy. If you like, I could dig it out and bring it up. Wouldn't be a problem.'

By the time they've finished, he's completely knackered and that hungry he could eat a horse. Once or twice his stomach rumbled so loudly he was sure she must have heard him. But rumblings or no rumblings, he doesn't regret staying back. Doesn't regret hauling the rug back up again, either, or regrouping the desks into two long lines. Doesn't even regret telling her to get on home while he stays behind to give everything a wipe-down and a vacuum before he pops the stepladder back in the storeroom and heads home himself.

Rebecca

They arrive early, close to an hour early. At eleven o'clock they are greeted by a thin man who wears a suit but no tie and they follow him into a small room with a table and three chairs. Once they are inside, the man motions for Rebecca and Emmanuel to sit together while he takes a seat on the other side of the table.

He has papers and a file in front of him. In front of Rebecca, there is a pen and a writing pad. In front of Emmanuel, there is nothing.

To one side of the table is a recording device and before he says a word, the man flicks a switch on the machine. A red button lights up. Only then does the man introduce himself. He is Mr Robert Parker, from the Department of Immigration. He is Rebecca's case officer. Emmanuel's, too. But because Emmanuel has made no claims himself, it is Rebecca's story he wishes to hear. Emmanuel can stay, if that is what Rebecca would like. Alternatively, Rebecca can ask to be interviewed alone.

She tells him she would like to have Emmanuel with her.

Mr Robert Parker is, it seems, a very busy man, and although he doesn't exactly rush her through the questions, neither does he encourage her to take her time.

So when he asks her why she left her country, she gives him only the salient points. She says that she is well known in her country. She tells him this so he will understand why she cannot, now, simply slip back into the country unnoticed, unseen. Because everywhere she goes there, she is seen, and noticed.

He meets this with some scepticism. How then had she been able to leave the country at all, if, indeed, she is so well known? She starts to tell him about her passport, her name, the hairstyle, the clothes, but none of these things seem to interest him.

Instead he asks her if she is a religious woman. No, she replies, and this is the honest answer. And when he asks her about her political affiliations, her political activities, there is nothing she can tell him. All she can do is explain, as simply as she can, why it was she had to leave her country and why it is she cannot return there. She tells him everything she has already told Emmanuel: she had been arrested, she had been questioned, she had been released.

Only once does she hesitate, at the very end of the interview, when he asks her if there is anything more.

'No,' she says eventually, 'there is nothing more.'

Terry

For a hardware shop, it's a big one, and Jim Williams has owned it for as long as Terry can remember. Terry likes Jim, always has: likes the way he keeps the place well-stocked, likes that he's happy to order in anything he's asked for. And Terry's always been a good customer, so he knows the shop well. Which comes in handy now.

It's the uniform he doesn't like so much: a bright yellow polo shirt with *Jim's Hardware* embroidered on the pocket, teamed with a pair of navy King Gees. He can see why Jim thinks having a uniform is a good idea. It keeps the staff looking neat during shifts, even if they dress like slobs at home, and it's easy for the customers to find someone when they need help. Bright yellow is good as a beacon, too, he'll concede that much. Although that's about all it's good for.

That first week, they gave him three eight-hour shifts. No big deal, he thought at the time, but by the end of the week his legs were killing him. Three weeks down, and with two extra shifts thrown in, he's slowly starting to get used to it. Although there are still things that leave him floundering. Being on the cash register, for example:

trying to locate the blimmin' barcode on whatever item he's got in front of him, and starting to panic when he can't. That's when he's supposed to ring the bell beside the register and wait for Matt—or whoever's working with him that day—to grab the product, work out where it's from, then hightail it back with a replacement that's got a working barcode. That's the theory of it, except Matt isn't the brightest cookie in the jar, or the quickest, and half the time, Terry just ends up eyeballing the customer while they both wait and the line of customers gets longer.

When he's not needed on the register, he spends his time on the floor, and he likes that: keeping the shelves stocked up; answering whatever questions come his way. Generally, they're dead easy, and if they aren't, he makes it his business to find out the right answer.

It's not what he'd have chosen, working at Jim's, but it sure as hell beats pacing the lounge room. And he's got Sid to thank for it: Jim was looking for someone, and Sid suggested Terry. Well, Jim had him on the books before Terry had a chance to say, *Give me a day to think about it.* Which is just as well because with his head the way it's been, chances are he'd have got spooked and turned it down.

Instead he spends the day with a tape measure in his back pocket. But it's a decent job—close to home, too—and he's grateful to have it.

Today, the time's gone quickly. When he checks his watch, it's already three o'clock, which is his break time. There's a lunchroom at the back of the shop, and that's where he heads now. It's nothing to write home about, the lunchroom: no windows, no natural light even, and some might find it claustrophobic. But Terry doesn't mind. It's got a table and chairs, sink, kettle, microwave. And because they all take their breaks in shifts, mostly he has the place to himself.

He sits down to check what Michelle's packed for him. Today it's a muffin: raspberry and white chocolate. Terrific, he thinks. Terrific.

She'd gone quiet when he let her know about the job.

'As much work as I want,' he'd told her, 'part time, full time, it's up to me.'

'Good,' she'd answered without a smile, her voice indistinct. 'That's good.'

'Decent of Jim, really, to put me on.' He'd said this in his jolly voice, his upbeat voice, a voice he hadn't had much call for of late. Not after all the—what would you call it?—the furore.

He saw her struggle to match his cheeriness; watched her mouth turn up in what could have been a smile but came out more as a grimace; saw the rise of her shoulders as she took a breath in and let a breath out.

'Don't you think so?' he said, a desperate edge creeping into his voice.

Maybe it was this that did it.

'No,' she blurted out, her voice muffled. 'I don't think so.'

Her answer confused him. 'Sorry, love?'

'I don't want to be pitied, Terry. And I don't feel like being grateful for a job like that.'

She stopped then, and he thought she might cry, but she didn't; she kept going.

'Every time I go to the shops, there's someone who asks about you. Some that think you're still there at the school and tell me about Jess or Joe, who were in your class once, or maybe they weren't—it doesn't seem to matter—they tell me anyway. And I just nod and say, *Well done*, or, *Terry'll be pleased to hear it*, or, *Isn't that great?*

Trying not to get into a conversation, trying not to say that you've left, that you aren't there anymore. Because I don't want to talk about it. I don't want them to ask why.'

She'd pulled her lips in then, like she was trying to gather herself up. 'Then there's the ones who do know, but want to find out a bit more. And I'm never sure how much they really know, how much they've been told. So I say nothing, because I'm scared I'll say too much, that I'll give them more than they've already got. Feeling like a bloody idiot when I say, *Yes, that's right, he's retired.* It kills me, Terry; it kills me what happened. So then when you say, *Jim's given me a job and isn't that great?*, what do you expect me to say? Yes, it's great? When I think of all the kids you saw through that place. Kids you taught to read, kids you taught to write—kids who'd have had no chance of any bloody job if you hadn't got them sorted in the first place. Kids doing all sorts of things now, and I'm supposed to be turning handstands because someone's got you a job stacking shelves. What am I supposed to say to that, Terry? Yep, Jim Williams sure is a good guy for taking you on?'

He'd nodded then and kept nodding until he was able to speak. 'Love, you wanted me to be working. And I am. I'm working. And the thing is,' he said, 'I'd be hard pressed to find anyone else who would take me on now.'

She'd stared at him then. Really stared at him, so hard, so unflinchingly it seemed she was trying to peer into him.

Watching her, his heart had started to pound. 'What, Chelle? What is it?'

Finally she'd dropped her eyes and turned away from him. 'Nothing,' she said softly. 'Nothing.'

❧

It's almost closing time when he hears her voice.

'Dad?' she's calling. And when there's no answer, she calls again, louder this time, so loud her voice booms through the shop. 'Dad?' If Len's in the shop at all, he's got to have heard her this time.

What are they doing here? Terry wonders. Len can't use a screwdriver let alone find his way around a hardware shop.

'Dad?' he hears her call out once more. This time Len answers her.

'Elsie,' he calls back, 'where did you get to?'

'I just lost you, Dad,' she says. 'I just lost you in the shop.'

Terry is in aisle four, restocking paints. When, from the corner of his eye, he sees the two of them at the end of his aisle, he doesn't know why, but he starts to panic. As they come closer, ambling slowly up the aisle, Terry bends close into the shelf so that his face is shielded and he won't be recognised.

As he stays there, statue-like, he hears their loud voices right beside him.

'Letterboxes,' Len is saying to her, 'the row for letterboxes, that's what we need. Have you seen it, Elsie, the row where they've got letterboxes?'

Elsie hasn't seen the letterboxes, she tells her father; she hasn't even seen one letterbox. Then she reconsiders. Yes, she corrects herself, she did see one, but that was on the way in and it was the shop one. And you couldn't buy that, could you, because then where would they put the shop letters?

'We need to find the letterboxes, Else,' Len says loudly. 'We need to keep looking until we find them.'

Aisle nine, Terry directs them silently. *You need to look in aisle nine.*

But instead of saying it out loud, he buries his head further into the shelf, in so far he'll risk bumping his head if he doesn't watch himself. That's when he realises that he's holding his breath. Holding it in so hard that when he finally lets go, he finds himself gasping for air.

You blithering fool, he scolds himself. What the hell are you doing hiding from poor old Len and Elsie?

But still he keeps himself out of sight until their voices fade away. Only then does he pull his head out of the shelf, and only once he's double-checked they're really gone does he stand up to rub the stiffness out of his legs.

He's shaking, he discovers. He's shaking so much he has to reach out to hold on to the shelving to steady himself.

Hearing her voice behind him makes him jump.

'Mr P!' she shouts, her voice so excited it sounds like she's about to burst. 'Mr P, Mr P, it's me, Elsie.'

His first impulse is to run, to just take off, but he turns around and forces a smile to his lips. 'So it is, Elsie, so it is.'

She gives him a delighted smile. 'How come you're here, Mr P?' she asks. 'Is this your job now, because we've got Mrs Foreman?'

So her name is Foreman. He didn't know that. Tania had spoken of a Tina or a Nina but hadn't mentioned her last name. And he hadn't asked. Probably because it made his lungs contract to think about it; to think about someone in his class, with his kids, in his school.

'Is that why you left, Mr P? Because you work here now instead?'

He gives her the smallest of smiles. 'Tell you what, I'd rather hear about you. What brings you here today, Elsie?'

'Dad and me,' she says, 'we're buying another letterbox because the old one got blown right up.'

That's a surprise. 'It got blown up?'

'Yes, Mr P, yes it did. It got blown up in the night when I was asleep but my dad wasn't, he was still awake. And he went out to see what was going on. And that's what was going on, the letterbox was blown up, so we need to get another one, otherwise we'll never get any more letters because there won't be a letterbox to put them in.'

He gives her a nod. 'You want me to show you where they are, the letterboxes?'

That's exactly what she wants. And as he walks her over, he feels her hand—her warm little hand—slip into his and squeeze. He should drop it. He should say, *No, Elsie, you can't do that. Not here. Not now.* But how can he? How can he do anything but squeeze her hand back as he leads her over to aisle nine?

Nina

And so now they've moved in together, Steve and Sue. Finally, he has admitted it to her. Through the phone, his voice cuts Nina to pieces. *Oh*, she hears herself say, her mind on autopilot and, strangely, the word *congratulations* sitting on her tongue.

She imagines telling Marina. *I almost congratulated him*, she'd say with a laugh. *Can you imagine? I had to stop myself.*

But when she thinks about it, when she thinks about the two of them in the house that's now theirs, her mouth turns dry. The thought of dropping Emily over to them makes her feel physically sick.

Not Emily. Emily is thrilled about it. So thrilled she spends the hour-long car trip singing in the back seat. Nina makes herself smile. 'I like your song, sweetheart,' she says. It's a song she hasn't heard before. 'Where did you learn it?'

Emily keeps singing. Only when she gets to the end of the song does she answer. 'From Paige,' she says.

Nina stiffens.

'And you know what, Mummy?' she continues. 'Paige says I'm her *stepsister*.' She pronounces the word carefully, almost reverently.

Nina feels the back of her neck become even tighter. 'Is that what Daddy says, too?' She tries not to spit the words out. Her eyes on the rear-view mirror, she watches for her daughter's reaction.

Emily looks pensive. 'I haven't asked him,' she says and then, as an afterthought, 'Do you want me to?'

'No.' This Nina says too quickly, too loudly. 'No,' she says again, more quietly. 'No, that's fine.' Already she can feel the prickling of tears behind her eyes. It's going to take all her focus, all her will-power not to lose it now. And she can't lose it. Not yet.

As a test to herself, she parks in front of the house. Right in front of the house. But once she's stopped, she finds she can't move. She actually can't move. Behind her, Emily starts to fidget. 'Mummy,' she says, 'I want to get out.'

When Nina doesn't answer her, she gets louder. 'Out, Mummy!' she shouts. 'I want to get out!'

And when Nina still doesn't answer, the little girl starts to cry. 'Let me out,' she sobs. 'Let me out.'

Nina forces her hands from the steering wheel, unbuckles her seatbelt, gets out of the car and walks around to Emily's side. When she opens the door, her daughter's breath is ragged and her face is wet with tears. 'I was waiting, Mummy,' she reproaches her. 'I was waiting for you.'

Nina doesn't have the energy to answer. All she can do is bundle her up and, holding her tight, carry her up to the house.

Closing her eyes, she presses the bell. When Steve answers the door, her stomach churns as she tries for a smile. Not that it matters— he doesn't meet her eye anyway. And because she can't think of anything to say, she says nothing at all. Instead, she squeezes Emily hard before she hands her over to him. 'See you soon, my darling,' she says, trying her best not to cry. 'See you soon.'

Cheery now in her father's arms, Emily waves. 'Guess what, Mummy?' she says. 'Tonight I'm going to sleep with Paige in her room.'

⁓

On Sunday afternoon, Emily is back again, silently transferred from Steve's arms into her own. Once he has gone—as quickly as he can—Nina burrows her face into the little girl's hair, breathing in the smell of her, breathing her daughter right back into her.

'How was your weekend, sweetie?' she asks. It's a dangerous question—there are so many things she doesn't want to know—but still she asks it. Every single time she asks it.

'It was Poppy's birthday,' Emily tells her, 'and we had a party.'

Nina gives her a wide, beaming, fake smile. 'At Poppy's place?'

Emily nods. 'Yes, at Poppy's place.'

Nina's stomach lurches but she presses on. 'And who else came to the party, sweetheart?'

'Yvette and Auntie Jen and Uncle Brett.'

'Is that all?'

Emily laughs. 'And Daddy, of course, and Sue and Paige. And Paige got to put some of the candles on the cake and I got to put some on and Yvette got to put some on.'

Nina's smile fades.

'Then we all had to sing "Happy Birthday" but Paige didn't sing the real "Happy Birthday" song, she sang another one. Do you want me to sing it?'

Nina doesn't want to hear the song but Emily starts up before she can answer. 'Happy birthday to you, happy birthday to you, you act like a monkey and you smell like one too.' She sings it loudly and gleefully before collapsing into exaggerated shrieks of laughter. 'That's a funny one, Mummy, isn't it?'

'Is that the song you sang for Poppy?' Nina's voice is sharp. 'That he smells like a monkey? Do you think that's a nice thing to sing for your poppy?'

Emily looks confused. 'It was a funny song,' she says. 'It was just Paige's funny song.'

That's all it takes for Nina to snap. 'Well, I don't think it's a funny song, Emily. I think it's a very rude song and I think Paige was very rude to sing it at Poppy's party. Very rude.'

Emily's lip starts to tremble. 'Well, Daddy thought it was funny,' she says defiantly. 'Daddy said it was funny and Sue said it was funny. And Poppy was laughing and Auntie Jen was laughing too.'

Nina can't stand to listen to it. But she must. Trying her best, she manages to squeeze out a smile. 'Well, I like the real birthday song,' she says brightly. 'Was it a yummy birthday cake?'

Emily nods. 'Sue and Paige and me, we made it together. It was a vanilla cake with chocolate icing and I did the sprinkles. You should have seen it, Mummy. You should have seen how good it was.' Her face is hopeful, now: so hopeful, so confused and so desperate to please that Nina suddenly feels ashamed of herself.

'It sounds beautiful,' she says softly. 'It sounds really, really beautiful.'

⤝

She's just got Emily to bed when the phone rings. On the other end of the line, Marina is breathless.

'You won't believe what happened today. You will not believe it.'

Nina waits for it. God knows what Marina's been up to this time.

'*Steve* was there at pick-up time today,' she says. 'Your Steve.'

Nina doesn't want her to continue, but Marina doesn't stop. 'I almost fell over when I saw him,' she says, 'and you know why he was there?'

'No,' Nina whispers weakly, but she thinks she does know.

'To pick up Paige,' she reveals, her voice loud and indignant. 'Can you believe it?'

Nina can believe it. More than that, she has to believe it. And she has to get used to it. To all of it, to everything about their happy family life together. But she wishes Marina hadn't told her.

Now that she has, she starts to imagine them all together: her husband, their daughter, that woman and Paige. Pushing herself even further—just to see how much she can take—she pictures the two of them alone, Steve and Sue: his hand on her leg, her hand on his face, his lips on her neck.

In the background, Marina is still talking, but Nina is praying for the call to end.

At last, Marina rings off; things have been crazy at school, she explains, and she'll be preparing lessons all night if she doesn't get on with it.

Nina needs to prepare, too, and once the call is over, she turns on the computer to get started. There are six new emails in her inbox. One is from Steve. As usual, her heart drops at the sight of his name. The subject heading is *Next weekend.*

We'll need to swap weekends, he writes. *Meg and Paul have invited us down the coast this weekend. We'll take Emily with us, so can you have her next weekend instead?*

She stares at the computer screen in disbelief, anger rising in her. She can actually feel it rising. It starts low, right down in her groin, expands into her stomach and travels up to her chest, making her arms rigid and bringing a dull pressure to the back of her eyes. 'No!' she shouts at the screen. 'No!'

There will be no swap this weekend and Emily will not be going down the coast with you.

This is what she'll tell him.

Her fingers banging hard on the keyboard, she types quickly.

No, Steve, I will not be swapping weekends with you. Too bad if this mucks up your plans. Because you know what? My plans have been mucked up, too: they've been mucked up by you and that woman. And if you think you can simply push me out of your life and insert her into it, then you might like to think again. I'm not sure what Paul thinks about Sue Rankin, but I can tell you what Meg thinks: Meg thinks she's disgusting. So good luck with Meg and Sue getting on like a house on fire.

Once she has finished, she leans back to reread it. She is satisfied with what she has written. Satisfied with every word of it. Sated, somehow, by the very act of writing it.

Later, when she returns to it, she is still pleased with it, still satisfied by it. Only reluctantly does she delete it and start again.

Dear Steve, she writes instead.

I'm happy to have Emily next weekend so she can go away with you this weekend.

N

The effort of it has her so wired, she can't go to sleep. Instead, she stays up to finish off name tags for the class. She even laminates them.

◦⌣◦

The next morning, Elsie is first into the room. Her mouth drops as she takes it all in: the desks back in a horseshoe shape, the red rug back at the front of the room.

Behind her, the rest of the class starts to pile in. 'Hey,' Kurt yells out, 'it's back! Mr P's rug is back. And we've got name tags. With plastic and everything.'

Ethan almost trips over in his haste to find his. Nina smiles when he does: she's put him next to Kurt, opposite Sebastian. Jade she's pushed up to the end with Cody, and Bridie she's kept at the front of the room.

Kurt sticks his hand up and grunts until she picks him. 'Miss,' he says, 'this is heaps better. Not like Mr P, but heaps better than before.'

Nina gives him a wry smile. 'Thanks,' she says. 'Thanks for letting me know.'

The rug and the horseshoe make for a better week—her best yet. For the first time, the week flies by and suddenly it is Friday afternoon and the bell has gone, the classroom has emptied and the place is quiet. Nina is busy sorting through her desk when she hears a noise and looks up. Tania is there, standing in the doorway.

She gives Nina a smile. 'Sorry,' she says, 'didn't mean to scare you. Belinda and I were about to head off for a drink. I thought you might want to come.'

It's the first time she's been asked and a sparkle of shy excitement surges through her, making her tongue-tied.

'Don't worry if you can't,' Tania tells her. 'It's just that Sarah's with Dean, so I've got the night off.'

'No, I'm not busy,' Nina stammers. 'Not at all.' Which is true: now that Emily is with Steve all weekend, she's completely free.

Take advantage of it, for God's sake. This is what Marina keeps telling her. *Go out dancing, go to the pub, have a one-night stand, just do something.*

Okay, she thinks, okay.

'Thanks,' she tells Tania. 'I'd love to come.'

So they pick Belinda up from her classroom and together they walk down to the car park. On the way, they pass Laurie. 'Enjoy your weekend,' she says, her voice strangely high, almost strained.

Tania gives her a bland smile. 'You too,' she calls back. 'As if, you workaholic,' she adds under her breath.

Belinda turns away so she won't be caught laughing.

Uncomfortable now, Nina gives Laurie an awkward wave. 'See you,' she calls out, a little too softly. When Laurie meets Nina's eye, she seems wistful, upset even.

They should ask her to join them, Nina thinks. It would be easy enough to say, *Laurie, we're having a drink, do you want to join us?* But it's not up to her. She's lucky to have been asked herself. So she doesn't say anything. Instead, she just keeps walking.

Tania waits until Laurie is out of earshot. 'You reckon she's got a camp bed set up?'

Belinda titters and Nina allows herself a smile. 'Why do you think she works so hard?'

Tania shrugs. 'Because she hasn't got a life. Because she's a nasty bitch who probably hasn't got any friends.'

Belinda steps back in mock horror. 'Language, Ms Rossi, language.'

But Tania doesn't look like she's about to apologise. 'Well, it's true, isn't it? She's a nasty bitch who probably hasn't got any friends.

I mean, look at what she did to Terry. Would you risk getting close? Me, I'll be keeping my distance.'

Belinda nods. 'At least it's only until the end of the year.'

'Don't be too confident—look what she's managed to do so far. I reckon she could get rid of the lot of us if she tried hard enough.'

'What do you mean?'

Tania gives Nina the once-over. 'Not you—she seems to like you; it's troublemakers like me she doesn't want.'

'You seriously think she'd try to get rid of you?'

Tania laughs. 'No idea—but if she can do it to Terry, she can do it to anyone.'

❧

They go to Tania's favourite pub, in Raleigh. Once they've ordered their drinks, they grab a table in the bar area. The bar stools are high and because Belinda is so short, it takes her a couple of tries to get up.

Tania grins at her. 'Remember when Terry tried to give you a leg up?'

For a small woman, Belinda has a throaty laugh. 'I think he forgot I wasn't one of the kids. Tell you what, though, it got me practising. The next time, I almost sprinted over so I could hoick myself up before he tried to step in again.'

Tania tilts her head towards Nina. 'I've been meaning to ask you,' she says, 'how are you going with the show?'

Nina's stomach drops. She'd forgotten about the show; completely forgotten about it. 'Not very well,' she says.

Tania looks a bit startled. 'You'll need to get a move on if you're going to have it ready on time.'

'Maybe we could just skip it this year?' she ventures.

Tania and Belinda both look stunned. 'What, cancel the whole thing?' Belinda asks her.

'Well, it wouldn't be cancelled if it didn't even get started, would it?' She says it as a joke but neither of them laughs.

Tania doesn't even smile. 'The kids would be gutted, completely gutted,' she says. 'The Year 6 show, it's like their—what would you call it?—their rite of passage, I suppose. Their farewell to the school. You can't just not do it.'

'But I don't even know where to begin.' She's starting to panic now.

Tania softens her tone. 'Don't worry,' she says, 'I'll give you a hand.'

❧

By six o'clock, Belinda and Tania are both hungry. Nina is starting to get peckish, too.

It's cash only at the bistro but there's an ATM near the bar. Which is just as well because Nina is almost out of cash. So she walks over to the ATM, slots in her card, hits sixty and waits for her money. Instead, the screen flashes her a warning: *You have insufficient funds to complete this transaction.*

Pulling her card out, she tries once more. Again, the warning appears. It must be a problem with the machine. Her pay won't go in until Tuesday but Steve's child support will have already come through, so even with the rent and childcare fees taken out, she should still have two hundred dollars in the account. Maybe she punched in the wrong number. Maybe she pressed six hundred instead of sixty. She has a third go at it: carefully this time, so there's no chance of a mistake. It still doesn't work. So she asks for an account balance instead of a withdrawal. This time the machine does what she asks, and gives her the balance. Only it's not what she's anticipated. According to the slip of paper, she has eighteen dollars fifty left in her account. And twenty dollars is the minimum withdrawal amount. Apart from that, she's got eight dollars eighty left in her purse.

In a brief moment of optimism, she checks the blackboard menu for something under eight dollars. There's nothing. Even the soup costs ten dollars. Which means she won't be staying for dinner after all. Her humiliation is so sharp it makes her want to cry. If it was Marina, she could tell her the truth: that she can't pay for dinner. But she can't say that to Tania and Belinda; she scarcely knows them.

'I just got a text from Steve,' she tells them instead. 'Emily's sick. She won't settle. So I'm going to have to go.'

Belinda makes a sad face. 'What a bummer,' she says.

Tania is more probing. 'You're not upset about the show, are you?'

The question surprises her. 'It's not that.' This, at least, is truthful. 'It's just Emily,' she says weakly, too spent to add anything more to the lie.

In the car she kicks herself for having been so stupid: for not having noticed her account was so low. But she can't work out how it could have happened, where the extra money would have gone.

When she gets home, she logs into online banking and scrolls through her statement. There aren't any extra withdrawals, just the usual: rent, childcare, groceries. The entry marked *Steve Foreman monthly deposit* is there too: transferred, as usual, on the fourteenth of the month. But as her eyes follow the entry to the end of the row, she sees that something is different: the amount is short by two hundred dollars. Instead of nine hundred dollars, he has paid her seven hundred.

The bank must have made a mistake, she decides. She should ring Steve to let him know, so it can be sorted out quickly. She dials his number.

He answers straightaway. 'Hello?' he says, his voice wary.

'It's me,' she says. 'You got a minute?'

When he doesn't answer, she clears her throat. 'I just wanted to talk about the money.'

'What money?'

'My money.' The words are out before she can get them back. 'I mean, the money for Emily. I've checked and there's only seven hundred this month.'

He stays quiet.

'And I thought, well, I thought maybe they'd got it wrong. The bank. I thought the bank might have made a mistake. Something like that.' She's gabbling now.

Still he says nothing.

'Did they?' she asks softly, her voice suddenly croaky. 'Did they get it wrong?'

Finally he answers her. 'It's gone down,' he says.

She doesn't understand what he's saying. 'What do you mean? What's gone down?'

She hears him clear his throat. 'The child support amount. What I'm supposed to pay.'

'I'm sorry?' Her voice is cooling now.

'Because of Paige. They count her now, so the amount, it's lower.'

'Because of Paige?'

'That's right.'

'And that's why you're paying less? Because of *Paige*?' She can feel her cheeks start to burn. Calm down, she tells herself, calm down. This is not the child's fault. This is not Paige's fault.

'Look, it's not like I'm ripping you off. I'm paying what I'm supposed to pay.' His voice is less certain now but more defensive.

'I was out with friends from my new school,' she tells him. 'They invited me out but there was no money in my account so I had to come home.' She stops to catch herself. 'Steve,' she pleads, willing him to comfort her, 'I couldn't even pay for a bowl of soup.'

Afterwards, she is so agitated she can't keep still.

She needs to eat, that's what she needs to do. So she gets out a couple of eggs then goes back to the fridge for the milk. Scrambled eggs. She'll make herself some scrambled eggs on toast.

But there's no milk. She can't believe it. 'Shit!' she shouts aloud. Instead of getting milk on the way home from school, she went to the pub. And now she's back home again, cranky, tired and hungry, and there's no milk. And it's his fault. His fault she's here on her own in this house; his fault there's no milk.

Frustration consumes her, and she doesn't know what to do.

Then it dawns on her.

The neighbour.

She could ask the neighbour. She searches for her name. Jean. Yes, Jean. She could ask Jean for some milk.

Joan

The knock at the door so startles her, she almost jumps out of her armchair. When she looks at the clock on top of the television, she sees that it is almost eight o'clock. Fear makes her cautious. Someone at the door at this hour? She should ignore it. It could be a burglar—or worse.

The screen door is locked, her mother reminds her, *so you'll be fine to open the front door.*

Still Joan hesitates. Who could it be?

When the second knock comes, curiosity decides her. Standing up, she tightens the sash of her dressing-gown and makes her way to the door.

'Hello?' she calls out softly. When there is no answer, she opens the front door a fraction, leaving the chain latched. 'Hello?' she says again, her eyes straining into the darkness. There is a porch light above the door but the bulb has gone and because the fitting's tricky, she hasn't replaced it. Now she wishes she'd tried a bit harder. 'Hello?'

'Sorry to bother you,' she hears. 'It's Nina, from next door. I—I've got a favour to ask you.'

Nina! She hasn't spoken to her for weeks. Strange how they can live so close but never see each other. Not that Joan hasn't been keeping an eye out for her. Especially when she's in the yard. Sometimes she sees Emily, but not often. Once she'd even called over to her, from over the fence. 'Hello, there!' she'd called out, but it can't have been loud enough because the girl didn't look up and Joan, suddenly shy, hadn't tried a second time.

'Nina,' she says now, 'yes, yes, of course.'

Ask her in, her mother urges. *Ask her in right now.*

Thinking about it makes Joan's hands clammy and she swallows hard before quickly, too quickly, she blurts it out. 'Come in, Nina, come in.'

And to Joan's amazement, she does. Without a word, she comes inside and follows Joan through to the kitchen.

There, Nina turns to her and, with tears in her eyes, tells her that she has no milk.

Taken aback by the tears, Joan is flustered. 'Don't cry about that,' she says. 'Please don't cry about that. I've got milk. You can have my milk.'

Nina wipes her eyes with the back of her hand. 'I'm sorry,' she whispers. 'I was supposed to be going out for dinner and then I couldn't, so I started to make some scrambled eggs and realised I didn't have any milk. I'm sorry,' she says, her voice starting to crack. 'I'm sorry to bother you like this.'

Bother?

If only she knew.

Quickly, Joan heads for the fridge. She has a little less than a litre of milk left; she will give it all to Nina. She'll make do with black tea in the morning and later in the day she'll go to the shops.

But her mother is in her ear again now. *Make the girl some dinner, for God's sake, Joanie. Look at the poor thing. She needs looking after more than she needs your milk, that's clear as day. Sit her down and make her something to eat. She can just as easily eat scrambled eggs here as eat them there. But don't give her a choice. Be a bit assertive, Joan. Don't give her a chance to say no.*

'Sit down,' Joan says aloud, hoping she doesn't sound as nervous as she feels. 'I'll make you some eggs.'

But Nina shakes her head. 'No,' she says, 'it's okay. I'm just being silly. I'll be fine.'

What now, Joan thinks, what do I do now?

Tell her, Joan: just tell her to sit down.

So she does. 'Sit down,' she says, 'while I make them.'

And her neighbour Nina does just that. She sits on one of the kitchen chairs and waits quietly while Joan cooks. It's only when Joan is scooping the eggs onto a plate that she remembers.

'Where's Emily?' she asks.

Nina's face turns red. 'She's with her father for the weekend,' she says.

And although Joan doesn't ask her anything more, still she keeps going. 'He—we've separated,' she says, her words tripping together. 'My husband and I are separated.'

Joan doesn't know what to say, so she says nothing at all.

'Thank you,' Nina says softly. 'Thank you for being so kind to me, Jean.'

Shy now, and embarrassed, Joan just nods. It's not the time, she thinks, to say that her name isn't Jean, it's Joan.

Nina

That night, Nina sleeps well. Better, in fact, than she has for weeks. And when she wakes up the next morning, she almost feels refreshed.

For the rest of the weekend, she tries to come up with ideas for the Year 6 show. A play, she thinks, but she can't find anything with enough parts for all the kids.

It's too much, she decides. She's left it too late and she won't be able to do it. It's as simple as that.

But when she gets to school on Monday, there's a book on her desk with a sticky-note stuck to its cover.

Hi Nina, the note says. *There are some good pieces in here—see what you think. Tania.*

Nina picks up the book and has a flick through it. It's a book of plays for kids. Forget it, she thinks. But when she has a closer look at it over recess, she finds herself wavering. The pieces are simple enough, and not too long. She takes the book home with her and, once Emily is in bed, rings Marina to talk about it. Within an hour, Marina has convinced her.

The Year 6 show will be going ahead. It is with some trepidation that Nina announces this to the class the next day.

If she's honest, she'd have expected some appreciation; nothing over the top, just a small show of enthusiasm.

They aren't exactly indifferent to the news. Unconvinced would be a better way to describe it. Kurt leads the discussion.

'These plays you've suggested, miss, I think you'll find we're a bit too old for them, seeing as we'll be in high school soon.'

Cody is quick to support him. 'What Kurt said, miss—well, he's right and that.'

Nina scans the classroom. 'Anyone else?'

Ethan is also keen for a word. 'Miss, I think we should do a play about something else.'

'For example?'

Put on the spot, he shoots a look at Kurt and Cody. Kurt has nothing to offer and Cody just shrugs. 'Dunno, miss, exactly.' After a moment or two he brightens. 'Maybe something about fighting or that.'

'Or maybe something not lame,' says Jade. 'Something cool.'

Nina lets them keep talking.

Cool is good. Everyone in the classroom agrees. Even Elsie wants cool.

'So, something cool,' Nina starts. She tries to sound a bit hesitant, just hesitant enough to make it sound like she's trying her best to think of something that might work. 'You mean, something like . . . rap?'

All over the classroom, heads flick up.

His eyes narrowed, Kurt scrutinises her. 'Did you say rap, miss?'

Yes, she thinks, it's working. She tries to hold herself back. Keep it cool, she tells herself, don't look too excited, just keep it cool.

Rap-style cool. 'Yes, Kurt,' she says, keeping her voice very, very casual, 'that's exactly what I said.'

He contemplates this. 'You mean, we'd all be rapping?'

'That's right.'

'Like Kanye West?' He's testing her, she knows that, but today she's ready for it.

'I was thinking more like Eminem,' she tells him.

Eyes widen and Ethan doesn't even bother checking with Kurt before he pipes up, 'Eminem, miss, he rocks, he so rocks.'

Even Jade is looking interested.

But Kurt is still sceptical. 'Why do you like him, miss?'

She gives him a nod that is part concession, part victory. His instinct, to query her credentials, is right: before yesterday she had none. Not that he needs to know this. Because after a night of cramming with Marina, she's got everything she needs.

Marina knows about all of them, all the big-name rappers, but there's only been time for Nina to focus on one. Now she's an expert.

She takes her time to answer him. She even lets her eyes go a bit dreamy. 'I just love what he's got to say, Kurt,' she says. 'And his rhythm, it's fantastic.'

He's still not convinced. 'What are your favourite songs, miss?'

She's written them all out—the ten songs Marina has chosen as her favourites—and has the list right there in front of her, ready for just this question. She steals a quick glance at it. 'Look, Kurt,' she says, 'like everyone else, I love "Lose Yourself"—I mean, you have to, don't you?'

Ethan and Cody are hers now, she can see it, their eyes wide with newfound respect, their heads nodding hard. But Kurt still needs more. And that's okay, because she's got more.

'But if I'm honest, Kurt, it's "When I'm Gone" that does it for me, because it's about his little girl, and I've got a little girl too, so I feel like we've got something in common, Eminem and me.'

And with that, she's done it. He's hers.

'Girls always like that one,' he tells her. It feels like a confidence. 'Even my mum likes that one. But my brother and me, we like the other stuff.'

'"Like Toy Soldiers"?' She tries not to sound too smug, tries not to look triumphant, but it's not easy.

Kurt takes a moment to consider. '"Like Toy Soldiers" isn't bad. But "Just Lose It", that's even better.' He lowers his voice. 'Except the video's a bit inappropriate and that.'

She hasn't seen the video and doesn't want him to start describing it now. So she gives him a nod to let him know—as one Eminem fan to another—that this is something best kept between the two of them. 'That's why I prefer some of his other stuff,' she tells him, 'because it's suitable for a younger audience too.'

That makes him thoughtful. 'I get your point, miss.'

'Thanks, Kurt,' she says solemnly. Inside, she is dancing. Inside, she is doing cartwheels.

And sure enough, once Kurt is with her, there's no problem selling it to the rest of the class. It's a simple enough idea: two plays, each of them performed in rap. The first one—*The Wolf*—is the rap version of 'Little Red Riding Hood' and the second—*The Bears*—is the rap version of 'Goldilocks and the Three Bears'.

To decide the cast, she takes nominations from the class.

Immediately, Kurt, Cody and Ethan come together in a mini scrum. Ethan flicks his head across to Jade, who smiles and sidles over. Over in the corner, Sebastian is standing alone. Kurt gives Ethan a nudge and lifts his chin up in Sebastian's direction. Immediately Ethan scowls and shakes his head. But Kurt persists, pulling his head in close and whispering to him, his voice urgent. When, finally, Ethan pulls back, his face resigned, Kurt gives a whistle.

'Hey, Sebastian,' he calls. 'Come here.'

Sebastian looks over but doesn't move. Kurt doesn't like being kept waiting, so he gives Sebastian another whistle. 'Come on,' he calls out again. Still Sebastian takes his time.

'Are you a rapper?' Kurt asks once he has joined them.

When Sebastian looks confused, Kurt tries again.

'I mean, when you're at home with your family, do you all do rap together? You know, because you're all black and that—no offence or anything. We thought you'd be good to have in our group because you probably rap heaps already.'

It's clear that Sebastian does want to be part of the group; Nina can tell by the way his eyes stay fixed on Kurt, listening hard. And yet seconds pass before he answers.

'Yes,' he says finally, 'that's true. We do rap a lot at home.'

Kurt, Cody and Ethan move into a huddle for a quick conference. Then Kurt holds out his hand. Sebastian offers his up for a handshake but instead Kurt rotates his hand around, takes hold of Sebastian's thumb then slides his palm away. 'Welcome, bro,' he says.

To the clique, Nina adds Elsie and Bridie. Together, they'll form the cast of *The Wolf*. The rest of the class will be in *The Bears*.

She'll need some parent volunteers, she tells the class, because there's a lot to organise. When she mentions this, Kurt's hand shoots up. 'Seeing as Sebastian's dad is a rapper and that, he probably should come in to show us his best moves. Like, so he could teach us and that.'

Nina looks to Sebastian for confirmation. His eyes flicker as he answers. 'Yes, miss,' he says, 'he could definitely do that.'

Rebecca

Fork in hand, Emmanuel looks up from his meal. He seems so shocked, Rebecca is scared he'll choke.

'What do you mean my best moves? I've never rapped in my life.'

Sebastian keeps his eyes on the floor.

'And anyway,' Emmanuel continues, 'why on earth would any-one think I'm a rapper? Do I look like a rapper to you?'

Rebecca looks at her husband. Tonight he is wearing his brown trousers, a checked shirt fastened up to the neck and a dark blue cardigan. She stifles a smile—rapper is not the first word that comes to mind.

But Emmanuel isn't stifling a smile; he's becoming worked up. For him, this is an unusual thing.

'Well, Sebastian,' he says, 'is there anything about me that screams rap artist to you? I'm an engineer, for God's sake. Why would anyone think I'm a rapper?'

Sebastian's answer is very low, so low Rebecca can't hear it and Emmanuel has to ask him to speak up.

Sebastian does raise his voice but he doesn't look up. 'It's because we're black,' he says. 'They think we do rap at home because we're black.'

Rebecca feels her mouth starting to twitch. She can't laugh. She can't let herself laugh, not when Emmanuel is taking it all so seriously.

'That's what they think, do they? That we come home, kick off our shoes, start rapping and don't stop?' He is both angry and flustered now.

The questions are for Sebastian, but Sebastian still won't look up.

Rebecca is going to have to step in. She tries to think of something that will calm Emmanuel down, something to make him less upset. Instead, an image comes into her head. It's an image that is a bit like a Bollywood film, only it's not Bollywood, it's rap; it's rap at home with the Chumas. Non-stop rap with the Chumas. It's a stupid thought, but it makes her laugh. Just a chuckle at first, but then she finds she can't stop herself, and soon she's laughing so hard she's starting to cry, the tears streaming down her cheeks.

When she looks at Emmanuel and Sebastian, they are both staring at her open-mouthed. This just makes her laugh harder. And God, it feels good. God, it feels good to laugh. It has been a long, long time since she has laughed like this.

'Can you imagine?' she asks them, when at last she is able to speak. 'Just think of the possibilities—there could be the dinner rap, the washing-up rap, the shower rap, the clean-the-house rap.'

That makes Sebastian smile, but not Emmanuel. Emmanuel is still stony-faced.

'It's fine for you,' he tells her. 'You don't have to become a rapping guru by next week.'

Well, the thought of it, the thought of her staid, brown-trousered husband as a rapping guru, just sets her off again.

'We'll just have to find you something to wear,' she says, 'so it looks like you've just come from the hood.'

'And where exactly is the hood, Rebecca?' Emmanuel asks her. 'Because strange as it may seem—black as I am—I've never actually been there.'

Rebecca tries to stop laughing—she does try, but still she can't. 'Looks like you'll have to pretend.'

Emmanuel stares at her. 'I can't rap, Rebecca. I can't sing, I can't dance and I certainly can't rap. How am I supposed to give a masterclass in something I've never even done before?'

Rebecca shakes her head. 'You'll just have to wing it.'

'You could do it,' he says to her, his voice becoming softer. 'You're good at all that performance stuff. You could do it instead of me. Couldn't you?'

'I've never rapped either,' she says. 'Not seriously.'

'But you could work something out, you know you could.' He is almost pleading with her. 'Please, Rebecca,' he says.

The plays are scripted, which means there'll be no ad-libbing. So the rapping itself isn't the issue: it's the dancing that has to go with it. And Rebecca has never been a dancer.

Sitting in front of Emmanuel's computer, she types in the words *rap dance moves*. She gets three million hits. She adds the word *easy*. Then she just clicks on sites at random. Many people like to dance to rap in their own living rooms, she finds. And of the many who do, some choose to dance only in G-strings. These are not the videos she opts to use as a teaching aid.

Instead, she chooses T-Rap Thomas. He is, he claims,

choreographer to the world's greatest rappers. T-Rap Thomas has a great smile but he's one of life's fast talkers and, try as she might, she can't follow him past step two of his Easy Hip-hop Moves.

In the end, it is a home video by an eight-year-old that proves most helpful. Two nights later, she's ready to showcase what she's learnt. She pushes the coffee table aside and moves the sofa up against the wall, then invites Emmanuel and Sebastian to witness her performance.

The robot, that's the dance she's been practising most. Of all the ones she's watched, it's the one she finds easiest: stiff legs, elbows bent, head turned to the side. This is how she starts and ends the sequence. In between, she lifts one leg up, and one leg down, she bends at the waist and swivels to the side, she rotates one arm up, then the other. Keeping her face completely expressionless, she moves her head first up then down, to one side, then to the other.

Once she has finished—legs still stiff, elbows still bent, head still to the side—she feels proud of the performance.

Emmanuel claps hard and for a long time. Sebastian is more subdued.

'What did you think?' she asks him.

He hesitates. 'You were a very good robot,' he tells her. 'You were just like a robot. But I don't know how robots would fit in with the plays. I mean, one's about a wolf and the other's about bears. I'm not sure how a robot would fit in.'

Rebecca's face falls. She hadn't considered that. All she'd thought about was finding something easy.

She thinks quickly. 'It might work for the bears. At the beginning, perhaps they could robot out of the house?'

For a long time, Sebastian stays silent. 'I think it would look a bit strange if the bears did the robot dance out of their house. I don't think it would be very good.' There is a hint of panic in his voice now.

Rebecca takes a deep breath. 'Okay,' she says, 'I'll work on something else.'

Her first lesson is with the cast of *The Wolf*. For Rebecca, who has only ever had to deal with one child, this is a frightening prospect.

She's remembered their names, so that's a start, but she's going to need more than that to keep things under control. She'll need to assert her authority. And so, from the depths of her diaphragm, she brings out a strong, deep voice: so loud and so low, it shocks even her. For the cast of *The Wolf*, it is astonishingly effective: immediately they fall silent.

'Thank you,' she says. Now she needs to get them into some order. 'Two rows,' she tells them. 'Elsie, Kurt and Cody, you'll be in the front row—Sebastian, you too. Jade, Bridie and Ethan, you can line up behind them.'

And that's exactly what they do: without any fuss, they arrange themselves into two lines.

'As you know,' she says, 'Sebastian and I, we've got a bit of experience in rapping. In our house, that's how we like to relax, by rapping as we go about our business.'

There is a lot of nodding as she says this. Only Sebastian looks doubtful.

After a moment, Kurt raises his hand. With some apprehension, Rebecca nods at him.

'I was just wondering,' he says, 'when you're rapping, are you always freestyling?'

She has absolutely no idea what he's talking about.

To buy some time, she clears her throat. 'Good question,' she tells him, 'and as a matter of fact, we do spend a lot of time free-styling. So you're right about that.'

Fearing more questions, she moves on quickly. 'Today, I'll be teaching you a couple of basic hip-hop moves to use when you're rapping. When you're a bit more experienced—like we are in our family—you'll be able to work on some more complicated routines. But for today, we'll be keeping it simple.'

She's brought along a CD of rap hits and a step-by-step plan of the routine she's managed to cobble together. She sweeps her eyes over the plan as she gets herself into position: knees bent, shoulders forward, hands by her side.

Then she turns on the music. 'Okay,' she says, 'let's begin with a warm-up.'

In position already, Kurt starts to bob his head up and down to the music. When Rebecca nods to let him know she's impressed, he surprises her with a wink. He does it with such confidence and such panache, she finds it hard not to laugh. But she can't laugh: what-ever she does, she can't laugh. Instead, she turns away and, putting a hand up to her mouth, pretends to cough. Then she turns back to the class and starts to shake her hands. 'All right,' she says, 'I want you to shake your hands. Shake them out, shake them right out.'

So they all start shaking. All except Sebastian, who stands there rigid: knees locked, arms motionless.

'Do it,' she mouths at him.

But he doesn't do it; he just stands there looking mortified.

'Do it,' she mouths again. If he doesn't, she'll end up looking like a complete fool.

Slowly, he shakes his head then makes a flicking motion with his hand.

'Don't watch,' he mouths back.

A wave of resentment rockets through her. Don't watch? *Don't watch?* How about the room full of children watching her? If she could, she'd grab him by the arm and give him a shake. *You're the reason I'm doing this*, she'd hiss at him. *You're the reason I'm up here looking like an idiot. You're why I'm pretending to be some rap queen, when I've got no idea what I'm doing.*

But all she can do is glare at him before, with an exaggerated sweep, she tosses her head away from him.

She switches her focus to Elsie, who is not only shaking out her hands, she's shaking out her whole body: legs, feet, fingers, head.

Cody isn't; he's just rocking to the music. She likes the way he moves: likes the way he just does it, as though he's not even thinking about it, as though he's just letting his body take the lead. Just shaking and rocking and shaking and rocking. It's almost mesmerising and for a moment she stops to watch him.

But she's not supposed to be watching, she's supposed to be teaching. And the dance she's supposed to be teaching them today is the Walk it Out dance.

She turns the music off to explain it to them. 'Okay,' she says, 'this is one of your basic hip-hop steps. You can do it while you're rapping. It's really just twisting while you walk. Keep your knees bent and, as you step forward, twist to one side, then twist to the other side. So you're walking out and twisting at the same time.' She shows them then turns the music back on again. 'Now you try it.'

They're nothing if not enthusiasts. In the second row, Jade is tossing her hair around with such vigour it whips across Ethan's face. Turning to face each other, Kurt and Cody walk it out towards one another until they collide. And although Elsie is still shaking instead of stepping, her face is lit up with pleasure. Beside her, Bridie frowns in concentration as she keeps her eyes fixed on Rebecca.

'A bit more twisting,' Rebecca tells her. 'A bit more twisting while you're stepping out.'

With grim focus, the girl does just that. Her face set, she twists as she steps, her fists tightly clenched, her teeth biting down on her lip.

'Good girl,' Rebecca tells her gently.

When she can, she ventures a look in Sebastian's direction. To her surprise, he's dancing now, too. There's nothing ostentatious about the way he moves—his steps are small and he keeps his head down—but his rhythm is good and his style is fluid. A surge of pride floods through her.

When she turns back to address the class, she has to shout to be heard over the music. 'Well, you've got the legs,' she tells them. 'How about the arms?'

And as she talks them through the steps, she keeps on walking it out: to the front, to the side, to the back. She's really starting to enjoy herself now. 'I like to start with my arms lifted high,' she tells them. 'Arms high, elbows bent, then you just groove them out and groove them back in again. When you've got that sorted, you can improvise a little: cross one arm over the other, roll your arm over your head, whatever you like.'

There's a change of song then, to one that Rebecca has started to enjoy. It's the refrain she likes best:

Here I am; it's me in the middle now
Me in the middle now;
Me in the middle

She doesn't know what it's supposed to mean but it doesn't matter; there's something about the music that makes her want to sing along. Soon, the children are joining in too. For the most part they just hum along, out of tune and out of time, but Rebecca loves it. When she steals a look over at Sebastian, she sees that he is singing, too. And when he catches her looking at him, this time he smiles.

She smiles then too: a big, broad, beaming smile. And as she smiles, a strong sensation of wellbeing engulfs her, filling her up from the soles of her feet to the top of the head. It is a feeling that makes her light-headed with joy.

It hits her then: this is the first time in many weeks she has felt happy.

More than that, even. This is the first time in many weeks that she has felt something other than trepidation; the first time she has not been consumed with that one question, that one ever-circling, ever-present question. Will they be allowed to stay?

Joan

Joan feels a surge of delight when she hears Nina's car pull up. She hasn't checked the letterbox all day. Deliberately. Because this will give her an excuse to be outside when Nina arrives home.

Now she hurries to the front door. Once she's outside, she forces herself to slow down, to take her time getting to the letterbox. By the time she's there, Nina is taking Emily out of the car. Only then does Joan check for the mail.

It works like a treat.

'Jean!' Nina calls out to her. 'Jean!'

She forces herself not to look up straightaway. When she does, she tries to look surprised. 'Nina,' she says, 'and Emily, hello.'

Nina smiles but Emily, who is being carried, buries her face in her mother's shoulder. 'Sorry,' Nina says. 'Long day at childcare. I think she's tired.'

At that, the little girl's head pops up. An enormous frown shadows her eyes. 'I'm not tired,' she says. 'I'm just a bit shy.'

This makes Nina laugh, so Joan laughs, too.

'When I'm at big school,' Emily tells her, 'I'm going to be Goldilocks and the Three Bears.'

Nina looks over her daughter's head. 'My class is putting on a couple of plays at the end of the year. I was telling Emily about it and now she wants to be Goldilocks.'

'And I'll get a Goldilocks dress, too,' the little girl pipes up.

When she hears this, an idea pops into Joan's head. She surprises herself by giving voice to it. 'I could make you one,' she says.

Emily's eyes light up. 'For me?'

Joan ducks her head at the question, embarrassed she hasn't checked with Nina first.

But Nina is looking pleased. 'That's a lovely offer, Jean—as long as it's no trouble.'

Joan shakes her head. 'It's no trouble at all,' she says. 'I used to be a dressmaker.'

෴

No trouble is less than the truth and Joan spends hours getting the costume right. In her house, there are no books for children, so on Saturday morning, she walks down to the library and looks through the picture-book section until she finds what she needs. In the book she chooses, Goldilocks wears a simple yellow-waisted frock, and this is what she uses as her model.

All day she works on it and it is evening before she is finished. Holding the gingham dress out in front of her—pressed now and on a coathanger—she is caught by a wave of delight.

Without stopping to think, she hurries next door. Only after she has knocked does it occur to her that this may not be a good time to visit: perhaps it is already dinner time or bath time or bedtime.

As soon as Nina opens the door, these thoughts disappear as a burst of uncontained excitement rushes through her. 'I've finished!' she exclaims.

Nina smiles. 'Come in,' she says. 'Please, come in.'

Joan's pulse quickens. 'Yes,' she says. 'Thank you.'

Inside, she scarcely recognises the place. Shyly, gingerly even, she walks down the hallway of the house she used to know well. Stripped of its wallpaper and painted white, it is foreign to her now: the same shape, the same proportions, but strangely unrecognisable, like an old friend with a new face.

Nina leads her into the lounge room. When Mr Edwards was living here, it had a brown striped sofa in it; that and a television fitted inside a wooden sideboard. Now the room has a red sofa and two orange armchairs. Little Emily is lying on the sofa, curled up, watching television.

'Look what Jean made for you,' Nina calls to her.

Emily's eyes widen when she sees the dress. 'Is that for me?' she asks.

Joan flushes with pride. 'Yes,' she says, 'it is.'

Although it is almost time for bed, the little one wants to try it on immediately.

'Why not?' says Nina.

So carefully, very carefully, Joan slips the dress over Emily's head, fastens the zipper and ties the bow at the back.

The little girl is radiant. 'This is my best dress ever!' she says.

Joan's heart swells to hear it. 'I'm so glad,' she says. 'I'm so glad you like it.'

'Are you going to make all the dresses?' the little girl asks her. 'Are you going to do all of them, for everybody in Mummy's class?'

339

The question confuses Joan and she looks to Nina for help. But Nina just shakes her head as though she doesn't understand the question, either.

Only when the little girl keeps asking does she step in.

'Don't be silly,' Nina says, looking embarrassed. 'Jean made a lovely dress just for you. Imagine how long it would take to make a costume for everybody!'

That's when Joan remembers. 'The plays,' she says, 'does she mean the costumes for the plays?'

When Nina nods, Joan again surprises herself. 'I can make them for you,' she says.

She's nervous and she's excited. She's not sure if she's more excited than nervous, or more nervous than excited. More nervous, she decides. But not so nervous as to back out. The meeting is starting at 7.30 pm. It is not quite six, but already she is dressed and ready. She is wearing a frock she made some years ago. It's wool crepe, in blues and greens, like swirls of sky and grass mixed up together.

She's made a batch of chocolate-chip biscuits to take with her. Once they've cooled, she arranges them on one of the good plates and covers them with cling wrap. There's nothing left to do, then, but wait.

How slowly the time passes. So very slowly. But it does pass and finally—finally!—it is time to go next door.

As always, it is hard to leave the house: twice she almost does it, and twice she turns back again. Once to check the oven (it was off) and once to check the heater (it was off, too). It is an effort not to turn back a third time. When she still hesitates, it is her mother who urges her forward. *Keep going,* she whispers. *This is a special night, Joanie love, so you need to keep going.*

Outside, is it very dark, and with the porch light still out it is difficult to see properly. And only once she's shut the door behind her does she realise she's forgotten to bring a torch. For a moment or two she swivels on the spot, turning back then forward, back then forward.

Don't worry about it, love, her mother reassures her. *You haven't far to go and the streetlights are on.*

This is true. The streetlights are on and they throw just enough light for her to make her way across to Nina's. To save time, she could simply cut across the lawn—it is the quickest way there—but tonight it feels more official, more appropriate to use the footpath.

When she gets there, she presses the doorbell then steps back to wait. She hears nothing: no footsteps, no voices. Perhaps, she thinks, she has made a mistake. Perhaps it is the wrong night. Perhaps it was last night. Perhaps she's missed it.

Steady on, Joanie, her mother warns her. *Give the poor girl a moment.*

It is good advice, for now there are footsteps coming down the hall. Then the door opens and there she is, Nina herself, all dressed up and looking beautiful.

'Hi,' she says. 'Thanks so much for coming.'

Joan presses the plate of biscuits into Nina's hands and follows her down the hallway. There are two doors on the right. Both of them are closed but as they pass the second one, Nina pushes it open. 'I told Emily you'd be in to say goodnight,' she says. 'She wants to show you something.'

Tucked up in bed, the little girl grins up at her. 'Look,' she says, 'I'm wearing my new dress.'

When Joan looks closer, she sees that this is right: Emily is dressed for bed in her Goldilocks costume.

'Do you think I look lovely?' she asks.

Joan nods. 'Yes,' she says, 'I do.' Oh, the joy of it; the joy of looking at that lovely little face smiling up at her.

Nina taps her on the arm. 'Come on, Jean,' she says, 'I want to introduce you to the others.'

There are two women sitting in the lounge room. One of them is vaguely familiar but it is the other one Joan can't keep her eyes off. A black woman! A black woman—black as the ace of spades— right here in Brindle. Joan can't help marvelling at her. And then the woman is standing up to greet her; standing up and stretching a hand out to her. To her surprise, the woman's palm is light—not white, but so much paler than the rest of her. How strange, Joan thinks, how strange, and quickly she glances at her own palm to check whether it, too, is a shade lighter.

The black woman is talking to her. 'I'm Rebecca,' she's saying. 'It's so lovely to meet you.'

Joan would not have expected her to have a voice like that. Such a beautiful voice; the sort of voice you'd expect to hear on the radio. Yes, she thinks to herself, that's what it is: it's a radio voice. A wonderfully rich radio voice and when Joan replies, 'It's lovely to meet you too,' her own sounds thin and scratchy.

'Rebecca's son is in my class,' Nina tells her. 'Mel's son, too.'

Mel is the other woman. The two of them, Mel and Rebecca, are sitting together on the red sofa. On the coffee table in front of them, there's a plate of lemon slice. Nina sets Joan's biscuits beside it.

Mel leans in to look at them. 'Chocolate chip?' she asks, and when Joan blushes and murmurs that yes, they are, Mel pats her stomach and says she can't wait to try them.

From the front of the house comes the sound of the doorbell. 'That'll be Sid,' Nina tells them as she hurries to answer it.

Moments later, the sound of a man's laughter echoes down the hallway. It's a good sound, throaty and infectious, and Joan is curious to see who it is. When he steps into the lounge room—Nina right behind him—Joan can't believe her eyes.

It's him.

The lovely man from the bakery; the lovely man from the library. He's here, in Nina's house.

How can that be?

Nina introduces him. 'This is Sid,' she says. 'Sid Charlton.'

And when he looks over at Joan, he smiles. 'Nice to see you again,' he says.

Joan feels her face burn with embarrassment and pleasure. He remembers me, she thinks; how lovely that he should remember me.

'Jean is a dressmaker,' Nina explains. 'She'll be making all the costumes.'

When he hears that, Sid gives a low whistle. 'My word,' he says, 'that'll be a job and a half.'

Joan's palms are beginning to sweat. 'But I love sewing,' she says.

The five of them are a committee: the Year 6 play committee. Nina herself is the producer, Rebecca is the director, Mel is in charge of photography, make-up and set design, and Sid is in charge of props. Joan has a title, too: costume designer. *Costume designer.* She's the costume designer.

They have three months to get everything ready. This is what

Nina tells them. She sounds anxious but Rebecca tells them not to worry: all they need to do is stay focused. Rebecca has experience in production work, Mel explains; she used to be on television.

Television—she's not radio, she's television. Of course she is, Joan thinks: her voice is a television voice and her face—so smooth and perfect-looking—is a television face, too. There is something magnetic about her. Something that draws the eye, that makes it hard to look away. So Joan doesn't look away. She tries to listen, too; she tries to concentrate on what's being said. But there is a lot to take in—a lot of information about scripts and rehearsals and spreadsheets and timetables—and after a while, she finds herself fading.

Sid is sitting across from her and when she looks over at him, she sees that he is fading, too. This comforts her: she's not the only one getting tired. He must feel her glance on him, for quickly he straightens up again.

When the meeting itself is over, they all stay for coffee. Sid reaches for one of Joan's biscuits. 'These are beaut,' he tells her, 'just how I like them.'

Later, when he stands to leave, he offers her a lift home.

She blushes and shakes her head. 'I'm just next door,' she tells him.

So he walks her home instead. On the way, he starts to tell her a bit about himself, and a bit about the work he does at the school. Suddenly, Joan wishes she lived further away, streets away, a much longer conversation away.

When they get to the door, he waits for her to let herself in. But without the porch light, she can hardly see a thing. She certainly can't find the right key.

When she does find it, she struggles to fit it in the lock. 'Could do with a bit of light here,' he murmurs.

'The globe's gone,' she tells him, shamefaced. 'I wanted to change it but I can't get the old one out.'

When, finally, she has managed to get the door open and turns to thank him—for keeping her company, for walking her home—he leans slightly towards her. For a moment, for the very smallest of moments, she thinks he might kiss her.

He doesn't. Instead, he straightens up, pushes a hand through his hair and tells her that he'd best be off. And so, with a wave and something of a smile, he makes his way up the pathway and over to a car that is parked just before Nina's house.

She watches from the doorway until he is in the car and has driven off. When she closes the door behind her, she leans against it.

'Sid,' she murmurs to herself. 'His name is Sid.'

Term 4

Sid

At the hardware store, he has a quick look up the aisles for Terry. When he's sure the coast is clear, he hurries to the end of the aisle where Jim keeps the light globes. He picks out a few of them, a mixture of bayonet and screw fittings, and has them cradled in his arms when he hears his name being called. He turns, and one of the boxes falls out of his hands. He hears the glass shatter as it hits the ground.

'Hey, you!' the voice is calling. 'What do you think you're doing?' It's Terry, of course.

Sid tries to laugh. 'Just destroying the joint.' In truth, he's cursing himself for being so clumsy.

Terry picks up the box and gives it a shake. 'Faulty stock, by the looks of it,' he says, as he hands Sid a replacement. 'What do you need all these for, anyway?'

'Stocking up for school,' he lies. It's not a good lie, though, and he waits for Terry to ask him the obvious question: why he doesn't just order them through the school, along with everything else.

That's not what he asks. 'What, in the holidays? Why don't you wait until next term?'

And when he mumbles something about wanting to keep on top of things, Terry doesn't pursue it, he just nods.

As they walk down to the register, Terry is quiet at first. Finally he asks, 'So how's it going at school?'

Sid hesitates. 'All right,' he says cautiously. 'Not much to report really.'

'What about the kids?'

'Good, pretty good.'

Terry nods slowly. 'So, she's shaping up all right then, is she?'

Sid isn't sure what he means.

'The new one,' says Terry, and this time there's an edge of impatience in his voice. 'The new teacher. Is she doing all right?'

It's hard to know what sort of answer he's after: if he just wants to hear that Nina's not a patch on him or if he's looking for an update.

'I'd say she's going okay,' he ventures.

Terry considers this for a moment. 'But what's she been doing with them?'

At first he keeps it vague. 'Oh, the usual, I'd say.'

Still, Terry keeps at him. 'Anything in particular?'

'Well, they're rehearsing a couple of plays for the Year 6 show,' he offers.

Terry sucks at his top lip. 'Good,' he says, his voice stiff, 'good to hear. Which plays?'

It's this question that does it. It's this question that fills Sid with a feeling of such pride he starts tripping over his words in his rush to tell Terry all about it. To tell him that they aren't just normal plays, they're rap plays; that there's a committee, and he's part of it. And not just part of it: he's in charge of props. Plus they've got themselves a proper director—who used to be in television, he adds casually. They've even got a costume designer who's a professional.

'Her name's Jean,' Sid tells him, and saying her name out loud makes him feel so good he says it again. 'Jean,' he says. 'She's Nina's neighbour. Nina, the new teacher,' he clarifies. 'Nina Foreman.'

Only then does he notice that while Terry's lips are still fixed in a smile, the rest of his face has fallen. 'Everything sounds good, then,' he murmurs.

That's when Sid kicks himself for having been so thoughtless, for having gone on about it so much. For having said anything at all.

'Things aren't bad,' he says, trying to play it down. And that's the truth of it: things aren't bad at the school. It could even be said that things are good, despite all the trouble, despite everything.

A silence follows, and for the first time since they've known each other, it isn't an easy one.

In the end, it's Terry who breaks it and who says, in the voice of a man who has other things to do, 'How about I leave you with Leonie, then? She'll pop everything through for you.'

Sid nods and, without speaking, the two of them make their way down to the front of the shop.

Standing at the register is a woman with a name tag that says *Hello, I'm Leonie*. Terry gives her a wink. 'Watch out for him, won't you, love?' He nods in Sid's direction.

The woman laughs as she starts to ring the items through.

'See you, mate!' Terry calls out in a jovial voice.

Sid tries hard to match his tone. 'See you, Terry!' he calls back, his palms clammy. 'See you soon.'

∽

In the daylight, the house looks different: brighter and more welcoming. Welcoming enough to give him the confidence to walk up to the front door and ring the bell.

He hears the lock click before the door opens a fraction.

'Hello?' she asks, her voice guarded.

Her wariness makes Sid nervous and he hastens to explain himself: that he just popped around to take a look at the porch light, to see if he can't fix it.

When he's said all that, the door opens wider and there she is, right in front of him. She looks nice, he thinks, in a green dress that's just about the colour of her eyes.

'Thanks for coming,' she says softly.

This makes him feel chuffed. 'It's a pleasure,' he says, 'a real pleasure.'

He's brought a stepladder with him and she stays at the door, watching, as he climbs up it. 'Water's starting to warm up again,' he tells her, trying to make conversation. 'You swim much?'

She shakes her head. 'Not much.'

He makes a clicking sound with his tongue. 'That's no good. Because, tell you what, it's God's own country over here and we've got to take advantage of it. The rock pool, for example. From now through to May, it's beautiful. Especially if you're down there early.'

He throws her a quick look, keeping hold of the side of the ladder so he won't lose his balance. 'Come down one morning. You won't regret it, I promise you that.'

She nods and says she'll think about it. It's all the encouragement he needs. 'How about Tuesday, then?' he says, trying to sound casual. 'If you're free, that is.'

But this suggestion seems to alarm her and his heart sinks to see it.

'No pressure,' he says. 'I just thought it might be nice.' He tries for a light-hearted tone, but his voice just comes out hoarse.

She looks up at him, then, her eyes shy and her face suddenly crimson. 'I can't swim,' she blurts out. 'I've never learnt.'

Relief pumps through his body so fast he finds it hard to keep his hand from shaking as he replaces the globe. 'So, I'll teach you then,' he says.

Joan

Her sleep is fitful and she finds herself awake before first light. As she lies in bed, waiting for a hint of sunlight to push through the curtains, she thinks about him. About Sid. It is not the first time she has found herself thinking about him. To be honest, she has spent a lot of time thinking about him.

She imagines the rock pool and how it will be when she meets him there this morning.

She can't swim, that is true enough, but she does have a swimming costume. She just hasn't worn it in years. Not since she and her mother would take the bus to Raleigh Beach and spend the morning there, just the two of them, paddling in the water.

It's not a fancy swimming costume: it's just plain black with a built-in bra. At the time, she'd hankered after something bright, striped or even floral, but black was always going to be the sensible choice, especially for a woman of her shape.

Once it is light, she gets out of bed and starts to get ready. She lifts the nightdress over her head, steps out of her underpants and ventures a glimpse in the mirror. Yet again she is dismayed by what she sees: breasts spilling down to a stomach that falls over itself, thick veins running down legs that no longer narrow nicely at the ankles.

She could cancel. She has his telephone number. She could give him a ring to say she doesn't feel up to it. A raincheck. She could ask him for a raincheck. He wouldn't mind. *Sure*, he'd say, *take a raincheck, that's fine.*

But her mother won't let her off the hook so easily. *Joanie*, she says, *you're going. No ifs, no buts, you're going.*

So instead of cancelling, she steps into her swimming costume. Pulling it up over her stomach, she lifts the straps over her shoulders as she drops her breasts into the bra insert. She flinches as she turns back to the mirror.

But this time what she sees surprises her. It would be too much to say she looks sleek, but it wouldn't be wrong to say that the swimming costume has given her a different body: in it, her breasts are high and her stomach has flattened. Heartened now, she slips on her favourite sundress.

In the kitchen, she makes herself a cup of tea and puts a piece of bread in the toaster. No time for an egg this morning. Not that she has the appetite for it anyway; she can scarcely even finish her toast.

When she steps outside, the morning is bright. It is still a little early, but quickly she checks next door for Emily, to see if she is where she so often is these days: sitting on the front steps. She isn't, but her sandshoes have been left out on the lawn. With a soft smile, Joan gathers them up and leaves them beside the door.

It is a decent walk there and by the time she reaches the steps leading down to the pool, she is out of breath. There is a bench and she lowers herself onto it. All at once, anxiety engulfs her. She should have cancelled. He'd have understood. And if she were to turn around now and head back home, surely he'd understand that, too. Once she's rung to explain. Once she's apologised. Another time, that's what she'll say; that they'll have to do it another time.

His voice catches her off guard. 'Well, hello there,' he says, sitting down beside her. 'Fancy meeting you here.'

His voice is jolly, but when he looks her way, he doesn't quite meet her eye. 'You still up for a swim?' he asks.

His question gives her an out. She could still say no. *You go in,* she could say. *I'll watch.*

'Looks lovely in,' he adds.

From where they are sitting, she can see over to the pool. He's right—it's a beautiful morning and already the water is sparkling.

'It does,' she says.

He takes that as a yes, she's still up for a swim, because not only does he stand up, he also reaches out to carry her bag.

All the benches surrounding the pool are free. Sid claims one with his towel and gently puts her bag beside it.

Then, almost before she realises what is happening, he has taken off his shorts and his shirt, and is down to his swimming trunks. Embarrassed, she looks away.

When she looks up again, he hasn't moved. Only then does she realise he is waiting for her. He is waiting for her to get ready, too.

She slips off her sandals first. Slowly, then, she starts to unbutton her dress. After the third button, she is so self-conscious she has to stop. Quickly, she glances over at him. To her relief, he isn't looking her way at all. Instead, he is looking out at the water. For a moment she, too, follows his gaze and watches the tiny waves that spill over the wall of the pool and into the bay. He is right, she thinks: it is a beautiful place.

With a deep breath, she undoes the fourth button on her dress, then the fifth and the sixth until, finally, the dress parts to reveal her swimming costume. Shyly, she slips off her dress and lays it over the bench. From her bag, she takes out her mother's old swimming cap and puts it over her head, tucking her hair in at the front, at the back, at the sides.

Only then does he turn to look at her. 'Ready?'

She finds she can't answer him. She can't look at him either, paralysed as she is by the question that vibrates through her head: *Am I good enough?*

Lightly, his fingertips touch the back of her hand. 'Once you're in, you'll love it,' he promises.

And so, tentatively, very tentatively, she follows him over to the ladder at the shallow end of the pool. She should use it to get in, he tells her. So, holding on tight to the handrails, she uses the ladder to lower herself into the water. And although it is so cold it makes her gasp, still she keeps going until it is up to her thighs. With the next step down, she feels not another metal rung but only water. Stifling her fear, she keeps hold of the rail with one hand and reaches out to the water with the other. Then she lets go. The water is deeper than she has expected, coming over her stomach. But at least she can still stand in it, so she won't drown. Slowly, her fear gives way to a creeping sense of pride.

Sid is sitting beside the pool ladder, his feet dangling in the water. He catches her eye. 'How about that? You're in.'

She gives him a shy smile. 'Yes,' she says, 'I am.'

Slipping into the water himself now, he swims the length of the pool, arms pushing in front of him, head out of the water. Fascinated, she watches and watches, until warily, self-consciously, she begins to copy him. Still standing, she brings her arms out in front of her, then pulls them back again. Again and again she does it, walking in circles through the water, over and over, so focused she doesn't notice him swim up behind her.

'Hi there!' he calls out. Surprised, she turns around to him. With his hair wet and slicked back, he looks different. Boyish. His arms, she sees, are strong, although the skin around them is loose. She sees, too, that he is practically hairless; that the only hair he has is clustered around his nipples. Embarrassed, she looks away again.

'Not too cold for you?' he asks.

She blinks. 'Sorry?'

'The water. Is it a bit cold for you?'

She isn't sure: she's stopped noticing whether she's cold or whether she isn't.

'Some people,' he tells her, 'they get nervous in the rock pool. 'Cause it's hard to see the bottom. You one of those people?'

His voice, so unhurried, relaxes her. 'Probably,' she says.

'That's okay. But you might find it a bit easier if you hang on to me.'

She nods, but when he clasps her hand in his, she feels herself start to shake.

'Let's get you swimming,' he says.

She can't talk, so she just nods. His hand is big and makes hers seem very small. At first, she lets her hand lies loosely in his; but his hold is strong and eventually she, too, tightens her clasp. She cannot remember when she has last felt so happy.

He turns to her with a smile. 'You right to give it a shot?'

'Yes,' she whispers, though she still isn't sure.

'Can you float?'

'I think so,' she says.

He tells her to lie on her back. 'Don't worry,' he says, 'I'll help you. I'll put my hand on your back to keep you straight.'

She swallows. 'All right,' she says, her voice scarcely audible.

'I'll hold you,' he reassures her. 'I won't let you fall.'

As she leans back, she feels his hand on the small of her back, pushing up until she finds herself horizontal, feet and legs on the surface, floating.

'That's good,' he says as, slowly, he takes his hand away. 'That's really good.'

Afterwards, when she is upright again, he is triumphant. 'See?' he tells her. 'You were floating by yourself; you didn't even need me.' His tone is so excited, he is almost cheering her. 'Come down every morning, and you'll be swimming by Christmas. Mark my words, Jean, you'll be a swimmer by Christmas.'

And when he says that, something like a bubble forms inside her and travels upwards, from her stomach to her chest then right up to her throat, filling her with a momentum that makes the words rush out of her: 'My name is Joan.'

Sid puts his head to one side. 'What was that?'

She isn't sure whether she can say it again. But he's waiting, so she shuts her eyes tight, takes a breath and forces it out. 'My name isn't Jean, it's Joan.'

He laughs then, shakes his head and laughs. 'Why do they call you Jean, then?'

'I'm not sure,' she says, 'it just happened.' She doesn't know how else to explain it.

Again he laughs. 'Which do you like best, Jean or Joan?'

She hesitates.

'Yes?' he prompts.

'I like Joan,' she says, 'because that's my name.'

Rebecca

Soon it will be two months since the interview and still they have not heard anything. Sometimes she succeeds in convincing herself that this is a positive sign; that the time is being used to attend to those administrative tasks required to issue a visa. These things take time, she understands that. She understands, too, that she should be patient. And she will be patient, truly she will be. If only someone would reassure her that all will be well.

At home, she and Emmanuel have stopped discussing it. For what is there to say? The same thing they have been saying to each other for weeks now: that surely the application will be successful. Surely, they will be accepted. There is nothing else to be said; nothing else they can dare contemplate. Indeed, there are times when she even laughs about it. Not a belly-aching sort of laugh, more a laugh of incredulity. For who could have dreamt it: that she, of all people, should find herself in such a dilemma? How has it come to this: that she should find herself on the other side of the world, unable to return to the place that is hers? It is all so ridiculous. So absolutely ridiculous.

And now they are making her wait. There are times when the stress of it threatens to tear her apart; when the stress of it so fills her body that she feels she will burst.

Tell me, she wants to scream at Mr Robert Parker—that small serious man in that empty room—*just tell me what is happening.*

But she cannot scream at him. Both because that would be unwise and because the correspondence they have received warns them not to contact the Department of Immigration for an update. The processing of an application takes time, they have been advised, and such queries will only further delay the decision-making process itself. So they have not called. Instead, they have waited.

To better manage the frustration of this, Rebecca has taken to humming. Whenever she thinks about the decision and when it will come, she starts a low hum. There is something comforting about this: it slows the anxiety, slows the panic that might otherwise completely overwhelm her.

So this is what she does now as she walks Sebastian to school: she hums.

From the corner of her eye, she notices a car beside them, a car driving more slowly than they are walking. She feels her stomach lurch. Why is that? she asks herself. Why should a car be driving so slowly beside them?

Alarm rises in her when she realises what is happening: they are being followed. Oh God, she thinks, oh God. Fortunately, the school is ahead: the school with its gate and its safety. But they are not yet there and it is still not close enough. Panic engulfs her, a blinding panic that makes her reach out for Sebastian and pull him towards her, so suddenly and with such force that he shouts out in protest, 'What? What are you doing?'

She doesn't let go. Instead, she clutches him, hissing at him to keep walking, to look ahead and keep walking. Her insistence silences him into obedience. Only then does she dare to glance at the car that is still moving slowly behind them.

As she does, the front window slides down, and Rebecca sees Ethan Thompson sitting in the front seat. Mel's voice rings out from the driver's side. 'Rebecca, hi.'

Confusion blocks her thoughts. 'It's Ethan's mother,' Sebastian whispers to her. 'It's just Ethan's mother.'

She should be able to laugh at herself for being so stupid, for letting herself be scared witless by something so ridiculous. But the fright of it has made her nauseous, so nauseous she can't trust herself to speak. Breathe, she tells herself, just breathe.

'Hey, Rebecca,' Mel calls. 'It's me.'

With another breath, Rebecca turns her lips up into a smile. 'So it is,' she says.

Mel pulls into the kerb to park. As soon as the car is stationary, Ethan jumps out and, running past Sebastian, heads for the school gate. When Mel gets out, she makes a face at Sebastian. 'Sorry my son's such a dickhead, mate.' She holds up a cigarette. 'You want a smoke?' she asks Rebecca.

It has been years since Rebecca was a smoker, but now she craves a cigarette.

They need to cross over to the park, Mel tells her. 'The new one—Ms Mathews—she threatened to arrest me if I lit up within sight of the school gate.'

Concentrating hard, Rebecca tries to slow her breathing. Calm down, she tells herself, calm down, you are fine. You are safe. She manages to turn to Mel with a wry smile. 'Could she actually arrest you?'

Mel looks solemn. 'Citizen's arrest.'

Rebecca's eyes widen. 'Really?'

Mel's face relaxes into a broad grin. 'Had you, didn't I? I reckon she would, though, if she saw me.'

Once they're in the park, Mel passes her a cigarette and leans over to light it for her. 'So,' she says, 'how's it hanging?'

Rebecca is confused. 'Sorry?'

Mel blows smoke at the ground. 'How's it hanging? You know, how's it going?'

Rebecca smiles as she inhales. 'Of course,' she says. 'How's it hanging.'

Mel looks bemused. 'And?'

And? For a moment, Rebecca toys with telling her the truth. All of it. To tell her exactly how it's hanging.

Then she thinks better of it. They are here for Emmanuel's work, that's all anyone knows. As for the rest of it, well, where would she start?

She catches herself in time. How's it hanging, that's all Mel wants to know. She doesn't want a life story, she doesn't want some epic.

So she takes another puff of the cigarette, exhales, then gives Mel a smile. 'I'm well,' she says, 'really well.'

For the rest of the morning, Rebecca will be rehearsing with the children. She'll take the cast of *The Wolf* while Nina will work with those in *The Bears*. And Mel will spend the time filming so it can all be played back to the children afterwards. It's the best way to show them what they're doing wrong and how they can make it better.

An early hitch—not enough parts for everyone—has been dealt with. Instead of having one narrator for *The Wolf*, there will be three. Three narrators, one Wolf, one Little Red Riding Hood, one Granny and one Woodcutter. That way, all the children get an onstage role.

Today, they're working on the denouement.

Rebecca nods at Kurt. 'Okay, Mr Wolf,' she says, 'take it away.'

Because they're still waiting on a real bed to use, they have to make do with nothing. So Kurt just lies down on the floor. Elsie, who is Granny, also lies on the floor, but just behind Kurt, which would be fine if he didn't keep flicking her elbow with his finger while they wait for Little Red Riding Hood to arrive. Jade, who has been waiting in the wings, takes her time. As she struts onstage, it is clear—yet again—that she is not the demure Little Red Riding Hood Rebecca has been asking for.

'Nervous, Jade,' Rebecca calls out to her, 'you're supposed to be nervous. You've come to see Granny but there seems to be something wrong. So you're looking nervous, all right?'

Jade gives her a big, happy smile. 'Sure thing.'

Rebecca turns her attention to Bridie, who is standing to one side of the stage. She looks so pale Rebecca thinks she might be ill. 'Are you all right?' she asks her.

Bridie gives her a tiny smile. 'I'm okay,' she murmurs.

'Good. Now this part of the play is quite dramatic,' Rebecca tells her. 'You're one of the narrators, so you have to show that to the audience. Do you think you can do it?'

The little girl looks unconvinced.

'Bridie?'

Bridie opens her mouth to answer but says nothing.

Rebecca tries again. 'Bridie,' she says, 'are you ready to try it now?'

This time she gives Rebecca a quick nod. With a breath in, she shuts her eyes, pauses, then pushes out the first of her lines. Her voice, when it comes, is quiet and shaky.

When she saw those big teeth
Staring out from the bed
Little Red Riding Hood
Clutched at her head.

'A bit louder, sweetheart,' Rebecca says. 'Just a bit louder.'

Biting her lip, the girl gives another nod before she tries again. This time she is slightly louder.

Filled with fright,
She tried not to cry
Oh why was her grandmother
Looking so sly?

Rebecca nods. 'Well done,' she says. 'Much better.'

The girl smiles but later, after the rehearsal has finished, she comes to Rebecca in tears. 'I don't think I should be a narrator,' she whispers.

Rebecca has to bend down to hear her properly. 'Why not?'

'Because I'm not very loud and I'm not very good and sometimes I think I won't be able to remember all my lines.'

Rebecca slips an arm around her waist. 'Listen, we can get you a microphone, so having a soft voice isn't a problem. And not thinking you're very good isn't a problem either because we're still rehearsing. Everyone feels like that when they rehearse. And if you forget your lines, I'll whisper them out to you. Okay?'

The girl nods but her eyes stay solemn.

Rebecca pulls her closer. 'It'll be fine, I promise.'

When she leaves the school to walk home, there is a lightness inside her she scarcely recognises.

It's because of the children, she thinks. Because they're doing so well. Because—barring the odd hiccup—with each rehearsal they are improving. And today, especially today, when Sebastian stood up on stage—so tall and so confident—she thought she would burst at the sight of him. Her son, her beautiful son—Narrator No. 1—who is doing so well. Her son, who has new friends. Her son, who, so quickly, has become part of this small school. How it comforts her to see this.

She smiles, now, to think of it, and doesn't stop when she bumps into Mrs Davies from down the street. Only recently have they begun to speak. Before that, the old lady had simply ignored her. Out of shyness, Rebecca had assumed, though she had seen her greet others.

Over time, Rebecca had become so irked by the slight, she made it her mission to wear the woman down. So she began to call out loud, cheery greetings each time they crossed paths.

After a week she received a grunt in reply; after a fortnight a mumbled *good morning.* That night, she had laughed to Emmanuel about it.

He had found it less amusing. 'Why push it? What does it matter if a woman on the street fails to greet you? Why does that matter?'

'It matters,' she replied, her lips tightening. 'It matters that people in this country lift up their heads to greet me when I greet them. It matters.'

Buoyed by the small victory, she began to ask questions of the woman. Just simple ones, like 'Beautiful day, isn't it?' or 'Strange weather, hasn't it been?' until, finally, the woman gave in. One day she gave Rebecca her name; the next, details of the cold she hadn't managed to shake.

Today, it is Rebecca who has something for her: an invitation to the Year 6 show.

If she is surprised by the invitation, Mrs Davies doesn't show it. 'See how I go,' she mumbles.

'You should come,' Rebecca tells her. 'I'm the director.'

The woman's expression changes. '*You're* the director?'

Rebecca nods.

'Can you really do that sort of thing, the directing sort of thing?'

She holds her head high. 'Yes,' she says, 'I can.'

The woman is interested now. 'Is that what you did back there?' she asks. 'Were you a director?'

An accurate answer would be too complicated, so Rebecca just inclines her head.

The woman takes a good look at her. 'A director,' she says. 'Fancy that.' There is grudging admiration in her tone and Rebecca finds herself gratified by it.

She gives the woman a proud smile. 'Yes,' she says, 'fancy that.'

She is still smiling when she stops to check the letterbox. Usually it is filled with junk mail but today, caught between a flyer for a pizza outlet and one for cleaning services, is a letter. It has an official look about it and she sees it has been sent by the Department of Immigration. Her stomach lurches, both with fear and anticipation, and quickly she takes it inside with her.

Only then does she dare to open it. Her hands shake as she pulls at the envelope.

I'm sorry to inform you. These are the first words she sees. *I'm sorry to inform you.*

And as soon as she has seen this, she knows she doesn't have to read any further.

Instead, she sits on the sofa, her mind blank; her mind so blank it might well have been erased.

Some hours later, she picks up the letter again and forces herself to read it in its entirety.

If she wants to, the apologetic officer tells her, she can go to a tribunal and ask for the decision to be reviewed. There, her case will be considered again. Otherwise, she will need to leave the country; she and her husband and her son. They will all have to go.

Mel

She's started an hour early this morning. It's the only way she'll be able to make it to the committee meeting on time; Nina wants them there by eleven. It's a Saturday but the boys are at rugby with Adam, which means she won't have to drag them along with her. All she needs to do is finish the house and get out. It's not a difficult job: Andrew Hill lives by himself and there's only a certain amount of mess one person can make in a week. Not that he doesn't give it his best shot.

As usual, he's left the cash on the kitchen bench but today there's a note with it: *Away for the weekend so please check everything's locked when you leave.*

As far as notes to cleaners go, it's not such a bad one—some of them are like bloody decrees: do this, do that, with no please or thank you. It still gives her the shits, though. What the hell does he think: that she'd planned on leaving the place wide open? Quite frankly, he'd be better taking a leaf out of his own book instead of wasting time leaving notes like that. She can't count the number of times she's come in to find him gone and the back door still open.

As it happens, being a bit pissed off isn't such a bad thing in her line of business: the energy it gives her always makes her work faster. So now, once she's screwed up the note and pocketed the cash, she gets to it.

She starts on the kitchen, which looks out onto the yard. It's a wild, unkempt sort of yard that would drive Adam mad but Mel thinks is beautiful, so beautiful she often finds herself just standing at the sink and gazing out at it. There's something about it that makes her thoughtful, that makes her stop and think about things she wouldn't usually dwell on. Like how life might have panned out if she hadn't fallen pregnant with Ethan; if she'd just moseyed her way through school instead and done all her exams with the rest of them.

Who knows, she might have even got in to uni. It wouldn't have been impossible, so long as she'd pulled her finger out and started to apply herself. And perhaps she would have. Then she could have been . . . what? Maybe a scientist or a geologist or a zoologist. A zoologist: that makes her smile. She doesn't even know what a bloody zoologist does. Feed the elephants? Or why not aim a bit higher? How about a doctor or a lawyer? Lawyer to the stars: that's what she could have been. Lawyer to the frigging stars. This makes her laugh.

She likes to work with the radio up high so she can sing the time away. Which is what she does today. Once she's done, she does another quick whip around the house; partly to check she hasn't missed anything and partly because she likes to admire her handiwork before she leaves. And, of course, to check she's locked all the doors.

There's no time to go home before the meeting but that's okay, she's brought everything she needs with her: a change of clothes, bit of make-up, a stick of deodorant and some perfume. Because she has to make some effort, doesn't she, now that she's hanging out with supermodel Rebecca Chuma. Even now, Mel has to stop herself from staring at her, open-mouthed—she's that beautiful. Not a lookin'-good-today beautiful, more freak-of-nature beautiful. It's the whole thing: the skin, the big brown eyes, the neck, the legs, everything. And how can she possibly compete with that? She said as much to Adam one day. Not in a boo-hoo-poor-me sort of way, just in passing.

And God love him, straightaway he was pulling her right up to him—the way those dirty dancers do—and running his hand over her bum before giving it a good squeeze.

'Tell you what, darling,' he said, 'I don't know about Miss Supermodel, but I can tell you this much: you've still got the best bum in Brindle.'

Bless him.

Before she heads out, she takes a look at herself in the bedroom mirror and tries to give herself an honest appraisal: the belly could do with some work but her legs are looking good, so that's something. A bit of lippy, some mascara and a squirt of Nina Ricci and no one would guess she'd just come from scrubbing out Andrew Hill's toilet.

❧

She's late getting to Nina's place. When she arrives, the others are all there, gathered in the lounge room.

'Where's Emily?' she asks Nina. It's an innocent enough question, more small talk than anything. So she's astonished when Nina's face turns bright red. 'She's, um, she's at her father's this weekend.' There's a stutter in her voice as she speaks.

Oh. She had no idea Nina was a single mum. It's the last thing she'd have imagined.

'Okay, right.' But she needs to say something more than that; something to fill the silence. 'Must be good to get a bit of child-free time,' she ventures.

Nina pauses. 'Actually, I really miss her when she's away,' she says.

She looks so sad and so lost that Mel just wants to wrap her arms around her. But she can't do that, can she? She can't go throwing herself on Ethan's teacher. So all she can do is watch as Nina tries to compose herself.

'Sorry,' she says, her voice thick. 'Sorry for being so silly. I'm just a bit new to it.'

There is another silence then, until Sid pipes up with a suggestion. 'How about I make us all a cuppa before we get started?'

Nina starts to protest that she's fine, that she can do it, but Sid is already headed for the kitchen. Seconds later, Jean gets up to follow him. 'I'll give him a hand,' she volunteers.

Rebecca is sitting on the sofa. She's looking sensational, as usual. Though it's only early November, it's already hot and today she's in shorts and a T-shirt. Not those skimpy denim shorts, the ones that are so short the lining of the pockets peeps through—although with her legs, Mel wouldn't be holding back. Rebecca's are more like walk shorts. They still look fantastic, though.

'Looking good,' she tells her.

Normally that would make Rebecca laugh but today she doesn't even smile.

'You okay?' Mel asks.

Rebecca nods, but almost immediately, her eyes fill with tears.

Fuck, she's setting them all off today. 'What's wrong?' she asks as she sits down beside her.

Rebecca shakes her head but now there are tears dripping down her cheeks and spilling onto her T-shirt.

Mel starts to get worried. 'Is Sebastian okay?'

Rebecca nods.

'Emmanuel?'

Again, she nods.

'So what is it?'

Nina is sitting in the chair opposite them. Mel gives her a puzzled look. 'What's wrong?' she mouths. But Nina just shakes her head.

Mel reaches over to take Rebecca's hand. 'What is it, Rebecca? What's happened?'

She takes a while to answer. When she does, her voice is very soft. 'They said no,' she says. 'They said we can't stay.'

Mel is confused. 'What do you mean?'

'We can't stay.' She is hunched in her seat now. 'You know, we never intended staying. But there are problems now. There are problems for me. At home. So we thought to stay. Because we can't return. But we can't stay here either.'

Mel tries to take make sense of the other woman's words. *What problems?* she wants to ask. But she can't just come out with it like that, not here. Instead, she keeps hold of Rebecca's hand as the three of them—Mel, Rebecca and Nina—sit in silence.

Only when Sid and Jean return with the tea does Rebecca hasten to wipe her eyes.

If they notice she's been crying, neither Sid nor Jean let on. Jean just hands her a cup of tea while Sid goes back to the kitchen and returns with a plate of chocolate-chip biscuits.

Nina touches Jean's arm with her hand. 'Thanks for bringing the biscuits, Jean,' she says.

When Jean just smiles, Sid gives her a bit of a prod. 'Go on,' he says.

Jean flushes red and shakes her head.

'Go on,' he insists.

Now what? Mel thinks. It seems like everyone's got something happening this morning.

'You say,' Jean whispers to Sid. 'You tell them.'

Sid clears his throat. 'Her name's not Jean,' he announces. 'It's Joan.'

Rebecca

They wait, with others, in a foyer filled with tables and chairs. There is talking in the room, but it is low, almost murmuring.

She has been told to be there by 9.45 am. They have arrived much earlier.

Her name is called out just before ten and a woman hurries over to them. She is thin with darting eyes and slightly rounded shoulders, her hands clutching a single sheet of paper. 'Mrs Rebecca Chuma?' she asks.

When Rebecca nods, the woman looks over to Emmanuel, who is also standing now. 'My husband,' Rebecca tells her. 'Dr Emmanuel Chuma.'

The woman looks interested. 'Oh,' she says, 'are you a doctor, then?'

Emmanuel inclines his head. 'I am a doctor of engineering.'

'So not a hospital doctor or anything like that?'

Emmanuel's eyelids close for a second. 'I'm afraid not.'

Rebecca feels her body stiffen. Why has the woman asked him this? Are they already being assessed, even here in the foyer? She looks for a clue but the woman's eyes are lowered now, focused on her paper.

'Please follow me,' she says.

They follow her through a door that leads into a courtroom. This is a surprise: Rebecca has not expected such formality. On the back wall is a crest fashioned out of metal. The woman directs Rebecca to a table in front of a raised bench and Emmanuel to the row of seats lined up against the back of the room. Then she leaves them there, alone. In one corner Rebecca sees electrical equipment. That's when it occurs to her that perhaps they are already being recorded, even before the hearing has started; perhaps this is what they do here when they wish to discover the truth—they secretly record people. Perhaps this is why the woman has left, to make them think they are alone, when really they are not.

So when Emmanuel calls over to her, she shakes her head as she turns around, pointing a hand to the equipment with its row of illuminated buttons. When he looks confused, again she jabs a finger at the equipment, then puts a finger to her lips. He raises an eyebrow but she is relieved when he stays silent.

Laying her hands in her lap, she tries to relax. But her hands won't stay still. And even when she slides them under her legs to press the movement out of them, still they shake.

Some minutes pass before the woman returns. This time, she enters through a far door behind the bench and this time she is not alone. Instead, she is accompanied by a tall white woman, who sits herself at the bench behind a name plate that says *Tribunal Member Maxine Kelly*.

Tribunal Member Maxine Kelly has blue eyes, startlingly blue, and dark hair. Dyed hair, Rebecca sees: at the roots it is lighter, perhaps greying. Apart from this, there are few clues to her age. More than forty, Rebecca thinks, but not yet fifty.

Her voice, when finally it comes, is a surprise. She doesn't speak in the rushed way of many people here, their words muffled and swallowed. Rather, she speaks slowly, with a lilt and intonation that mark her as a foreigner. Strange, Rebecca thinks, that a foreign-born woman should hold a position such as this.

She has read Rebecca's statement, she tells her, and has some questions for her. But first, Emmanuel should leave the room. Rebecca feels her heart lurch. But what can she do? There is nothing she can do.

Almost immediately, the questions begin. At first, they are easy ones: simple questions about her family, her childhood, her schooling, her career. She is not unused to this: these are questions journalists would often ask her, questions she has frequently answered.

Slowly, then, the questions change.

'Why did you leave your country?' the tribunal member asks her.

'I couldn't stay,' Rebecca stammers. 'I wasn't safe.'

But more is needed than that.

Rebecca nods. She will try, she hears herself say, she will try to explain it.

'The day of your arrest. Can you tell me about that?'

'Yes,' she answers. Yes, she will talk about it. Even though her skin prickles to think of it.

There were eight police officers. Inside the house, there were eight of them. Or perhaps it was only seven. They took her to a police station on the outskirts of the city. Not only her—Grace too, and Johnson, and three other men Rebecca had never seen before. It is a well-known police station, a somewhat notorious one, but if the tribunal member has heard of it, she doesn't say. At first they were kept together. Later, they were separated. Later still, she was taken to a man in an office.

'Who was he?' the tribunal member asks her.

'I don't know,' she says. 'I don't know who he was.'

But she does know.

The member is insistent. 'Who was he?' she repeats.

She is frightened to tell her. She is frightened to say. Even here, so far away, she is fearful.

'I need his name. I need you to tell me his name.'

Rebecca has to force the words out. 'Joseph Muponda,' she says. 'His name is Joseph Muponda.'

'Is that what he told you?'

'Yes,' she says, but this is not the absolute truth.

'Tell me about him.'

No.

No.

But she does.

'I believe he is one of the chief investigators,' she says softly. 'He asked me questions. About Johnson and about Grace. I told him the truth—that we were no more than neighbours. He asked me about the ACC and I told him that I had no involvement in it.'

The tribunal member thinks the ACC is a political party.

Rebecca shakes her head. Not a political party, an association: the Association for Constitutional Change.

'Then what happened?'

She hesitates. 'Then I was released.'

'Just like that?'

She swallows but says nothing.

The tribunal member thumbs through the papers in front of her. 'In your interview with the department, you told the delegate you were so frightened you made arrangements to leave the country as soon as you could.'

'Yes,' Rebecca says.

'Even though you were simply questioned and released?'

'That's right.'

'You weren't kept there overnight?'

She shakes her head.

'You weren't questioned any further about your involvement with Grace and Johnson?'

'No.'

'You weren't asked any more questions about the ACC?'

'No.'

'You were simply released without charge?'

She bites on her lip to stop herself from crying. 'That's right.'

'Then why are you seeking protection?' For the first time, there is an impatience in the woman's voice. 'From your evidence, it seems that you aren't of interest to the police, you weren't able to give them information, you weren't kept in custody, you weren't threatened with arrest, you were simply released. How, then, are you in need of protection?'

Rebecca lowers her head so she no longer has to meet the woman's eyes. She tries to swallow so that she might then be able to speak, but she can only cry, and although she tries to stop herself, she cannot. The tears slide down her face and drip onto the table. 'I'm sorry,' she tries to whisper, but still no words come.

'Mrs Chuma,' the tribunal member asks her softly, 'do you have something more to tell me?'

Slowly, Rebecca looks up.

The woman's eyes are more compassionate now, and her voice is gentle as she says, 'Tell me.'

'I recognised him,' Rebecca says quietly, her head lowered. 'This is why I knew his name. Because we had been at school together. And because, even then, he was well known. His father had been a long-time supporter of the party, even before they came to power. For this loyalty, he had been rewarded with land. It was from this land the family became wealthy.'

'Your family, were they also wealthy?'

The question makes her bristle. 'My family were hard workers. They made their own wealth.'

'So they *were* wealthy?'

'To attend the school I went to, there had to be some wealth. My parents bought a business, which became successful. This is how they made their money.'

The tribunal member nods. 'Tell me what happened at the police station,' she says.

And so Rebecca does. Finally, she tells it all. And how it frightens her to tell it. Even though she is here, even though she is no longer there, still, how it frightens her.

It has been a long time since I last saw you, Rebecca Vera. His first words to her, lilting, unhurried, amused even.

Joey—Joey Muponda, she had replied, for this was what he had always been called.

He tut-tutted her, as though she were a child. *Joseph, not Joey.* Then he laughed. *I would not have taken you for a political agitator, Rebecca Vera.*

And when she said no, that she had never been a political agitator, this, too, had made him laugh. He had always found politics a worthwhile endeavour, he told her. A helpful one, too. One, he suggested, that might also be helpful for her.

The suggestion had made her laugh in turn. Now, she is hard pressed to explain why; why, in the circumstances, she should have laughed. Better to have screamed or cried or wept.

Because it was Joey Muponda, this was why she had laughed. It is the only answer she has. Because it was Joey Muponda, pretending to be important.

Her laughing had upset him. *You might be well known in this country,* he told her, *but here, you are nobody, and here, I am to be shown respect.*

Had she been wiser, she would have apologised. Instead, she'd said nothing.

In retrospect, she could claim it as an act of bravery. Sometimes she can still convince herself that this was what it was: an act of brave defiance. In fact, it had been nothing of the kind. She had simply stayed silent.

Just as she had continued to stay silent when, from one of the drawers, he took out a gun and laid it on the desk.

A curious thing, thinking back on it now, to see it there, lying right beside his pen holder, his writing pad, his teacup.

The tribunal member wants to know more about it, about the gun.

But Rebecca knows little of guns.

It was small. She can tell her that much. Small enough, in any case, for him to pick it up and twirl it around in his hands, around and around as though it were nothing more than a plaything.

'Is that all he did? Picked up the gun and played with it?'

Rebecca's eyes flick up before settling on the tabletop in front of her. 'No,' she says, trying to sound casual, trying to curb the fear spreading through her, 'that is not all he did.' And Rebecca describes how, for a time, Joseph Muponda had continued to play with it, running a fingertip along it, up and down it. How, then, with the gun in his hand, he stood up and walked around the desk until he was standing close to her. Too close. So close she would have stepped back had she been standing. But she had not been standing, she was still seated, so she couldn't move away.

'And then?'

'And then,' Rebecca says, 'he began to stroke my cheek with his finger. At first, he stroked me softly, but as he continued, the pressure increased until soon he was stroking so hard, I suspected it would leave a mark on my face.'

Now, too, she feels his hand on her face again; now, too, she feels his breath as he leans down to whisper that she would do well to answer when she was spoken to.

It had been a stupid thing to spit at him.

She keeps her eyes averted from the woman. 'After that, he told me to stand. When I was not quick enough, he pulled me up. Roughly. By the arm. He pushed me against the wall. Then he . . . then he violated me.'

She has said it.

After all this time, she has said it. Aloud.

And to a stranger.

She has told a stranger what she has told no one else. Not even Emmanuel. And the shame of it is so sharp it makes her want to retch. Now again, she feels it; she feels every second of it, as the shocking realisation returns to her: that rather than speeding time up, terror should instead slow it right down. Right, right down: his face so close it grazes her cheek, his breath warm and meaty, his hands grasping. Even now the fear of it makes her shake and weep—loud, heaving sobs—sounds she has only ever allowed herself when alone.

The tribunal member suggests a break. But Rebecca doesn't want a break. She just wants to be finished.

So they continue.

'And afterwards?'

'Afterwards, I was allowed to leave.'

'Just like that?'

She gives the woman the smallest of smiles. 'Just like that. He even walked me out. No one stopped him. No one stopped me. Because he was a man of power, that was clear. As we walked out, he spoke as he would to an acquaintance, his manner straightforward, friendly even, as though he was suddenly a completely different person. Only once we were out of the building and on the street did he grab my arm and pull me close to him, close enough so he could whisper to me.'

'What did he say?'

Again she feels her composure slipping, and again she struggles to push the words out of her mouth. 'He told me he'd see me soon, very soon. He told me he'd had so much fun, he was looking forward to spending more time with me. Very, very soon. And that I should tell him—I must tell him—anything I found out about Grace and Johnson. He'd be interested in that, he told me, very interested.'

'And then?'

'And then he just left me there in the street. I didn't know what to do. I had nothing with me: not my phone, not my handbag, no money; nothing at all. I knew only that I needed to get away from this place, as quickly as I could. So I started to walk. I walked until I came to a main road and I found a taxicab. I told the driver I had no money with me, but that I had money in my house. This is how I managed to get home.'

'And when did you decide to leave the country?'

'That day. That day, I decided we would leave. Earlier than planned. I needed only to change the tickets.'

The tribunal member nods. 'Thank you,' she says.

And then it is over: there are no more questions. The tribunal member leaves the bench and Rebecca finds herself being ushered back into the foyer, blinking hard, as though emerging from the cinema.

Emmanuel is there waiting for her. He smiles to see her. She has no smile in return—not here, not yet—but how she is comforted when he reaches for her hand.

Nina

The weeks are passing quickly. So quickly it's making Nina nervous. Only three weeks until the show and there's still such a lot to be done. Tickets are on sale in the office from Thursday, but to make sure no one misses out, Nina wants to give the class a couple of days' head start.

To get an idea of numbers, she needs a show of hands: one hand up for one guest; both hands up for two.

Straightaway, Kurt shoots both his hands up. They'll both be there, he tells her, his mum and his dad.

Ethan looks doubtful. 'You reckon your dad'll come back from overseas?'

For Kurt, it's a no-brainer. 'He'll be there all right. Definitely.'

'But he didn't even come back for your birthday,' Cody reminds him. 'Remember? You said he would and then he didn't.'

Slowly Kurt puts his hands down. 'Yeah,' he says, 'but that was because of his business and everything. He was going to fly over but he had to stay because there was a problem with the builders and that.'

Nina is curious. 'The builders?'

Kurt becomes businesslike. 'Yep, miss, my dad, he's building all these huts like a resort sort of thing to rent out to tourists and that. And when they're all finished, when we go over—Jordan and me—we'll get one for ourselves. Not sharing with Dad and Sari or anything, just us.'

Nina is impressed. 'Sounds good.'

'I'll show you all the pictures, miss, when he comes back for the show.'

'But what happens if he doesn't come?' Despite the softness of her voice, Bridie's question rings out.

Kurt frowns. 'He'll be there. I've been telling him about it on Skype. He's stoked I'm the wolf so he'll definitely be there.'

When Bridie still doesn't sound convinced, Kurt has his own question for her. There is the hint of a smirk as he asks it. 'How about your dad, is he coming? Or will it be just your nan—*again*?'

'My dad's coming too,' she tells him. 'He'll be there.'

Kurt widens his eyes like he can't believe it, then gives Cody a dig with his elbow. 'But we've never even seen your dad. How come he never comes to school, like, ever?'

'He works away a lot.'

'A lot? You mean all the time? You mean every day of the year? Because I've never seen him. Never ever.'

'That's because his work is really important and he can't leave.' Her voice is raised now, high and shrill.

'But he's coming to see you in the show, isn't he, sweetheart?' To calm things down, Nina keeps her own voice very steady.

The little girl gives her a searching look, a confused searching look, as though she herself is surprised by the question. 'Have you talked to my nan about it?' she asks, her voice hopeful.

This time it's Nina's turn to feel confused. 'Do you want me to talk to her about it? Is that what you'd like?'

'Mr P,' she says, 'he'd talk to my nan sometimes.'

Kurt joins in now. 'Because her mum's dead. That's why Mr P used to talk to her nan. Because her mum's dead and her dad doesn't come to the school or nothing. Just her nan.'

The little girl looks harder at Nina, as though waiting for her to step in. But Nina doesn't know what she can do, or even what Bridie is expecting of her. 'Well, it'll be nice to have your dad come this time then, won't it?' It's all she can think of to say.

This time, Bridie's eyes light up. 'Do you know that my dad's coming to the play?'

Nina gives her an uncertain smile. 'If that's what he told you, sweetheart.'

But it's as though the girl hasn't heard her. 'And that will be okay, miss, that he comes and everything?'

Now Nina is completely perplexed. 'I can't see why not.'

'Well, I bet he won't come,' Kurt pipes up again, 'because he never does.'

After lunch, once the kids are back in the classroom, Bridie's seat is empty. This is unusual: Bridie isn't a dawdler. In fact, she's always one of the first back to class.

'Has anyone seen Bridie?' Nina asks the other students.

No one has. She sends Jade to check the toilets, but Bridie's not there either. Nina begins to worry.

'Who played with Bridie over lunch?' she asks.

No answer.

'Anyone?' she asks, her voice rising. There's still no answer.

In her top drawer, Nina keeps a list of phone contacts for the children. There's no mobile number beside Bridie's name, just a landline. When she rings the number, there's no answer and no answering machine. When she tries a second time, again the number rings out.

Slipping her phone back into her pocket, she turns to the class. 'Does anyone know where Bridie could be?' She tries not to sound panicked.

No answer.

'This is very important,' she says. 'No one will be getting into trouble; I just want to know where she is. I just need to know that she's safe. Does anyone have any idea where she could have gone?'

Kurt shrugs his shoulders. 'No idea, miss. Except maybe she went home or something.'

Elsie raises her hand. 'Sometimes she goes to see Mr P.'

Nina is gobsmacked. 'She does what?' She's almost yelling now.

Elsie doesn't answer her. Instead, her mouth gapes and her eyes fill with tears.

Nina tries hard to lower her voice. 'When you say she goes to see Mr P,' she says, 'what do you mean?'

Elsie has started to sniffle. 'In his shop, miss,' she says. 'She goes to visit him in his shop. Quite a lot.'

More than ever, it's an effort for Nina to contain herself. 'Elsie,' she says, keeping her voice as steady as she can, 'can you tell me where the shop is?'

This time, it's Kurt who answers. 'It's the hardware shop, miss. It's pretty close, even. You can just walk there. Me and Ethan and Cody, we've all walked there, no problem.'

Her voice rises again. 'What do you mean, you've all walked there? Did Mr Pritchard ask you to go there? Did he tell you to come and see him there?'

Kurt becomes defensive. 'He never told us to come. Elsie told us she seen him there. She said he was working there. But we didn't believe her. We said, what would he be doing working at a hardware shop when he's a teacher and that? So we went to the shop to see if he was really there. We couldn't find him but Cody spoke to one of the shop ladies and she said Mr P was working there but not that day, because it was his day off, so we just went home.'

Just listening to him makes Nina feel sick.

She hurries next door to see Tania. She doesn't have time to tell her everything—just that she needs her to keep an eye on the class while she tries to find Bridie.

She goes to Bridie's house first, just in case, but there's no one there, so she heads to the hardware shop.

There's a woman at the entrance of the shop, sitting at the cash register.

Nina tries to keep her voice calm. 'Does Terry Pritchard work here?' she asks.

The woman nods. 'But he's just gone on his break,' she says.

'I need to speak to him, urgently,' Nina says. 'Can you tell me where I might find him?'

The woman scratches the side of her face. 'He might be in the tearoom. That's mostly where he goes. It's at the back of the shop. But you can't go in!' she calls after her as Nina heads off. 'It's staff only.'

❧

Without knocking, Nina nudges the door open a fraction. She can't see much but what she does see is enough to make her cry out. It's a piece of uniform—Brindle Public uniform—partly covered by a man's hand.

Panicked, she pushes at the door so hard it swings open. 'What the hell are you doing?' she cries out. 'What the hell are you doing with her?'

Startled eyes turn towards her. Two pairs of startled eyes.

'Bridie,' she says to the girl. 'Bridie.' The little girl is sitting on a man's lap. So this is him, Nina thinks. This is Terry Pritchard. The sight of him disgusts her.

When neither the child nor the man moves, Nina screams at Bridie to get off him.

The girl, clearly frightened now, doesn't budge. The man pats her leg—his hand still too high, too large, too awful—then gives Bridie a gentle push that forces her forward and onto her feet. 'Off you get, darling,' he whispers.

Rushing to the girl, Nina pulls her close and holds her tight, one arm wrapped around her narrow shoulders, the other stroking her back.

'I'm here,' she says. 'It's all right, I'm here.' And when Bridie tries to pull away, Nina tightens her grip on the girl, pulling her even closer until, finally, Bridie relents and goes limp against her.

Nina's voice, when she turns to him, is clipped and icy. 'I'm Nina Foreman, her teacher,' she tells him. 'You know I'm going to call the police, don't you?'

She watches him tap a finger against the side of his face. 'That'll only make things worse,' he says softly. His voice, rich and gentle, comes as a surprise.

She can't believe his gall. 'Worse for you, you mean?'

He shakes his head. 'Not for me.'

Nina feels Bridie start to tremble. 'I'm sorry,' she says. 'For running away. I'm really sorry.'

Nina keeps the girl close. 'It's okay,' she says. 'It's okay.'

Bridie pulls back so she can see Nina's face. 'Are you still going to call the police?'

'You won't be in trouble,' Nina tells her. 'I promise.'

Terry Pritchard leans forward in his seat. 'What's say we go and find Leonie?' he suggests to Bridie. 'Maybe you could help her on the register while I sort things out here.'

This makes Nina bridle. How dare he try to take over? How dare he have the nerve to suggest anything at all?

Instead of falling silent, he keeps talking. 'They get on well,' he says. 'Leonie's always happy to give her a go on the register. And, quite frankly, she'd be better doing that than staying here listening to us.'

I'm her teacher, Nina wants to tell him, *and I'll decide what she'd be better doing.* Instead she gives him a stiff nod.

Standing up, he walks over to the girl. 'Let's go, sweetie,' he says.

Bridie gives him a tentative smile and, to Nina's horror, slips her hand in his as they head towards the door.

Get your filthy hands off her, she wants to cry out. Only the thought of scaring the child stops her. But as she watches them disappear down the aisle, another fear seizes her. What if he were to simply take her out of the shop? What then?

Her mind racing, she follows them towards the exit doors. And when she fears he will do just that—he will walk out with her—he stops at the cash register.

'Leonie,' he calls out, lifting the hand still clutching Bridie, 'thought you might need a bit of back-up help.'

Leonie is a plain woman, her lank hair tied back in a loose ponytail, but when she sees Bridie, her face lights up. 'That's good news for me. You going to be my offsider for a bit?'

Bridie nods as Leonie lets her into the register area.

Terry Pritchard gives them both a wink. 'Let the boss know I'll be in the tearoom. There's just something I need to sort out.' He says all this with an easy smile; a smile he drops as soon as he turns back to Nina.

In the tearoom, he offers her a seat then sits down across from her. Leaning back in his chair, he lays his hands on the table, palms out. 'Okay,' he says, 'so shoot.'

Nerves make her own hands shake as she takes a breath. 'What have you been doing to her?' she asks.

His answer comes quickly, without hesitation. 'Today,' he says, 'I was comforting her. Today she turned up on the verge of hysterics so I brought her in here to calm her down.'

Unlikely, she thinks. 'So that's why you had her on your lap, is it, to calm her down?'

He looks at her with distaste. 'Yes,' he says, 'that's why I had her on my lap.' The way he says this—with such disdain, with such scorn—fills her with rage.

How dare he? she thinks. How dare he treat her like that, given everything he's done?

'I know all about you,' she tells him, her voice hard.

To her astonishment, this makes him laugh.

'I doubt that,' he says.

She feels the colour rising up her neck. 'Laurie Mathews has told me everything.'

Again he laughs: a sarcastic, angry sort of laugh. 'And, of course, Laurie Mathews would be well placed to do this, wouldn't she? Given that she worked with me for, what, less than half a year?'

She doesn't have to listen to this. 'She told me why you had to leave,' she says.

His voice turns sharp. 'And what exactly did she tell you?'

'That you're not allowed to work with children. Under the—' she grapples for the right term '—child-protection laws.'

He gives her a dry smile. 'Which means I must be a paedophile, is that what you're trying to say?'

When she doesn't answer, he runs a finger over his lip. 'Let me help you out. I think you'll find that what I am is a "prohibited person" under the Prohibited Persons Act. I think that's the term you're looking for. Is that what Laurie told you?'

She's not sure. 'Something like that.'

He nods. 'All right, then. And since you know everything about me already, I'd imagine you know why it is that I'm a prohibited person.'

'Carnal knowledge,' she whispers, her voice tightening.

'Carnal knowledge,' he repeats, 'that's right. I have a conviction for carnal knowledge. And since Laurie told you everything, I assume she told you the circumstances. The agreed facts, that's what the police call them.'

Nina shakes her head. 'No, I don't think so.'

He seems unsurprised to hear this. 'Well, maybe I can help you out there. Make sure you're right: that you actually do know everything about me.' He cocks an eyebrow at her. 'So why don't we start with the facts, then, the agreed facts. Yes, there was a girl—Clare, that's her name—and yes, she was only fifteen and yes, because she was so young, I should have known better. I accept that. I'll wear that. But I'm not sure that makes me a paedophile.'

She doesn't want to hear his excuses. 'Well, what does it make you, then? She was a child, you've said it yourself. She was fifteen years old.'

'That's right,' he says, 'at fifteen she was a child, and I was an adult. So what I did was a crime. I accept that. But out of interest, did Laurie tell you how old I was when it all happened?'

She stays silent.

'Funny that,' he murmurs. 'Well, let me tell you, then. I was eighteen years old, and the victim—if that's what we're going to call her—was my girlfriend.'

Nina stares at him. 'You were eighteen?'

He nods. 'That's right. Eighteen. I was eighteen when she fell pregnant. And Clare, she was fifteen. Call me naive, but I thought we'd go ahead and have the baby. She'd have been sixteen by the time she gave birth; I'd have been nineteen. I wasn't earning a lot—I was a baby carpenter in those days—but I figured we'd get by.'

He pushes his thumb up against the edge of the table. 'Her parents, they were the only snag. They screamed blue murder. As far as they were concerned, there was no way she'd be keeping the baby. So she had an abortion instead. At least, that's what I heard. Because once they found out about the pregnancy, she wasn't allowed to have any contact with me. None. And the next thing I know, I'm being charged with carnal knowledge. Because she was a child and I was an adult. Simple as that.'

That can't be right, Nina thinks. It can't work like that.

'Of course, I could have denied it—denied being the father and all. That would have been a way out. But I was the father, wasn't I? Or at least I would have been. And that was the truth of it. So I pleaded guilty, copped a good-behaviour bond, and everyone told me how well I'd done to get it: they'd expected me to go to jail.'

When he looks across at her, he gives a soft chuckle. 'To be honest, I'd expected it too. And when I didn't, I just wanted to get away instead. So I moved down south, where no one knew me. And later, much later, my record was finally wiped—that's what they told me, anyway—and I didn't have to disclose the conviction anymore. So I didn't. By then, I'd started to get sick of the building caper—not that I didn't like carpentry, I just didn't like the industry—and I was looking for something else to do. We'd just got married, Michelle and me, and she suggested teaching. Said she thought I'd be suited to it, because I was good with kids.'

He lets out a laugh that isn't really a laugh at all. 'And how about this for a twist to the story? After the mess with Clare, it turned out Michelle and I couldn't have kids. Funny, isn't it, how these things pan out? So, long story short, I went to teachers' college, got the degree, then started teaching. And what a fabulous thing that turned out to be. What a marvellous thing that was.'

For moment, he is quiet. 'But it all came back again. Forty years later and it all came out. Because that's how it works, doesn't it? Doesn't matter how much time's gone by, doesn't matter what the situation was, once you've been done for something like that, you're cooked. And as it happened, Laurie Mathews was the one to get the ball rolling. She got the department to check up on me. And bingo, they struck gold. Carnal knowledge.'

Nina is confused. 'But couldn't you have explained the situation? Couldn't you have told them how old you were?'

He shakes his head. 'I've asked the lawyers, love—believe me, I've asked them—but it seems that there's no way around it. Once they find out you've been done for carnal knowledge, that's it, you're out. No appeal, nothing.'

For a moment, she feels herself wavering. What if it's true, she asks herself, what if everything he's told her is true? What if that's all there is to know?

But she's getting ahead of herself. Because even if it's all true—everything he's told her—it still doesn't explain what he was doing with a child on his lap and the door closed behind them.

So that's what she asks him.

Closing his eyes, he tilts back his head and takes a deep breath. 'Do you know how humiliating it is to be asked a question like that? Do you have any idea what it's like?'

When he opens his eyes again, he takes a good look at her. 'You want to know why Bridie came here? She came to me because she needed my help. She was that upset the first time she turned up—just out of the blue—and I didn't know what to do. I couldn't just send her packing, could I?'

Nina doesn't know what he's talking about.

'It was the bloody play,' he explains. 'She didn't think she could do it. Didn't think she'd be able to get up onstage; didn't think her voice would be loud enough; didn't think she'd be able to remember her lines. Didn't think she could do anything. And when she came here that first time, when she came to find me, she'd got herself into such a state, it took me half an hour to calm her down.'

There's a half-smile on his face now. 'You know what she wanted me to do? Join some bloody play committee so I could come to school to help with the rehearsals. How the hell could I tell her I wouldn't be able to do it because I wasn't even allowed to set foot in the school? That if Laurie Mathews so much as saw me on the school premises, she'd be setting the dogs on to me? So I told her I couldn't help out with the rehearsals because I had to work at the shop. That's the excuse I gave her. And you know what she said? She said she could come to me instead; she could come after school and just wait until I was free. How could I refuse her? You tell me. So I said we could give it a try and she started coming on a Thursday after school. I'd take my break, we'd come in here to get a bit of peace and quiet, then we'd go through her part.'

'But why you?' Nina asks him. 'Why didn't she just ask her grandmother to help?'

The question makes him laugh. 'Good old Vonnie. Why can't Vonnie stretch herself just a bit further? Vonnie's got a heart of gold, anyone will tell you that, but she's struggling. She's over seventy, for God's sake, and she's trying to raise a young girl. She can't do everything—it's a wonder she manages as well as she does. I've always tried to help out where I could.'

'Like buying her glasses?' She asks this deliberately, so he'll know that she knows all about it.

Again he laughs. 'Laurie's told you about it, has she? That I broke the kid's glasses so I could lure her into my car? Is that what she said?'

He's wearing her down now and she doesn't want to be worn down. And she doesn't have to answer any of his questions. Not when he's the one who's supposed to be answering her. 'I'm going to have to tell her,' she says.

He looks baffled. 'Tell who?'

'Laurie.'

'About what?'

'That I found Bridie here, with you. I'm going to have to tell her.'

His face falls. 'Do you have to?'

She hesitates before she answers. 'Yes,' she says, 'I do.'

He lets out a long sigh. 'Well, that's something for you to decide,' he says eventually. 'But let me say this: if you tell Laurie, I can guarantee you she'll contact the police—because it's me, and because of the whole palaver—and if she contacts the police, she'll also be contacting Family Services. And once she does that, it'll all be on.' He's becoming agitated now. 'Just so you know, this is how it goes: some Family Services officer will be brought on board, and they'll be overworked and under-experienced, but with any luck well meaning, and they'll have a close look into Bridie's situation to see what they can find. And if they look hard enough, you know what they'll find?'

When Nina shakes her head, he makes a clicking sound. 'Well, Nina,' he says, 'I know. I know exactly what they might find. The problem is I've been told a lot of it in confidence. And I'm not the sort of person who blabs about things. It's something I've always prided myself on. But you might appreciate that I'm in a bit of a tight spot here now: if I keep it all to myself, you'll be straight off to Laurie Mathews and the police and Family Services and what have you. And if I do tell you what I know—in the hope you might have a bit of a rethink—then I'll be breaking a confidence. So you can see how I'm caught: either I spill the beans or I sit by and watch the catastrophe unfold. The thing is,' he says, his voice thick now, 'that means we have to come to an arrangement: anything I tell you, you're going to have to promise to keep it to yourself.'

While he waits for her answer, a voice fills her head. It's Marina's voice, low and droll. *Sounds a bit freaky, love. Got himself banned from the school and now he wants you to keep his secrets for him? Sounds a bit problematic, Nina Ballerina.*

But she needs to find out. So she promises.

'How much do you know about Bridie, family-wise?' he begins.

Almost nothing, she admits. That her mother died, and that she lives with her grandmother. That's all she knows.

He takes a moment to consider this. 'And her father, what do you know about him?'

'Only that he's been working up north,' she says.

This makes him chuckle. 'Up north now, is he? It used to be out west. She's getting inventive, I'll give her that much. As it happens, he's not working up north, or out west, for that matter. He's not actually working at all, unless you count the roster they give them.'

She doesn't know what he's talking about.

'Trent's been inside pretty much since the day Bridie was born,' he tells her, 'and he'll be there until she's well and truly out of school. Twenty-two years he got, all up.'

'I had no idea,' she says quietly.

He seems pleased to hear it. 'Diane always took care to keep it under wraps. Strictly on a need-to-know basis. Bridie doesn't know that much herself. If you were to ask her, she'd say robbery. And there's probably some truth in that. But it still leaves a bit out. The bit the kid did to get himself such a long sentence. The bit about what happened to her mother.'

Nina can feel her eyes widen.

'Yes,' he says, 'comes as a bit of a shock, doesn't it?'

'How?' she whispers.

He shrugs. 'Nothing very original. Donna was at home with Bridie when Trent came home, tanked again. And maybe Donna said something to him, something that got him going, so he gave her what for. Only this time he went too far. This time, he killed her. Lucky he didn't kill Bridie while he was at it, I suppose. Stupid boy. Stupid, stupid boy. You couldn't have seen it coming. Leastways, I didn't.'

Nina can only whisper, 'You knew him?'

'Oh yes,' he says softly, 'I knew Trent Juckes. I had him in Year 6, you know, and by the end of the year, I thought I knew him like the back of my hand, little blighter that he was. A lot like Kurt Ward, really—always up to mischief, but bright, too, and funny with it. A bit rough, but all right. Never out of control. I can still see his cheeky little face looking up at me. Gave me the shock of my life to read about it afterwards. Thank God for Vonnie. Thank God she took over. I knew she would, mind you, I knew she'd step up. But when I saw her in the schoolyard with that little girl beside her, well, you could have knocked me for six. Dead ringer, she was, an absolute dead ringer for her father.'

He pulls at his hands until the knuckles crack. 'Trent and Donna, they were never married—they were still so young, weren't they—so officially Bridie was Simon, like her mother. Donna's name had been plastered all over the papers, and soon enough everyone would have put two and two together. They'd have worked out that Bridie was Donna's daughter. But here's the thing: Vonnie was Taylor, from her second marriage, so when Bridie turned up at the school, I suggested Vonnie change her name to Taylor, too. That way there wouldn't be a connection to either of them: to Donna or to Trent. Of course, Brindle's a small place and Vinnie's cohort, they'd have known—nothing to be done about that—but at least we could try to keep it a bit quiet where we could. So that's what happened. And up until now, it seems to have worked. The way I see it, the longer it stays like that the better. Because once the police or Family Services get a whiff of it, it'll all be on again and suddenly she won't be Bridie Taylor anymore, she'll be *that* kid. And I don't think she could cope with it. I don't think any of us could.'

Terry

Once they're in the car—she drives a small, zippy little thing—he stands by the entrance to the shop and waves them off. He's not sure what else to do, how else to behave. So he waves. And as he waves, he whacks a smile on his face in case Bridie is still watching. Only when the car is out of sight does he let it fade. Then he just stands there. When he feels his shoulders slump, quickly he pulls them back again. This is not the time to crack. This is the time to get back to work.

So he gets back to work. And for the rest of the afternoon and into the evening, he's as attentive to the customers as always: he listens to their questions, he gives them some suggestions, he even manages a joke or two. The only thing that makes it difficult is his throat: it's so dry it just about kills him to swallow.

When at last it is time to go, he waves at Leonie and gives her a wide smile as he walks out. Only when he's in the car does he start to wilt. But not for long. Don't come a cropper now, he warns himself as he starts the engine. Not now.

He's hoping he'll beat Michelle home. At least that'll give him a bit of time to compose himself.

But as it happens, she's already home, and as he walks through the door, her cheery voice greets him. 'Hi, love,' she calls from the kitchen, 'I'm making a cuppa—you want one?'

A cuppa's not going to fix it, love. That's what he's going to have to tell her. *A cuppa's not nearly going to fix it, love.*

And then he can't hold it back any longer. So there he is, bent over in the hallway, his face in his hands, his knees bent, his shoulders hunched. Crying. How he cries. He cries until the muscles in his stomach contract, his eyes sting and, once more, he can't swallow. He doesn't cry loudly. He is almost silent in his weeping, almost soundless.

When Michelle finds him like that, doubled over and sobbing, she starts to scream. 'Terry!' she screams, like she thinks he's having a heart attack or something. 'Terry! What is it? What is it?'

He can't tell her. He doesn't have the words for it. He has no words at all. He just wants to be alone.

But he isn't alone. He is at home and Michelle is there with him. So he lets her take him into the lounge room, lets her sit him down on the sofa, lets her sponge his face with a warm washer. And, later, he thanks her for the cup of tea she brings him.

She doesn't push him to speak. She just waits. She sits beside him on the sofa and she waits.

He starts slowly, cautiously. 'The new teacher,' he tells her, 'she came into the shop. She was looking for Bridie. Thought she might be with me. And she was, she was with me, all right. She'd taken off from school. And she was that upset, poor little blossom. That's why I took her to the tearoom, love, just to calm her down.'

When he turns to Michelle she gives him a tiny smile and, taking his hand, holds it tightly in hers. 'Love, I had her on my lap. I was holding her on my lap. And maybe I shouldn't have done that, but she was so upset, I didn't know what to do. I just—I just wanted to comfort her.'

Michelle's hand tightens around his. She makes a noise, a little noise, so he'll keep going. But he's not sure he can.

'When the new teacher saw me there, with Bridie on my lap like that, the look she gave me, it was like I was vermin. *No, no*, I wanted to say to her, *no, no. It's not like that. It's not what you're thinking.* But she wouldn't have heard; she was just screaming at the little one to get off me—when all I wanted was to keep my arms around her and hold her tight and keep her safe.'

It is so, so hard to speak now. 'The new teacher, she said she was going to tell Laurie Mathews. And I know what she'd do: she'd be on to the police. And I was thinking, for God's sake, we can't get the police mixed up in all this, not after everything we've done to keep Bridie away from all that. I panicked then, love. I panicked and I told her everything: everything about Bridie and Trent and Donna. I told her the lot. I didn't want to, love, I really didn't want to, but what could I do?' His voice cracks. 'And, love, I don't know if I can trust her, I don't know what she'll do with it, but I told her anyway. And all the while she was staring at me, staring at me like I was the most disgusting thing she'd ever seen.' Because he can't face looking at Michelle—he just can't face it—he keeps his head right down.

Michelle doesn't say anything. For the longest time, she doesn't say a thing. 'The other stuff,' she says finally. 'Did you tell her about the other stuff?'

He looks up, confused.

'About the girl,' she says. 'Did you tell her about the girl?'

For a moment he is still puzzled. The girl? What girl? Then he realises she means Clare. 'Yes,' he says, 'I told her about Clare.'

'And about the baby, did you tell her about that, too?'

She is speaking so quietly he can hardly hear her.

'I told her all of it, love. I told her everything.'

She is silent for a moment. 'But you've never really told me, Terry,' she says at last. 'Not properly. Not in any detail.'

It is his turn to fall silent. 'You know, love,' he says, when he can bring himself to speak again, 'after the fuss, I didn't even want to think about it. That's why I never talked about it.'

Slowly, gently even, she slips her hand from his. 'But I want to know about her. I want to talk about her.'

It's the last thing he wants to do. The last thing.

But after everything he's put her through, maybe that's not fair.

'She was nice, love,' he tells her softly. 'She was really nice. Fair hair, not so as you'd call it blonde, sort of silvery blonde-brown, something like that.'

'Ash,' Michelle murmurs. 'Ash-blonde, that's what it's called.'

He repeats that back to himself. 'Ash-blonde. That'd be it. And blue eyes and an olive sort of complexion. A bright spark, she was, too. Even at fifteen, I reckon she was running rings around me.'

God, it's hard to talk about her. Even now.

'It was a surprise—a big surprise, really—when she said she'd be my girlfriend.'

Beside him, Michelle is very quiet. He gives her hand a squeeze. 'You right, love?'

'Do you wish—I mean, do you wish she'd had the baby?' The question is whisper-quiet and when he looks at her, he sees that there are tears falling down her face.

'Oh, love,' he says. 'Oh, love.'

'Do you?' she repeats. 'Do you wish she'd had the baby?'

He can't bear the sadness in her voice. He can't bear it.

'Oh, darling,' he says, 'I wish I'd had a baby with *you*. That's what I wish. I wish *we'd* had a baby.'

She doesn't bother to wipe her tears away. She just lets them fall. 'But you could have had one with her. And it's my fault.' She falters. 'It's my fault we didn't have a baby.'

It breaks him to hear her. It almost breaks him. 'No,' he tells her. 'No, no. That's not what they said. You know that's not what they said. It just didn't happen, love. It just didn't happen.'

They are both crying then: they are both crying, their shoulders touching, their hands tightly clasped. They cry for a long time, for such a long time, and it is as though they might never stop. But they do stop. They stop, they wipe their eyes, they blow their noses then they stand up and, slowly, they make a start on dinner.

Nina

The concert doesn't start for an hour but already Nina has stage fright.

Breathe, she whispers to herself, breathe.

The kids are all backstage, but Kurt, it seems, has left half of his costume at home. Nina calls his mother to check but she doesn't pick up. 'It's Nina Foreman here,' she says when it kicks over to voicemail. 'Could you ring when you get this? It's about Kurt's costume.' Despite the breathing, she's still feeling panicked.

Almost immediately, her phone rings. But it's not Kurt's mother. It's the childcare centre. They're calling to say that Emily has conjunctivitis and, in accordance with the centre's policy, will need to be picked up immediately.

Steve doesn't pick up his mobile. She dials again but it goes to voicemail. She hates calling him at work but today there's no choice. In any case, the receptionist tells her he's not there.

When her phone rings, she grabs it without checking the screen. 'Steve?' she says hopefully.

But it's not Steve, it's Kay Ward to let her know she's got Kurt's costume and is on her way.

Colin. She'll call Colin. But Colin doesn't answer when she rings the home number and he doesn't have a mobile.

Now what?

There's one other possibility.

No, she tells herself, not her.

But any moment now, the childcare centre will be ringing again to find out what's happening.

Nina still has her number. She knows she does. And sure enough, when she scrolls through her contacts, there she is: SR. Squeezing her eyes, she presses call. As soon as the number starts ringing, she hangs up. Then she calls again. This time, she doesn't hang up.

The phone rings three times before it connects. 'Hello?' a woman answers, then, more tentatively, 'Hello? Is anyone there?' when Nina doesn't reply.

Nina clears her throat. 'Is that Sue?' she asks.

The voice is wary now. 'Yes, this is Sue.'

'It's Nina here,' she says. 'Nina Foreman.'

There's a pause. *Don't hang up*, Nina wills her, *don't hang up*.

She doesn't.

'It's Emily,' Nina tells her.

'Oh,' she says, her voice rising, 'is she all right?'

Nina tells her what has happened. 'I can't get on to Steve,' she says.

That's because he's away, she is told, and won't be back until the evening.

Nina is angry to hear this: angry that he isn't available and angry that this woman knows where he is when Nina has no idea. 'Right,' she replies, 'all right.' She sounds curt, she knows that, but she doesn't care.

'I could pick her up,' the woman says. 'I've been there before, with Steve, so they already know me.'

Nina bristles. What does she mean, she's been there before?

'And I'm pretty sure Steve's authorised me to pick her up, but you might need to check.'

Nina struggles to control herself. How the hell can she have the authority to pick up Emily when it's the first Nina's even heard about it?

Forget it, she wants to say. I'll go.

But she can't go. If there was ever a day she couldn't go, this is the one.

'I can be there in twenty minutes.' That's what she's telling Nina now. 'I'll take her straight home.'

Nina is confused. Home? What does she mean, home? It takes her a minute to register. She means her home with Steve. Their home together.

'What about a car seat?' Nina asks, her voice flat.

She already has one. In her car, in this woman's car, there is a car seat for Emily. The thought of it enrages her.

'Right,' she says. 'Right.' Forcing the words out, Nina thanks her. Then she hangs up.

Breathe, and breathe, and breathe.

Because now it's time.

There is talking in the audience and Nina's heart is loud as she walks onstage. When she stops in the middle of the stage, the talking stops, too. All eyes, then, are on her. It makes her want to vomit.

'Good afternoon,' she says. Her voice wobbles as she speaks. 'Welcome to the Year 6 show. The students have been working very hard and are very excited about it. We'll be starting with *The Bears*.' Through her nerves, she does her best to give the audience a smile. 'I know you'll all be familiar with the story, but I don't think you'll have seen it done quite this way before. So sit back, relax and enjoy the performance.'

With that, Belinda presses play on the sound system, Nina melts back into the wings, and the bears take over.

❧

Backstage, the cast of *The Wolf* is in disarray.

'Get moving,' Nina tells them. 'I need you all ready now.'

Immediately Elsie bursts into tears: she's left her bonnet somewhere and now she can't find it. The dressing-room is a mess so it could be anywhere. And because it's her job to make sure the kids are ready, Mel is down on her hands and knees searching around for the bloody thing. Once she finds it, she gives a whoop, and when Elsie joins in too, Nina has to hiss at them both to keep it down.

Ethan's shirt is hanging out. As Mel reaches over to tuck it in, he pulls back, scowling. 'Can you just stop it, Mum?' he growls. 'I'm not a baby.' Nina smiles to watch them. Beside him, Mel looks so young she could pass for his sister.

Adam is backstage, too, helping out with the sets. When he passes Ethan, he gives him a poke between his shoulder blades, which makes him jerk back. 'Mate,' he tells him, 'your mother's just trying to make sure you don't look ridiculous onstage. Show her a bit of respect, for God's sake.'

He looks like he's about to say something else, but he's interrupted by the sound of clapping. Loud, continuous clapping, and some whistling. The bears are finished.

'Five minutes,' Nina tells Mel. 'We'll need everyone in *The Wolf* ready in the wings in five minutes.'

Four minutes later, they're all there except for Bridie, who refuses to leave the dressing-room. Nina squats down beside her. 'What is it, darling?'

'What if I forget?' she murmurs. 'What if I forget what I'm supposed to say?'

Nina reaches out to hold her. 'You won't, sweetheart. As soon as you're up there, the words will just come out. And if they don't, Sebastian's mum will be there to prompt you. Okay?'

Bridie bites at her lip. 'Okay,' she whispers.

～

Bridie is in the wings now, too: all decked out in her silver narrator's cape. Silver shoes, too, she sees.

'Love your shoes,' Nina tells her. 'I really, really love your shoes.'

Bridie smiles. 'Mr P got them for me,' she says, 'when I told him about the cape. He got them for me so they were matching.'

Nina can't suppress a grimace. Why does he have to keep popping up, why can't he just disappear? And even though she doesn't say anything out loud, still the little girl's smile fades. Nina takes her hand and gives it a squeeze. 'They're beautiful,' she tells her. 'They're absolutely beautiful.'

Terry

He's taken the day off work and now he's sitting on the sofa, phone in hand, just waiting. When the call finally comes through, he answers it on the first ring.

'Terry, mate,' Sid whispers, 'I've got to keep it down. Can you hear me okay?'

He can. In fact, Sid's coming through crystal clear.

Sid sounds pleased. 'Rightio. *The Wolf*'s about to start so we'll do it the way we did it with *The Bears*, okay? I'll just hold the phone up again. That should do the trick.'

It does the trick, all right. As soon as Terry puts the phone on speaker, he can hear them all loud and clear. And by God, does that make him smile.

When it's Bridie's turn, his palms start to sweat; twice he has to wipe them on his trousers. Listening hard, he wills her to remember the lines, wills her to bat on, no matter what happens. God love her, she does. She keeps on going, her voice clear, her voice strong, her voice loud.

But not nearly as loud as Elsie, who yells her lines. Hearing her makes Terry want to laugh and cry and clap, all at once. It seems he's not the only one because from somewhere in the distance—from the back of the hall, he imagines—comes a cheer and a foghorn call. *Perfect, Else, that's perfect.* In his mind, Terry sees her up there, waving to her father like a maniac, as she hollers out the rest of her lines. Once again, he's got it right, has Len: she *is* perfect, she's a perfect orator; the only kid in the school who doesn't need a microphone to broadcast her words.

Except perhaps Kurt, who gives her a run for her money as he belts out his final lines:

> *Now that I've got you*
> *Here all alone*
> *What else should I do*
> *But eat you to the bone?*

There's a yell from the audience then. *Way to go, Kurt, way to go.* For a moment Terry thinks Sean's stopped island-hopping long enough to give his son some support. But when the yell goes out again and the words are slightly slurred, he realises that it's not Sean; it's Cody's dad, Scott, who's cheering the boy on. He's a good egg, that one. Terry's got to hand it to him.

And all at once, there he is again: right back in the classroom, all of them there in front of him, eyes to the front, smiles on their faces.

The thought of it.

God, the thought of it—it fills him with a sadness so piercing he has to draw breath.

From down the phone comes the sound of clapping: loud, raucous clapping that keeps on going and going. When, finally, it starts to die down, Sid comes on the line again. 'I think that's about it, mate,' he says.

Terry can't answer him. He has to inhale a couple of times before he can get anything out at all. 'Thanks, Sid,' he says finally. 'Thanks for that.'

'No problem, mate,' says Sid. 'No problem at all.'

And with that, he's gone—they're all gone. Every one of them.

Rebecca

They're still clapping. Clapping and clapping. The hall is filled with the sound of it. Rebecca is clapping, too, her hands outstretched in front of her.

Onstage, the kids are holding hands and bowing, Sebastian right in the middle of them. *Look at him*, she wants to shout. *Look at him*. At that moment, she is close to euphoric. They have done it.

The show is over and they have done it well.

So.

So now it's time.

Beside her, Emmanuel's eyes are on the stage. He doesn't even know the letter has arrived.

It is still unopened. All day, it has lain in her pocket, unopened. Now, with a small tug, she tears at the back of the envelope. Inside is just one piece of paper.

Once again, it is little more than a form letter.

And once again, she flinches as her eyes fix on the opening words.

This time, the words are different.

For a moment she just stares at them, unable to properly comprehend what they are saying. Only slowly does it register.

Carefully, she refolds the letter and passes it to Emmanuel. 'Read it,' she whispers.

When he is finished, he, too, refolds the letter before he passes it back to her. If she were to look at him, she knows she would dissolve, so instead she looks ahead.

All around her the clapping continues, strong and loud and joyful. And now, she joins in with it once more.

They will stay.

This is where they will belong.

And as she thinks of this, and all it might mean, she catches a glimpse of Mel, who is standing in the aisle, her camera pointed at the stage. All afternoon she has been taking photographs, this woman who is fast becoming her friend. She must have hundreds of them, hundreds of pictures of the show. It will be good, she thinks, to sift through them together. She will look forward to this with great pleasure.

A little closer, only a couple of seats down from her, are Sid and Joan. Rebecca smiles to watch them: their eyes glued to the stage, both of them transfixed. How delightful, she thinks. How lovely, too, that they have both made such an effort for the show: Joan's dress is a rainbow of colours and, in her hair, she's wearing a clip that sparkles. Sid's hair, as usual, is carefully slicked back and today he is wearing a tie. It's like they're out on a date, she thinks. It's like they're an old married couple out on a date.

It is only then that she notices it: Sid is holding Joan's hand.

No, it can't be.

But it is. It is. Sid's hand is clasped around Joan's and their shoulders are touching.

Imagine that, she thinks. And for some time longer, she keeps watching them until slowly, almost reluctantly, she turns her gaze back to the stage.

Nina

When the applause has died away and the children have disappeared down into the audience, Laurie comes on stage. Watching from the wings, Nina remembers, with a jolt, that it's her last day. She kicks herself for having forgotten. She could have at least bought her flowers.

Laurie keeps it brief. She talks about the year and about the school's achievements, and how she'll be sorry to leave.

There is applause when she finishes, but it is muted, and when Nina scans the audience, she sees that Tania isn't clapping at all. From somewhere in the back of the audience comes a shout: *What about Terry Pritchard, why'd ya sack him?* It's so loud Laurie must have heard it. But if she has, she gives no sign of it. Only when she walks back down the stairs to her seat does Nina see that her hands are trembling.

As soon as Laurie sits down, Tania stands up and makes her way to the stage. She waits until the hall falls silent.

'To prepare for Ms Thomas's return next year,' she says, 'I thought we should start exercising our vocal cords again. Brindle Public

School students, you won't need the words. Brindle Public parents, you probably won't either. Anyone else, just try your best. All right?'

There is only a faint response. Taking a step forward, Tania puts a hand behind her ear. 'Can't hear you, Brindle Public,' she says.

From the audience comes a sprinkle of laughter.

Tania takes a second step forward. She's at the edge of the stage now and when she takes a third step, she keeps her foot in mid-air. Another step, and she'll fall off the stage. 'Still can't hear you, Brindle Public!' she shouts.

Loud laughter fills the hall now. Still with her foot up, Tania calls out to the audience, 'I said, Brindle Public, are you ready for some music?'

This time, the response is overwhelming.

Putting her foot down, Tania looks pleased. 'That's more like it,' she says. To the left, Belinda is waiting by the PA system. Tania gives her a nod. 'Ready when you are, Ms Coote.'

A silence, then, before music starts to trickle through the system. It takes Nina only a couple of bars to recognise the song: 'Blame It on the Boogie'. She struggles to hold back a chortle.

The music gets louder then, louder and louder, and soon it's not just coming from the PA system, it's coming from everywhere.

Onstage, Tania is singing hard, pumping each word into the microphone, so that her voice reverberates throughout the hall. When the chorus comes, the audience erupts.

There are actions for the chorus. Fabulous actions, and onstage, Tania leads the audience through them: half-circles, stretched arms, twinkling fingers, twisting.

And although Tania is keeping time, there are problems in the audience. Some are stretching, some are twinkling, some are twisting, some are doing nothing. It's a fiasco. To one side of the hall, everyone from *The Wolf* is grouped together. They're all standing up, they're all facing Tania and they're all doing the actions, each one of them. Nina splutters with laughter when she sees them. Not because they can't do it, but because they're trying so hard: their faces earnest while their arms fly everywhere. And when they start to boogie, each of them twisting vigorously, each of them pointing a hand to the ceiling, each of them still absolutely serious, she can't hold back.

God, she laughs.

She laughs and laughs. More than she has in years. She laughs so much she starts to choke. And when she tries to control herself, a giggle catches in her throat, and still she keeps on laughing—how she laughs—even after the music is over and the dancing has finished.

Acknowledgements

I have long admired Jane Palfreyman and her stable of innovative and talented writers. To now be one of them still makes my heart leap. Thank you, Jane, for all your advice, care and support.

Ali Lavau's editing gave the book a clear and cohesive setting in time and place, Sarah Baker was meticulous with her suggestions and changes, Sarina Rowell was a careful and thoughtful proofreader and Alissa Dinallo designed a beautifully striking cover. Thank you, too, to the rest of the team at Allen & Unwin.

My agent, Margaret Connolly, is wise and practical and encouraging and always available. It's a delight to be her client and friend.

Claire Scobie read many early drafts of the work and her feedback was invaluable.

Richard Glover, Kathryn Heyman and Joanne Fedler were so very generous with their time and their feedback.

Megan Tipping (née James) read the manuscript with the eyes of a teacher and helped me navigate the world of primary schools.

Mandy Mashanyare's thoughtful suggestions were instrumental in making the work more credible and more authentic.

Juliet Lucy was a scrupulous proofreader and Kelly Barlow, queen of social media, organised me, revamped me and sent me out into the digital world.

My father, Barry Leal, has instilled in me a love of language and stories, and my mother, Roslyn Leal, has been an ever-present support to me.

Alex, Dominic and Xavier are my beautiful sons, and Miranda, our lovely little latecomer, completes us. I'm so very proud of you all.

David Barrow is my great love. As a husband, father and step-father, he is caring and funny and generous and wise. How lucky we are to have you!

About the author

Suzanne Leal began her career as a criminal lawyer with the Legal Aid Commission of NSW and has since held appointments to several tribunals, including the Refugee Review Tribunal. A former legal commentator on ABC Radio, Suzanne is an experienced interviewer at literary functions and events.

Curiosity about hidden stories and secret lives drives Suzanne's writing. It sparked her interest in the lives of her Czech landlords, Fred and Eva Perger, who inspired her first novel, *Border Street*, commended in the Asher Literary Award. Curiosity, too, prompted Suzanne to explore the intrigues of the schoolyard and bring them to life in this, her second novel.

Suzanne lives in Sydney with her husband, David, and her four children, Alex, Dominic, Xavier and Miranda.

suzanneleal.com